Emily of New Moon

AEVUM EDITIONS PUBLISHING

Printed or published to the highest ethical standard

Emily of New Moon

By L.M. Montgomery

Canada
1923

CONTENTS

CHAPTER I
THE HOUSE IN THE HOLLOW

THE house in the hollow was "a mile from anywhere"—so Maywood people said. It was situated in a grassy little dale, looking as if it had never been built like other houses but had grown up there like a big, brown mushroom. It was reached by a long, green lane and almost hidden from view by an encircling growth of young birches. No other house could be seen from it although the village was just over the hill. Ellen Greene said it was the lonesomest place in the world and vowed that she wouldn't stay there a day if it wasn't that she pitied the child.

Emily didn't know she was being pitied and didn't know what lonesomeness meant. She had plenty of company. There was Father—and Mike—and Saucy Sal. The Wind Woman was always around; and there were the trees—Adam-and-Eve, and the Rooster Pine, and all the friendly lady-birches.

And there was "the flash," too. She never knew when it might come, and the possibility of it kept her a-thrill and expectant.

Emily had slipped away in the chilly twilight for a walk. She remembered that walk very vividly all her life—perhaps because of a certain eerie beauty that was in it—perhaps because "the flash" came for the first time in weeks—more likely because of what happened after she came back from it.

It had been a dull, cold day in early May, threatening to rain but never raining. Father had lain on the sitting-room lounge all day. He had coughed a good deal and he had not talked much to Emily, which was a very unusual thing for him. Most of the time he lay with his hands clasped under his head and his large, sunken, dark-blue eyes fixed dreamily and unseeingly on the cloudy sky that was visible between the boughs of the two big spruces in the front yard—Adam-and-Eve, they always called those spruces, because of a whimsical resemblance Emily had traced between their position, with reference to a small apple-tree between them, and that of Adam and Eve and the Tree of Knowledge in an old-fashioned picture in one of Ellen Greene's books. The Tree of Knowledge looked exactly like the squat little apple-tree, and Adam and Eve stood up on either side as stiffly and rigidly as did the spruces.

Emily wondered what Father was thinking of, but she never bothered him with questions when his cough was bad. She only wished she had somebody to talk to. Ellen Greene wouldn't talk that day either.

She did nothing but grunt, and grunts meant that Ellen was disturbed about something. She had grunted last night after the doctor had whispered to her in the kitchen, and she had grunted when she gave Emily a bedtime snack of bread and molasses. Emily did not like bread and molasses, but she ate it because she did not want to hurt Ellen's feelings. It was not often that Ellen allowed her anything to eat before going to bed, and when she did it meant that for some reason or other she wanted to confer a special favor.

Emily expected the grunting attack would wear off over night, as it generally did; but it had not, so no company was to be found in Ellen. Not that there was a great deal to be found at any time. Douglas Starr had once, in a fit of exasperation, told Emily that "Ellen Greene was a fat, lazy old thing of no importance," and Emily, whenever she looked at Ellen after that, thought the description fitted her to a hair.

So Emily had curled herself up in the ragged, comfortable old wing-chair and read *The Pilgrim's Progress* all the afternoon. Emily loved *The Pilgrim's Progress*. Many a time had she walked the straight and narrow path with CHRISTIAN and CHRISTIANA—although she never liked CHRISTIANA'S adventures half as well as CHRISTIAN'S. For one thing, there was always such a crowd with CHRISTIANA. She had not half the fascination of that solitary, intrepid figure who faced all alone the shadows of the Dark Valley and the encounter with Apollyon. Darkness and hobgoblins were nothing when you had plenty of company. But to be ALONE—ah, Emily shivered with the delicious horror of it!

When Ellen announced that supper was ready Douglas Starr told Emily to go out to it.

"I don't want anything tonight. I'll just lie here and rest. And when you come in again we'll have a real talk, Elfkin."

He smiled up at her his old, beautiful smile, with the love behind it, that Emily always found so sweet. She ate her supper quite happily—though it wasn't a good supper. The bread was soggy and her egg was underdone, but for a wonder she was allowed to have both Saucy Sal and Mike sitting, one on each side of her, and Ellen only grunted when Emily fed them wee bits of bread and butter.

Mike had such a cute way of sitting up on his haunches and catching the bits in his paws, and Saucy Sal had HER trick of touching Emily's ankle with an almost human touch when her turn was too long in coming. Emily loved them both, but Mike was her favourite. He was a handsome, dark-grey cat with huge owl-like eyes, and he was so soft and fat and fluffy. Sal was always thin; no amount of feeding put any flesh on her bones. Emily liked her, but never cared to cuddle or stroke her because of her thinness. Yet there was a sort of weird beauty about her that appealed to Emily. She was grey-and-white—very white and very sleek, with a long, pointed face, very long ears and very green eyes. She was a redoubtable fighter, and strange cats were vanquished in one round. The fearless little spitfire would even attack dogs and rout them utterly.

Emily loved her pussies. She had brought them up herself, as she proudly said. They had been given to her when they were kittens by her Sunday School teacher.

"A LIVING present is so nice," she told Ellen, "because it keeps on getting nicer all the time."

But she worried considerably because Saucy Sal didn't have kittens.

"I don't know why she doesn't," she complained to Ellen Greene. "Most cats seem to have more kittens than they know what to do with."

After supper Emily went in and found that her father had fallen asleep. She was very glad of this; she knew he had not slept much for two nights; but she was a little disappointed that they were not going to have that "real talk." "Real" talks with Father were always such delightful things. But next best would be a walk—a lovely all-by-your-lonesome walk through the grey evening of the young spring. It was so long since she had had a walk.

"You put on your hood and mind you scoot back if it starts to rain," warned Ellen. "YOU can't monkey with colds the way some kids can."

"Why can't I?" Emily asked rather indignantly. Why must SHE be debarred from "monkeying with colds" if other children could? It wasn't fair.

But Ellen only grunted. Emily muttered under her breath for her own satisfaction, "You are a fat old thing of no importance!" and slipped upstairs to get her hood—rather reluctantly, for she loved to run bareheaded. She put the faded blue hood on over her long, heavy braid of glossy, jet-black hair, and smiled chummily at her reflection in the little greenish glass. The smile began at the corners of her lips and spread over her face in a slow, subtle, very wonderful way, as Douglas Starr often thought. It was her dead mother's smile—the thing that had caught and held him long ago when he had first seen Juliet Murray. It seemed to be Emily's only physical inheritance from her mother. In all else, he thought, she was like the Starrs—in her large, purplish-grey eyes with their very long lashes and black brows, in her high, white forehead—too high for beauty—in the delicate modeling of her pale oval face and sensitive mouth, in the little ears that were pointed just a wee bit to show that she was kin to tribes of elfland.

"I'm going for a walk with the Wind Woman, dear," said Emily. "I wish I could take you too. Do you EVER get out of that room, I wonder. The Wind Woman is going to be out in the fields to-night. She is tall and misty, with thin, grey, silky clothes blowing all about her—and wings like a bat's—only you can see through them—and shining eyes like stars looking through her long, loose hair. She can fly—but to-night she will walk with me all over the fields. She's a GREAT friend of mine—the Wind Woman is. I've known her ever since I was six. We're OLD, OLD friends—but not quite so old as you and I, little Emily-in-the-glass. We've been friends ALWAYS, haven't we?"

With a blown kiss to little Emily-in-the-glass, Emily-out-of-the-glass was off.

The Wind Woman was waiting for her outside—ruffling the little spears of striped grass that were sticking up stiffly in the bed under the sitting-room window—tossing the big boughs of Adam-and-Eve—whispering among the misty green branches of the birches—teasing the "Rooster Pine" behind the house—it really did look like an enormous, ridiculous rooster, with a huge, bunchy tail and a head thrown back to crow.

It was so long since Emily had been out for a walk that she was half crazy with the joy of it. The winter had been so stormy and the snow so deep that she was never allowed out; April had been a month of rain and wind; so on this May evening she felt like a released prisoner. Where should she go? Down the brook—or over the fields to the spruce barrens? Emily chose the latter.

She loved the spruce barrens, away at the further end of the long, sloping pasture. That was a place where magic was made. She came more fully into her fairy birthright there than in any other place. Nobody who saw Emily skimming over the bare field would have envied her. She was little and pale and poorly clad; sometimes she shivered in her thin jacket; yet a queen might have gladly given a crown for her visions—her dreams of wonder. The brown, frosted grasses under her feet were velvet piles. The old, mossy, gnarled half-dead spruce-tree, under which she paused for a moment to look up into the sky, was a marble column in a palace of the gods; the far dusky hills were the ramparts of a city of wonder. And for companions she had all the fairies of the countryside—for she could believe in them here—the fairies of the white clover and satin catkins, the little green folk of the grass, the elves of the young fir-trees, sprites of wind and wild fern and thistledown. Anything might happen there—everything might come true.

And the barrens were such a splendid place in which to play hide and seek with the Wind Woman. She was so very REAL there; if you could just spring quickly enough around a little cluster of spruces—only you never could—you would SEE her as well as feel her and hear her. There she was—that WAS the sweep of her grey cloak—no, she was laughing up in the very top of the taller trees—and the chase was on again—till, all at once, it seemed as if the Wind Woman were gone—and the evening was bathed in a wonderful silence—and there was a sudden rift in the curdled clouds westward, and a lovely, pale, pinky-green lake of sky with a new moon in it.

Emily stood and looked at it with clasped hands and her little black head upturned. She must go home and write down a description of it in the yellow account book, where the last thing written had been, "Mike's Biograffy." It would hurt her with its beauty until she wrote it down. Then she would read it to Father. She must not forget how the tips of the trees on the hill came out like fine black lace across the edge of the pinky-green sky.

And then, for one glorious, supreme moment, came "the flash."

Emily called it that, although she felt that the name didn't exactly describe it. It couldn't be described—not even to Father, who always seemed a little puzzled by it. Emily never spoke of it to any one else.

It had always seemed to Emily, ever since she could remember, that she was very, very near to a world of wonderful beauty. Between it and herself hung only a thin curtain; she could never draw the curtain aside—but sometimes, just for a moment, a wind fluttered it and then it was as if she caught a glimpse of the enchanting realm beyond—only a glimpse—and heard a note of unearthly music.

This moment came rarely—went swiftly, leaving her breathless with the inexpressible delight of it. She could never recall it—never summon it—never pretend it; but the wonder of it stayed with her for days. It never came twice with the same thing. To-night the dark boughs against that far-off sky had given it. It had come with a high, wild note of wind in the night, with a shadow wave over a ripe field, with a greybird lighting on her window-sill in a storm, with the singing of "Holy, holy, holy" in church, with a glimpse of the kitchen fire when she had come home on a dark autumn night, with the spirit-like blue of ice palms on a twilit pane, with a felicitous new word when she was writing down a "description" of something. And always when the flash came to her Emily felt that life was a wonderful, mysterious thing of persistent beauty.

She scuttled back to the house in the hollow, through the gathering twilight, all agog to get home and write down her "description" before the memory picture of what she had seen grew a little blurred. She knew just how she would begin it—the sentence seemed to shape itself in her mind: "The hill called to me and something in me called back to it."

She found Ellen Greene waiting for her on the sunken front-doorstep. Emily was so full of happiness that she loved everything at that moment, even fat things of no importance. She flung her arms around Ellen's knees and hugged them. Ellen looked down gloomily into the rapt little face, where excitement had kindled a faint wild-rose flush, and said, with a ponderous sigh:

"Do you know that your pa has only a week or two more to live?"

CHAPTER II
A Watch in the Night

EMILY stood quite still and looked up at Ellen's broad, red face—as still as if she had been suddenly turned to stone. She felt as if she had. She was as stunned as if Ellen had struck her a physical blow. The colour faded out of her little face and her pupils dilated until they swallowed up the irides and turned her eyes into pools of blackness. The effect was so startling that even Ellen Greene felt uncomfortable.

"I'm telling you this because I think it's high time you was told," she said. "I've been at your pa for months to tell you, but he's kept putting it off and off. I says to him, says I, 'You know how hard she takes things, and if you drop off suddent some day it'll most kill her if she hasn't been prepared. It's your duty to prepare her,' and he says, says he, 'There's time enough yet, Ellen.' But he's never said a word, and when the doctor told last night that the end might come any time now, I just made up my mind that I'd do what was right and drop a hint to prepare you. Laws-a-massy, child, don't look like that! You'll be looked after. Your ma's people will see to that—on account of the Murray pride, if for no other reason. They won't let one of their own blood starve or go to strangers—even if they have always hated your pa like p'isen. You'll have a good home—better'n you've ever had here. You needn't worry a mite. As for your pa, you ought to be thankful to see him at rest. He's been dying by inches for the last five years. He's kept it from you, but he's been a great sufferer. Folks say his heart broke when your ma died—it came on him so suddent-like—she was only sick three days. That's why I want you to know what's coming, so's you won't be all upset when it happens. For mercy's sake, Emily Byrd Starr, don't stand there staring like that! You give me the creeps! You ain't the first child that's been left an orphan and you won't be the last. Try and be sensible. And don't go pestering your pa about what I've told you, mind that. Come you in now, out of the damp, and I'll give you a cooky 'fore you go to bed."

Ellen stepped down as if to take the child's hand. The power of motion returned to Emily—she must scream if Ellen even touched her NOW. With one sudden, sharp, bitter little cry she avoided Ellen's hand, darted through the door and fled up the dark staircase.

Ellen shook her head and waddled back to her kitchen.

"Anyhow, I've done MY duty," she reflected. "He'd have just kept saying 'time enough' and put it off till he was dead and then there'd have been no managing her. She'll have time now to get used to it, and she'll brace up in a day or two. I will say for her she's got spunk—which is lucky, from all I've heard of the Murrays. They won't find it easy to overcrow HER. She's got a streak of their pride, too, and that'll help her through. I wish I dared send some of the Murrays word that he's dying, but I don't dast go that far. There's no telling what HE'd do. Well, I've stuck on here to the last and I ain't sorry. Not many women would 'a' done it, living as they do here. It's a shame the way that child's been brought up—never even sent to school. Well, I've told him often enough what I've thought of it—it ain't on MY conscience, that's one comfort. Here, you Sal-thing, you git out! Where's Mike, too?"

Ellen could not find Mike for the very good reason that he was upstairs with Emily, held tightly in her arms, as she sat in the darkness on her little cot bed. Amid her agony and desolation there was a certain comfort in the feel of his soft fur and round velvety head.

Emily was not crying; she stared straight into the darkness, trying to face the awful thing Ellen had told her. She did not doubt it—something told her it was true. Why couldn't she die, too? She couldn't go on living without Father.

"If I was God I wouldn't let things like this happen," she said.

She felt it was very wicked of her to say such a thing—Ellen had told her once that it was the wickedest thing any one could do to find fault with God. But she didn't care. Perhaps if she were wicked enough God would strike her dead and then she and Father could keep on being together.

But nothing happened—only Mike got tired of being held so tightly and squirmed away. She was all alone now, with this terrible burning pain that seemed all over her and yet was not of the body. She could never get rid of it. She couldn't help it by writing about it in the old yellow account book. She had written there about her Sunday School teacher going away, and of being hungry when she went to bed, and Ellen telling her she must be half crazy to talk of Wind Women and flashes; and after she had written down all about them these things hadn't hurt her any more. But this couldn't be written about. She could not even go to Father for comfort, as she had gone when she burned her hand so badly, picking up the red-hot poker by mistake. Father had held her in his arms all that night and told her stories and helped her to bear the pain. But Father, so Ellen had said, was going to die in a week or two. Emily felt as if Ellen had told her this years and years ago. It surely couldn't be less than an hour since she had been playing with the Wind Woman in the barrens and looking at the new moon in the pinky-green sky.

"The flash will never come again—it can't," she thought.

But Emily had inherited certain things from her fine old ancestors—the power to fight—to suffer—to pity—to love very deeply—to rejoice—to endure. These things were all in her and looked out at you through her purplish-grey eyes. Her heritage of endurance came to her aid now and bore her up. She must not let Father know what Ellen had told her—it might hurt him. She must keep it all to herself and LOVE Father, oh, so much, in the little while she could yet have him.

She heard him cough in the room below: she must be in bed when he came up; she undressed as swiftly as her cold fingers permitted and crept into the little cot bed which stood across the open window. The voices of the gentle spring night called to her all unheeded—unheard the Wind Woman whistled by the eaves. For the fairies dwell only in the kingdom of Happiness; having no souls they cannot enter the kingdom of Sorrow.

She lay there cold and tearless and motionless when her father came into the room. How very slowly he walked—how very slowly he took off his clothes. How was it she had never noticed these things before? But he was not coughing at all. Oh, what if Ellen were mistaken?—what if—a wild hope shot through her aching heart. She gave a little gasp.

Douglas Starr came over to her bed. She felt his dear nearness as he sat down on the chair beside her, in his old red dressing-gown. Oh, how she loved him! There was no other Father like him in all the world—there never could have been—so tender, so understanding, so wonderful! They had always been such chums—they had loved each other so much—it couldn't be that they were to be separated.

"Winkums, are you asleep?"

"No," whispered Emily.

"Are you sleepy, small dear?"

"No—no—not sleepy."

Douglas Starr took her hand and held it tightly.

"Then we'll have our talk, honey. I can't sleep either. I want to tell you something."

"Oh—I know it—I know it!" burst out Emily. "Oh, Father, I know it! Ellen told me."

Douglas Starr was silent for a moment. Then he said under his breath, "The old fool—the FAT old fool!"—as if Ellen's fatness was an added aggravation of her folly. Again, for the last time, Emily hoped. Perhaps it was all a dreadful mistake—just some more of Ellen's fat foolishness.

"It—it isn't true, is it, Father?" she whispered.

"Emily, child," said her father, "I can't lift you up—I haven't the strength—but climb up and sit on my knee—in the old way."

Emily slipped out of bed and got on her father's knee. He wrapped the old dressing-gown about her and held her close with his face against hers.

"Dear little child—little beloved Emilykin, it is quite true," he said, "I meant to tell you myself to-night. And now that old absurdity of an Ellen has told you—brutally, I suppose—and hurt you dreadfully. She has the brain of a hen and the sensibility of a cow. May jackals sit on her grandmother's grave! I wouldn't have hurt you, dear."

Emily fought something down that wanted to choke her.

"Father, I can't—I can't bear it."

"Yes, you can and will. You will live because there is something for you to do, I think. You have my gift—along with something I never had. You will succeed where I failed, Emily. I haven't been able to do much for you, sweetheart, but I've done what I could. I've taught you something, I think—in spite of Ellen Greene. Emily, do you remember your mother?"

"Just a little—here and there—like lovely bits of dreams."

"You were only four when she died. I've never talked much to you about her—I couldn't. But I'm going to tell you all about her to-night. It doesn't hurt me to talk of her now—I'll see her so soon again. You don't look like her, Emily—only when you smile. For the rest, you're like your namesake, my mother. When you were born I wanted to call you Juliet, too. But your mother wouldn't. She said if we called you Juliet then I'd soon take to calling her 'Mother' to distinguish between you, and she couldn't endure THAT. She said her Aunt Nancy had once said to her, 'The first time your husband calls you "Mother" the romance of life is over.' So we called you after my mother— HER maiden name was Emily Byrd. Your mother thought Emily the prettiest name in the world,—it was quaint and arch and delightful, she said. Emily, your mother was the sweetest woman ever made."

His voice trembled and Emily snuggled close.

"I met her twelve years ago, when I was sub-editor of the *Enterprise* up in Charlottetown and she was in her last year at Queen's. She was tall and fair and blue-eyed. She looked a little like your Aunt Laura, but Laura was never so pretty. Their eyes were very much alike—and their voices. She was one of the Murrays from Blair Water. I've never told you much about your mother's people, Emily. They live up on the old north shore at Blair Water on New Moon Farm—always have lived there since the first Murray came out from the Old Country in 1790. The ship he came on was called the *New Moon* and he named his farm after her."

"It's a nice name—the new moon is such a pretty thing," said Emily, interested for a moment.

"There's been a Murray ever since at New Moon Farm. They're a proud family—the Murray pride is a byword along the north shore, Emily. Well, they had some things to be proud of, that cannot be denied—but they carried it too far. Folks call them 'the chosen people' up there.

"They increased and multiplied and scattered all over, but the old stock at New Moon Farm is pretty well run out. Only your Aunts, Elizabeth and Laura, live there now, and their cousin, Jimmy Murray. They never married—could not find any one good enough for a Murray, so it used to be said. Your Uncle Oliver and your Uncle Wallace live in Summerside, your Aunt Ruth in Shrewsbury and your Great-Aunt Nancy at Priest Pond."

"Priest Pond—that's an INTERESTING name—not a pretty name like New Moon and Blair Water—but interesting," said Emily. Feeling Father's arm around her the horror had momentarily shrunk away. For just a little while she ceased to believe it.

Douglas Starr tucked the dressing-gown a little more closely around her, kissed her black head, and went on.

"Elizabeth and Laura and Wallace and Oliver and Ruth were old Archibald Murray's children. His first wife was their mother. When he was sixty he married again—a young slip of a girl—who died when your mother was born. Juliet was twenty years younger than her half-family, as she used to call them. She was very pretty and charming and they all loved and petted her and were very proud of her. When she fell in love with me, a poor young journalist, with nothing in the world but his pen and his ambition, there was a family earthquake. The Murray pride couldn't tolerate the thing at all. I won't rake it all up—but things were said I could never forget or forgive. Your mother married me, Emily—and the New Moon people would have nothing more to do with her. Can you believe that, in spite of it, she was never sorry for marrying me?"

Emily put up her hand and patted her father's hollow cheek.

"OF COURSE she wouldn't be sorry. OF COURSE she'd rather have you than all the Murrays of any kind of a moon."

Father laughed a little—and there was just a note of triumph in his laugh.

"Yes, she seemed to feel that way about it. And we were so happy—oh, Emilykin, there never were two happier people in the world. You were the child of that happiness. I remember the night you were born in the little house in Charlottetown. It was in May and a west wind was blowing silvery clouds over the moon. There was a star or two here and there. In our tiny garden—everything we had was small except our love and our happiness—it was dark and blossomy. I walked up and down the path between the beds of violets your mother had planted—and prayed. The pale east was just beginning to glow like a rosy pearl when some one came and told me I had a little daughter. I went in—and your mother, white and weak, smiled just that dear, slow, wonderful smile I loved, and said, 'We've—got—the only—baby—of any importance—in—the world, dear. Just—think—of that!'"

"I wish people could remember from the very moment they're born," said Emily. "It would be so very interesting."

"I dare say we'd have a lot of uncomfortable memories," said her father, laughing a little. "It can't be very pleasant getting used to living—no pleasanter than getting used to stopping it. But you didn't seem to find it hard, for you were a good wee kidlet, Emily. We had four more happy years and then—do you remember the time your mother died, Emily?"

"I remember the funeral, Father—I remember it DISTINCTLY. You were standing in the middle of a room, holding me in your arms, and Mother was lying just before us in a long, black box. And you were crying—and I couldn't think why—and I wondered why Mother looked so white and wouldn't open her eyes. And I leaned down and touched her cheek—and oh, it was so cold. It made me shiver. And somebody in the room said, 'Poor little thing!' and I was frightened and put my face down on your shoulder."

"Yes, I recall that. Your mother died very suddenly. I don't think we'll talk about it. The Murrays all came to her funeral. The Murrays have certain traditions and they live up to them very strictly. One of them is that nothing but candles shall be burned for light at New Moon—and another is that no quarrel must be carried past the grave. They came when she was dead—they would have come when she was ill if they had known, I will say that much for them. And they behaved very well—oh, very well indeed. They were not the Murrays of New Moon for nothing. Your Aunt Elizabeth wore her best black satin dress to the funeral. For any funeral but a Murray's the second best one would have done; and they made no serious objection when I said your mother would be buried in the Starr plot in Charlottetown cemetery. They would have liked to take her back to the old Murray burying-ground in Blair Water—they had their own private burying-ground, you know—no indiscriminate graveyard for THEM. But your Uncle Wallace handsomely admitted that a woman should belong to her husband's family in death as in life. And then they offered to take you and bring you up—to 'give you your mother's place.' I refused to let them have you—then. Did I do right, Emily?"

"Yes—yes—yes!" whispered Emily, with a hug at every "yes."

"I told Oliver Murray—it was he who spoke to me about you—that as long as I lived I would not be parted from my child. He said, 'If you ever change your mind, let us know.' But I did not change my mind—not even three years later when my doctor told me I must give up work. 'If you don't, I give you a year,' he said, 'if you do, and live out-of-doors all you can, I give you three—or possibly four.' He was a good prophet. I came out here and we've had four lovely years together, haven't we, small dear one?"

"Yes—oh, yes!"

"Those years and what I've taught you in them are the only legacy I can leave you, Emily. We've been living on a tiny income I have from a life interest that was left me in an old uncle's estate—an uncle who died before I was married. The estate goes to a charity now, and this little house is only a rented one. From a worldly point of view I've certainly been a failure. But your mother's people will care for you—I know that. The Murray pride will guarantee so much, if nothing else. And they can't help loving you. Perhaps I should have sent for them before—perhaps I ought to do it yet. But I have pride of a kind, too—the Starrs are not entirely traditionless—and the Murrays said some very bitter things to me when I married your mother. Will I send to New Moon and ask them to come, Emily?"

"No!" said Emily, almost fiercely.

She did not want any one to come between her and Father for the few precious days left. The thought was horrible to her. It would be bad enough if they had to come—afterwards. But she would not mind anything much—then.

"We'll stay together to the very end, then, little Emily-child. We won't be parted for a minute. And I want you to be brave. You mustn't be afraid of ANYTHING, Emily. Death isn't terrible. The universe is full of love—and spring comes everywhere—and in death you open and shut a door. There are beautiful things on the other side of the door. I'll find your mother there—I've doubted many things, but I've never doubted THAT. Sometimes I've been afraid that she would get so far ahead of me in the ways of eternity that I'd never catch up. But I feel NOW that she's waiting for me. And we'll wait for you—we won't hurry—we'll loiter and linger till you catch up with us."

"I wish you—could take me right through the door with you," whispered Emily.

"After a little while you won't wish that. You have yet to learn how kind time is. And life has something for you—I feel it. Go forward to meet it fearlessly, dear. I know you don't feel like that just now—but you will remember my words by and by."

"I feel just now," said Emily, who couldn't bear to hide anything from Father, "that I don't like God any more."

Douglas Starr laughed—the laugh Emily liked best. It was such a dear laugh—she caught her breath over the dearness of it. She felt his arms tightening round her.

"Yes, you do, honey. You can't help liking God. He is Love itself, you know. You mustn't mix Him up with Ellen Greene's God, of course."

Emily didn't know exactly what Father meant. But all at once she found that she wasn't afraid any longer—and the bitterness had gone out of her sorrow, and the unbearable pain out of her heart. She felt as if love was all about her and around her, breathed out from some great, invisible, hovering Tenderness. One couldn't be afraid or bitter where love was—and love was everywhere. Father was going through the door—no, he was going to lift a curtain—she liked THAT thought better, because a curtain wasn't as hard and fast as a door—and he would slip into that world of which the flash had given her glimpses. He would be there in its beauty—never very far away from her. She could bear anything if she could only feel that Father wasn't very far away from her—just beyond that wavering curtain.

Douglas Starr held her until she fell asleep; and then in spite of his weakness he managed to lay her down in her little bed.

"She will love deeply—she will suffer terribly—she will have glorious moments to compensate—as I have had. As her mother's people deal with her, so may God deal with them," he murmured brokenly.

CHAPTER III
A HOP OUT OF KIN

DOUGLAS STARR lived two weeks more. In after years when the pain had gone out of their recollection, Emily thought they were the most precious of her memories. They were beautiful weeks—beautiful and not sad. And one night, when he was lying on the couch in the sitting-room, with Emily beside him in the old wing-chair, he went past the curtain—went so quietly and easily that Emily did not know he was gone until she suddenly felt the strange STILLNESS of the room— there was no breathing in it but her own.

"Father—Father!" she cried. Then she screamed for Ellen.

Ellen Greene told the Murrays when they came that Emily had behaved real well, when you took everything into account. To be sure, she had cried all night and hadn't slept a wink; none of the Maywood people who came flocking kindly in to help could comfort her; but when morning came her tears were all shed. She was pale and quiet and docile.

"That's right, now," said Ellen, "that's what comes of being properly prepared. Your pa was so mad at me for warning you that he wasn't rightly civil to me since—and him a dying man. But I don't hold any grudge against him. I did my duty. Mrs. Hubbard's fixing up a black dress for you and it'll be ready by supper time. Your ma's people will be here tonight, so they've telegraphed, and I'm bound they'll find you looking respectable. They're well off and they'll provide for you. Your pa hasn't left a cent but there ain't any debts, I'll say THAT for him. Have you been in to see the body?"

"Don't call him THAT," cried Emily, wincing. It was horrible to hear Father called THAT.

"Why not? If you ain't the queerest child! He makes a better looking corpse than I thought he would, what with being so wasted and all. He was always a pretty man, though too thin."

"Ellen Greene," said Emily suddenly, "if you say any more of— those things—about Father, I will put the black curse on you!"

Ellen Greene stared.

"I don't know what on earth you mean. But that's no way to talk to me, after all I've done for you. You'd better not let the Murrays hear you talking like that or they won't want much to do with you. The black curse indeed! Well, here's gratitude!"

Emily's eyes smarted. She was just a lonely, solitary little creature and she felt very friendless. But she was not at all remorseful for what she had said to Ellen and she was not going to pretend she was.

"Come you here and help me wash these dishes," ordered Ellen. "It'll do you good to have something to take up your mind and then you won't be after putting curses on people who have worked their fingers to the bone for you."

Emily, with an eloquent glance at Ellen's hands, went and got the dish towel.

"Your hands are fat and pudgy," she said. "The bones don't show at all."

"Never mind sassing back! It's awful, with your poor pa dead in there. But if your Aunt Ruth takes you she'll soon cure you of that."

"Is Aunt Ruth going to take me?"

"I don't know, but she ought to. She's a widow with no chick or child, and well-to-do."

"I don't think I want Aunt Ruth to take me," said Emily deliberately, after a moment's reflection.

"Well, YOU won't have the choosing likely. You ought to be thankful to get a home anywhere. Remember you're not of much importance."

"I am important to myself," cried Emily proudly.

"It'll be some chore to bring YOU up," muttered Ellen. "Your Aunt Ruth is the one to do it, in my opinion. SHE won't stand no nonsense. A fine woman she is and the neatest housekeeper on P. E. Island. You could eat off her floor."

"I don't want to eat off her floor. I don't care if a floor is dirty as long as the tablecloth is clean."

"Well, her tablecloths are clean too, I reckon. She's got an elegant house in Shrewsbury with bow windows and wooden lace all round the roof. It's very stylish. It would be a fine home for you. She'd learn you some sense and do you a world of good."

"I don't want to learn sense and be done a world of good to," cried Emily with a quivering lip. "I—I want somebody to love me."

"Well, you've got to behave yourself if you want people to like you. You're not to blame so much—your pa has spoiled you. I told him so often enough, but he just laughed. I hope he ain't sorry for it now. The fact is, Emily Starr, you're queer, and folks don't care for queer children."

"How am I queer?" demanded Emily.

"You talk queer—and you act queer—and at times you look queer. And you're too old for your age—though that ain't YOUR fault. It comes of never mixing with other children. I've always threaped at your father to send you to school—learning at home ain't the same thing—but he wouldn't listen to me, of course. I don't say but what you are as far along in book learning as you need to be, but what you want is to learn how to be like other children. In one way it would be a good thing if your Uncle Oliver would take you, for he's got a big family. But he's not as well off as the rest, so it ain't likely he will. Your Uncle Wallace might, seeing as he reckons himself the head of the family. He's only got a grown-up daughter. But his wife's delicate—or fancies she is."

"I wish Aunt Laura would take me," said Emily. She remembered that Father had said Aunt Laura was something like her mother.

"Aunt Laura! SHE won't have no say in it—Elizabeth's boss at New Moon. Jimmy Murray runs the farm, but he ain't quite all there, I'm told—"

"What part of him isn't there?" asked Emily curiously.

"Laws, it's something about his mind, child. He's a bit simple—some accident or other when he was a youngster, I've heard. It addled his head, kind of. Elizabeth was mixed up in it some way—I've never heard the rights of it. I don't reckon the New Moon people will want to be bothered with you. They're awful set in their ways. You take my advice and try to please your Aunt Ruth. Be polite—and well-behaved—mebbe she'll take a fancy to you. There, that's all the dishes. You'd better go upstairs and be out of the way."

"Can I take Mike and Saucy Sal?" asked Emily.

"No, you can't."

"They'd be company for me," pleaded Emily.

"Company or no company, you can't have them. They're outside and they'll stay outside. I ain't going to have them tracking all over the house. The floor's been scrubbed."

"Why didn't you scrub the floor when Father was alive?" asked Emily. "He liked things to be clean. You hardly ever scrubbed it then. Why do you do it now?"

"Listen to her! Was I to be always scrubbing floors with my rheumatiz? Get off upstairs and you'd better lie down awhile."

"I'm going upstairs, but I'm not going to lie down," said Emily. "I've got a lot of thinking to do."

"There's one thing I'd advise you to do," said Ellen, determined to lose no chance of doing her duty, "and that is to kneel down and pray to God to make you a good and respectful and grateful child."

Emily paused at the foot of the stairs and looked back.

"Father said I wasn't to have anything to do with your God," she said gravely.

Ellen gasped foolishly, but could not think of any reply to this heathenish statement. She appealed to the universe.

"Did any one ever hear the like!"

"I know what YOUR God is like," said Emily. "I saw His picture in that Adam-and-Eve book of yours. He has whiskers and wears a nightgown. I don't like Him. But I like Father's God."

"And what is your father's God like, if I may ask?" demanded Ellen sarcastically.

Emily hadn't any idea what Father's God was like, but she was determined not to be posed by Ellen.

"He is clear as the moon, fair as the sun, and terrible as an army with banners," she said triumphantly.

"Well, you're bound to have the last word, but the Murrays will teach you what's what," said Ellen, giving up the argument. "They're strict Presbyterians and won't hold by any of your father's awful notions. Get off upstairs."

Emily went up to the south room, feeling very desolate.

"There isn't anybody in the world who loves me now," she said, as she curled up on her bed by the window. But she was determined she would not cry. The Murrays, who had hated her father, should not see her crying. She felt that she detested them all—except perhaps Aunt Laura. How very big and empty the world had suddenly become. Nothing was interesting any more. It did not matter that the little squat apple-tree between Adam-and-Eve had become a thing of rose-and-snow beauty—that the hills beyond the hollow were of green silk, purple-misted—that the daffodils were out in the garden—that the birches were hung all over with golden tassels—that the Wind Woman was blowing white young clouds across the sky. None of these things had any charm or consolation for her now. In her inexperience she believed they never would have again.

"But I promised Father I'd be brave," she whispered, clenching her little fists, "and I will. And I WON'T let the Murrays see I'm afraid of them—I won't BE afraid of them!"

When the far-off whistle of the afternoon train blew beyond the hills, Emily's heart began to beat. She clasped her hands and lifted her face.

"Please help me, Father's God—NOT Ellen's God," she said. "Help me to be brave and not cry before the Murrays."

Soon after there was the sound of wheels below—and voices—loud, decided voices. Then Ellen came puffing up the stairs with the black dress—a sleazy thing of cheap merino.

"Mrs. Hubbard just got it done in time, thanks be. I wouldn't 'a' had the Murrays see you not in black for the world. They can't say I haven't done my duty. They're all here—the New Moon people and Oliver and his wife, your Aunt Addie, and Wallace and his wife, your Aunt Eva, and Aunt Ruth—Mrs. Dutton, HER name is. There, you're ready now. Come along."

"Can't I put my Venetian beads on?" asked Emily.

"Did ever any mortal! Venetian beads with a mourning dress! Shame on you! Is this a time to be thinking of vanity?"

"It isn't vanity!" cried Emily. "Father gave me those beads last Christmas—and I want to show the Murrays that I've got SOMETHING!"

"No more of your nonsense! Come along, I say! Mind your manners—there's a good deal depends on the impression you make on them."

Emily walked rigidly downstairs before Ellen and into the parlour. Eight people were sitting around it—and she instantly felt the critical gaze of sixteen stranger eyes. She looked very pale and plain in her black dress; the purple shadows left by weeping made her large eyes look too large and hollow. She was desperately afraid, and she knew it—but she would not let the Murrays see it. She held up her head and faced the ordeal before her gallantly.

"This," said Ellen, turning her around by the shoulder, "is your Uncle Wallace."

Emily shuddered and put out a cold hand. She did not like Uncle Wallace—she knew that at once—he was black and grim and ugly, with frowning, bristly brows and a stern, unpitying mouth. He had big pouches under his eyes, and carefully-trimmed black side-whiskers. Emily decided then and there that she did not admire side-whiskers.

"How do you do, Emily?" he said coldly—and just as coldly he bent forward and kissed her cheek.

A sudden wave of indignation swept over Emily's soul. How DARED he kiss her—he had hated her father and disowned her mother! She would have none of his kisses! Flash-quick, she snatched her handkerchief from her pocket and wiped her outraged cheek.

"Well—WELL!" exclaimed a disagreeable voice from the other side of the room.

Uncle Wallace looked as if he would like to say a great many things but couldn't think of them. Ellen, with a grunt of despair, propelled Emily to the next sitter.

"Your Aunt Eva," she said.

Aunt Eva was sitting huddled up in a shawl. She had the fretful face of the imaginary invalid. She shook hands with Emily and said nothing. Neither did Emily.

"Your Uncle Oliver," announced Ellen.

Emily rather liked Uncle Oliver's appearance. He was big and fat and rosy and jolly-looking. She thought she would not mind so much if HE kissed her, in spite of his bristly white moustache. But Uncle Oliver had learned Uncle Wallace's lesson.

"I'll give you a quarter for a kiss," he whispered genially. A joke was Uncle Oliver's idea of being kind and sympathetic, but Emily did not know this, and resented it.

"I don't SELL my kisses," she said, lifting her head as haughtily as any Murray of them all could do.

Uncle Oliver chuckled and seemed infinitely amused and not a bit offended. But Emily heard a sniff across the room.

Aunt Addie was next. She was as fat and rosy and jolly-looking as her husband and she gave Emily's cold hand a nice, gentle squeeze.

"How are you, dear?" she said.

That "dear" touched Emily and thawed her a trifle. But the next in turn froze her up instantly again. It was Aunt Ruth—Emily knew it was Aunt Ruth before Ellen said so, and she knew it was Aunt Ruth who had "well—welled" and sniffed. She knew the cold, grey eyes, the prim, dull brown hair, the short, stout figure, the thin, pinched, merciless mouth.

Aunt Ruth held out the tips of her fingers, but Emily did not take them.

"Shake hands with your Aunt," said Ellen in an angry whisper.

"She does not want to shake hands with me," said Emily, distinctly, "and so I am not going to do it."

Aunt Ruth folded her scorned hands back on her black silk lap.

"You are a very ill-bred child," she said; "but of course it was only what was to be expected."

Emily felt a sudden compunction. Had she cast a reflection on her father by her behaviour? Perhaps after all she should have shaken hands with Aunt Ruth. But it was too late now—Ellen had already jerked her on.

"This is your Cousin, Mr. James Murray," said Ellen, in the disgusted tone of one who gives up something as a bad job and is only anxious to be done with it.

"Cousin Jimmy—Cousin Jimmy," said that individual. Emily looked steadily at him, and liked him at once without any reservations.

He had a little, rosy, elfish face with a forked grey beard; his hair curled over his head in a most un-Murray-like mop of glossy brown; and his large, brown eyes were as kind and frank as a child's. He gave Emily a hearty handshake, though he looked askance at the lady across from him while doing it.

"Hello, pussy!" he said.

Emily began to smile at him, but her smile was, as always, so slow in developing that Ellen had whisked her on before it was in full flower, and it was Aunt Laura who got the benefit of it. Aunt Laura started and paled.

"Juliet's smile!" she said, half under her breath. And again Aunt Ruth sniffed.

Aunt Laura did not look like any one else in the room. She was almost pretty, with her delicate features and the heavy coils of pale, sleek, fair hair, faintly greyed, pinned closely all around her head. But it was her eyes that won Emily. They were such round blue, BLUE eyes. One never quite got over the shock of their blueness. And when she spoke it was in a beautiful, soft voice.

"You poor, dear, little child," she said, and put her arm around Emily for a gentle hug.

Emily returned the hug and had a narrow escape then from letting the Murrays see her cry. All that saved her was the fact that Ellen suddenly pushed her on into the corner by the window.

"And this is your Aunt Elizabeth."

Yes, this was Aunt Elizabeth. No doubt about that—and she had on a stiff, black satin dress, so stiff and rich that Emily felt sure it must be her very best. This pleased Emily. Whatever Aunt Elizabeth thought of her father, at least she had paid him the respect of her best dress. And Aunt Elizabeth was quite fine looking in a tall, thin, austere style, with clear-cut features and a massive coronet of iron-grey hair under her black lace cap. But her eyes, though steel-blue, were as cold as Aunt Ruth's, and her long, thin mouth was compressed severely. Under her cool, appraising glance Emily retreated into herself and shut the door of her soul. She would have liked to please Aunt Elizabeth—who was "boss" at New Moon—but she felt she could not do it.

Aunt Elizabeth shook hands and said nothing—the truth being that she did not know exactly what to say. Elizabeth Murray would not have felt "put about" before King or Governor-General. The Murray pride would have carried her through there; but she did feel disturbed in the presence of this alien, level-gazing child who had already shown that she was anything but meek and humble. Though Elizabeth Murray would never have admitted it, she did not want to be snubbed as Wallace and Ruth had been.

"Go and sit on the sofa," ordered Ellen.

Emily sat on the sofa with her eyes cast down, a slight, black, indomitable little figure. She folded her hands on her lap and crossed her ankles. They should see she had manners.

Ellen had retreated to the kitchen, thanking her stars that THAT was over. Emily did not like Ellen but she felt deserted when Ellen had gone. She was alone now before the bar of Murray opinion. She would have given anything to be out of the room. Yet in the back of her mind a design was forming of writing all about it in the old account book. It would be interesting. She could describe them all—she knew she could. She had the very word for Aunt Ruth's eyes—"stone-grey." They were just like stones—as hard and cold and relentless. Then a pang tore through her heart. Father could never again read what she wrote in the account book.

Still—she felt that she would rather like to write it all out. How could she best describe Aunt Laura's eyes? They were such beautiful eyes—just to call them "blue" meant nothing—hundreds of people had blue eyes—oh, she had it—"wells of blue"—that was the very thing.

And then the flash came!

It was the first time since the dreadful night when Ellen had met her on the doorstep. She had thought it could never come again—and now in this most unlikely place and time it HAD come—she had seen, with other eyes than those of sense, the wonderful world behind the veil. Courage and hope flooded her cold little soul like a wave of rosy light. She lifted her head and looked about her undauntedly—"brazenly" Aunt Ruth afterwards declared.

Yes, she WOULD write them all out in the account book—describe every last one of them—sweet Aunt Laura, nice Cousin Jimmy, grim old Uncle Wallace, and moon-faced Uncle Oliver, stately Aunt Elizabeth and detestable Aunt Ruth.

"She's a delicate-looking child," said Aunt Eva, suddenly, in her fretful, colourless voice.

"Well, what else could you expect?" said Aunt Addie, with a sigh that seemed to Emily to hold some dire significance. "She's too pale—if she had a little colour she wouldn't be bad-looking."

"I don't know who she looks like," said Uncle Oliver, staring at Emily.

"She is not a Murray, that is plain to be seen," said Aunt Elizabeth, decidedly and disapprovingly.

"They are talking about me just as if I wasn't here," thought Emily, her heart swelling with indignation over the indecency of it.

"I wouldn't call her a Starr either," said Uncle Oliver. "Seems to me she's more like the Byrds—she's got her grandmother's hair and eyes."

"She's got old George Byrd's nose," said Aunt Ruth, in a tone that left no doubt as to her opinion of George's nose.

"She's got her father's forehead," said Aunt Eva, also disapprovingly.

"She has her mother's smile," said Aunt Laura, but in such a low tone that nobody heard her.

"And Juliet's long lashes—hadn't Juliet very long lashes?" said Aunt Addie.

Emily had reached the limit of her endurance.

"You make me feel as if I was made up of scraps and patches!" she burst out indignantly.

The Murrays stared at her. Perhaps they felt some compunction—for, after all, none of them were ogres and all were human, more or less. Apparently nobody could think of anything to say, but the shocked silence was broken by a chuckle from Cousin Jimmy—a low chuckle, full of mirth and free from malice.

"That's right, puss," he said. "Stand up to them—take your own part."

"Jimmy!" said Aunt Ruth.

Jimmy subsided.

Aunt Ruth looked at Emily.

"When I was a little girl," she said, "I never spoke until I was spoken to."

"But if nobody ever spoke until they were spoken to there would be no conversation," said Emily argumentatively.

"I never answered back," Aunt Ruth went on severely. "In those days little girls were trained properly. We were polite and respectful to our elders. We were taught our place and we kept it."

"I don't believe you ever had much fun," said Emily—and then gasped in horror. She hadn't meant to say that out loud—she had only meant to THINK it. But she had such an old habit of thinking aloud to Father.

"Fun!" said Aunt Ruth, in a shocked tone. "I did not think of fun when I was a little girl."

"No, I know," said Emily gravely. Her voice and manner were perfectly respectful, for she was anxious to atone for her involuntary lapse. Yet Aunt Ruth looked as if she would like to box her ears. This child was PITYING her—insulting her by being sorry for HER—because of her prim, impeccable childhood. It was unendurable—especially in a Starr. And that abominable Jimmy was chuckling again! Elizabeth should suppress him!

Fortunately Ellen Greene appeared at this juncture and announced supper.

"You've got to wait," she whispered to Emily. "There ain't room for you at the table."

Emily was glad. She knew she could not eat a bite under the Murray eyes. Her aunts and uncles filed out stiffly without looking at her—all except Aunt Laura, who turned at the door and blew her a tiny, furtive kiss. Before Emily could respond Ellen Greene had shut the door.

Emily was left all alone in the room that was filling with twilight shadows. The pride that had sustained her in the presence of the Murrays suddenly failed her and she knew that tears were coming. She went straight to the closed door at the end of the parlour, opened it, and went in. Her father's coffin stood in the centre of the small room which had been a bedroom. It was heaped with flowers—the Murrays had done the proper thing in that as in all else. The great anchor of white roses Uncle Wallace had brought stood up aggressively on the small table at the head. Emily could not see her father's face for Aunt Ruth's heavily-fragrant pillow of white hyacinths lying on the glass, and she dared not move it. But she curled herself up on the floor and laid her cheek against the polished side of the casket. They found her there asleep when they came in after supper. Aunt Laura lifted her up and said,

"I'm going to take the poor child up to bed—she's worn right out."
Emily opened her eyes and looked drowsily about her.

"Can I have Mike?" she said.

"Who is Mike?"

"My cat—my big grey cat."

"A cat!" exclaimed Aunt Elizabeth in a shocked tone. "You must not have a cat in your bedroom!"

"Why not—for once?" pleaded Laura.

"Certainly not!" said Aunt Elizabeth. "A cat is a most unwholesome thing in a sleeping apartment. I'm surprised at you, Laura! Take the child up to bed and see that there are plenty of bedclothes. It's a cold night—but let me hear no more talk of sleeping with cats."

"Mike is a clean cat," said Emily. "He washes himself—every day."

"Take her up to bed, Laura!" said Aunt Elizabeth, ignoring Emily.

Aunt Laura yielded meekly. She carried Emily upstairs, helped her undress, and tucked her into bed. Emily was very sleepy. But before she was wholly asleep she felt something, soft and warm and purry and companionable, snuggling down by her shoulder. Aunt Laura had sneaked down, found Mike and brought him up to her. Aunt Elizabeth never knew and Ellen Greene dared not say a word in protest—for was not Laura a Murray of New Moon?

CHAPTER IV
A FAMILY CONCLAVE

EMILY wakened at daylight the next morning. Through her low, uncurtained window the splendour of the sunrise was coming in, and one faint, white star was still lingering in the crystal-green sky over the Rooster Pine. A fresh sweet wind of dawn was blowing around the eaves. Ellen Greene was sleeping in the big bed and snoring soundly. Except for that the little house was very still. It was the chance for which Emily had waited.

Very carefully she slipped from her bed, tiptoed across the room and opened the door. Mike uncoiled himself from the mat on the middle of the floor and followed her, rubbing his warm sides against her chilly little ankles. Almost guiltily she crept down the bare, dark staircase. How the steps creaked—surely it would waken everybody! But nobody appeared and Emily got down and slipped into the parlour, drawing a long breath of relief as she closed the door. She almost ran across the room to the other door.

Aunt Ruth's floral pillow still covered the glass of the casket. Emily, with a tightening of the lips that gave her face an odd resemblance to Aunt Elizabeth, lifted up the pillow and set it on the floor.

"Oh, Father—Father!" she whispered, putting her hand to her throat to keep something down. She stood there, a little shivering, white-clad figure, and looked at her father. This was to be her good-bye; she must say it when they were alone together—she would not say it before the Murrays.

Father looked so beautiful. All the lines of pain had vanished—his face looked almost like a boy's except for the silver hair above it. And he was smiling—such a nice, whimsical, wise little smile, as if he had suddenly discovered something lovely and unexpected and surprising. She had seen many nice smiles on his face in life but never one just like this.

"Father, I didn't cry before them," she whispered. "I'm sure I didn't disgrace the Starrs. Not shaking hands with Aunt Ruth wasn't disgracing the Starrs, was it? Because she didn't really want me to—oh, Father, I don't think any of them like me, unless perhaps Aunt Laura does a little. And I'm going to cry a little bit now, Father, because I can't keep it back ALL the time."

She laid her face on the cold glass and sobbed bitterly but briefly. She must say good-bye before any one found her. Raising her head she looked long and earnestly at the beloved face.

"Good-bye, dearest darling," she whispered chokingly.

Dashing away her blinding tears she replaced Aunt Ruth's pillow, hiding her father's face from her forever. Then she slipped out, intent on speedily regaining her room. At the door she almost fell over Cousin Jimmy, who was sitting on a chair before it, swathed in a huge, checked dressing-gown, and nursing Mike.

"S-s-h!" he whispered, patting her on the shoulder. "I heard you coming down and followed you. I knew what you wanted. I've been sitting here to keep them out if any of them came after you. Here, take this and hurry back to your bed, small pussy."

"This" was a roll of peppermint lozenges. Emily clutched it and fled, overcome with shame at being seen by Cousin Jimmy in her nightgown. She hated peppermints and never ate them, but the fact of Cousin Jimmy Murray's kindness in giving them to her sent a thrill of delight to her heart. And he called her "small pussy," too,—she liked that. She had thought nobody would ever call her nice pet names again. Father had had so many of them for her—"sweetheart" and "darling" and "Emily-child" and "dear wee kidlet" and "honey" and "elfkin." He had a pet name for every mood and she had loved them all. As for Cousin Jimmy, he was nice. Whatever part of him was missing it wasn't his heart. She felt so grateful to him that after she was safely in her bed again she forced herself to eat one of the lozenges, though it took all her grit to worry it down.

The funeral was held that forenoon. For once the lonesome little house in the hollow was filled. The coffin was taken into the parlour and the Murrays as mourners sat stiffly and decorously all round it, Emily among them, pale and prim in her black dress. She sat between Aunt Elizabeth and Uncle Wallace and dared not move a muscle. No other Starr was present. Her father had no near living relatives. The Maywood people came and looked at his dead face with a freedom and insolent curiosity they would never have presumed on in life. Emily hated to have them looking at her father like that. They had no right— they hadn't been friendly to him while he was alive—they had said harsh things of him—Ellen Greene had sometimes repeated them. Every glance that fell on him hurt Emily; but she sat still and gave no outward sign. Aunt Ruth said afterwards that she had never seen a child so absolutely devoid of all natural feeling.

When the service was over the Murrays rose and marched around the coffin for a dutiful look of farewell. Aunt Elizabeth took Emily's hand and tried to draw her along with them but Emily pulled it back and shook her head. She had said her good-bye already. Aunt Elizabeth seemed for a moment to be on the point of insisting; then she grimly swept onward, alone, looking every inch a Murray. No scene must be made at a funeral.

Douglas Starr was to be taken to Charlottetown for burial beside his wife. The Murrays were all going but Emily was not to go. She watched the funeral procession as it wound up the long, grassy hill, through the light grey rain that was beginning to fall. Emily was glad it was raining; many a time she had heard Ellen Greene say that happy was the corpse the rain fell on; and it was easier to see Father go away in that soft, kind, grey mist than through sparkling, laughing sunshine.

"Well, I must say the funeral went off fine," said Ellen Greene at her shoulder. "Everything's been done regardless. If your father was looking down from heaven at it, Emily, I'm sure he'd be pleased."

"He isn't in heaven," said Emily.

"Good gracious! Of all the children!" Ellen could say no more.

"He isn't there YET. He's only on the way. He said he'd wait around and go slow until I died, too, so that I could catch up with him. I hope I'll die soon."

"That's a wicked, wicked thing to wish," rebuked Ellen.

When the last buggy had disappeared Emily went back to the sitting-room, got a book out of the bookcase, and buried herself in the wing-chair. The women who were tidying up were glad she was quiet and out of the way.

"It's well she can read," said Mrs. Hubbard gloomily. "Some little girls couldn't be so composed—Jennie Hood just screamed and shrieked after they carried her mother out—the Hoods are all such a FEELING people."

Emily was not reading. She was thinking. She knew the Murrays would be back in the afternoon; and she knew her fate would probably be settled then. "We'll talk the matter over when we come back," she had heard Uncle Wallace saying that morning after breakfast. Some instinct told her just what "the matter" was; and she would have given one of her pointed ears to hear the discussion with the other. But she knew very well she would be sent out of the way. So she was not surprised when Ellen came to her in the twilight and said:

"You'd better go upstairs, Emily. Your aunts and uncles are coming in here to talk over the business."

"Can't I help you get supper?" asked Emily, who thought that if she were going and coming around the kitchen she might catch a word or two.

"No. You'd be more bother than help. March, now."

Ellen waddled out to the kitchen, without waiting to see if Emily marched. Emily got up reluctantly. How could she sleep to-night if she did not know what was going to happen to her? And she felt quite sure she would not be told till morning, if then.

Her eyes fell on the oblong table in the centre of the room. Its cloth was of generous proportions, falling in heavy folds to the floor. There was a flash of black stockings across the rug, a sudden disturbance of drapery, and then—silence. Emily, on the floor under the table, arranged her legs comfortably and sat triumphant. She would hear what was decided and nobody would be any the wiser.

She had never been told that it was not considered strictly honourable to eavesdrop, no occasion for such instruction ever having arisen in her life with her father; and she considered that it was a bit of pure luck that she had thought of hiding under the table. She could even see dimly through the cloth. Her heart beat so loudly in her excitement that she was afraid they would hear it; there was no other sound save the soft, faraway singing of frogs through the rain, that sounded through the open window.

In they came; down they sat around the room; Emily held her breath; for a few minutes nobody spoke, though Aunt Eva sighed long and heavily. Then Uncle Wallace cleared his throat and said,

"Well, what is to be done with the child?"

Nobody was in a hurry to answer. Emily thought they would NEVER speak. Finally Aunt Eva said with a whine,

"She's such a difficult child—so odd. I can't understand her at all."

"I think," said Aunt Laura timidly, "that she has what one might call an artistic temperament."

"She's a spoiled child," said Aunt Ruth very decidedly. "There's work ahead to straighten out HER manners, if you ask me."

(The little listener under the table turned her head and shot a scornful glance at Aunt Ruth through the tablecloth. "I think that your own manners have a slight curve." Emily did not dare even to murmur the words under her breath, but she shaped them with her mouth; this was a great relief and satisfaction.)

"I agree with you," said Aunt Eva, "and I for one do not feel equal to the task."

(Emily understood that this meant Uncle Wallace didn't mean to take her and she rejoiced thereat.)

"The truth is," said Uncle Wallace, "Aunt Nancy ought to take her. She has more of this world's goods than any of us."

"Aunt Nancy would never dream of taking her and you know it well enough!" said Uncle Oliver. "Besides, she's entirely too old to have the bringing up of a child—her and that old witch Caroline. Upon my soul, I don't believe either of them is human. I would like to take Emily—but I feel that I can hardly do it. I've a large family to provide for."

"She'll not likely live long to bother any one," said Aunt Elizabeth crisply. "She'll probably die of consumption same as her father did."

("I won't—I won't!" exclaimed Emily—at least she THOUGHT it with such vim that it almost seemed that she exclaimed it. She forgot that she had wanted to die soon, so that she could overtake Father. She wanted to live now, just to put the Murrays in the wrong. "I haven't ANY intention of dying. I'm going to live—for ages—and be a famous AUTHORESS—you'll just see if I don't, Aunt Elizabeth Murray!")

"She IS a weedy looking child," acknowledged Uncle Wallace.

(Emily relieved her outraged feelings by making a face at Uncle Wallace through the tablecloth. "If I ever possess a pig I am going to name it after YOU," she thought—and then felt quite satisfied with her revenge.)

"Somebody has to look after her as long as she's alive though, you know," said Uncle Oliver.

("It would serve you all right if I DID die and you suffered terrible remorse for it all the rest of your lives," Emily thought. Then in the pause that happened to follow, she dramatically pictured out her funeral, selected her pall-bearers, and tried to choose the hymn verse that she wanted engraved on her tombstone. But before she could settle this Uncle Wallace began again.)

"Well, we are not getting anywhere. We have to look after the child—"

("I WISH you wouldn't call me 'THE CHILD,'" thought Emily bitterly.)

"—and some of us must give her a home. Juliet's daughter must not be left to the mercy of strangers. Personally, I feel that Eva's health is not equal to the care and training of a child—"

"Of SUCH a child," said Aunt Eva.

(Emily stuck her tongue out at Aunt Eva.)

"Poor little soul," said Aunt Laura gently.

(Something frozen in Emily's heart melted at that moment. She was pitifully pleased over being called "poor little soul" so tenderly.)

"I do not think you need pity her overmuch, Laura," said Uncle Wallace decidedly. "It is evident that she has very little feeling. I have not seen her shed a tear since we came here."

"Did you notice that she would not even take a last look at her father?" said Aunt Elizabeth.

Cousin Jimmy suddenly whistled at the ceiling.

"She feels so much that she has to hide it," said Aunt Laura.

Uncle Wallace snorted.

"Don't you think WE might take her, Elizabeth?" Laura went on timidly.

Aunt Elizabeth stirred restlessly.

"I don't suppose she'd be contented at New Moon, with three old people like us."

("I would—I would!" thought Emily.)

"Ruth, what about you?" said Uncle Wallace. "You're all alone in that big house. It would be a good thing for you to have some company."

"I don't like her," said Aunt Ruth sharply. "She is as sly as a snake."

("I'm NOT!" thought Emily.)

"With wise and careful training many of her faults may be cured," said Uncle Wallace, pompously.

("I don't WANT them cured!" Emily was getting angrier and angrier all the time under the table. "I like MY faults better than I do YOUR—YOUR—" she fumbled mentally for a word—then triumphantly recalled a phrase of her father's—"your ABOMINABLE virtues!")

"I doubt it," said Aunt Ruth, in a biting tone. "What's bred in the bone comes out in the flesh. As for Douglas Starr, I think that it was perfectly disgraceful for him to die and leave that child without a cent."

"Did he do it on purpose?" asked Cousin Jimmy blandly. It was the first time he had spoken.

"He was a miserable failure," snapped Aunt Ruth.

"He wasn't—he wasn't!" screamed Emily, suddenly sticking her head out under the tablecloth, between the end legs of the table.

For a moment the Murrays sat as silent and motionless as if her outburst had turned them to stone. Then Aunt Ruth rose, stalked to the table, and lifted the cloth, behind which Emily had retired in dismay, realising what she had done.

"Get up and come out of that, Em'ly Starr!" said Aunt Ruth.

"Em'ly Starr" got up and came out. She was not specially frightened—she was too angry to be that. Her eyes had gone black and her cheeks crimson.

"What a little beauty—what a regular little beauty!" said Cousin Jimmy. But nobody heard him. Aunt Ruth had the floor.

"You shameless little eavesdropper!" she said. "There's the Starr blood coming out—a Murray would never have done such a thing. You ought to be whipped!"

"Father wasn't a failure!" cried Emily, choking with anger. "You had no right to call him a failure. Nobody who was loved as much as he was could be a failure. I don't believe anybody EVER loved you. So it's YOU that's a failure. And I'm NOT going to die of consumption."

"Do you realize what a shameful thing you've been guilty of?" demanded Aunt Ruth, cold with anger.

"I wanted to hear what was going to become of me," cried Emily. "I didn't know it was such a dreadful thing to do—I didn't know you were going to say such horrid things about me."

"Listeners never hear any good of themselves," said Aunt Elizabeth impressively. "Your mother would NEVER have done that, Emily."

The bravado all went out of poor Emily. She felt guilty and miserable—oh, so miserable. She hadn't known—but it seemed she had committed a terrible sin.

"Go upstairs," said Aunt Ruth.

Emily went, without a protest. But before going she looked around the room.

"While I was under the table," she said, "I made a face at Uncle Wallace and stuck my tongue out at Aunt Eva."

She said it sorrowfully, desiring to make a clean breast of her transgressions; but so easily do we misunderstand each other that the Murrays actually thought that she was indulging in a piece of gratuitous impertinence. When the door had closed behind her they all—except Aunt Laura and Cousin Jimmy—shook their heads and groaned.

Emily went upstairs in a state of bitter humiliation. She felt that she had done something that gave the Murrays the right to despise her, and they thought it was the Starr coming out in her—and she had not even found out what her fate was to be.

She looked dismally at little Emily-in-the-glass.

"I didn't know—I didn't know," she whispered. "But I'll know after this," she added with sudden vim, "and I'll never, NEVER do it again."

For a moment she thought she would throw herself on her bed and cry. She COULDN'T bear all the pain and shame that were burning in her heart. Then her eyes fell on the old yellow account book on her little table. A minute later Emily was curled up on her bed, Turk-fashion, writing eagerly in the old book with her little stubby lead pencil. As her fingers flew over the faded lines her cheeks flushed and her eyes shone. She forgot the Murrays although she was writing about them—she forgot her humiliation—although she was describing what had happened; for an hour she wrote steadily by the wretched light of her smoky little lamp, never pausing, save now and then, to gaze out of the window into the dim beauty of the misty night, while she hunted through her consciousness for a certain word she wanted; when she found it she gave a happy sigh and fell to again.

When she heard the Murrays coming upstairs she put her book away. She had finished; she had written a description of the whole occurrence and of that conclave ring of Murrays, and she had wound up by a pathetic description of her own deathbed, with the Murrays standing around imploring her forgiveness. At first she depicted Aunt Ruth as doing it on her knees in an agony of remorseful sobs. Then she suspended her pencil—"Aunt Ruth couldn't EVER feel as bad as THAT over anything," she thought—and drew her pencil through the line.

In the writing, pain and humiliation had passed away. She only felt tired and rather happy. It HAD been fun, finding words to fit Uncle Wallace; and what exquisite satisfaction it had been to describe Aunt Ruth as "a dumpy little woman."

"I wonder what my uncles and aunts would say if they knew what I REALLY think of them," she murmured as she got into bed.

CHAPTER V
DIAMOND CUT DIAMOND

EMILY, who had been pointedly ignored by the Murrays at breakfast, was called into the parlour when the meal was over.

They were all there—the whole phalanx of them—and it occurred to Emily as she looked at Uncle Wallace, sitting in the spring sunshine, that she had not just found the exact word after all to express his peculiar quality of grimness.

Aunt Elizabeth stood unsmilingly by the table with slips of paper in her hand.

"Emily," she said, "last night we could not decide who should take you. I may say that none of us feel very much like doing so, for you have behaved very badly in many respects—"

"Oh, Elizabeth,—" protested Laura. "She—she is our sister's child."

Elizabeth lifted a hand regally.

"I am doing this, Laura. Have the goodness not to interrupt me. As I was saying, Emily, we could not decide as to who should have the care of you. So we have agreed to Cousin Jimmy's suggestion that we settle the matter by lot. I have our names here, written on these slips of paper. You will draw one and the one whose name is on it will give you a home."

Aunt Elizabeth held out the slips of paper. Emily trembled so violently that at first she could not draw one. This was terrible—it seemed as if she must blindly settle her own fate.

"Draw," said Aunt Elizabeth.

Emily set her teeth, threw back her head with the air of one who challenges destiny, and drew. Aunt Elizabeth took the slip from the little shaking hand and held it up. On it was her own name—"Elizabeth Murray." Laura Murray suddenly put her handkerchief to her eyes.

"Well, that's settled," said Uncle Wallace, getting up with an air of relief. "And if I'm going to catch that train I've got to hurry. Of course, as far as the matter of expense goes, Elizabeth, I'll do my share."

"We are not paupers at New Moon," said Aunt Elizabeth rather coldly. "Since it has fallen to me to take her, I shall do all that is necessary, Wallace. I do not shirk my duty."

"I am her duty," thought Emily. "Father said nobody ever liked a duty. So Aunt Elizabeth will never like me."

"You've got more of the Murray pride than all the rest of us put together, Elizabeth," laughed Uncle Wallace.

They all followed him out—all except Aunt Laura. She came up to Emily, standing alone in the middle of the room, and drew her into her arms.

"I'm so glad, Emily—I'm so glad," she whispered. "Don't fret, dear child. I love you already—and New Moon is a nice place, Emily."

"It has—a pretty name," said Emily, struggling for self-control. "I've—always hoped—I could go with you, Aunt Laura. I think I am going to cry—but it's not because I'm sorry I'm going there. My manners are NOT as bad as you may think, Aunt Laura—and I wouldn't have listened last night if I'd known it was wrong."

"Of course you wouldn't," said Aunt Laura.

"But I'm not a Murray, you know."

Then Aunt Laura said a queer thing—for a Murray.

"Thank heaven for that!" said Aunt Laura.

Cousin Jimmy followed Emily out and overtook her in the little hall. Looking carefully around to ensure privacy, he whispered,

"Your Aunt Laura is a great hand at making an apple turnover, pussy."

Emily thought apple turnover sounded nice, though she did not know what it was. She whispered back a question which she would never have dared ask Aunt Elizabeth or even Aunt Laura.

"Cousin Jimmy, when they make a cake at New Moon, will they let me scrape out the mixing-bowl and eat the scrapings?"

"Laura will—Elizabeth won't," whispered Cousin Jimmy solemnly.

"And put my feet in the oven when they get cold? And have a cooky before I go to bed?"

"Answer same as before," said Cousin Jimmy. "I'LL recite my poetry to you. It's very few people I do that for. I've composed a thousand poems. They're not written down—I carry them here." Cousin Jimmy tapped his forehead.

"Is it very hard to write poetry?" asked Emily, looking with new respect at Cousin Jimmy.

"Easy as rolling off a log if you can find enough rhymes," said Cousin Jimmy.

They all went away that morning except the New Moon people. Aunt Elizabeth announced that they would stay until the next day to pack up and take Emily with them.

"Most of the furniture belongs to the house," she said, "so it won't take us long to get ready. There are only Douglas Starr's books and his few personal belongings to pack."

"How shall I carry my cats?" asked Emily anxiously.

Aunt Elizabeth stared.

"Cats! You'll take no cats, miss."

"Oh, I must take Mike and Saucy Sal!" cried Emily wildly. "I can't leave them behind. I can't live without a cat."

"Nonsense! There are barn cats at New Moon, but they are never allowed in the house."

"Don't you like cats?" asked Emily wonderingly.

"No, I do NOT."

"Don't you like the FEEL of a nice, soft, fat cat?" persisted Emily.

"No; I would as soon touch a snake."

"There's a lovely old wax doll of your mother's up there," said Aunt Laura. "I'll dress it up for you."

"I don't like dolls—they can't talk," exclaimed Emily.

"Neither can cats."

"Oh, can't they! Mike and Saucy Sal can. Oh, I MUST take them. Oh, PLEASE, Aunt Elizabeth. I LOVE those cats. And they're the only things left in the world that love me. Please!"

"What's a cat more or less on two hundred acres?" said Cousin Jimmy, pulling his forked beard. "Take 'em along, Elizabeth."

Aunt Elizabeth considered for a moment. She couldn't understand why anybody should want a cat. Aunt Elizabeth was one of those people who never do understand anything unless it is told them in plain language and hammered into their heads. And THEN they understand it only with their brains and not with their hearts.

"You may take ONE of your cats," she said at last, with the air of a person making a great concession. "One—and no more. No, don't argue. You may as well learn first as last, Emily, that when I say a thing I mean it. That's enough, Jimmy."

Cousin Jimmy bit off something he had tried to say, stuck his hands in his pockets, and whistled at the ceiling.

"When she won't, she won't—Murray like. We're all born with that kink in us, small pussy, and you'll have to put up with it—more by token that you're full of it yourself, you know. Talk about your not being Murray! The Starr is only skin deep with you."

"It isn't—I'm ALL Starr—I WANT to be," cried Emily. "And, oh, how can I choose between Mike and Saucy Sal?"

This was indeed a problem. Emily wrestled with it all day, her heart bursting. She liked Mike best—there was no doubt of that; but she COULDN'T leave Saucy Sal to Ellen's tender mercies. Ellen had always hated Sal; but she rather liked Mike and she would be good to him. Ellen was going back to her own little house in Maywood village and she wanted a cat. At last in the evening, Emily made her bitter decision. She would take Saucy Sal.

"Better take the Tom," said Cousin Jimmy. "Not so much bother with kittens you know, Emily."

"Jimmy!" said Aunt Elizabeth sternly. Emily wondered over the sternness. Why weren't kittens to be spoken of? But she didn't like to hear Mike called "the Tom." It sounded insulting, someway.

And she didn't like the bustle and commotion of packing up. She longed for the old quiet and the sweet, remembered talks with her father. She felt as if he had been thrust far away from her by this influx of Murrays.

"What's this?" said Aunt Elizabeth suddenly, pausing for a moment in her packing. Emily looked up and saw with dismay that Aunt Elizabeth had in her hands the old account book—that she was opening it—that she was READING in it. Emily sprang across the floor and snatched the book.

"You mustn't read that, Aunt Elizabeth," she cried indignantly, "that's mine,—my own PRIVATE PROPERTY."

"Hoity-toity, Miss Starr," said Aunt Elizabeth, staring at her, "let me tell you that I have a right to read your books. I am responsible for you now. I am not going to have anything hidden or underhanded, understand that. You have evidently something there that you are ashamed to have seen and I mean to see it. Give me that book."

"I'm NOT ashamed of it," cried Emily, backing away, hugging her precious book to her breast. "But I won't let you—or ANYBODY— see it."

Aunt Elizabeth followed.

"Emily Starr, do you hear what I say? Give me that book— at ONCE."

"No—no!" Emily turned and ran. She would NEVER let Aunt Elizabeth see that book. She fled to the kitchen stove—she whisked off a cover—she crammed the book into the glowing fire. It caught and blazed merrily. Emily watched it in agony. It seemed as if part of herself were burning there. But Aunt Elizabeth should never see it— see all the little things she had written and read to Father—all her fancies about the Wind Woman, and Emily-in-the-glass—all her little cat dialogues—all the things she had said in it last night about the Murrays. She watched the leaves shrivel and shudder, as if they were sentient things, and then turn black. A line of white writing came out vividly on one. "Aunt Elizabeth is very cold and HAWTY." What if Aunt Elizabeth had seen THAT? What if she were seeing it now! Emily glanced apprehensively over her shoulder. No, Aunt Elizabeth had gone back to the room and shut the door with what, in anybody but a Murray, would have been called a bang. The account book was a little heap of white film on the glowing coals. Emily sat down by the stove and cried. She felt as if she had lost something incalculably precious. It was terrible to think that all those dear things were gone. She could never write them again—not just the same; and if she could she wouldn't dare—she would never dare to write ANYTHING again, if Aunt Elizabeth must see everything. Father never insisted on seeing them. She liked to read them to HIM—but if she hadn't wanted to do it he would never have made her. Suddenly Emily, with tears glistening on her cheeks, wrote a line in an imaginary account book.

"Aunt Elizabeth is cold and hawty; and she is NOT FAIR."

Next morning, while Cousin Jimmy was tying the boxes at the back of the double-seated buggy, and Aunt Elizabeth was giving Ellen her final instructions, Emily said good-bye to everything—to the Rooster Pine and Adam-and-Eve—"they'll miss me so when I'm gone; there won't be any one here to love them," she said wistfully—to the spider crack in the kitchen window—to the old wing-chair—to the bed of striped grass—to the silver birch-ladies. Then she went upstairs to the window of her own old room. That little window had always seemed to Emily to open on a world of wonder. In the burned account book there had been one piece of which she was especially proud. "A deskripshun of the vew from my Window." She had sat there and dreamed; at night she used to kneel there and say her little prayers. Sometimes the stars shone through it—sometimes the rain beat against it—sometimes the little greybirds and swallows visited it—sometimes airy fragrances floated in from apple and lilac blossom—sometimes the Wind Woman laughed and sighed and sang and whistled round it— Emily had heard her there in the dark nights and in wild, white winter storms. She did not say good-bye to the Wind Woman, for she knew the Wind Woman would be at New Moon, too; but she said good-bye to the little window and the green hill she had loved, and to her fairy-haunted barrens and to little Emily-in-the-glass. There might be another Emily-in-the-glass at New Moon, but she wouldn't be the same one. And she unpinned from the wall and stowed away in her pocket the picture of the ball dress she had cut from a fashion sheet. It was such a wonderful dress—all white lace and wreaths of rosebuds, with a long, long, train of lace flounces that must reach clear across a room. Emily had pictured herself a thousand times wearing that dress, sweeping, a queen of beauty, across a ballroom floor.

Downstairs they were waiting for her. Emily said good-bye to Ellen Greene rather indifferently—she had never liked Ellen Greene at any time, and since the night Ellen had told her her father was going to die she had hated and feared her.

Ellen amazed Emily by bursting into tears and hugging her—begging her not to forget her—asking her to write to her—calling her "my blessed child."

"I am not your blessed child," said Emily, "but I will write to you. And will you be very good to Mike?"

"I b'lieve you feel worse over leaving that cat than you do over leaving me," sniffed Ellen.

"Why, of course I do," said Emily, amazed that there could be any question about it.

It took all her resolution not to cry when she bade farewell to Mike, who was curled up on the sun-warm grass at the back door.

"Maybe I'll see you again sometime," she whispered as she hugged him. "I'm sure GOOD pussy cats go to heaven."

Then they were off in the double-seated buggy with its fringed canopy, always affected by the Murrays of New Moon. Emily had never driven in anything so splendid before. She had never had many drives. Once or twice her father had borrowed Mr. Hubbard's old buckboard and grey pony and driven to Charlottetown. The buckboard was rattly and the pony slow, but Father had talked to her all the way and made the road a wonder.

Cousin Jimmy and Aunt Elizabeth sat in front, the latter very imposing in black lace bonnet and mantle. Aunt Laura and Emily occupied the seat behind, with Saucy Sal between them in a basket, shrieking piteously.

Emily glanced back as they drove up the grassy lane, and thought the little, old, brown house in the hollow had a broken-hearted look. She longed to run back and comfort it. In spite of her resolution, the tears came into her eyes; but Aunt Laura put a kid-gloved hand across Sal's basket and caught Emily's in a close, understanding squeeze.

"Oh, I just love you, Aunt Laura," whispered Emily.
And Aunt Laura's eyes were very, very blue and deep and kind.

CHAPTER VI
NEW MOON

EMILY found the drive through the blossomy June world pleasant. Nobody talked much; even Saucy Sal had subsided into the silence of despair; now and then Cousin Jimmy made a remark, more to himself, as it seemed, than to anybody else. Sometimes Aunt Elizabeth answered it, sometimes not. She always spoke crisply and used no unnecessary words.

They stopped in Charlottetown and had dinner. Emily, who had had no appetite since her father's death, could not eat the roast beef which the boarding-house waitress put before her. Whereupon Aunt Elizabeth whispered mysteriously to the waitress, who went away and presently returned with a plateful of delicate, cold chicken—fine white slices, beautifully trimmed with lettuce frills.

"Can you eat THAT?" said Aunt Elizabeth sternly, as to a culprit at the bar.

"I'll—try," whispered Emily.

She was too frightened just then to say more, but by the time she had forced down some of the chicken she had made up her small mind that a certain matter must be put right.

"Aunt Elizabeth," she said.

"Hey, what?" said Aunt Elizabeth, directing her steel-blue eyes straight at her niece's troubled ones.

"I would like you to understand," said Emily, speaking very primly and precisely so that she would be sure to get things right, "that it was not because I did not like the roast beef I did not eat it. I was not hungry at all; and I just et some of the chicken to oblige you, not because I liked it any better."

"Children should eat what is put before them and never turn up their noses at good, wholesome food," said Aunt Elizabeth severely. So Emily felt that Aunt Elizabeth had not understood after all and she was unhappy about it.

After dinner Aunt Elizabeth announced to Aunt Laura that they would do some shopping.

"We must get some things for the child," she said.

"Oh, please don't call me 'the child,'" exclaimed Emily. "It makes me feel as if I didn't belong anywhere. Don't you like my name, Aunt Elizabeth? Mother thought it so pretty. And I don't need any 'things.' I have two whole sets of underclothes—only one is patched.——"

"S-s-sh!" said Cousin Jimmy, gently kicking Emily's shins under the table.

Cousin Jimmy only meant that she would better let Aunt Elizabeth buy "things" for her when she was in the humour for it; but Emily thought he was rebuking her for mentioning such matters as underclothes and subsided in scarlet conviction. Aunt Elizabeth went on talking to Laura as if she had not heard.

"She must not wear that cheap black dress in Blair Water. You could sift oatmeal through it. It is nonsense expecting a child of ten to wear black at all. I shall get her a nice white dress with black sash for good, and some black-and-white-check gingham for school. Jimmy, we'll leave the child with you. Look after her."

Cousin Jimmy's method of looking after her was to take her to a restaurant down street and fill her up with ice-cream. Emily had never had many chances at ice-cream and she needed no urging, even with lack of appetite, to eat two saucerfuls. Cousin Jimmy eyed her with satisfaction.

"No use my getting anything for you that Elizabeth could see," he said. "But she can't see what is inside of you. Make the most of your chance, for goodness alone knows when you'll get any more."

"Do you never have ice-cream at New Moon?"

Cousin Jimmy shook his head.

"Your Aunt Elizabeth doesn't like new-fangled things. In the house, we belong to fifty years ago, but on the farm she has to give way. In the house—candles; in the dairy, her grandmother's big pans to set the milk in. But, pussy, New Moon is a pretty good place after all. You'll like it some day."

"Are there any fairies there?" asked Emily, wistfully.

"The woods are full of 'em," said Cousin Jimmy. "And so are the columbines in the old orchard. We grow columbines there on purpose for the fairies."

Emily sighed. Since she was eight she had known there were no fairies anywhere nowadays; yet she hadn't quite given up the hope that one or two might linger in old-fashioned, out-of-the-way spots. And where so likely as at New Moon?

"Really-truly fairies?" she questioned.

"Why, you know, if a fairy was really-truly it wouldn't BE a fairy," said Uncle Jimmy seriously. "Could it, now?"

Before Emily could think this out the aunts returned and soon they were all on the road again. It was sunset when they came to Blair

Water—a rosy sunset that flooded the long, sandy sea-coast with colour and brought red road and fir-darkened hill out in fleeting clearness of outline. Emily looked about her on her new environment and found it good. She saw a big house peering whitely through a veil of tall old trees—no mushroom growth of yesterday's birches but trees that had loved and been loved by three generations— a glimpse of silver water glistening through the dark spruces—that was the Blair Water itself, she knew—and a tall, golden-white church spire shooting up above the maple woods in the valley below. But it was none of these that brought her the flash—THAT came with the sudden glimpse of the dear, friendly, little dormer window peeping through vines on the roof—and right over it, in the opalescent sky, a real new moon, golden and slender. Emily was tingling all over with it as Cousin Jimmy lifted her from the buggy and carried her into the kitchen.

She sat on a long wooden bench that was satin-smooth with age and scrubbing, and watched Aunt Elizabeth lighting candles here and there, in great, shining, brass candlesticks—on the shelf between the windows, on the high dresser where the row of blue and white plates began to wink her a friendly welcome, on the long table in the corner. And as she lighted them, elvish "rabbits' candles" flashed up amid the trees outside the windows.

Emily had never seen a kitchen like this before. It had dark wooden walls and low ceiling, with black rafters crossing it, from which hung hams and sides of bacon and bunches of herbs and new socks and mittens, and many other things, the names and uses of which Emily could not imagine. The sanded floor was spotlessly white, but the boards had been scrubbed away through the years until the knots in them stuck up all over in funny little bosses, and in front of the stove they had sagged, making a queer, shallow little hollow. In one corner of the ceiling was a large square hole which looked black and spookish in the candlelight, and made her feel creepy. SOMETHING might pop down out of a hole like that if one hadn't behaved just right, you know. And candles cast such queer wavering shadows. Emily didn't know whether she liked the New Moon kitchen or not. It was an interesting place—and she rather thought she would like to describe it in the old account book, if it hadn't been burned—but Emily suddenly found herself trembling on the verge of tears.

"Cold?" said Aunt Laura kindly. "These June evenings are chilly yet. Come into the sitting-room—Jimmy has kindled a fire in the stove there."

Emily, fighting desperately for self-control, went into the sitting-room. It was much more cheerful than the kitchen. The floor was covered with gay-striped homespun, the table had a bright crimson cloth, the walls were hung with pretty, diamond-patterned paper, the curtains were of wonderful pale-red damask with a design of white ferns scattered all over them. They looked very rich and imposing and Murray-like. Emily had never seen such curtains before. But best of all were the friendly gleams and flickers from the jolly hardwood fire in the open stove that mellowed the ghostly candlelight with something warm and rosy-golden. Emily toasted her toes before it and felt reviving interest in her surroundings. What lovely little leaded glass doors closed the china closets on either side of the high, black, polished mantel! What a funny, delightful shadow the carved ornament on the sideboard cast on the wall behind it—just like a negro's side-face, Emily decided. What mysteries might lurk behind the chintz-lined glass doors of the bookcase! Books were Emily's friends wherever she found them. She flew over to the bookcase and opened the door. But before she could see more than the backs of rather ponderous volumes, Aunt Elizabeth came in, with a mug of milk and a plate whereon lay two little oatmeal cakes.

"Emily," said Aunt Elizabeth sternly, "shut that door. Remember that after this you are not to meddle with things that don't belong to you."

"I thought books belonged to everybody," said Emily.

"Ours don't," said Aunt Elizabeth, contriving to convey the impression that New Moon books were in a class by themselves. "Here is your supper, Emily. We are all so tired that we are just having a lunch. Eat it and then we will go to bed."

Emily drank the milk and worried down the oat-cakes, still gazing about her. How pretty the wallpaper was, with the garland of roses inside the gilt diamond! Emily wondered if she could "see it in the air." She tried—yes, she could—there it hung, a yard from her eyes, a little fairy pattern, suspended in mid-air like a screen. Emily had discovered that she possessed this odd knack when she was six. By a certain movement of the muscles of her eyes, which she could never describe, she could produce a tiny replica of the wallpaper in the air before her—could hold it there and look at it as long as she liked—could shift it back and forth, to any distance she chose, making it larger or smaller as it went farther away or came nearer. It was one of her secret joys when she went into a new room anywhere to "see the paper in the air." And this New Moon paper made the prettiest fairy paper she had ever seen.

"What are you staring at nothing in that queer way for?" demanded Aunt Elizabeth, suddenly returning.

Emily shrank into herself. She couldn't explain to Aunt Elizabeth—Aunt Elizabeth would be like Ellen Greene and say she was "crazy."

"I—I wasn't staring at nothing."

"Don't contradict. I say you were," retorted Aunt Elizabeth. "Don't do it again. It gives your face an unnatural expression. Come now—we will go upstairs. You are to sleep with me."

Emily gave a gasp of dismay. She had hoped it might be with Aunt Laura. Sleeping with Aunt Elizabeth seemed a very formidable thing. But she dared not protest. They went up to Aunt Elizabeth's big, sombre bedroom where there was dark, grim wallpaper that could never be transformed into a fairy curtain, a high black bureau, topped with a tiny swing-mirror, so far above her that there could be no Emily-in-the-glass, tightly closed windows with dark-green curtains, a high bedstead with a dark-green canopy, and a huge, fat, smothering feather-bed, with high, hard pillows.

Emily stood still, gazing about her.

"Why don't you get undressed?" asked Aunt Elizabeth.

"I—I don't like to undress before you," faltered Emily.

Aunt Elizabeth looked at Emily through her cold, spectacled eyes.

"Take off your clothes, AT ONCE," she said.

Emily obeyed, tingling with anger and shame. It was abominable—taking off her clothes while Aunt Elizabeth stood and watched her. The outrage of it was unspeakable. It was even harder to say her prayers before Aunt Elizabeth. Emily felt that it was not much good to pray under such circumstances. Father's God seemed very far away and she suspected that Aunt Elizabeth's was too much like Ellen Greene's.

"Get into bed," said Aunt Elizabeth, turning down the clothes.

Emily glanced at the shrouded window.

"Aren't you going to open the window, Aunt Elizabeth?"

Aunt Elizabeth looked at Emily as if the latter had suggested removing the roof.

"Open the window—and let in the night air!" she exclaimed. "Certainly not!"

"Father and I always had our window open," cried Emily.

"No wonder he died of consumption," said Aunt Elizabeth. "Night air is poison."

"What air is there at night but night air?" asked Emily.

"Emily," said Aunt Elizabeth icily, "get—into—bed."

Emily got in.

But it was utterly impossible to sleep, lying there in that engulfing bed that seemed to swallow her up, with that cloud of blackness above her and not a gleam of light anywhere—and Aunt Elizabeth lying beside her, long and stiff and bony.

"I feel as if I was in bed with a griffin," thought Emily. "Oh—oh—oh—I'm going to cry—I know I am."

Desperately and vainly she strove to keep the tears back—they WOULD come. She felt utterly alone and lonely—there in that darkness, with an alien, hostile world all around her—for it seemed hostile now. And there was such a strange, mysterious, mournful sound in the air—far away, yet clear. It was the murmur of the sea, but Emily did not know that and it frightened her. Oh, for her little bed at home—oh, for Father's soft breathing in the room—oh, for the dancing friendliness of well-known stars shining down through her open window! She MUST go back—she couldn't stay here—she would never be happy here! But there wasn't any "back" to go to—no home—no father—. A great sob burst from her—another followed and then another. It was no use to clench her hands and set her teeth—and chew the inside of her cheeks—nature conquered pride and determination and had her way.

"What are you crying for?" asked Aunt Elizabeth.

To tell the truth Aunt Elizabeth felt quite as uncomfortable and disjointed as Emily did. She was not used to a bedfellow; she didn't want to sleep with Emily any more than Emily wanted to sleep with her. But she considered it quite impossible that the child should be put off by herself in one of the big, lonely New Moon rooms; and Laura was a poor sleeper, easily disturbed; children always kicked, Elizabeth Murray had heard. So there was nothing to do but take Emily in with her; and when she had sacrificed comfort and inclination to do her unwelcome duty this ungrateful and unsatisfactory child was not contented.

"I asked you what you were crying for, Emily?" she repeated.

"I'm—homesick, I guess," sobbed Emily.

Aunt Elizabeth was annoyed.

"A nice home you had to be homesick for," she said sharply.

"It—it wasn't as elegant—as New Moon," sobbed Emily, "but—FATHER was there. I guess I'm Father-sick, Aunt Elizabeth. Didn't you feel awfully lonely when YOUR father died?"

Elizabeth Murray involuntarily remembered the ashamed, smothered feeling of relief when old Archibald Murray had died—the handsome, intolerant, autocratic old man who had ruled his family with a rod of iron all his life and had made existence at New Moon miserable with the petulant tyranny of the five years of invalidism that had closed his career. The surviving Murrays had behaved impeccably, and wept decorously, and printed a long and flattering obituary. But had one genuine feeling of regret followed Archibald Murray to his tomb? Elizabeth did not like the memory and was angry with Emily for evoking it.

"I was resigned to the will of Providence," she said coldly. "Emily, you must understand right now that you are to be grateful and obedient and show your appreciation of what is being done for you. I won't have tears and repining. What would you have done if you had no friends to take you in? Answer me that."

"I suppose I would have starved to death," admitted Emily—instantly beholding a dramatic vision of herself lying dead, looking exactly like the pictures she had seen in one of Ellen Greene's missionary magazines depicting the victims of an Indian famine.

"Not exactly—but you would have been sent to some orphanage where you would have been half-starved, probably. You little know what you have escaped. You have come to a good home where you will be cared for and educated properly."

Emily did not altogether like the sound of being "educated properly." But she said humbly,

"I know it was very good of you to bring me to New Moon, Aunt Elizabeth. And I won't bother you long, you know. I'll soon be grown-up and able to earn my own living. What do you think is the earliest age a person can be called grown-up, Aunt Elizabeth?"

"You needn't think about that," said Aunt Elizabeth shortly. "The Murray women have never been under any necessity for earning their own living. All we require of you is to be a good and contented child and to conduct yourself with becoming prudence and modesty."

This sounded terribly hard.

"I WILL be," said Emily, suddenly determining to be heroic, like the girl in the stories she had read. "Perhaps it won't be so very hard after all, Aunt Elizabeth,"—Emily happened at this point to recall a speech she had heard her father use once, and thought this a good opportunity to work it in—"because, you know, God is good and the devil might be worse."

Poor Aunt Elizabeth! To have a speech like that fired at her in the darkness of the night from that unwelcome little interloper into her orderly life and peaceful bed! Was it any wonder that for a moment or so she was too paralyzed to reply! Then she exclaimed in tones of horror,

"Emily, NEVER say that again."

"All right," said Emily meekly. "But," she added defiantly under her breath, "I'll go on thinking it."

"And now," said Aunt Elizabeth, "I want to say that I am not in the habit of talking all night if you are. I tell you to go to sleep, and I EXPECT you to obey me. Good-night."

The tone of Aunt Elizabeth's good-night would have spoiled the best night in the world. But Emily lay very still and sobbed no more, though the noiseless tears trickled down her cheeks in the darkness for some time. She lay so still that Aunt Elizabeth imagined she was asleep and went to sleep herself.

"I wonder if anybody in the world is awake but me," thought Emily, feeling a sickening loneliness. "If I only had Saucy Sal here! She isn't so cuddly as Mike but she'd be better than nothing. I wonder where she is. I wonder if they gave her any supper."

Aunt Elizabeth had handed Sal's basket to Cousin Jimmy with an impatient, "Here—look to this cat," and Jimmy had carried it off. Where had he put it? Perhaps Saucy Sal would get out and go home—Emily had heard cats always went back home. She wished SHE could get out and go home—she pictured herself and her cat running eagerly along the dark, starlit roads to the little house in the hollow—back to the birches and Adam-and-Eve and Mike, and the old wing-chair and her dear little cot and the open window where the Wind Woman sang to her and at dawn one could see the blue of the mist on the homeland hills.

"Will it ever be morning?" thought Emily. "Perhaps things won't be so bad in the morning."

And then—she heard the Wind Woman at the window—she heard the little, low, whispering murmur of the June night breeze—cooing, friendly, lovesome.

"Oh, you're out there, are you, dearest one?" she whispered, stretching out her arms. "Oh, I'm so glad to hear you. You're such company, Wind Woman. I'm not lonesome any more. And the flash came, too! I was afraid it might never come at New Moon."

Her soul suddenly escaped from the bondage of Aunt Elizabeth's stuffy feather-bed and gloomy canopy and sealed windows. She was out in the open with the Wind Woman and the other gipsies of the night—the fireflies, the moths, the brooks, the clouds. Far and wide she wandered in enchanted reverie until she coasted the shore of dreams and fell soundly asleep on the fat, hard pillow, while the Wind Woman sang softly and luringly in the vines that clustered over New Moon.

CHAPTER VII
THE BOOK OF YESTERDAY

THAT first Saturday and Sunday at New Moon always stood out in Emily's memory as a very wonderful time, so crowded was it with new and generally delightful impressions. If it be true that we "count time by heart throbs" Emily lived two years in it instead of two days. Everything was fascinating from the moment she came down the long, polished staircase into the square hall that was filled with a soft, rosy light coming through the red glass panes of the front door. Emily gazed through the panes delightedly. What a strange, fascinating, red world she beheld, with a weird red sky that looked, she thought, as if it belonged to the Day of Judgment.

There was a certain charm about the old house which Emily felt keenly and responded to, although she was too young to understand it. It was a house which aforetime had had vivid brides and mothers and wives, and the atmosphere of their loves and lives still hung around it, not yet banished by the old-maidishness of the régime of Elizabeth and Laura.

"Why—I'm going to LOVE New Moon," thought Emily, quite amazed at the idea.

Aunt Laura was setting the breakfast table in the kitchen, which seemed quite bright and jolly in the glow of morning sunshine. Even the black hole in the ceiling had ceased to be spookish and become only a commonplace entrance to the kitchen loft. And on the red-sandstone doorstep Saucy Sal was sitting, preening her fur as contentedly as if she had lived at New Moon all her life. Emily did not know it, but Sal had already drunk deep the delight of battle with her peers that morning and taught the barn cats their place once and for all. Cousin Jimmy's big yellow Tom had got a fearful drubbing, and was minus several bits of his anatomy, while a stuck-up, black lady-cat, who fancied herself considerably, had made up her mind that if that grey-and-white, narrow-faced interloper from goodness knew where was going to stay at New Moon, SHE was not.

Emily gathered Sal up in her arms and kissed her joyously, to the horror of Aunt Elizabeth, who was coming across the platform from the cook-house with a plate of sizzling bacon in her hands.

"Don't ever let me see you kissing a cat again," she ordered.

"Oh, all right," agreed Emily cheerfully. "I'll only kiss her when you don't see me after this."

"I don't want any of your pertness, miss. You are not to kiss cats at all."

"But, Aunt Elizabeth, I didn't kiss her on her mouth, OF COURSE. I just kissed her between her ears. It's nice—won't you just try it for once and see for yourself?"

"That will do, Emily. You have said quite enough." And Aunt Elizabeth sailed on into the kitchen majestically, leaving Emily momentarily wretched. She felt that she had offended Aunt Elizabeth, and she hadn't the least notion why or how.

But the scene before her was too interesting to worry long over Aunt Elizabeth. Delicious smells were coming from the cook-house—a little, slant-roofed building at the corner where the big cooking-stove was placed in summer. It was thickly overgrown with hop vines, as most of the New Moon buildings were. To the right was the "new" orchard, very wonderful now in blossom, but a rather commonplace spot after all, since Cousin Jimmy cultivated it in most up-to-date fashion and had grain growing in the wide spaces between the straight rows of trees that looked all alike. But on the other side of the barn lane, just behind the well, was the "old orchard," where Cousin Jimmy said the columbines grew and which seemed to be a delightful place where trees had come up at their own sweet will, and grown into individual shapes and sizes, where blue-eyed ivy twined about their roots and wild-briar roses rioted over the grey paling fence. Straight ahead, closing the vista between the orchards, was a little slope covered with huge white birches, among which were the big New Moon barns, and beyond the new orchard a little, lovable red road looped lightly up and up, over a hill, until it seemed to touch the vivid blue of the sky.

Cousin Jimmy came down from the barns, carrying brimming pails of milk, and Emily ran with him to the dairy behind the cook-house. Such a delightful spot she had never seen or imagined. It was a snow-white little building in a clump of tall balm-of-gileads. Its grey roof was dotted over with cushions of moss like fat green-velvet mice. You went down six sandstone steps, with ferns crowding about them, and opened a white door with a glass panel in it, and went down three more steps. And then you were in a clean, earthy-smelling, damp, cool place with an earthen floor and windows screened by the delicate emerald of young hop-vines, and broad wooden shelves all around, whereon stood wide, shallow pans of glossy brown ware, full of milk coated over with cream so rich that it was positively yellow.

Aunt Laura was waiting for them and she strained the milk into empty pans and then skimmed some of the full ones. Emily thought skimming was a lovely occupation and longed to try her hand at it. She also longed to sit right down and write a description of that dear dairy; but alas, there was no account book; still, she could write it in her head. She squatted down on a little three-legged stool in a dim corner and proceeded to do it, sitting so still that Jimmy and Laura forgot her and went away and later had to hunt for her a quarter of an hour. This delayed breakfast and made Aunt Elizabeth very cross. But Emily had found just the right sentence to define the clear yet dim green light that filled the dairy and was so happy over it that she didn't mind Aunt Elizabeth's black looks a bit.

After breakfast Aunt Elizabeth informed Emily that henceforth it would be one of her duties to drive the cows to pasture every morning.

"Jimmy has no hired man just now and it will save him a few minutes."

"And don't be afraid," added Aunt Laura, "the cows know the way so well they'll go of themselves. You have only to follow and shut the gates."

"I'm not afraid," said Emily.

But she was. She knew nothing about cows; still, she was determined that the Murrays should not suspect a Starr was scared. So, her heart beating like a trip-hammer, she sallied valiantly forth and found that what Aunt Laura had said was true and cows were not such ferocious animals after all. They went gravely on ahead and she had only to follow, through the old orchard and then through the scrub maple growth beyond, along a twisted ferny path where the Wind Woman was purring and peeping around the maple clumps.

Emily loitered by the pasture gate until her eager eyes had taken in all the geography of the landscape. The old pasture ran before her in a succession of little green bosoms right down to the famous Blair Water—an almost perfectly round pond, with grassy, sloping, treeless margins. Beyond it was the Blair Water valley, filled with homesteads, and further out the great sweep of the white-capped gulf. It seemed to Emily's eyes a charming land of green shadows and blue waters. Down in one corner of the pasture, walled off by an old stone dyke, was the little private graveyard where the dead-and-gone Murrays were buried.

Emily wanted to go and explore it, but was afraid to trust herself in the pasture.

"I'll go as soon as I get better acquainted with the cows," she resolved.

Off to the right, on the crest of a steep little hill, covered with young birches and firs, was a house that puzzled and intrigued Emily. It was grey and weather-worn, but it didn't look old. It had never been finished; the roof was shingled but the sides were not, and the windows were boarded over. Why had it never been finished? And it was meant to be such a pretty little house—a house you could love—a house where there would be nice chairs and cozy fires and bookcases and lovely, fat, purry cats and unexpected corners; then and there she named it the Disappointed House, and many an hour thereafter did she spend finishing that house, furnishing it as it should be furnished, and inventing the proper people and animals to live in it.

To the left of the pasture field was another house of a quite different type—a big, old house, tangled over with vines, flat-roofed, with mansard windows, and a general air of indifference and neglect about it. A large, untidy lawn, overgrown with unpruned shrubs and trees, straggled right down to the pond, where enormous willows drooped over the water. Emily decided that she would ask Cousin Jimmy about these houses when she got a good chance.

She felt that, before she went back, she must slip along the pasture fence and explore a certain path which she saw entering the grove of spruce and maple further down. She did—and found that it led straight into Fairyland,—along the bank of a wide, lovely brook—a wild, dear, little path with lady-ferns beckoning and blowing along it, the shyest of elfin June-bells under the firs, and little whims of loveliness at every curve. She breathed in the tang of fir-balsam and saw the shimmer of gossamers high up in the boughs, and everywhere the frolic of elfin lights and shadows. Here and there the young maple branches interlaced as if to make a screen for dryad faces—Emily knew all about dryads, thanks to her father—and the great sheets of moss under the trees were meet for Titania's couch.

"This is one of the places where dreams grow," said Emily happily.

She wished the path might go on forever, but presently it veered away from the brook, and when she had scrambled over a mossy, old board fence she found herself in the "front-garden" of New Moon, where Cousin Jimmy was pruning some spirea bushes.

"Oh, Cousin Jimmy, I've found the dearest little road," said Emily breathlessly.

"Coming up through Lofty John's bush?"

"Isn't it our bush?" asked Emily, rather disappointed.

"No, but it ought to be. Fifty years ago Uncle Archibald sold that jog of land to Lofty John's father—old Mike Sullivan. He built a little house down near the pond and lived there till he quarrelled with Uncle Archibald—which wasn't long, of course. Then he moved his house across the road—and Lofty John lives there now. Elizabeth has tried to buy the land back from him—she's offered him far more than it's worth—but Lofty John won't sell—just for spite, seeing that he has a good farm of his own and this piece isn't much good to him. He only pastures a few young cattle on it through the summer, and what was cleared is all growing up with scrub maple. It's a thorn in Elizabeth's side and likely to be as long as Lofty John nurses his spite."

"Why is he called Lofty John?"

"Because he's a high and lofty fellow. But never mind him. I want to show you round my garden, Emily. It's mine. Elizabeth bosses the farm; but she lets me run the garden—to make up for pushing me into the well."

"DID she do that?"

"Yes. She didn't mean to, of course. We were just children—I was here on a visit—and the men were putting a new hood on the well and cleaning it. It was open—and we were playing tag around it. I made Elizabeth mad—forget what I said—'twasn't HARD to make her mad, you understand—and she made to give me a bang on the head. I saw it coming—and stepped back to get out of the way—and down I went, head first. Don't remember anything more about it. There was nothing but mud at the bottom—but my head struck the stones at the side. I was took up for dead—my head all cut up. Poor Elizabeth was—" Cousin Jimmy shook his head, as if to intimate that it was impossible to describe how or what poor Elizabeth was. "I got about after a while, though—pretty near as good as new. Folks say I've never been quite right since—but they only say that because I'm a poet, and because nothing ever worries me. Poets are so scarce in Blair Water folks don't understand them, and most people worry so much, they think you're not right if you don't worry."

"Won't you recite some of your poetry to me, Cousin Jimmy?" asked Emily eagerly.

"When the spirit moves me I will. It's no use to ask me when the spirit don't move me."

"But how am I to know when the spirit moves you, Cousin Jimmy?"

"I'll begin of my own accord to recite my compositions. But I'll tell you this—the spirit generally moves me when I'm boiling the pigs' potatoes in the fall. Remember that and be around."

"Why don't you write your poetry down?"

"Paper's too scarce at New Moon. Elizabeth has some pet economies and writing paper of any kind is one of them."

"But haven't you any money of your own, Cousin Jimmy?"

"Oh, Elizabeth pays me good wages. But she puts all my money in the bank and just doles out a few dollars to me once in a while. She says I'm not fit to be trusted with money. When I came here to work for her she paid me my wages at the end of the month and I started for Shrewsbury to put it in the bank. Met a tramp on the road—a poor, forlorn creature without a cent. I gave HIM the money. Why not? I had a good home and a steady job and clothes enough to do me for years. I s'pose it was the foolishest thing I ever did—and the nicest. But Elizabeth never got over it. SHE'S managed my money ever since. But come you now, and I'll show you my garden before I have to go and sow turnips."

The garden was a beautiful place, well worthy Cousin Jimmy's pride. It seemed like a garden where no frost could wither or rough wind blow—a garden remembering a hundred vanished summers. There was a high hedge of clipped spruce all around it, spaced at intervals by tall lombardies. The north side was closed in by a thick grove of spruce against which a long row of peonies grew, their great red blossoms splendid against its darkness. One big spruce grew in the center of the garden and underneath it was a stone bench, made of flat shore stones worn smooth by long polish of wind and wave. In the southeast corner was an enormous clump of lilacs, trimmed into the semblance of one large drooping-boughed tree, gloried over with purple. An old summer house, covered with vines, filled the southwest corner. And in the northwest corner there was a sun-dial of grey stone, placed just where the broad red walk that was bordered with striped grass, and picked out with pink conchs, ran off into Lofty John's bush. Emily had never seen a sun-dial before and hung over it enraptured.

"Your great-great grandfather, Hugh Murray, had that brought out from the Old Country," said Cousin Jimmy. "There isn't as fine a one in the Maritime Provinces. And Uncle George Murray brought those conchs from the Indies. He was a sea-captain."

Emily looked about her with delight. The garden was lovely and the house quite splendid to her childish eyes. It had a big front porch with Grecian columns. These were thought very elegant in Blair Water, and went far to justify the Murray pride. A schoolmaster had said they gave the house a classical air. To be sure, the classical effect was just now rather smothered in hop vines that rioted over the whole porch and hung in pale-green festoons above the rows of potted scarlet geraniums that flanked the steps.

Emily's heart swelled with pride.

"It's a noble house," she said.

"And what about my garden?" demanded Cousin Jimmy jealously.

"It's fit for a queen," said Emily, gravely and sincerely.

Cousin Jimmy nodded, well pleased, and then a strange sound crept into his voice and an odd look into his eyes.

"There is a spell woven round this garden. The blight shall spare it and the green worm pass it by. Drought dares not invade it and the rain comes here gently."

Emily took an involuntary step backward—she almost felt like running away. But now Cousin Jimmy was himself again.

"Isn't this grass about the sun-dial like green velvet? I've taken some pains with it, I can tell you. You make yourself at home in this garden." Cousin Jimmy made a splendid gesture. "I confer the freedom of it upon you. Good-luck to you, and may you find the Lost Diamond."

"The Lost Diamond?" said Emily wonderingly. What fascinating thing was this?

"Never hear the story? I'll tell it to-morrow—Sunday's lazy day at New Moon. I must get off to my turnips now or I'll have Elizabeth out looking at me. She won't say anything—she'll just LOOK. Ever seen the real Murray look?"

"I guess I saw it when Aunt Ruth pulled me out from under the table," said Emily ruefully.

"No—no. That was the Ruth Dutton look—spite and malice and all uncharitableness. I hate Ruth Dutton. She laughs at my poetry—not that she ever hears any of it. The spirit never moves when Ruth is around. Dunno where they got her. Elizabeth is a crank but she's sound as a nut, and Laura's a saint. But Ruth's worm-eaten. As for the Murray look, you'll know it when you see it. It's as well-known as the Murray pride. We're a darn queer lot—but we're the finest people ever happened. I'll tell you all about us to-morrow."

Cousin Jimmy kept his promise while the aunts were away at church. It had been decided in family conclave that Emily was not to go to church that day.

"She has nothing suitable to wear," said Aunt Elizabeth. "By next Sunday we will have her white dress ready."

Emily was disappointed that she was not to go to church. She had always found church very interesting on the rare occasions when she got there. It had been too far at Maywood for her father to walk but sometimes Ellen Greene's brother had taken her and Ellen.

"Do you think, Aunt Elizabeth," she said wistfully, "that God would be much offended if I wore my black dress to church? Of course it's cheap—I think Ellen Greene paid for it herself—but it covers me all up."

"Little girls who do not understand things should hold their tongues," said Aunt Elizabeth. "I do not choose that Blair Water people should see my niece in such a dress as that wretched black merino. And if Ellen Greene paid for it we must repay her. You should have told us that before we came away from Maywood. No, you are not going to church to-day. You can wear the black dress to school to-morrow. We can cover it up with an apron."

Emily resigned herself with a sigh of disappointment to staying home; but it was very pleasant after all. Cousin Jimmy took her for a walk to the pond, showed her the graveyard and opened the book of yesterday for her.

"Why are all the Murrays buried here?" asked Emily. "Is it really because they are too good to be buried with common people?"

"No—no, pussy. We don't carry our pride as far as THAT. When old Hugh Murray settled at New Moon there was nothing much but woods for miles and no graveyards nearer than Charlottetown. That's why the old Murrays were buried here—and later on we kept it up because we wanted to lie with our own, here on the green, green banks of the old Blair Water."

"That sounds like a line out of a poem, Cousin Jimmy," said Emily.

"So it is—out of one of my poems."

"I kind of like the idea of a 'sclusive burying-ground like this," said Emily decidedly, looking around her approvingly at the velvet grass sloping down to the fairy-blue pond, the neat walks, the well-kept graves.

Cousin Jimmy chuckled.

"And yet they say you ain't a Murray," he said. "Murray and Byrd and Starr—and a dash of Shipley to boot, or Cousin Jimmy Murray is much mistaken."

"Shipley?"

"Yes—Hugh Murray's wife—your great-great-grandmother—was a Shipley—an Englishwoman. Ever hear of how the Murrays came to New Moon?"

"No."

"They were bound for Quebec—hadn't any notion of coming to P. E. I. They had a long rough voyage and water got scarce, so the captain of the *New Moon* put in here to get some. Mary Murray had nearly died of sea-sickness coming out—never seemed to get her sea-legs—so the captain, being sorry for her, told her she could go ashore with the men and feel solid ground under her for an hour or so. Very gladly she went and when she got to shore she said, 'Here I stay.' And stay she did; nothing could budge her; old Hugh—he was young Hugh then, of course—coaxed and stormed and raged and argued—and even cried, I've been told—but Mary wouldn't be moved. In the end he gave in and had his belongings landed and stayed, too. So that is how the Murrays came to P. E. Island."

"I'm glad it happened like that," said Emily.

"So was old Hugh in the long run. And yet it rankled, Emily—it rankled. He never forgave his wife with a whole heart. Her grave is over there in the corner—that one with the flat red stone. Go you and look at what he had put on it."

Emily ran curiously over. The big flat stone was inscribed with one of the long, discursive epitaphs of an older day. But beneath the epitaph was no scriptural verse or pious psalm. Clear and distinct, in spite of age and lichen, ran the line, "Here I stay."

"THAT'S how he got even with her," said Cousin Jimmy. "He was a good husband to her—and she was a good wife and bore him a fine family—and he never was the same after her death. But that rankled in him until it had to come out."

Emily gave a little shiver. Somehow, the idea of that grim old ancestor with his undying grudge against his nearest and dearest was rather terrifying.

"I'm glad I'm only HALF Murray," she said to herself. Aloud—"Father told me it was a Murray tradition not to carry spite past the grave."

"So 'tis now—but it took its rise from this very thing. His family were so horrified at it, you see. It made considerable of a scandal. Some folks twisted it round to mean that old Hugh didn't believe in the resurrection, and there was talk of the session taking it up, but after a while the talk died away."

Emily skipped over to another lichen-grown stone.

"Elizabeth Burnley—who was she, Cousin Jimmy?"

"Old William Murray's wife. He was Hugh's brother, and came out here five years after Hugh did. His wife was a great beauty and had been a belle in the Old Country. She didn't like the P. E. Island woods. She was homesick, Emily—scandalous homesick. For weeks after she came here she wouldn't take off her bonnet—just walked the floor in it, demanding to be taken back home."

"Didn't she take it off when she went to bed?" asked Emily.

"Dunno if she did go to bed. Anyway, William wouldn't take her back home so in time she took off her bonnet and resigned herself. Her daughter married Hugh's son, so Elizabeth was your great-great-grandmother."

Emily looked down at the sunken green grave and wondered if any homesick dreams haunted Elizabeth Burnley's slumber of a hundred years.

"It's dreadful to be homesick—I know," she thought sympathetically.

"Little Stephen Murray is buried over there," said Cousin Jimmy. "His was the first marble stone in the burying-ground. He was your grandfather's brother—died when he was twelve. He has," said Cousin Jimmy solemnly, "become a Murray tradition."

"Why?"

"He was so beautiful and clever and good. He hadn't a fault—so of course he couldn't live. They say there never was such a handsome child in the connection. And lovable—everybody loved him. He has been dead for ninety years—not a Murray living to-day ever saw him—and yet we talk about him at family gatherings—he's more real than lots of living people. So you see, Emily, he must have been an extraordinary child—but it ended in that—" Cousin Jimmy waved his hand towards the grassy grave and the white, prim headstone.

"I wonder," thought Emily, "if any one will remember ME ninety years after I'm dead."

"This old yard is nearly full," reflected Cousin Jimmy. "There's just room in yonder corner for Elizabeth and Laura—and me. None for you, Emily."

"I don't want to be buried here," flashed Emily. "I think it's splendid to have a graveyard like this in the family—but I am going to be buried in Charlottetown graveyard with Father and Mother. But there's one thing worries me Cousin Jimmy, do YOU think I'm likely to die of consumption?"

Cousin Jimmy looked judicially down into her eyes.

"No," he said, "no, Miss Puss. You've got enough life in YOU to carry you far. You aren't meant for death."

"I feel that, too," said Emily, nodding. "And now, Cousin Jimmy, WHY is that house over there disappointed?"

"Which one?—oh, Fred Clifford's house. Fred Clifford began to build that house thirty years ago. He was to be married and his lady picked out the plan. And when the house was just as far along as you see she jilted him, Emily—right in the face of day she jilted him. Never another nail was driven in the house. Fred went out to British Columbia. He's living there yet—married and happy. But he won't sell that lot to any one—so I reckon he feels the sting yet."

"I'm so sorry for that house. I WISH it had been finished. It WANTS to be—even yet it WANTS to be."

"Well, I reckon it never will. Fred had a bit of Shipley in him, too, you see. One of old Hugh's girls was his grandmother. And Doctor Burnley up there in the big grey house has more than a bit."

"Is he a relation of ours, too, Cousin Jimmy?"

"Forty-second cousin. Way back he had a cousin of Mary Shipley's for a great-something. That was in the Old Country—his forebears came out here after we did. He's a good doctor but an odd stick—odder by far than I am, Emily, and yet nobody ever says he's not all there. Can you account for that? HE doesn't believe in God—and I am not such a fool as that."

"Not in ANY God?"

"Not in any God. He's an infidel, Emily. And he's bringing his little girl up the same way, which I think is a shame, Emily," said Cousin Jimmy confidentially.

"Doesn't her mother teach her things?"

"Her mother is—dead," answered Cousin Jimmy, with a little odd hesitation. "Dead these ten years," he added in a firmer tone. "Ilse

Burnley is a great girl—hair like daffodils and eyes like yellow diamonds."

"Oh, Cousin Jimmy, you promised you'd tell me about the Lost Diamond," cried Emily eagerly.

"To be sure—to be sure. Well, it's there—somewhere in or about the old summer-house, Emily. Fifty years ago Edward Murray and his wife came here from Kingsport for a visit. A great lady she was, and wearing silks and diamonds like a queen, though no beauty. She had a ring on with a stone in it that cost two hundred pounds, Emily. That was a big lot of money to be wearing on one wee woman-finger, wasn't it? It sparkled on her white hand as she held her dress going up the steps of the summer house; but when she came down the steps it was gone."

"And was it NEVER found?" asked Emily breathlessly.

"Never—and for no lack of searching. Edward Murray wanted to have the house pulled down—but Uncle Archibald wouldn't hear of it—because he had built it for his bride. The two brothers quarrelled over it and were never good friends again. Everybody in the connection has taken a spell hunting for the diamond. Most folks think it fell out of the summer house among the flowers or shrubs. But I know better, Emily. I know Miriam Murray's diamond is somewhere about that old house yet. On moonlit nights, Emily, I've seen it glinting—glinting and beckoning. But never in the same place—and when you go to it—it's gone, and you see it laughing at you from somewhere else."

Again there was that eerie, indefinable something in Cousin Jimmy's voice or look that gave Emily a sudden crinkly feeling in her spine. But she loved the way he talked to her, as if she were grown-up; and she loved the beautiful land around her; and, in spite of the ache for her father and the house in the hollow which persisted all the time and hurt her so much at night that her pillow was wet with secret tears, she was beginning to be a little glad again in sunset and bird song and early white stars, in moonlit nights and singing winds. She knew life was going to be wonderful here—wonderful and interesting, what with outdoor cook-houses and cream-girdled dairies and pond paths and sundials, and Lost Diamonds, and Disappointed Houses and men who didn't believe in ANY God—not even Ellen Greene's God. Emily hoped she would soon see Dr. Burnley. She was very curious to see what an infidel looked like. And she had already quite made up her mind that she would find the Lost Diamond.

CHAPTER VIII
TRIAL BY FIRE

AUNT ELIZABETH drove Emily to school the next morning. Aunt Laura had thought that, since there was only a month before vacation, it was not worth while for Emily to "start school." But Aunt Elizabeth did not yet feel comfortable with a small niece skipping around New Moon, poking into everything insatiably, and was resolved that Emily must go to school to get her out of the way. Emily herself, always avid for new experiences, was quite keen to go, but for all that she was seething with rebellion as they drove along. Aunt Elizabeth had produced a terrible gingham apron and an equally terrible gingham sunbonnet from somewhere in the New Moon garret, and made Emily put them on. The apron was a long sack-like garment, high in the neck, with SLEEVES. Those sleeves were the crowning indignity. Emily had never seen any little girl wearing an apron with sleeves. She rebelled to the point of tears over wearing it, but Aunt Elizabeth was not going to have any nonsense. Emily saw the Murray look then; and when she saw it she buttoned her rebellious feelings tightly up in her soul and let Aunt Elizabeth put the apron on her.

"It was one of your mother's aprons when she was a little girl, Emily," said Aunt Laura comfortingly, and rather sentimentally.

"Then," said Emily, uncomforted and unsentimental, "I don't wonder she ran away with Father when she grew up."

Aunt Elizabeth finished buttoning the apron and gave Emily a none too gentle push away from her.

"Put on your sunbonnet," she ordered.

"Oh, please, Aunt Elizabeth, don't make me wear that horrid thing."

Aunt Elizabeth, wasting no further words, picked up the bonnet and tied it on Emily's head. Emily had to yield. But from the depths of the sunbonnet issued a voice, defiant though tremulous.

"Anyway, Aunt Elizabeth, you can't boss God," it said.

Aunt Elizabeth was too cross to speak all the way to the schoolhouse. She introduced Emily to Miss Brownell, and drove away. School was already "in," so Emily hung her sunbonnet on the porch nail and went to the desk Miss Brownell assigned her. She had already made up her mind that she did not like Miss Brownell and never would like her.

Miss Brownell had the reputation in Blair Water of being a fine teacher—due mainly to the fact that she was a strict disciplinarian and kept excellent "order." She was a thin, middle-aged person with a colourless face, prominent teeth, most of which she showed when she laughed, and cold, watchful grey eyes—colder even than Aunt Ruth's. Emily felt as if those merciless agate eyes saw clean through her to the core of her sensitive little soul. Emily could be fearless enough on occasion; but in the presence of a nature which she instinctively felt to be hostile to hers she shrank away in something that was more repulsion than fear.

She was a target for curious glances all the morning. The Blair Water school was large and there were at least twenty little girls of about her own age. Emily looked back curiously at them all and thought the way they whispered to each other behind hands and books when they looked at her very ill-mannered. She felt suddenly unhappy and homesick and lonesome—she wanted her father and her old home and the dear things she loved.

"The New Moon girl is crying," whispered a black-eyed girl across the aisle. And then came a cruel little giggle.

"What is the matter with you, Emily?" said Miss Brownell suddenly and accusingly.

Emily was silent. She could not tell Miss Brownell what was the matter with her—especially when Miss Brownell used such a tone.

"When I ask one of my pupils a question, Emily, I am accustomed to having an answer. Why are you crying?"

There was another giggle from across the aisle. Emily lifted miserable eyes and in her extremity fell back on a phrase of her father's.

"It is a matter that concerns only myself," she said.

A red spot suddenly appeared in Miss Brownell's sallow cheek. Her eyes gleamed with cold fire.

"You will remain in during recess as a punishment for your impertinence," she said—but she left Emily alone the rest of the day.

Emily did not in the least mind staying in at recess, for, acutely sensitive to her environment as she was, she realized that, for some reason she could not fathom, the atmosphere of the school was antagonistic. The glances cast at her were not only curious but ill-natured. She did not want to go out to the playground with those girls. She did not want to go to school in Blair Water. But she would not cry any more. She sat erect and kept her eyes on her book. Suddenly a soft, malignant hiss came across the aisle.

"Miss Pridey—Miss Pridey!"

Emily looked across at the girl. Large, steady, purplish-grey eyes gazed into beady, twinkling, black ones—gazed unquailingly—with something in them that cowed and compelled. The black eyes wavered and fell, their owner covering her retreat with another giggle and toss of her short braid of hair.

"I can master HER," thought Emily, with a thrill of triumph.

But there is strength in numbers and at noon hour Emily found herself standing alone on the playground facing a crowd of unfriendly faces. Children can be the most cruel creatures alive. They have the herd instinct of prejudice against any outsider, and they are merciless in its indulgence. Emily was a stranger and one of the proud Murrays—two counts against her. And there was about her, small and ginghamed and sunbonneted as she was, a certain reserve and dignity and fineness that they resented. And they resented the level way she looked at them, with that disdainful face under cloudy black hair, instead of being shy and drooping as became an interloper on probation.

"You are a proud one," said Black-eyes. "Oh, my, you may have buttoned boots, but you are living on charity."

Emily had not wanted to put on the buttoned boots. She wanted to go barefoot as she had always done in summer. But Aunt Elizabeth had told her that no child from New Moon had ever gone barefoot to school.

"Oh, just look at the baby apron," laughed another girl, with a head of chestnut curls.

Now Emily flushed. This was indeed the vulnerable point in her armour. Delighted at her success in drawing blood the curled one tried again.

"Is that your grandmother's sunbonnet?"

There was a chorus of giggles.

"Oh, she wears a sunbonnet to save her complexion," said a bigger girl. "That's the Murray pride. The Murrays are rotten with pride, my mother says."

"You're awful ugly," said a fat, squat little miss, nearly as broad as she was long. "Your ears look like a cat's."

"You needn't be so proud," said Black-eyes. "Your kitchen ceiling isn't plastered even."

"And your Cousin Jimmy is an idiot," said Chestnut-curls.

"He isn't!" cried Emily. "He has more sense than any of you. You can say what you like about me but you are not going to INSULT MY

FAMILY. If you say one more word about them I'll look you over with the evil eye."

Nobody understood what this threat meant, but that made it all the more effective. It produced a brief silence. Then the baiting began again in a different form.

"Can you sing?" asked a thin, freckled girl, who yet contrived to be very pretty in spite of thinness and freckles.

"No," said Emily.

"Can you dance?"

"No."

"Can you sew?"

"No."

"Can you cook?"

"No."

"Can you knit lace?"

"No."

"Can you crochet?"

"No."

"Then what CAN you do?" said the freckled-one in a contemptuous tone.

"I can write poetry," said Emily, without in the least meaning to say it. But at that instant she knew she COULD write poetry. And with this queer unreasonable conviction came—the flash! Right there, surrounded by hostility and suspicion, fighting alone for her standing, without backing or advantage, came the wonderful moment when soul seemed to cast aside the bonds of flesh and spring upward to the stars. The rapture and delight on Emily's face amazed and enraged her foes. They thought it a manifestation of Murray pride in an uncommon accomplishment.

"You lie," said Black-eyes bluntly.

"A Starr does not lie," retorted Emily. The flash was gone, but its uplift remained. She looked them all over with a cool detachment that quelled them temporarily.

"Why don't you like me?" she asked directly.

There was no reply. Emily looked straight at Chestnut-curls and repeated her question. Chestnut-curls felt herself compelled to answer it.

"Because you ain't a bit like us," she muttered.

"I wouldn't want to be," said Emily scornfully.

"Oh, my, you are one of the Chosen People," mocked Black-eyes.

"Of course I am," retorted Emily.

She walked away to the schoolhouse, conqueror in that battle.

But the forces against her were not so easily cowed. There was much whispering and plotting after she had gone in, a conference with some of the boys, and a handing over of bedizened pencils and chews of gum for value received.

An agreeable sense of victory and the afterglow of the flash carried Emily through the afternoon in spite of the fact that Miss Brownell ridiculed her for her mistakes in spelling. Miss Brownell was very fond of ridiculing her pupils. All the girls in the class giggled except one who had not been there in the morning and was consequently at the tail. Emily had been wondering who she was. She was as unlike the rest of the girls as Emily herself, but in a totally different style. She was tall, oddly dressed in an overlong dress of faded, striped print, and barefooted. Her thick hair, cut short, fluffed out all around her head in a bushy wave that seemed to be of brilliant spun gold; and her glowing eyes were of a brown so light and translucent as to be almost amber. Her mouth was large, and she had a saucy, pronounced chin. Pretty she might not be called, but her face was so vivid and mobile that Emily could not drag her fascinated eyes from it. And she was the only girl in class who did not, sometime through the lesson, get a barb of sarcasm from Miss Brownell, though she made as many mistakes as the rest of them.

At recess one of the girls came up to Emily with a box in her hand. Emily knew that she was Rhoda Stuart and thought her very pretty and sweet. Rhoda had been in the crowd around her at the noon hour but she had not said anything. She was dressed in crispy pink gingham; she had smooth, lustrous braids of sugar-brown hair, big blue eyes, a rose-bud mouth, doll-like features and a sweet voice. If Miss Brownell could be said to have a favourite it was Rhoda Stuart, and she seemed generally popular in her own set and much petted by the older girls.

"Here is a present for you," she said sweetly.

Emily took the box unsuspectingly. Rhoda's smile would have disarmed any suspicion. For a moment Emily was happily anticipant as she removed the cover. Then with a shriek she flung the box from her, and stood pale and trembling from head to foot. There was a snake in the box—whether dead or alive she did not know and did not care. For any snake Emily had a horror and repulsion she could not overcome. The very sight of one almost paralyzed her.

A chorus of giggles ran around the porch.

"Before I'd be so scared of an old dead snake!" scoffed Black-eyes.

"Can you write poetry about THAT?" giggled Chestnut-curls.

"I HATE you—I hate you!" cried Emily. "You are mean, hateful girls!"

"Calling names isn't ladylike," said the Freckled-one. "I thought a Murray would be too grand for that."

"If you come to school to-morrow, MISS Starr," said Black-eyes deliberately, "we are going to take that snake and put it around your neck."

"Let me see you do it!" cried a clear, ringing voice. Into their midst with a bound came the girl with amber eyes and short hair. "Just let me SEE you do it, Jennie Strang!"

"This isn't any of your business, Ilse Burnley," muttered Jennie, sullenly.

"Oh, isn't it? Don't you sass me, Piggy-eyes." Ilse walked up to the retreating Jennie and shook a sunburned fist in her face. "If I catch you teasing Emily Starr to-morrow with that snake again I'll take IT by the tail and YOU by YOUR tail, and slash you across the face with it. Mind that, Piggy-eyes. Now you go and pick up that precious snake of yours and throw it down on the ash pile."

Jennie actually went and did it. Ilse faced the others.

"Clear out, all of you, and leave the New Moon girl alone after this," she said. "If I hear of any more meddling and sneaking I'll slit your throats, and rip out your hearts and tear your eyes out. Yes, and I'll cut off your ears and wear them pinned on my dress!"

Cowed by these ferocious threats, or by something in Ilse's personality, Emily's persecutors drifted away. Ilse turned to Emily.

"Don't mind them," she said contemptuously. "They're jealous of you, that's all—jealous because you live at New Moon and ride in a fringed top-buggy and wear buttoned boots. You smack their mugs if they give you any more of their jaw."

Ilse vaulted the fence and tore off into the maple bush without another glance at Emily. Only Rhoda Stuart remained.

"Emily, I'm awful sorry," she said, rolling her big blue eyes appealingly. "I didn't know there was a snake in that box, cross my heart I didn't. The girls just told me it was a present for you. You're not mad at me, are you? Because I like you."

Emily had been "mad" and hurt and outraged. But this little bit of friendliness melted her instantly. In a moment she and Rhoda had their arms around each other, parading across the playground.

"I'm going to ask Miss Brownell to let you sit with me," said Rhoda. "I used to sit with Annie Gregg but she's moved away. You'd like to sit with me, wouldn't you?"

"I'd love it," said Emily warmly. She was as happy as she had been miserable. Here was the friend of her dreams. Already she worshipped Rhoda.

"We OUGHT to sit together," said Rhoda importantly. "We belong to the two best families in Blair Water. Do you know that if my father had his rights he would be on the throne of England?"

"England!" said Emily, too amazed to be anything but an echo.

"Yes. We are descended from the kings of Scotland," said Rhoda. "So of course we don't 'sociate with everybody. My father keeps store and I'm taking music lessons. Is your Aunt Elizabeth going to give you music lessons?"

"I don't know."

"She ought to. She is very rich, isn't she?"

"I don't know," said Emily again. She wished Rhoda would not ask such questions. Emily thought it was hardly good manners. But surely a descendant of the Stuart kings ought to know the rules of breeding, if anybody did.

"She's got an awful temper, hasn't she?" asked Rhoda.

"No, she hasn't!" cried Emily.

"Well, she nearly killed your Cousin Jimmy in one of her rages," said Rhoda. "That's true—Mother told me. Why doesn't your Aunt Laura get married? Has she got a beau? What wages does your Aunt Elizabeth pay your Cousin Jimmy?"

"I don't know."

"Well," said Rhoda, rather disappointedly. "I suppose you haven't been at New Moon long enough to find things out. But it must be very different from what you've been used to, I guess. Your father was as poor as a church mouse, wasn't he?"

"My father was a very, VERY rich man," said Emily deliberately.

Rhoda stared.

"I thought he hadn't a cent."

"Neither he had. But people can be rich without money."

"I don't see how. But anyhow, YOU'LL be rich some day—your Aunt Elizabeth will likely leave you all her money, Mother says. So I don't care if you ARE living on charity—I love you and I'm going to stick up for you. Have you got a beau, Emily?"

"No," cried Emily, blushing violently and quite scandalized at the idea. "Why, I'm only eleven."

"Oh, everybody in our class has a beau. Mine is Teddy Kent. I shook hands with him after I'd counted nine stars for nine nights without missing a night. If you do that the first boy you shake hands with afterwards is to be your beau. But it's awful hard to do. It took me all winter. Teddy wasn't in school to-day—he's been sick all June. He's the best-looking boy in Blair Water. You'll have to have a beau, too, Emily."

"I won't," declared Emily angrily. "I don't know a thing about beaux and I won't have one."

Rhoda tossed her head.

"Oh, I s'pose you think there's nobody good enough for you, living at New Moon. Well, you won't be able to play Clap-in-and-clap-out if you haven't a beau."

Emily knew nothing of the mysteries of Clap-in-and-clap-out, and didn't care. Anyway, she wasn't going to have a beau and she repeated this in such decided tones that Rhoda deemed it wise to drop the subject.

Emily was rather glad when the bell rang. Miss Brownell granted Rhoda's request quite graciously and Emily transferred her goods and chattels to Rhoda's seat. Rhoda whispered a good deal during the last hour and Emily got scolded for it but did not mind.

"I'm going to have a birthday party the first week in July, and I'm going to invite you, if your aunts will let you come. I'm not going to have Ilse Burnley though."

"Don't you like her?"

"No. She's an awful tomboy. And then her father is an infidel. And so's she. She always spells 'God' with a little 'g' in her dictation. Miss Brownell scolds her for it but she does it right along. Miss Brownell won't whip HER because she's setting her cap for Dr. Burnley. But Ma says she won't get him because he hates women. I don't think it's proper to 'sociate with such people. Ilse is an awful wild queer girl and has an awful temper. So has her father. She doesn't chum with anybody. Isn't it ridic'lus the way she wears her hair? YOU ought to have a bang, Emily. They're all the rage and you'd look well with one because you've such a high forehead. It would make a real beauty of you. My, but you have lovely hair, and your hands are just lovely. All the Murrays have pretty hands. And you have the SWEETEST eyes, Emily."

Emily had never received so many compliments in her life. Rhoda laid flattery on with a trowel. Her head was quite turned and she went home from school determined to ask Aunt Elizabeth to cut her hair in a bang. If it would make a beauty of her it must be compassed somehow. And she would also ask Aunt Elizabeth if she might wear her Venetian beads to school next day.

"The other girls may RESPECT me more then," she thought.

She was alone from the crossroads, where she had parted company with Rhoda, and she reviewed the events of the day with a feeling that, after all, she had kept the Starr flag flying, except for a temporary reverse in the matter of the snake. School was very different from what she had expected it to be, but that was the way in life, she had heard Ellen Greene say, and you just had to make the best of it. Rhoda was a darling; and there was something about Ilse Burnley that one liked; and as for the rest of the girls Emily got square with them by pretending she saw them all being hanged in a row for frightening her to death with a snake, and felt no more resentment towards them, although some of the things that had been said to her rankled bitterly in her heart for many a day. She had no father to tell them to, and no account book to write them out in, so she could not exorcise them.

She had no speedy chance to ask for a bang, for there was company at New Moon and her aunts were busy getting ready an elaborate supper. But when the preserves were brought on Emily snatched the opportunity of a lull in the older conversation.

"Aunt Elizabeth," she said, "can I have a bang?"

Aunt Elizabeth looked her disdain.

"No," she said, "I do not approve of bangs. Of all the silly fashions that have come in now-a-days, bangs are the silliest."

"Oh, Aunt Elizabeth, DO let me have a bang. It would make a beauty of me,—Rhoda says so."

"It would take a good deal more than a bang to do that, Emily. We will not have bangs at New Moon—except on the Molly cows. THEY are the only creatures that should wear bangs."

Aunt Elizabeth smiled triumphantly around the table—Aunt Elizabeth DID smile sometimes when she thought she had silenced some small person by exquisite ridicule. Emily understood that it was no use to hope for bangs. Loveliness did not lie that way for her. It was mean of Aunt Elizabeth—mean. She heaved a sigh of disappointment and dismissed the idea for the present. There was something else she wanted to know.

"Why doesn't Ilse Burnley's father believe in God?" she asked.

"'Cause of the trick her mother played him," said Mr. Slade, with a chuckle. Mr. Slade was a fat, jolly-looking old man with bushy hair and whiskers. He had already said some things Emily could not understand and which had seemed greatly to embarrass his very lady-like wife.

"What trick did Ilse's mother play?" asked Emily, all agog with interest.

Now Aunt Laura looked at Aunt Elizabeth and Aunt Elizabeth looked at Aunt Laura. Then the latter said:

"Run out and feed the chickens, Emily."

Emily rose with dignity.

"You might just as well tell me that Ilse's mother isn't to be talked about and I would obey you. I understand PERFECTLY what you mean," she said as she left the table.

CHAPTER IX
A SPECIAL PROVIDENCE

EMILY was sure on that first day at school that she would never like it. She must go, she knew, in order to get an education and be ready to earn her own living; but it would always be what Ellen Greene solemnly called "a cross." Consequently Emily felt quite astonished when, after going to school a few days, it dawned upon her that she was liking it. To be sure, Miss Brownell did not improve on acquaintance; but the other girls no longer tormented her—indeed, to her amazement, they seemed suddenly to forget all that had happened and hailed her as one of themselves. She was admitted to the fellowship of the pack and, although in some occasional tiff she got a dig about baby aprons and Murray pride, there was no more hostility, veiled or open. Besides, Emily was quite able to give "digs" herself, as she learned more about the girls and their weak points, and she could give them with such merciless lucidity and irony that the others soon learned not to provoke them. Chestnut-curls, whose name was Grace Wells, and the Freckled-one, whose name was Carrie King, and Jennie Strang became quite chummy with her, and Jennie sent chews of gum and tissue thumb-papers across the aisle instead of giggles. Emily allowed them all to enter the outer court of her temple of friendship but only Rhoda was admitted to the inner shrine. As for Ilse Burnley, she did not appear after that first day. Ilse, so Rhoda said, came to school or not, just as she liked. Her father never bothered about her. Emily always felt a certain hankering to know more of Ilse, but it did not seem likely to be gratified.

Emily was insensibly becoming happy again. Already she felt as if she belonged to this old cradle of her family. She thought a great deal about the old Murrays; she liked to picture them revisiting the glimpses of New Moon—Great-grandmother rubbing up her candlesticks and making cheeses; Great-aunt Miriam stealing about looking for her lost treasure; homesick Great-great-aunt Elizabeth stalking about in her bonnet; Captain George, the dashing, bronzed sea-captain, coming home with the spotted shells of the Indies; Stephen, the beloved of all, smiling from its windows; her own mother dreaming of Father—they all seemed as real to her as if she had known them in life.

She still had terrible hours when she was overwhelmed by grief for her father and when all the splendours of New Moon could not stifle the longing for the shabby little house in the hollow where they had loved each other so. Then Emily fled to some secret corner and cried her heart out, emerging with red eyes that always seemed to annoy Aunt Elizabeth. Aunt Elizabeth had become used to having Emily at New Moon but she had not drawn any nearer to the child. This hurt Emily always; but Aunt Laura and Cousin Jimmy loved her and she had Saucy Sal and Rhoda, fields creamy with clover, soft dark trees against amber skies, and the madcap music the Wind Woman made in the firs behind the barns when she blew straight up from the gulf; her days became vivid and interesting, full of little pleasures and delights, like tiny, opening, golden buds on the tree of life. If she could only have had her old yellow account book, or some equivalent, she could have been fully content. She missed it next to her father, and its enforced burning was something for which she held Aunt Elizabeth responsible and for which she felt she could never wholly forgive her. It did not seem possible to get any substitute. As Cousin Jimmy had said, writing paper of any kind was scarce at New Moon. Letters were seldom written, and when they were a sheet of note-paper sufficed. Emily dared not ask Aunt Elizabeth for any. There were times when she felt she would burst if she couldn't write out some of the things that came to her. She found a certain safety valve in writing on her slate in school; but these scribblings had to be rubbed off sooner or later—which left Emily with a sense of loss—and there was always the danger that Miss Brownell would see them. That, Emily felt, would be unendurable. No stranger eyes must behold these sacred productions. Sometimes she let Rhoda read them, though Rhoda rasped her by giggling over her finest flights. Emily thought Rhoda as near perfection as a human being could be, but giggling was her fault.

But there is a destiny which shapes the ends of young misses who are born with the itch for writing tingling in their baby fingertips, and in the fulness of time this destiny gave to Emily the desire of her heart—gave it to her, too, on the very day when she most needed it. That was the day, the ill-starred day, when Miss Brownell elected to show the fifth class, by example as well as precept, how the *Bugle Song* should be read.

Standing on the platform Miss Brownell, who was not devoid of a superficial, elocutionary knack, read those three wonderful verses. Emily, who should have been doing a sum in long division, dropped her pencil and listened entranced. She had never heard the *Bugle Song* before—but now she heard it—and SAW it—the rose-red splendour falling on those storied, snowy summits and ruined castles—the lights that never were on land or sea streaming over the lakes—she heard the wild echoes flying through the purple valleys and the misty passes—the mere sound of the words seemed to make an exquisite echo in her soul—and when Miss Brownell came to "Horns of elf-land faintly blowing" Emily trembled with delight. She was snatched out of herself. She forgot everything but the magic of that unequalled line—she sprang from her seat, knocking her slate to the floor with a clatter, she rushed up the aisle, she caught Miss Brownell's arm.

"Oh, teacher," she cried with passionate earnestness, "read that line over again—oh, read that line over again!"

Miss Brownell, thus suddenly halted in her elocutionary display, looked down into a rapt, uplifted face where great purplish-grey eyes were shining with the radiance of a divine vision—and Miss Brownell was angry. Angry with this breach of her strict discipline—angry with this unseemly display of interest in a third class atom whose attention should have been focused on long division. Miss Brownell shut her book and shut her lips and gave Emily a resounding slap on her face.

"Go right back to your seat and mind your own business, Emily Starr," said Miss Brownell, her cold eyes malignant with her fury.

Emily, thus dashed to earth, moved back to her seat in a daze. Her smitten cheek was crimson, but the wound was in her heart. One moment ago in the seventh heaven—and now THIS—pain, humiliation, misunderstanding! She could not bear it. What had she done to deserve it? She had never been slapped in her life before. The degradation and the injustice ate into her soul. She could not cry—this was "a grief too deep for tears"—she went home from school in a suppressed anguish of bitterness and shame and resentment—an anguish that had no outlet, for she dared not tell her story at New Moon. Aunt Elizabeth, she felt sure, would say that Miss Brownell had done quite right, and even Aunt Laura, kind and sweet as she was, would not understand. She would be grieved because Emily had misbehaved in school and had had to be punished.

"Oh, if I could only tell Father all about it!" thought Emily.

She could not eat any supper—she did not think she would ever be able to eat again. And oh, how she hated that unjust, horrid Miss Brownell! She could never forgive her—never! If there were only some way in which she could get square with Miss Brownell! Emily, sitting small and pale and quiet at the New Moon supper table, was a seething volcano of wounded feeling and misery and pride—ay, pride! Worse even than the injustice was the sting of humiliation over this thing that had happened. She, Emily Byrd Starr, on whom no hand had ever before been ungently laid, had been slapped like a naughty baby before the whole school. Who could endure this and live?

Then destiny stepped in and drew Aunt Laura to the sitting-room bookcase to look in its lower compartment for a certain letter she wanted to see. She took Emily with her to show her a curious old snuff-box that had belonged to Hugh Murray, and in rummaging for it lifted out a big, flat bundle of dusty paper—paper of a deep pink colour in oddly long and narrow sheets.

"It's time these old letter-bills were burned," she said. "What a pile of them! They've been here gathering dust for years and they are no earthly good. Father once kept the post-office here at New Moon, you know, Emily. The mail came only three times a week then, and each day there was one of these long red 'letter-bills,' as they were called. Mother always kept them, though when once used they were of no further use. But I'm going to burn them right away."

"Oh, Aunt Laura," gasped Emily, so torn between desire and fear that she could hardly speak. "Oh, don't do that—give them to me—PLEASE give them to me."

"Why, child, what ever do you want of them?"

"Oh, Aunty, they have such lovely blank backs for writing on. Please, Aunt Laura, it would be a SIN to burn those letter-bills."

"You can have them, dear. Only you'd better not let Elizabeth see them."

"I won't—I won't," breathed Emily.

She gathered her precious booty into her arms and fairly ran upstairs—and then upstairs again into the garret, where she already had her "favourite haunt," in which her uncomfortable habit of thinking of things thousands of miles away could not vex Aunt Elizabeth. This was the quiet corner of the dormer window, where shadows always moved about, softly and swingingly, and beautiful mosaics patterned the bare floor. From it one could see over the tree-tops right down to the Blair Water. The walls were hung around with great bundles of soft fluffy rolls, all ready for spinning, and hanks of untwisted yarn. Sometimes Aunt Laura spun on the great wheel at the other end of the garret and Emily loved the whirr of it.

In the recess of the dormer window she crouched—breathlessly she selected a letter-bill and extracted a lead pencil from her pocket. An old sheet of cardboard served as a desk; she began to write feverishly.

"Dear Father"—and then she poured out her tale of the day—of her rapture and her pain—writing heedlessly and intently until the sunset faded into dim, star-litten twilight. The chickens went unfed—Cousin Jimmy had to go himself for the cows—Saucy Sal got no new milk—Aunt Laura had to wash the dishes—what mattered it? Emily, in the delightful throes of literary composition, was lost to all worldly things.

When she had covered the backs of four letter-bills she could see to write no more. But she had emptied out her soul and it was once more free from evil passions. She even felt curiously indifferent to Miss Brownell. Emily folded up her letter-bills and wrote clearly across the packet,

MR. DOUGLAS STARR,

ON THE ROAD TO HEAVEN.

Then she stepped softly across to an old, worn-out sofa in a far corner and knelt down, stowing away her letter and her "letter-bills" snugly on a little shelf formed by a board nailed across it underneath. Emily had discovered this one day when playing in the garret and had noted it as a lovely hiding-place for secret documents. Nobody would ever come across them there. She had writing paper enough to last for months—there must be hundreds of those jolly old letter-bills.

"Oh," cried Emily, dancing down the garret stairs, "I feel as if I was made out of star-dust."

Thereafter few evenings passed on which Emily did not steal up to the garret and write a letter, long or short, to her father. The bitterness died out of her grief. Writing to him seemed to bring him so near; and she told him everything, with a certain honesty of confession that was characteristic of her—her triumphs, her failures, her joys, her sorrows, everything went down on the letter-bills of a Government which had not been so economical of paper as it afterwards became. There was fully half a yard of paper in each bill and Emily wrote a small hand and made the most of every inch.

"I like New Moon. It's so STATELY and SPLENDID here," she told her father. "And it seems as if we must be very aristokratik when we have a sun dyal. I can't help feeling proud of it all. I am afraid I have too much pride and so I ask God every night to take MOST of it away but not quite all. It is very easy to get a repputation for pride in Blair Water school. If you walk straight and hold your head up you are a proud one. Rhoda is proud, too, because her father ought to be King of England. I wonder how Queen Victoria would feel if she knew that.

It's very wonderful to have a friend who would be a princess if every one had their rites. I love Rhoda with all my heart. She is so sweet and kind. But I don't like her giggles. And when I told her I could see the school wallpaper small in the air she said You lie. It hurt me awfully to have my dearest friend say that to me. And it hurt me worse when I woke up in the night and thought about it. I had to stay awake ever so long, too, because I was tired lying on one side and I was afraid to turn over because Aunt Elizabeth would think I was figitting.

"I didn't dare tell Rhoda about the Wind Woman because I suppose that really is a kind of lie, though she seems so real to me. I hear her now singing up on the roof around the big chimneys. I have no Emily-in-the-glass here. The looking-glasses are all too high up in the rooms I've been in. I've never been in the look-out. It is always locked. It was Mother's room and Cousin Jimmy says her father locked it up after she ran away with you and Aunt Elizabeth keeps it locked still out of respect to his memory, though Cousin Jimmy says Aunt Elizabeth used to fight with her father something scandalus when he was alive though no outsider knew of it because of the Murray pride. I feel that way myself. When Rhoda asked me if Aunt Elizabeth burned candles because she was old-fashioned I answered hawtily no, it was a Murray tradishun. Cousin Jimmy has told me all the tradishuns of the Murrays. Saucy Sal is very well and bosses the barns but still she will not have kittens and I can't understand it. I asked Aunt Elizabeth about it and she said nice little girls didn't talk about such things but I cannot see why kittens are impropper. When Aunt Elizabeth is away Aunt Laura and I smuggle Sal into the house but when Aunt Elizabeth comes back I always feel gilty and wish I hadn't. BUT THE NEXT TIME I DO IT AGAIN. I think that very strange. I never hear about dear Mike. I wrote Ellen Greene and asked about him and she replyed and never mentioned Mike but told me all about her roomatism. As if I cared about her roomatism.

"Rhoda is going to have a birthday party and she is going to invite me. I am so exited. You know I never was to a party before. I think about it a great deal and picture it out. Rhoda is not going to invite all the girls but only a favered few. I hope Aunt Elizabeth will let me ware my white dress and good hat. Oh, Father, I pinned that lovely picture of the lace ball dress up on the wall of Aunt Elizabeth's room, just like I had it at home and Aunt Elizabeth took it down and burned it and skolded me for making pin marks in the paper. I said Aunt Elizabeth you should not have burned that picture. I wanted to have it when I grow up to have a dress made like it for balls. And Aunt Elizabeth said Do you expect to attend many balls if I may ask and I said Yes when I am rich and famus and Aunt Elizabeth said Yes when the moon is made of green cheese.

"I saw Dr. Burnley yesterday when he came over to buy some eggs from Aunt Elizabeth. I was disappointed because he looks just like other people. I thought a man who didn't believe in God would look queer in some way. He did not sware either and I was sorry for I have never heard any one sware and I am very angshus to. He has big yellow eyes like Ilse and a loud voice and Rhoda says when he gets mad you can hear him yelling all over Blair Water. There is some mistery about Ilse's mother which I cannot fathum. Dr. Burnley and Ilse live alone. Rhoda says Dr. Burnley says he will have no devils of women in that house. That speech is wikked but striking. Old Mrs. Simms goes over and cooks dinner and supper for them and then vamooses and they get their own breakfast. The doctor sweeps out the house now and then and Ilse never does anything but run wild. The doctor never smiles so Rhoda says. He must be like King Henry the Second.

"I would like to get akwanted with Ilse. She isn't as sweet as Rhoda but I like her looks, too. But she doesn't come to school much and Rhoda says I mustn't have any chum but her or she will cry her eyes out. Rhoda loves me as much as I love her. We are both going to pray that we may live together all our lives and die the same day.

"Aunt Elizabeth always puts up my school dinner for me. She won't give me anything but plain bread and butter but she cuts good thick slices and the butter is thick too and never has the horrid taste Ellen Greene's butter used to have. And Aunt Laura slips in a cooky or an apple turnover when Aunt Elizabeth's back is turned. Aunt Elizabeth says apple turnovers are not helthy for me. Why is it that the nicest things never are helthy, Father? Ellen Greene used to say that too.

"My teacher's name is Miss Brownell. I don't like the cut of her jib. (That is a naughtical frays that Cousin Jimmy uses. I know frays is not spelled right but there is no dixonary at New Moon but that is the sound of it.) She is too sarkastik and she likes to make you rediklus. Then she laughs at you in a disagreable, snorting way. But I forgave her for slapping me and I took a boquet to her to school next day to make up. She receeved it very coldly and let it fade on her desk. In a story she would have wepped on my neck. I don't know whether it is any use forgiving people or not. Yes, it is, it makes you feel more comfortable yourself. You never had to ware baby aprons and sunbonnets because you were a boy so you can't understand how I feel about it. And the aprons are made of such good stuff that they will never ware out and it will be years before I grow out of them. But I have a white dress for church with a black silk sash and a white legorn hat with black bows and black kid slippers, and I feel very elegant in them. I wish I could have a bang but Aunt Elizabeth will not hear to it. Rhoda told me I had beautiful eyes. I wish she hadn't. I have always suspekted my eyes were beautiful but I was not sure. Now that I know they are I'm afraid I'll always be wondering if people notis it. I have to go to bed at half past eight and I don't like it but I sit up in bed and look out of the window till it gets dark, so I get square with Aunt Elizabeth that way, and I listen to the sound the sea makes. I like it now though it always makes me feel sorrowful, but it's a kind of a nice sorrow. I have to sleep with Aunt Elizabeth and I don't like that either because if I move ever so little she says I figit but she admits that I don't kick. And she won't let me put the window up. She doesn't like fresh air or light in the house. The parlour is dark as a toomb. I went in one day and rolled up all the blinds and Aunt Elizabeth was horrifyed and called me a little hussy and gave me the Murray look. You would suppose I had committed a crime. I felt so insulted that I came up to the garret and wrote a deskription of myself being drowned on a letter-bill and then I felt better. Aunt Elizabeth said I was never to go into the parlour again without permission but I don't want to. I am afraid of the parlour. All the walls are hung over with pictures of our ancestors and there is not one good-looking person among them except Grand-father Murray who looks handsome but very cross. The spare room is upstairs and is just as gloomy as the parlour. Aunt Elizabeth only lets distingwished people sleep there. I like the kitchen in daytime, and the garret and the cook-house and the sitting-room and the hall because of the lovely red front door and I love the dairy, but I don't like the other New Moon rooms. Oh, I forgot the cellar cubbord. I love to go down there and look at the beautiful rows of jam and jelly pots. Cousin Jimmy says it is a New Moon tradishun that the jam pots must never be empty. What a lot of tradishuns New Moon has. It is a very spashus house, and the trees are lovely. I have named the three lombardys at the garden gate the Three Princesses and I have named the old summer house Emily's Bower, and the big apple tree by the old orchard gate the Praying Tree because it holds up its long boughs exactly as Mr. Dare holds up his arms in church where he prays.

"Aunt Elizabeth has given me the little right hand top burow drawer to keep my things in.

"Oh, Father dear, I have made a great diskoverry. I wish I had made it when you were alive for I think you'd have liked to know. I CAN WRITE POETRY. Perhaps I could have written it long ago if I'd tried. But after that first day in school I felt I was bound in honnour to try and it is so easy. There is a little curly black-covered book in Aunt Elizabeth's bookcase called Thompson's Seasons and I decided I would write a poem on a season and the first three lines are,

Now Autumn comes ripe with the peech and pear,
The sportsman's horn is heard throughout the land,
And the poor partridge fluttering falls dead.

"Of course there are no peeches in P. E. Island and I never heard a sportsman's horn here either, but you don't have to stick too close to facts in poetry. I filled a whole letter-bill with it and then I ran and read it to Aunt Laura. I thought she would be overjoyed to find she had a niece who could write poetry but she took it very coolly and said it didn't sound much like poetry. It's blank verse I cryed. VERY blank said Aunt Elizabeth sarkastically though I hadn't asked HER opinion. But I think I will write ryming poetry after this so that there will be no mistake about it and I intend to be a poetess when I grow up and become famus. I hope also that I will be silph-like. A poetess should be silph-like. Cousin Jimmy makes poetry too. He has made over 1000 pieces but he never writes any down but carries them in his head. I offered to give him some of my letter-bills—for he is very kind to me—but he said he was too old to learn new habits. I haven't heard any of his poetry yet because the spirit hasn't moved him but I am very angshus to and I am sorry they don't fatten the pigs till the fall. I like Cousin Jimmy more and more all the time, except when he takes his queer spells of looking and talking. Then he fritens me but they never last long. I have read a good many of the books in the New Moon bookcase. A history of the reformation in France, very relijus and sad. A little fat book deskribing the months in England and the afoursaid Thompson's Seasons. I like to read them because they have so many pretty words in them, but I don't like the feel of them. The paper is so rough and thick it makes me creepy. Travels in Spain, very fassinating, with lovely smooth shiny paper, a missionary book on the Paciffic Islands, pictures very interesting because of the way the heathen chiefs arange their hair. After they became Christians they cut it off which I think was a pity. Mrs. Hemans Poems. I am passhunately fond of poetry, also of stories about desert islands. Rob Roy, a novel, but I only read a little of it when Aunt Elizabeth said I must stop because I must not read novels. Aunt Laura says to read it on the sly. I don't see why it wouldn't be all right to obey Aunt Laura but I have a queer feeling about it and I haven't yet. A lovely Tiger-book, full of pictures and stories of tigers that make me feel so nice and shivery. The Royal Road, also relijus but some fun in it so very good for Sundays. Reuben and Grace, a story but not a novel, because Reuben and Grace are brother and sister and there is no getting married. Little Katy and Jolly Jim, same as above but not so exciting and traggic. Nature's Mighty Wonders which is good and improving. Alice in Wonderland, which is perfectly lovely, and the Memoirs of Anzonetta B. Peters who was converted at seven and died at twelve. When anybody asked for a question she answered with a hym verse. That is after she was converted. Before that she spoke English. Aunt Elizabeth told me I ought to try to be like Anzonetta. I think I might be an Alice under more faverable circumstances but I am sure I can never be as good as Anzonetta was and I don't believe I want to be because she never had any fun. She got sick as soon as she was converted and suffered aggonies for years. Besides I am sure that if I talked hyms to people it would exite ridicule. I tried it once. Aunt Laura asked me the other day if I would like blue stripes better than red in my next winter's stockings and I ansered just as Anzonetta did when asked a similar question, only different, about a sack,

> Jesus Thy blood and rightchusness
> My beauty are, my glorious dress.

And Aunt Laura said was I crazy and Aunt Elizabeth said I was ireverent. So I know it wouldn't work. Besides, Anzonetta couldn't eat anything for years having ulsers in her stomach and I am pretty fond of good eating.

"Old Mr. Wales on the Derry Pond Road is dying of canser. Jennie Strang says his wife has her morning all ready.

"I wrote a biograffy of Saucy Sal to-day and a deskripshun of the road in Lofty John's bush. I will pin them to this letter so you can read them too. Good night my beloved Father.

"Yours most obedient humble servant,

"EMILY B. STARR.

"P. S. I think Aunt Laura loves me. I like to be loved, Father dear.

"E. B. S."

CHAPTER X
GROWING PAINS

THERE was a great deal of suppressed excitement in school during the last week in June, the cause thereof being Rhoda Stuart's birthday party, which was to take place early in July. The amount of heart burning was incredible. Who was to be invited? That was the great question. There were some who knew they wouldn't and some who knew they would; but there were more who were in truly horrible suspense. Everybody paid court to Emily because she was Rhoda's dearest friend and might conceivably have some voice in the selection of guests. Jennie Strang even went as far as bluntly to offer Emily a beautiful white box with a gorgeous picture of Queen Victoria on the cover, to keep her pencils in, if she would procure her an invitation. Emily refused the bribe and said grandly that she could not interfere in such a delicate matter. Emily really did put on some airs about it. SHE was sure of her invitation. Rhoda had told her about the party weeks before and had talked it all over with her. It was to be a very grand affair—a birthday cake covered with pink icing and adorned with ten tall pink candles—ice-cream and oranges—and written invitations on pink, gilt-edged notepaper SENT THROUGH THE POST-OFFICE—this last being an added touch of exclusiveness. Emily dreamed about that party day and night and had her present all ready for Rhoda—a pretty hair ribbon which Aunt Laura had brought from Shrewsbury.

On the first Sunday in July Emily found herself sitting beside Jennie Strang in Sunday School for the opening exercises. Generally she and Rhoda sat together, but now Rhoda was sitting three seats ahead with a strange little girl—a very gay and gorgeous little girl, dressed in blue silk, with a large, flower-wreathed leghorn hat on her elaborately curled hair, white lace-work stockings on her pudgy legs and a bang that came clean down to her eyes. Not all her fine feathers could make a really fine bird of her, however; she was not in the least pretty and her expression was cross and contemptuous.

"Who is the girl sitting with Rhoda?" whispered Emily.

"Oh, she's Muriel Porter," answered Jennie. "She's a towny, you know. She's come out to spend her vacation with her aunt, Jane Beatty. I hate her. If I was her I'd never DREAM of wearing blue with a skin as dark as hers. But the Porters are rich and Muriel thinks she's a wonder. They say Rhoda and her have been AWFUL THICK since she came out—Rhoda's always chasing after anybody she thinks is up in the world."

Emily stiffened up. She was not going to listen to disparaging remarks about her friends. Jennie felt the stiffening and changed her note.

"Anyway, I'm GLAD I'm not invited to Rhoda's old party. I wouldn't WANT to go when Muriel Porter will be there, putting on her airs."

"How do you know you are not invited?" wondered Emily.

"Why, the invitations went out yesterday. Didn't you get yours?"

"No—o—o."

"Did you get your mail?"

"Yes—Cousin Jimmy got it."

"Well, maybe Mrs. Beecher forgot to give it to him. Likely you'll get it to-morrow."

Emily agreed that it was likely. But a queer cold sensation of dismay had invaded her being, which was not removed by the fact that after Sunday School Rhoda strutted away with Muriel Porter without a glance at any one else. On Monday Emily herself went to the post-office, but there was no pink envelope for her. She cried herself to sleep that night, but did not quite give up hope until Tuesday had passed. Then she faced the terrible truth—that she—she, Emily Byrd Starr, of New Moon—had not been invited to Rhoda's party. The thing was incredible. There MUST be a mistake somewhere. Had Cousin Jimmy lost the invitation on the road home? Had Rhoda's grown-up sister who wrote the invitations overlooked her name? Had,—Emily's unhappy doubts were forever resolved into bitter certainty by Jennie, who joined her as she left the post-office. There was a malicious light in Jennie's beady eyes. Jennie liked Emily quite well by now, in spite of their passage-at-arms on the day of their first meeting, but she liked to see her pride humbled for all that.

"So you're not invited to Rhoda's party after all."

"No," admitted Emily.

It was a very bitter moment for her. The Murray pride was sorely wrung—and, beneath the Murray pride, something else had been grievously wounded but was not yet quite dead.

"Well, I call it dirt mean," said Jennie, quite honestly sympathetic in spite of her secret satisfaction. "After all the fuss she's made over you, too! But that's Rhoda Stuart all over. Deceitful is no name for HER."

"I don't think she's deceitful," said Emily, loyal to the last ditch. "I believe there's some mistake about my not being invited."

Jennie stared.

"Then you don't know the reason? Why, Beth Beatty told me the whole story. Muriel Porter hates you and she just up and told Rhoda that she would not go to her party if you were invited. And Rhoda was so crazy to have a town girl there that she promised she wouldn't invite you."

"Muriel Porter doesn't know me," gasped Emily. "How can she hate me?"

Jennie grinned impishly.

"I can tell you. She's DEAD STUCK on Fred Stuart and Fred knows it and he teased her by praising YOU up to her—told her you were the sweetest girl in Blair Water and he meant to have you for HIS GIRL when you were a little older. And Muriel was so mad and jealous she made Rhoda leave you out. I wouldn't care if I was you. A Murray of New Moon is away above such trash. As for Rhoda not being deceitful, I can tell you she IS. Why, she told you that she didn't know that snake was in the box, when it was her thought of doing it in the first place."

Emily was too crushed to reply. She was glad that Jennie had to switch off down her own lane and leave her alone. She hurried home, afraid that she could not keep the tears back until she got there. Disappointment about the party—humiliation over the insult—all were swallowed up in the anguish of a faith betrayed and a trust outraged. Her love of Rhoda was quite dead now and Emily smarted to the core of her soul with the pain of the blow that had killed it. It was a child's tragedy—and all the more bitter for that, since there was no one to understand. Aunt Elizabeth told her that birthday parties were all nonsense and that the Stuarts were not a family that the Murrays had ever associated with. And even Aunt Laura, though she petted and comforted, did not realize how deep and grievous the hurt had been—so deep and grievous that Emily could not even write about it to her father, and had no outlet for the violence of emotion that racked her being.

The next Sunday Rhoda was alone in Sunday School, Muriel Porter having been suddenly summoned back to town by her father's illness; and Rhoda looked sweetly towards Emily. But Emily sailed past her with a head held very high and scorn on every lineament. She would NEVER have anything to do with Rhoda Stuart again—she couldn't. She despised Rhoda more than ever for trying to get back with her, now that the town girl for whom she had sacrificed her was gone. It was not for Rhoda she mourned—it was for the friendship that had been so dear to her. Rhoda HAD been dear and sweet on the surface at least, and Emily had found intense happiness in their companionship. Now it was gone and she could never, NEVER love or trust anybody again. THERE lay the sting.

It poisoned everything. Emily was of a nature which, even as a child, did not readily recover from or forget such a blow. She moped about New Moon, lost her appetite and grew thin. She hated to go to Sunday School because she thought the other girls exulted in her humiliation and her estrangement from Rhoda. Some slight feeling of the kind there was, perhaps, but Emily morbidly exaggerated it. If two girls whispered or giggled together she thought she was being discussed and laughed at. If one of them walked home with her she thought it was out of condescending pity because she was friendless. For a month Emily was the most unhappy little being in Blair Water.

"I think I must have been put under a curse at birth," she reflected disconsolately.

Aunt Elizabeth had a more prosaic idea to account for Emily's languor and lack of appetite. She had come to the conclusion that Emily's heavy masses of hair "took from her strength" and that she would be much stronger and better if it were cut off. With Aunt Elizabeth to decide was to act. One morning she coolly informed Emily that her hair was to be "shingled."

Emily could not believe her ears.

"You don't mean that you are going to cut off my hair, Aunt Elizabeth," she exclaimed.

"Yes, I mean exactly that," said Aunt Elizabeth firmly. "You have entirely too much hair especially for hot weather. I feel sure that is why you have been so miserable lately. Now, I don't want any crying."

But Emily could not keep the tears back.

"Don't cut it ALL off," she pleaded. "Just cut a good big bang. Lots of the girls have their hair banged clean from the crown of their heads. That would take half my hair off and the rest won't take too much strength."

"There will be no bangs here," said Aunt Elizabeth. "I've told you so often enough. I'm going to shingle your hair close all over your head for the hot weather. You'll be thankful to me some day for it."

Emily felt anything but thankful just then.

"It's my one beauty," she sobbed, "it and my lashes. I suppose you want to cut off my lashes too."

Aunt Elizabeth DID distrust those long, upcurled fringes of Emily's, which were an inheritance from the girlish stepmother, and too un-Murray-like to be approved; but she had no designs against them. The hair must go, however, and she curtly bade Emily wait there, without any fuss, until she got the scissors.

Emily waited—quite hopelessly. She must lose her lovely hair—the hair her father had been so proud of. It might grow again in time—if Aunt Elizabeth let it—but that would take years, and meanwhile what a fright she would be! Aunt Laura and Cousin Jimmy were out; she had no one to back her up; this horrible thing must happen.

Aunt Elizabeth returned with the scissors; they clicked suggestively as she opened them; that click, as if by magic, seemed to loosen something—some strange formidable power in Emily's soul. She turned deliberately around and faced her aunt. She felt her brows drawing together in an unaccustomed way—she felt an uprush as from unknown depths of some irresistible surge of energy.

"Aunt Elizabeth," she said, looking straight at the lady with the scissors, "MY HAIR IS NOT GOING TO BE CUT OFF. Let me hear no more of this."

An amazing thing happened to Aunt Elizabeth. She turned pale—she laid the scissors down—she looked aghast for one moment at the transformed or possessed child before her—and then for the first time in her life Elizabeth Murray turned tail and fled—literally fled—to the kitchen.

"What is the matter, Elizabeth?" cried Laura, coming in from the cook-house.

"I saw—Father—looking from her face," gasped Elizabeth, trembling. "And she said, 'Let me hear no more of this,'—just as HE always said it—his very words."

Emily overheard her and ran to the sideboard mirror. She had had, while she was speaking, an uncanny feeling of wearing somebody else's face instead of her own. It was vanishing now—but Emily caught a glimpse of it as it left—the Murray look, she supposed. No wonder it had frightened Aunt Elizabeth—it frightened herself—she was glad that it had gone. She shivered—she fled to her garret retreat and cried; but somehow, she knew that her hair would not be cut.

Nor was it; Aunt Elizabeth never referred to the matter again. But several days passed before she meddled much with Emily.

It was a rather curious fact that from that day Emily ceased to grieve over her lost friend. The matter had suddenly become of small importance. It was as if it had happened so long ago that nothing, save the mere emotionless memory of it, remained. Emily speedily regained appetite and animation, resumed her letters to her father and found that life tasted good again, marred only by a mysterious prescience that Aunt Elizabeth had it in for her in regard to her defeat in the matter of her hair and would get even sooner or later.

Aunt Elizabeth "got even" within the week. Emily was to go on an errand to the shop. It was a broiling day and she had been allowed to go barefooted at home; but now she must put on boots and stockings. Emily rebelled—it was too hot—it was too dusty—she couldn't walk that long half-mile in buttoned boots. Aunt Elizabeth was inexorable. No Murray must be seen barefooted away from home—and on they went. But the minute Emily was outside the New Moon gate she deliberately sat down, took them off, stowed them in a hole in the dyke, and pranced away barefooted.

She did her errand and returned with an untroubled conscience. How beautiful the world was—how softly blue was the great, round Blair Water—how glorious that miracle of buttercups in the wet field below Lofty John's bush! At sight of it Emily stood stock still and composed a verse of poetry.

"Buttercup, flower of the yellow dye,
I see thy cheerful face
Greeting and nodding everywhere
Careless of time and place.
"In boggy field or public road
Or cultured garden's pale
You sport your petals satin-soft,
And down within the vale."

So far, so good. But Emily wanted another verse to round the poem off properly and the divine afflatus seemed gone. She walked dreamily home, and by the time she reached New Moon she had got her verse and was reciting it to herself with an agreeable sense of completion.

"You cast your loveliness around
Where'er you chance to be,
And you shall always, buttercup,
Be a flower dear to me."

Emily felt very proud. This was her third poem and undoubtedly her best. Nobody could say IT was very blank. She must hurry up to the garret and write it on a letter-bill. But Aunt Elizabeth was confronting her on the steps.

"Emily, where are your boots and stockings?"

Emily came back from cloudland with a disagreeable jolt. She had forgotten all about boots and stockings.

"In the hole by the gate," she said flatly.

"You went to the store barefooted?"

"Yes."

"After I had told you not to?"

This seemed to Emily a superfluous question and she did not answer it. But Aunt Elizabeth's turn had come.

CHAPTER XI
ILSE

EMILY was locked in the spare-room and told that she must stay there until bedtime. She had pleaded against such a punishment in vain. She had tried to give the Murray look but it seemed that—in her case at any rate—it did not come at will.

"Oh, don't shut me up alone there, Aunt Elizabeth," she implored. "I know I was naughty—but don't put me in the spare-room."

Aunt Elizabeth was inexorable. She knew that it was a cruel thing to shut an over-sensitive child like Emily in that gloomy room. But she thought she was doing her duty. She did not realize and would not have for a moment believed that she was really wreaking her own smothered resentment with Emily for her defeat and fright on the day of the threatened hair-cutting. Aunt Elizabeth believed she had been stampeded on that occasion by a chance family resemblance coming out under stress, and she was ashamed of it. The Murray pride had smarted under that humbling, and the smart ceased to annoy her only when she turned the key of the spare-room on the white-faced culprit.

Emily, looking very small and lost and lonely, her eyes full of such fear as should have no place in a child's eyes, shrank close against the door of the spare-room. It was better that way. She could not imagine things behind her then. And the room was so big and dim that a dreadful number of things could be imagined in it. Its bigness and dimness filled her with a terror against which she could not strive. Ever since she could remember she had had a horror of being shut up alone in semi-darkness. She was not frightened of twilight out-of-doors, but this shadowy, walled gloom made of the spare-room a place of dread.

The window was hung with heavy, dark-green material, reinforced by drawn slat-blinds. The big canopied bed, jutting out from the wall into the middle of the floor, was high and rigid and curtained also with dark draperies. ANYTHING might jump at her out of such a bed. What if some great black hand should suddenly reach out of it—reach right across the floor—and pluck at her? The walls, like those of the parlour, were adorned with pictures of departed relatives. There WAS such a large connection of dead Murrays. The glasses of their frames gave out weird reflections of the spectral threads of light struggling through the slat blinds. Worst of all, right across the room from her, high up on the top of the black wardrobe, was a huge, stuffed white Arctic owl, staring at her with uncanny eyes. Emily shrieked aloud when she saw it, and then cowered down in her corner aghast at the sound she had made in the great, silent, echoing room. She wished that something WOULD jump out of the bed and put an end to her.

"I wonder what Aunt Elizabeth would feel like if I was found here DEAD," she thought, vindictively.

In spite of her fright she began to dramatize it and felt Aunt Elizabeth's remorse so keenly that she decided only to be unconscious and come back to life when everybody was sufficiently scared and penitent. But people HAD died in this room—dozens of them. According to Cousin Jimmy it was a New Moon tradition that when any member of the family was near death he or she was promptly removed to the spare-room, to die amid surroundings of proper grandeur. Emily could SEE them dying, in that terrible bed. She felt that she was going to scream again, but she fought the impulse down. A Starr must not be a coward. Oh, that owl! Suppose, when she looked away from it and then looked back she would find that it had silently hopped down from the wardrobe and was coming towards her. Emily dared not look at it for fear that was just what had happened. DIDN'T the bed curtains stir and waver! She felt beads of cold perspiration on her forehead.

Then something did happen. A beam of sunlight struck through a small break in one of the slats of the blind and fell directly athwart the picture of Grandfather Murray hanging over the mantel-piece. It was a crayon "enlargement" copied from the old daguerreotype in the parlour below. In that gleam of light his face seemed veritably to leap out of the gloom at Emily with its grim frown strangely exaggerated. Emily's nerve gave way completely. In an ungovernable spasm of panic she rushed madly across the room to the window, dashed the curtains aside, and caught up the slat blind. A blessed flood of sunshine burst in. Outside was a wholesome, friendly, human world. And, of all wonders, there, leaning right against the window-sill was a ladder! For a moment Emily almost believed that a miracle had been worked for her escape.

Cousin Jimmy had tripped that morning over the ladder, lying lost among the burdocks under the balm-of-gileads behind the dairy. It was very rotten and he decided it was time it was disposed of. He had shouldered it up against the house so that he would be sure to see it on his return from the hayfield.

In less time than it takes to write of it Emily had got the window up, climbed out on the sill, and backed down the ladder. She was too intent on escaping from that horrible room to be conscious of the shakiness of the rotten rungs. When she reached the ground she bolted through the balm-of-gileads and over the fence into Lofty John's bush, nor did she stop running till she reached the path by the brook.

Then she paused for breath, exultant. She was full of a fearful joy with an elfin delight running through it. Sweet was the wind of freedom that was blowing over the ferns. She had escaped from the spare-room and its ghosts—she had got the better of mean old Aunt Elizabeth.

"I feel as if I was a little bird that had just got out of a cage," she told herself; and then she danced with joy of it all along her fairy path to the very end, where she found Ilse Burnley huddled up on the top of a fence panel, her pale-gold head making a spot of brilliance against the dark young firs that crowded around her. Emily had not seen her since that first day of school and again she thought she had never seen or pretended anybody just like Ilse.

"Well, Emily of New Moon," said Ilse, "where are you running to?"

"I'm running away," said Emily frankly. "I was bad—at least, I was a little bad—and Aunt Elizabeth locked me in the spare-room. I hadn't been bad enough for THAT—it wasn't fair—so I got out of the window and down the ladder."

"You little cuss! I didn't think you'd gimp enough for that," said Ilse.

Emily gasped. It seemed very dreadful to be called a little cuss. But Ilse had said it quite admiringly.

"I don't think it was gimp," said Emily, too honest to take a compliment she didn't deserve. "I was too scared to stay in that room."

"Well, where are you going now?" asked Ilse. "You'll have to go somewhere—you can't stay outdoors. There's a thunderstorm coming up."

So there was. Emily did not like thunderstorms. And her conscience smote her.

"Oh," she said, "do you suppose God is bringing up that storm to punish me because I've run away?"

"No," said Ilse scornfully. "If there is any God he wouldn't make such a fuss over nothing."

"Oh, Ilse, don't you believe there is a God?"

"I don't know. Father says there isn't. But in that case how did things happen? Some days I believe there's a God and some days I don't. You'd better come home with me. There's nobody there. I was so dodgastedly lonesome I took to the bush."

Ilse sprang down and held out her sunburned paw to Emily. Emily took it and they ran together over Lofty John's pasture to the old Burnley house which looked like a huge grey cat basking in the warm late sunshine, that had not yet been swallowed up by the menacing thunderheads. Inside, it was full of furniture that must have been quite splendid once; but the disorder was dreadful and the dust lay thickly over everything. Nothing was in the right place apparently, and Aunt Laura would certainly have fainted with horror if she had seen the kitchen. But it was a good place to play. You didn't have to be careful not to mess things up. Ilse and Emily had a glorious game of hide and seck all over the house until the thunder got so heavy and the lightning so bright that Emily felt she must huddle on the sofa and nurse her courage.

"Aren't you ever afraid of thunder?" she asked Ilse.

"No, I ain't afraid of anything except the devil," said Ilse.

"I thought you didn't believe in the devil either—Rhoda said you didn't."

"Oh, there's a devil all right, Father says. It's only God he doesn't believe in. And if there IS a devil and no God to keep him in order, is it any wonder I'm scared of him? Look here, Emily Byrd Starr, I like you—heaps. I've always liked you. I knew you'd soon be good and sick of that little, white-livered, lying sneak of a Rhoda Stuart. I never tell lies. Father told me once he'd kill me if he ever caught me telling a lie. I want you for MY chum. I'd go to school regular if I could sit with you."

"All right," said Emily off-handedly. No more sentimental Rhodian vows of eternal devotion for her. THAT phase was over.

"And you'll tell me things—nobody ever tells me things. And let ME tell YOU things—I haven't anybody to tell things to," said Ilse. "And you won't be ashamed of me because my clothes are always queer and because I don't believe in God?"

"No. But if you knew Father's God you'd believe in HIM."

"I wouldn't. Besides, there's only one God if there is any at all."

"I don't know," said Emily perplexedly. "No, it can't be like that. Ellen Greene's God isn't a bit like Father's, and neither is Aunt Elizabeth's. I don't think I'd LIKE Aunt Elizabeth's, but He is a DIGNIFIED God at least, and Ellen's isn't. And I'm sure Aunt Laura's is another one still—nice and kind but not wonderful like Father's."

"Well never mind—I don't like talking about God," said Ilse uncomfortably.

"I do," said Emily. "I think God is a very interesting subject, and I'm going to pray for you, Ilse, that you can believe in Father's God."

"Don't you dast!" shouted Ilse, who for some mysterious reason did not like the idea. "I won't be prayed for!"

"Don't you ever pray yourself, Ilse?"

"Oh, now and then—when I feel lonesome at night—or when I'm in a scrape. But I don't want any one else to pray for me. If I catch you doing it, Emily Starr, I'll tear your eyes out. And don't you go sneaking and praying for me behind my back either."

"All right, I won't," said Emily sharply, mortified at the failure of her well-meant offer. "I'll pray for every single soul I know, but I'll leave you out."

For a moment Ilse looked as if she didn't like this either. Then she laughed and gave Emily a volcanic hug.

"Well, anyway, please like me. Nobody likes me, you know."

"Your father MUST like you, Ilse."

"He doesn't," said Ilse positively. "Father doesn't care a hoot about me. I think there's times when he hates the sight of me. I wish he DID like me because he can be awful nice when he likes any one. Do you know what I'm going to be when I grow up? I'm going to be an elo-cu-tion-ist."

"What's that?"

"A woman who recites at concerts. I can do it dandy. What are you going to be?"

"A poetess."

"Golly!" said Ilse, apparently overcome. "I don't believe YOU can write poetry," she added.

"I can so, too," cried Emily. "I've written three pieces—'Autumn' and 'Lines to Rhoda'—only I burned THAT—and 'An Address to a Buttercup.' I composed it to-day and it is my—my masterpiece."

"Let's hear it," ordered Ilse.

Nothing loth, Emily proudly repeated her lines. Somehow she did not mind letting Ilse hear them.

"Emily Byrd Starr, you DIDN'T make that out of your own head?"

"I did."

"Cross your heart?"

"Cross my heart."

"Well"—Ilse drew a long breath—"I guess you ARE a poetess all right."

It was a very proud moment for Emily—one of the great moments of life, in fact. Her world had conceded her standing. But now other things had to be thought of. The storm was over and the sun had set. It was twilight—it would soon be dark. She must get home and back into the spare-room before her absence was discovered. It was dreadful to think of going back but she must do it lest a worse thing come upon her at Aunt Elizabeth's hands. Just now, under the inspiration of Ilse's personality, she was full of Dutch courage. Besides, it would soon be her bedtime and she would be let out. She trotted home through Lofty John's bush, that was full of the wandering, mysterious lamps of the fireflies, dodged cautiously through the balm-of-gileads—and stopped short in dismay. The ladder was gone!

Emily went around to the kitchen door, feeling that she was going straight to her doom. But for once the way of the transgressor was made sinfully easy. Aunt Laura was alone in the kitchen.

"Emily dear, where on earth did you come from?" she exclaimed. "I was just going up to let you out. Elizabeth said I might—she's gone to prayer-meeting."

Aunt Laura did not say that she had tiptoed several times to the spare-room door and had been racked with anxiety over the silence behind it. Was the child unconscious from fright? Not even while the thunderstorm was going on would relentless Elizabeth allow that door to be opened. And here was Miss Emily walking unconcernedly in out of the twilight after all this agony. For a moment even Aunt Laura was annoyed. But when she heard Emily's tale her only feeling was thankfulness that Juliet's child had not broken her neck on that rotten ladder.

Emily felt that she had got off better than she deserved. She knew Aunt Laura would keep the secret; and Aunt Laura let her give Saucy Sal a whole cupful of strippings, and gave her a big plummy cooky and put her to bed with kisses.

"You oughtn't to be so good to me because I WAS bad to-day," Emily said, between delicious mouthfuls. "I suppose I disgraced the Murrays going barefoot."

"If I were you I'd hide my boots every time I went out of the gate," said Aunt Laura. "But I wouldn't forget to put them on before I came back. What Elizabeth doesn't know will never hurt her."

Emily reflected over this until she had finished her cooky. Then she said,

"That would be nice, but I don't mean to do it any more. I guess I must obey Aunt Elizabeth because she's the head of the family."

"Where do you get such notions?" said Aunt Laura.

"Out of my head. Aunt Laura, Ilse Burnley and I are going to be chums. I like her—I've always felt I'd like her if I had a chance. I don't believe I can ever LOVE any girl again, but I LIKE her."

"Poor Ilse!" said Aunt Laura, sighing.

"Yes, her father doesn't like her. Isn't it dreadful?" said Emily. "Why doesn't he?"

"He does—really. He only thinks he doesn't."

"But WHY does he think it?"

"You are too young to understand, Emily."

Emily hated to be told she was too young to understand. She felt that she could understand perfectly well if only people would take the trouble to explain things to her and not be so mysterious.

"I wish I could pray for her. It wouldn't be fair, though, when I know how she feels about it. But I've always asked God to bless all my friends so she'll be in THAT and maybe some good will come of it. Is 'golly' a proper word to say, Aunt Laura?"

"No—no!"

"I'm sorry for that," said Emily, seriously, "because it's very striking."

CHAPTER XII
THE TANSY PATCH

EMILY and Ilse had a splendid fortnight of fun before their first fight. It was really quite a terrible fight, arising out of a simple argument as to whether they would or would not have a parlour in the playhouse they were building in Lofty John's bush. Emily wanted a parlour and Ilse didn't. Ilse lost her temper at once, and went into a true Burnley tantrum. She was very fluent in her rages and the volley of abusive "dictionary words" which she hurled at Emily would have staggered most of the Blair Water girls. But Emily was too much at home with words to be floored so easily; she grew angry too, but in the cool, dignified, Murray way which was more exasperating than violence. When Ilse had to pause for breath in her diatribes, Emily, sitting on a big stone with her knees crossed, her eyes black and her cheeks crimson, interjected little sarcastic retorts that infuriated Ilse still further. Ilse was crimson, too, and her eyes were pools of scintillating, tawny fire. They were both so pretty in their fury that it was almost a pity they couldn't have been angry all the time.

"You needn't suppose, you little puling, snivelling chit, that you are going to boss ME, just because you live at New Moon," shrieked Ilse, as an ultimatum, stamping her foot.

"I'm not going to boss you—I'm not going to associate with you ever again," retorted Emily, disdainfully.

"I'm glad to be rid of you—you proud, stuck-up, conceited, top-lofty BIPED," cried Ilse. "Never you speak to me again. And don't you go about Blair Water saying things about me, either."

This was unbearable to a girl who NEVER "said things" about her friends or once-friends.

"I'm not going to SAY things about you," said Emily deliberately. "I am just going to THINK them."

This was far more aggravating than speech and Emily knew it. Ilse was driven quite frantic by it. Who knew what unearthly things Emily might be thinking about her any time she took the notion to? Ilse had already discovered what a fertile invention Emily had.

"Do you suppose I care what you think, you insignificant serpent? Why, you haven't ANY sense."

"I've got something then that's far better," said Emily, with a maddening superior smile. "Something that YOU can NEVER have, Ilse Burnley."

Ilse doubled her fists as if she would like to demolish Emily by physical force.

"If I couldn't write better poetry than you, I'd hang myself," she derided.

"I'll lend you a dime to buy a rope," said Emily.

Ilse glared at her, vanquished.

"You go to the devil!" she said.

Emily got up and went, not to the devil, but back to New Moon. Ilse relieved HER feelings by knocking the boards of their china closet down, and kicking their "moss gardens" to pieces, and departed also.

Emily felt exceedingly badly. Here was another friendship destroyed—a friendship, too, that had been very delightful and satisfying. Ilse HAD been a splendid chum—there was no doubt about that. After Emily had cooled down she went to the dormer window and cried.

"Wretched, wretched me!" she sobbed, dramatically, but very sincerely.

Yet the bitterness of her break with Rhoda was not present. THIS quarrel was fair and open and above-board. She had not been stabbed in the back. But of course she and Ilse would never be chums again. You couldn't be chums with a person who called you a chit and a biped, and a serpent, and told you to go to the devil. The thing was impossible. And besides, Ilse could NEVER forgive HER— for Emily was honest enough to admit to herself that she had been very aggravating, too.

Yet, when Emily went to the playhouse next morning, bent on retrieving her share of broken dishes and boards, there was Ilse, skipping around, hard at work, with all the shelves back in place, the moss garden re-made, and a beautiful parlour laid out and connected with the living-room by a spruce arch.

"Hello, you. Here's your parlour and I hope you'll be satisfied now," she said gaily. "What's kept you so long? I thought you were never coming."

This rather posed Emily after her tragic night, wherein she had buried her second friendship and wept over its grave. She was not prepared for so speedy a resurrection. As far as Ilse was concerned it seemed as if no quarrel had ever taken place.

"Why, that was YESTERDAY," she said in amazement, when Emily, rather distantly, referred to it. Yesterday and to-day were two entirely different things in Ilse's philosophy. Emily accepted it—she found she had to. Ilse, it transpired, could no more help flying into tantrums now and then than she could help being jolly and affectionate between them. What amazed Emily, in whom things were bound to rankle for a time, was the way in which Ilse appeared to forget a quarrel the moment it was over. To be called a serpent and a crocodile one minute and hugged and darling-ed the next was somewhat disconcerting until time and experience took the edge off it.

"Aren't I nice enough between times to make up for it?" demanded Ilse. "Dot Payne never flies into tempers, but would you like HER for a chum?"

"No, she's too stupid," admitted Emily.

"And Rhoda Stuart is never out of temper, but you got enough of HER. Do you think I'd ever treat you as she did?"

No, Emily had no doubt on this point. Whatever Ilse was or was not, she was loyal and true.

And certainly Rhoda Stuart and Dot Payne compared to Ilse were "as moonlight unto sunlight and as water unto wine"—or would have been if Emily had as yet known anything more of her Tennyson than the *Bugle Song*.

"You can't have everything," said Ilse. "I've got Dad's temper and that's all there is to it. Wait till you see HIM in one of his rages."

Emily had not seen this so far. She had often been down in the Burnley's house but on the few occasions when Dr. Burnley had been home he had ignored her save for a curt nod. He was a busy man, for, whatever his shortcomings were, his skill was unquestioned and the bounds of his practice extended far. By the sickbed he was as gentle and sympathetic as he was brusque and sarcastic away from it. As long as you were ill there was nothing Dr. Burnley would not do for you; once you were well he had apparently no further use for you. He had been absorbed all through July trying to save Teddy Kent's life up at the Tansy Patch. Teddy was out of danger now and able to be up, but his improvement was not speedy enough to satisfy Dr. Burnley. One day he held up Emily and Ilse, who were heading through the lawn to the pond, with fishing-hooks and a can of fat, abominable worms—the latter manipulated solely by Ilse—and ordered them to betake themselves up to the Tansy Patch and play with Teddy Kent.

"He's lonesome and moping. Go and cheer him up," said the doctor.

Ilse was rather loth to go. She liked Teddy, but it seemed she did not like his mother. Emily was secretly not averse. She had seen Teddy Kent but once, at Sunday School the day before he was taken seriously ill, and she had liked his looks. It had seemed that he liked hers, too, for she caught him staring shyly at her over the intervening pews several times. He was very handsome, Emily decided. She liked his thick, dark-brown hair and his black-browed blue eyes, and for the first time it occurred to her that it might be rather nice to have a boy playmate, too. Not a "beau" of course. Emily hated the school jargon that called a boy your "beau" if he happened to give you a pencil or an apple and picked you out frequently for his partner in the games.

"Teddy's nice but his mother is queer," Ilse told her on their way to the Tansy Patch. "She never goes out anywhere—not even to church— but I guess it's because of the scar on her face. They're not Blair Water people—they've only been living at the Tansy Patch since last fall. They're poor and proud and not many people visit them. But Teddy is awfully nice, so if his mother gives us some black looks we needn't mind."

Mrs. Kent gave them no black looks, though her reception was rather distant. Perhaps she, too, had received some orders from the doctor. She was a tiny creature, with enormous masses of dull, soft, silky, fawn hair, dark, mournful eyes, and a broad scar running slantwise across her pale face. Without the scar she must have been pretty, and she had a voice as soft and uncertain as the wind in the tansy. Emily, with her instinctive faculty of sizing up people she met, felt that Mrs. Kent was not a happy woman.

The Tansy Patch was east of the Disappointed House, between the Blair Water and the sand-dunes. Most people considered it a bare, lonely, neglected place, but Emily thought it was fascinating. The little clap-boarded house topped a small hill, over which tansy grew in a hard, flaunting, aromatic luxuriance, rising steeply and abruptly from a main road. A straggling rail fence, almost smothered in wild rosebushes, bounded the domain, and a sagging, ill-used little gate gave ingress from the road. Stones were let into the side of the hill for steps up to the front door. Behind the house was a tumble-down little barn, and a field of flowering buckwheat, creamy green, sloping down to the Blair Water. In front was a crazy veranda around which a brilliant band of red poppies held up their enchanted cups.

Teddy was unfeignedly glad to see them, and they had a happy afternoon together. There was some colour in Teddy's clear olive skin when it ended and his dark-blue eyes were brighter. Mrs. Kent took in these signs greedily and asked the girls to come back, with an eagerness that was yet not cordiality. But they had found the Tansy Patch a charming place and were glad to go again. For the rest of the vacation there was hardly a day when they did not go up to it—preferably in the long, smoky, delicious August evenings when the white moths sailed over the tansy plantation and the golden twilight faded into dusk and purple over the green slopes beyond and fireflies lighted their goblin torches by the pond. Sometimes they played games in the tansy patch, when Teddy and Emily somehow generally found themselves on the same side and then no more than a match for agile, quick-witted Ilse; sometimes Teddy took them to the barn loft and showed them his little collection of drawings. Both girls thought them very wonderful without knowing in the least how wonderful they really were. It seemed like magic to see Teddy take a pencil and bit of paper and with a few quick strokes of his slim brown fingers bring out a sketch of Ilse or Emily or Smoke or Buttercup, that looked ready to speak—or meow.

Smoke and Buttercup were the Tansy Patch cats. Buttercup was a chubby, yellow, delightful creature hardly out of kittenhood. Smoke was a big Maltese and an aristocrat from the tip of his nose to the tip of his tail. There was no doubt whatever that he belonged to the cat caste of Vere de Vere. He had emerald eyes and a coat of plush. The only white thing about him was an adorable dicky.

Emily thought of all the pleasant hours spent at the Tansy Patch the pleasantest were those, when, tired with play, they all three sat on the crazy veranda steps in the mystery and enchantment of the borderland 'tween light and dark when the little clump of spruce behind the barn looked like beautiful, dark, phantom trees. The clouds of the west faded into grey and a great round yellow moon rose over the fields to be reflected brokenly in the pond, where the Wind Woman was making wonderful, woven lights and shadows.

Mrs. Kent never joined them, though Emily had a creepy conviction that she was watching them stealthily from behind the kitchen blind. Teddy and Ilse sang school ditties, and Ilse recited, and Emily told stories; or they sat in happy silence, each anchored in some secret port of dreams, while the cats chased each other madly over the hill and through the tansy, tearing round and round the house like possessed creatures. They would spring up at the children with sudden pounces and spring as suddenly away. Their eyes gleamed like jewels, their tails swayed like plumes. They were palpitating with nervous, stealthy life.

"Oh, isn't it good to be alive—like this?" Emily said once. "Wouldn't it be dreadful if one had never lived?"

Still, existence was not wholly unclouded—Aunt Elizabeth took care of that. Aunt Elizabeth only permitted the visits to the Tansy Patch under protest, and because Dr. Burnley had ordered them.

"Aunt Elizabeth does not aprove of Teddy," Emily wrote in one of her letters to her father—which epistles were steadily mutiplying on the old garret sofa shelf. "The first time I asked her if I might go and play with Teddy she looked at me SEVERELY and said, Who is this Teddy person. We do not know anything about these Kents. Remember, Emily, the Murrays do not assosiate with every one. I said I am a Starr—I am not a Murray, you said so yourself. Dear Father I did not mean to be impertnent but Aunt Elizabeth said I was and would not speak to me the rest of the day. She seemed to think that was a very bad punishment but I did not mind it much only it is rather unpleasant to have your own family preserve a disdaneful silence towards you. But since then she lets me go to the Tansy Patch because Dr. Burnley came and told her to. Dr. Burnley has a STRANGE INFLEWENCE over Aunt Elizabeth. I do not understand it. Rhoda said once that Aunt Elizabeth hoped Dr. Burnley and Aunt Laura would make a match of it—which, you know means get married—but that is not so. Mrs. Thomas Anderson was here one afternoon to tea. (Mrs. Thomas Anderson is a big fat woman and her grandmother was a Murray and there is nothing else to say about HER.) She asked Aunt Elizabeth if she thought Dr. Burnley would marry again and Aunt Elizabeth said no, he would not and she did not think it right for people to marry a second time. Mrs. Anderson said Sometimes I have thought he would take Laura. Aunt Elizabeth just swept her a hawty glance. There is no use in denying it, there are times when I am very proud of Aunt Elizabeth, even if I do not like her.

"Teddy is a very nice boy, Father. I think you would aprove of him. Should there be two p's in aprove? He can make splendid pictures and he is going to be a famus artist some day, and then he is going to paint my portrate. He keeps his pictures in the barn loft because his mother doesn't like to see them. He can whistle just like a bird. The Tansy Patch is a VERY QUANTE place—espesially at night. I love the twilight there. We always have such fun in the twilight. The Wind Woman makes herself small in the tansy just like a tiny, tiny fairy and the cats are so queer and creepy and delightful then. They belong to Mrs. Kent and Teddy is afraid to pet them much for fear she will drown them. She drowned a kitten once because she thought he liked it better than her. But he didn't because Teddy is VERY MUCH ATTATCHED to his mother. He washes the dishes for her and helps her in all the house work. Ilse says the boys in school call him sissy for that but I think it is noble and manley of him. Teddy wishes she would let him have a dog but she wont. I have thought Aunt Elizabeth was tirannical but Mrs. Kent is far worse in some ways. But then she loves Teddy and Aunt Elizabeth does not love me.

"But Mrs. Kent doesn't like Ilse or me. She never says so but we FEEL it. She never asks us to stay to tea—and we've always been so polite to her. I believe she is jellus of us because Teddy likes us. Teddy gave me the sweetest picture of the Blair Water he had painted on a big white cowhawk shell but he said I mustn't let his mother know about it because she would cry. Mrs. Kent is a very misterious person, very like some people you read of in books. I like misterious people but not too close. Her eyes always look hungry though she has plenty to eat. She never goes anywhere because she has a scar on her face where she was burned with a lamp exploding. It made my blood run cold, dear Father. How thankful I am that Aunt Elizabeth only burns candles. Some of the Murray tradishuns are very sensible. Mrs. Kent is very relijus—what she calls relijus. She prays even in the middle of the day. Teddy says that before he was born into this world he lived in another one where there were two suns, one red and one blue. The days were red and the nights blue. I don't know where he got the idea but it sounds atractive to me. And he says the brooks run honey instead of water. But what did you do when you were thirsty, I said. Oh, we were never thirsty there. But I think I would LIKE to be thirsty because then cold water tastes so good. I would like to live in the moon. It must be such a nice silvery place.

"Ilse says Teddy ought to like her best because there is more fun in her than in me but that is not true. There is just as much fun in me when my conshence doesn't bother me. I guess Ilse wants Teddy to like her best but she is not a jellus girl.

"I am glad to say that Aunt Elizabeth and Aunt Laura both aprove of my friendship with Ilse. It is so seldom they aprove of the same thing. I am getting used to fighting with Ilse now and don't mind it much. Besides I can fight pretty well myself when my blood is up. We fight about once a week but we make up right away and Ilse says things would be dull if there was never a row. I would like it better without rows but you can never tell what will make Ilse mad. She never gets mad twice over the same thing. She calls me dreadful names. Yesterday she called me a lousy lizard and a toothless viper. But somehow I didn't mind it much because I knew I wasn't lousy or toothless and she knew it too. I don't call names because that is unladylike but I smile and that makes Ilse far madder than if I skowled and stamped as she does, and that is why I do it. Aunt Laura says I must be careful not to pick up the words Ilse uses and try to set her a good example because the poor child has no one to look after her propperly. I wish I could use some of her words because they are so striking. She gets them from her father. I think my aunts are too perticular. One night when the Rev. Mr. Dare was here to tea I used the word bull in my conversashun. I said Ilse and I were afraid to go through Mr. James Lee's pasture where the old well was because he had a cross bull there. After Mr. Dare had gone Aunt Elizabeth gave me an awful skolding and told me I was never to use THAT WORD again. But she had been talking of tigers at tea—in connexshun with missionaries—and I can't understand why it is more disgraceful to talk about bulls than tigers. Of course bulls are feroshus animals but so are tigers. But Aunt Elizabeth says I am always disgracing them when they have company. When Mrs. Lockwood was here from Shrewsbury last week they were talking about Mrs. Foster Beck, who is a bride, and I said Dr. Burnley thought she was devilishly pretty. Aunt Elizabeth said EMILY in an awful tone. She was pale with rath. Dr. Burnley said it, I cryed, I am only kwoting. And Dr. Burnley did say it the day I stayed to dinner with Ilse and Dr. Jameson was there from Shrewsbury. I saw Dr. Burnley in one of his rages that afternoon over something Mrs. Simms had done in his office. It was a groosome sight. His big yellow eyes blazed and he tore about and kicked over a chair and threw a mat at the wall and fired a vase out of the window and said TERRIBLE THINGS. I sat on the sofa and stared at him like one fassinated. It was so interesting I was sorry when he cooled down which he soon did because he is like Ilse and never stays mad long. He never gets mad at Ilse though. Ilse says she wishes he would—it would be better than being taken no notis of. She is as much of an orfan as I am, poor child. Last Sunday she went to church with her old faded blue dress on. There was a tare right in front of it. Aunt Laura wepped when she came home and then spoke to Mrs. Simms about it because she did not dare speak to Dr. Burnley. Mrs. Simms was cross and said it was not her place to look after Ilses close but she said she had got

Dr. Burnley to get Ilse a nice sprigged muslin dress and Ilse had got egg stane on it, and when Mrs. Simms skolded her for being so careless Ilse flew into a rage and went upstairs and tore the muslin dress to pieces, and Mrs. Simms said she wasn't going to bother her head again about a child like that and there was nothing for her to ware but her old blue but Mrs. Simms didn't know it was tore. So I sneaked Ilses dress over to New Moon and Aunt Laura mended it neetly and hid the tare with a pocket. Ilse said she tore up her muslin dress one of the days she didn't believe in God and didn't care what she did. Ilse found a mouse in her bed one night and she just shook it out and jumped in. Oh, how brave. I could never be as brave as that. It is not true that Dr. Burnley never smiles. I have seen him do it but not often. He just smiles with his lips but not his eyes and it makes me feel uncomfortable. Mostly he laughs in a horrid sarkastic way like JOLLY JIM'S uncle.

"We had barley soup for dinner that day—very watery.

"Aunt Laura is giving me five cents a week for washing the dishes. I can only spend one cent of it and the other four have to be put in the toad bank in the sitting-room on the mantel. The toad is made of brass and sits on top of the bank and you put the cents in his mouth one at a time. He swallows them and they drop into the bank. It's very fassinating (I should not write fassinating again because you told me I must not use the same word too often but I cant think of any other that deskribes my feelings so well). The toad bank is Aunt Laura's but she said I could use it. I just hugged her. Of course I never hug Aunt Elizabeth. She is too rijid and bony. She does not aprove of Aunt Laura paying me for washing dishes. I tremble to think what she would say if she knew Cousin Jimmy gave me a whole dollar on the sly last week.

"I wish he had not given me so much. It worrys me. It is an awful responsibility. It will be so diffikult to spend it wisely also without Aunt Elizabeth finding out about it. I hope I shall never have a million dollars. I am sure it would crush me utterly. I keep my dollar hid on the shelf with my letters and I put it in an old envelope and wrote on it Cousin Jimmy Murray gave me this so that if I died suddenly and Aunt Elizabeth found it she would know I came by it honestly.

"Now that the days are getting cool Aunt Elizabeth makes me wear my thick flannel petticoat. I hate it. It makes me so bunchy. But Aunt Elizabeth says I must wear it because you died of consumption. I wish close could be both graceful and helthy. I read the story of Red Riding Hood to-day. I think the wolf was the most intresting caracter in it. Red Riding Hood was a stupid little thing so easily fooled.

"I wrote two poems yesterday. One was short and entitelled Lines Adressed to a blue-eyed-grass flower gathered in the Old Orchard. Here it is.

Sweet little flower thy modest face
Is ever lifted tords the sky
And a reflexshun of its face
Is caught within thine own blue eye.
The meadow queens are tall and fair
The columbines are lovely too
But the poor talent I possess
Shall laurel thee my flower of blue.

"The other poem was long and I wrote it on a letter-bill. It is called The Monark of the Forest. The Monark is the big birch in Lofty John's bush. I love that bush so much it hurts. Do you understand that kind of hurting. Ilse likes it too and we play there most of the time when we are not at the Tansy Patch. We have three paths in it. We call them the To-day Road, the Yesterday Road and the To-morrow Road. The To-day Road is by the brook and we call it that because it is lovely now. The Yesterday Road is out in the stumps where Lofty John cut some trees down and we call it that because it used to be lovely. The To-morrow Road is just a tiny path in the maple clearing and we call it that because it is going to be lovely some day, when the maples grow bigger. But oh Father dear I haven't forgotten the dear old trees down home. I always think of them after I go to bed. But I am happy here. It isn't wrong to be happy, is it Father. Aunt Elizabeth says I got over being homesick very quick but I am often homesick INSIDE. I have got akwanted with Lofty John. Ilse is a great friend of his and often goes there to watch him working in his carpenter shop. He says he has made enough ladders to get to heaven without the priest but that is just his joke. He is really a very devowt Catholic and goes to the chapel at White Cross every Sunday. I go with Ilse though perhaps I ought not to when he is an enemy of my family. He is of stately baring and refined manners—very sivil to me but I don't always like him. When I ask him a serius question he always winks over my head when he ansers. That is insulting. Of course I never ask any questions on relijus subjects but Ilse does. She likes him but she says he would burn us all at the stake if he had the power. She asked him right out if he wouldn't and he winked at me and said Oh, we wouldn't burn nice pretty little Protestants like you. We would only burn the old ugly ones. That was a frivellus reply. Mrs. Lofty John is a nice woman and not at all proud. She looks just like a little rosy rinkled apple.

"On rainy days we play at Ilse's. We can slide down the bannisters and do what we like. Nobody cares only when the doctor is home we have to be quiet because he cant bear any noise in the house except what he makes himself. The roof is flat and we can get out on it through a door in the garret ceiling. It is very exiting to be up on the roof of a house. We had a yelling contest there the other night to see which could yell the loudest. To my surprise I found I could. You never can tell what you can do till you try. But too many people heard us and Aunt Elizabeth was very angry. She asked me what made me do such a thing. That is an okward question because often I cant tell what makes me do things. Sometimes I do them just to find out what I feel like doing them. And sometimes I do them because I want to have some exiting things to tell my grandchildren. Is it impropper to talk about haveing grandchildren. I have discovered that it is impropper to talk about haveing children. One evening when people were here Aunt Laura said to me quite kindly What are you thinking so ernestly about, Emily, and I said I am picking names for my children. I mean to have ten. And after the company had gone Aunt Elizabeth said to Aunt Laura ICILLY I think it will be better in the future Laura if you do NOT ask that child what she is thinking of. If Aunt Laura doesnt I shall be sorry because when I have an intresting thought I like to tell it.

"School begins again next week. Ilse is going to ask Miss Brownell if I can sit with her. I intend to act as if Rhoda was not there at all. Teddy is going too. Dr. Burnley says he is well enough to go though his mother doesnt like the idea. Teddy says she never likes to have him go to school but she is glad that he hates Miss Brownell. Aunt Laura says the right way to end a letter to a dear friend is yours affeckshunately.

"So I am yours very affeckshunately.

"EMILY BYRD STARR.

"P. S. Because YOU are my VERY DEAREST FRIEND STILL, Father. Ilse says she loves me best of anything in the world and her red leather boots that Mrs. Simms gave her next."

CHAPTER XIII
A DAUGHTER OF EVE

NEW MOON was noted for its apples and on that first autumn of Emily's life there both the "old" and the "new" orchards bore a bumper crop. In the new were the titled and pedigreed apples; and in the old the seedlings, unknown to catalogues, that yet had a flavour wildly sweet and all their own. There was no taboo on any apple and Emily was free to eat all she wanted of each and every kind,—the only prohibition being that she must not take any to bed with her. Aunt Elizabeth, very properly, did not want her bed messed up with apple seeds; and Aunt Laura had a horror of any one eating apples in the dark lest they might eat an apple worm into the bargain. Emily, therefore, should have been able fully to satisfy her appetite for apples at home; but there is a certain odd kink in human nature by reason of which the flavour of the apples belonging to somebody else is always vastly superior to our own—as the crafty serpent of Eden very well knew. Emily, like most people, possessed this kink, and consequently thought that nowhere were there such delicious apples as those belonging to Lofty John. He was in the habit of keeping a long row of apples on one of the beams in his workshop and it was understood that she and Ilse might help themselves freely whenever they visited that charming, dusty, shaving-carpeted spot. Three varieties of Lofty John's apples were their especial favourites—the "scabby apples," that looked as if they had leprosy but were of unsurpassed deliciousness under their queerly blotched skins; the "little red apples," scarcely bigger than a crab, deep crimson all over and glossy as satin, that had such a sweet, nutty flavour; and the big green "sweet apples" that children usually thought the best of all. Emily considered that day wasted whose low descending sun had not beheld her munching one of Lofty John's big green sweets.

In the back of her mind Emily knew quite well that she should not be going to Lofty John's at all. To be sure, she had never been forbidden to go—simply because it had never occurred to her aunts that an inmate of New Moon could so forget the beloved old family feud between the houses of Murray and Sullivan belonging to two generations back. It was an inheritance that any proper Murray would live up to as a matter of course. But when Emily was off with that wild little Ishmaelite of an Ilse, traditions lost their power under the allurement of Lofty John's "reds" and "scabs."

She wandered rather lonesomely into his workshop one September evening at twilight. She had been alone since she came from school; her aunts and Cousin Jimmy had gone to Shrewsbury, promising to be back by sunset. Ilse was away also, her father, prodded thereto by Mrs. Simms, having taken her to Charlottetown to get her a winter coat. Emily liked being alone very well at first. She felt quite important over being in charge of New Moon. She ate the supper Aunt Laura had left on the cook-house dresser for her and she went into the dairy and skimmed six lovely big pans of milk. She had no business at all to do this but she had always hankered to do it and this was too good a chance to be missed. She did it beautifully and nobody ever knew— each aunt supposing the other had done it—and so she was never scolded for it. This does not point any particular moral, of course; in a proper yarn Emily should either have been found out and punished for disobedience or been driven by an uneasy conscience to confess; but I am sorry—or ought to be—to have to state that Emily's conscience never worried her about the matter at all. Still, she was doomed to suffer enough that night from an entirely different cause, to balance all her little peccadillos.

By the time the cream was skimmed and poured into the big stone crock and well stirred—Emily didn't forget THAT, either—it was after sunset and still nobody had come home. Emily didn't like the idea of going alone into the big, dusky, echoing house; so she hied her to Lofty John's shop, which she found unoccupied, though the plane halted midway on a board indicated that Lofty John had been working there quite recently and would probably return. Emily sat down on a round section of a huge log and looked around to see what she could get to eat. There was a row of "reds" and "scabs" clean across the side of the shop but no "sweet" among them; and Emily felt that what she needed just then was a "sweet" and nothing else.

Then she spied one—a huge one—the biggest "sweet" Emily had ever seen, all by itself on one of the steps of the stair leading up to the loft. She climbed up, possessed herself of it and ate it out of hand. She was gnawing happily at the core when Lofty John came in. He nodded to her with a seemingly careless glance around.

"Just been in to get my supper," he said. "The wife's away so I had to get it myself."

He fell to planing in silence. Emily sat on the stairs, counting the seeds of the big "sweet"—you told your fortunes by the seeds— listening to the Wind Woman whistling elfishly through a knot hole in the loft, and composing a "Deskripshun of Lofty John's Carpenter Shop By Lantern Light," to be written later on a letter-bill. She was lost in a mental hunt for an accurate phrase to picture the absurd elongated shadow of Lofty John's nose on the opposite wall when Lofty John whirled about, so suddenly that the shadow of his nose shot upward like a huge spear to the ceiling, and demanded in a startled voice,

"What's become av that big sweet apple that was on that stair?"

"Why—I—I et it," stammered Emily.

Lofty John dropped his plane, threw up his hands, and looked at Emily with a horrified face.

"The saints preserve us, child! Ye never et that apple—don't tell me ye've gone and et THAT apple!"

"Yes, I did," said Emily uncomfortably. "I didn't think it was any harm—I—"

"Harm! Listen to her, will you? That apple was poisoned for the rats! They've been plaguing me life out here and I had me mind made up to finish their fun. And now you've et the apple—it would kill a dozen av ye in a brace of shakes."

Lofty John saw a white face and a gingham apron flash through the workshop and out into the dark. Emily's first wild impulse was to get home at once—before she dropped dead. She tore across the field through the bush and the garden and dashed into the house. It was still silent and dark—nobody was home yet. Emily gave a bitter little shriek of despair—when they came they would find her stiff and cold, black in the face likely, everything in this dear world ended for her forever, all because she had eaten an apple which she thought she was perfectly welcome to eat. It wasn't fair—she didn't want to die.

But she must. She only hoped desperately that some one would come before she was dead. It would be so terrible to die there all alone in that great, big, empty New Moon. She dared not try to go anywhere for help. It was too dark now and she would likely drop dead on the way. To die out there—alone—in the dark—oh, that would be too dreadful. It did not occur to her that anything could be done for her; she thought if you once swallowed poison that was the end of you.

With hands shaking in panic she got a candle lighted. It wasn't quite so bad then—you COULD face things in the light. And Emily, pale, terrified, alone, was already deciding that this must be faced bravely. She must not shame the Starrs and the Murrays. She clenched her cold hands and tried to stop trembling. How long would it be before she died, she wondered. Lofty John had said the apple would kill her in a "brace of shakes." What did that mean? How long was a brace of shakes? Would it hurt her to die? She had a vague idea that poison did hurt you awfully. Oh; and just a little while ago she had been so happy! She had thought she was going to live for years and write great poems and be famous like Mrs. Hemans. She had had a fight with Ilse the night before and hadn't made it up yet—never could make it up now. And Ilse would feel so terribly. She must write her a note and forgive her. Was there time for that much? Oh, how cold her hands were! Perhaps that meant she was dying already. She had heard or read that your hands turned cold when you were dying. She wondered if her face was turning black. She grasped her candle and hurried up the stairs to the spare-room. There was a looking-glass there—the only one in the house hung low enough for her to see her reflection if she tipped the bottom of it back. Ordinarily Emily would have been frightened to death at the mere thought of going into that spare-room by dim, flickering candlelight. But the one great terror had swallowed up all lesser ones. She looked at her reflection, amid the sleek, black flow of her hair, in the upward-striking light on the dark background of the shadowy room. Oh, she was pale as the dead already. Yes, that was a dying face—there could be no doubt of it.

Something rose up in Emily and took possession of her—some inheritance from the good old stock behind her. She ceased to tremble—she accepted her fate—with bitter regret, but calmly.

"I don't want to die but since I have to I'll die as becomes a Murray," she said. She had read a similar sentence in a book and it came pat to the moment. And now she must hurry. That letter to Ilse must be written. Emily went to Aunt Elizabeth's room first, to assure herself that her right-hand top bureau drawer was quite tidy; then she flitted up the garret stairs to her dormer corner. The great place was full of lurking, pouncing shadows that crowded about the little island of faint candlelight, but they had no terrors for Emily now.

"And to think I was feeling so bad to-day because my petticoat was bunchy," she thought, as she got one of her dear letter-bills—the last she would ever write on. There was no need to write to Father—she would see him soon—but Ilse must have her letter—dear, loving, jolly, hot-tempered Ilse, who, just the day before had shrieked insulting epithets after her and who would be haunted by remorse all her life for it.

"Dearest Ilse," wrote Emily, her hand shaking a little but her lips firmly set. "I am going to die. I have been poisoned by an apple Lofty

John had put for rats. I will never see you again, but I am writing this to tell you I love you and you are not to feel bad because you called me a skunk and a bloodthirsty mink yesterday. I forgive you, so do not worry over it. And I am sorry I told you that you were beneath contemt because I didn't mean a word of it. I leave you all my share of the broken dishes in our playhouse and please tell Teddy good-bye for me. He will never be able to teach me how to put worms on a fish-hook now. I promised him I would learn because I did not want him to think I was a coward but I am glad I did not for I know what the worm feels like now. I do not feel sick yet but I dont know what the simptoms of poisoning are and Lofty John said there was enough to kill a dozen of me so I cant have long to live. If Aunt Elizabeth is willing you can have my necklace of Venetian beads. It is the only valuble possession I have. Don't let anybody do anything to Lofty John because he did not mean to poison me and it was all my own fault for being so greedy. Perhaps people will think he did it on purpose because I am a Protestant but I feel sure he did not and please tell him not to be hawnted by remorse. I think I feel a pain in my stomach now so I guess that the end draws ni. Fare well and remember her who died so young.

"Your own devoted,

"EMILY."

As Emily folded up her letter-bill she heard the sound of wheels in the yard below. A moment later Elizabeth and Laura Murray were confronted in the kitchen by a tragic-faced little creature, grasping a guttering candle in one hand and a red letter-bill in the other.

"Emily, what is the matter?" cried Aunt Laura.

"I'm dying," said Emily solemnly. "I et an apple Lofty John had poisoned for rats. I have only a few minutes to live, Aunt Laura."

Laura Murray dropped down on the black bench with her hand at her heart. Elizabeth turned as pale as Emily herself.

"Emily, is this some play-acting of yours?" she demanded sternly.

"No," cried Emily, quite indignantly. "It's the truth. Do you suppose a dying person would be play-acting? And oh, Aunt Elizabeth, please will you give this letter to Ilse—and please forgive me for being naughty—though I wasn't always naughty when you thought I was— and don't let any one see me after I'm dead if I turn black—especially Rhoda Stuart."

By this time Aunt Elizabeth was herself again.

"How long ago is it since you ate that apple, Emily?"

"About an hour."

"If you'd eaten a poisoned apple an hour ago you'd be dead or sick by now—"

"Oh," cried Emily transformed in a second. A wild, sweet hope sprang up in her heart—was there a chance for her after all? Then she added despairingly, "But I felt another pain in my stomach just as I came downstairs."

"Laura," said Aunt Elizabeth, "take this child out to the cook-house and give her a good dose of mustard and water at once. It will do no harm and MAY do some good, if there's anything in this yarn of hers. I'm going down to the doctor's—he may be back—but I'll see Lofty John on the way."

Aunt Elizabeth went out—and Aunt Elizabeth went out very quickly—if it had been any one else it might have been said she ran. As for Emily—well, Aunt Laura gave her that emetic in short order and two minutes later Emily had no doubt at all that she was dying then and there—and the sooner the better. When Aunt Elizabeth returned Emily was lying on the sofa in the kitchen, as white as the pillow under her head, and as limp as a faded lily.

"Wasn't the doctor home?" cried Aunt Laura desperately.

"I don't know—there's no need of the doctor. I didn't think there was from the first. It was just one of Lofty John's jokes. He thought he'd give Emily a fright—just for fun—HIS idea of fun. March you off to bed, Miss Emily. You deserve all you've got for going over there to Lofty John's at all and I don't pity you a particle. I haven't had such a turn for years."

"I DID have a pain in my stomach," wailed Emily, in whom fright and mustard-and-water combined had temporarily extinguished all spirit.

"Any one who eats apples from dawn to dark must expect a few pains in her stomach. You won't have any more to-night, I reckon—the mustard will remedy that. Take your candle and go."

"Well," said Emily, getting unsteadily to her feet, "I HATE that dod-gasted Lofty John."

"Emily!" said both aunts together.

"He DESERVES it," said Emily vindictively.

"Oh, Emily—that dreadful word you used!" Aunt Laura seemed curiously upset about something.

"Why, what's the matter with dod-gasted?" said Emily, quite mystified. "Cousin Jimmy uses it often, when things vex him. He used it to-day—he said that dod-gasted heifer had broken out of the graveyard pasture again."

"Emily," said Aunt Elizabeth, with the air of one impaling herself on the easiest horn of a dilemma, "your Cousin Jimmy is a man—and men sometimes use expressions, in the heat of anger, that are not proper for little girls."

"But what IS the matter with dod-gasted?" persisted Emily. "It isn't a swear word, is it? And if it isn't, why can't I use it?"

"It isn't a—a ladylike word," said Aunt Laura.

"Well, then, I won't use it any more," said Emily resignedly, "but Lofty John IS dod-gasted."

Aunt Laura laughed so much after Emily had gone upstairs that Aunt Elizabeth told her a woman of her age should have more sense.

"Elizabeth, you KNOW it was funny," protested Laura.

Emily being safely out of sight, Elizabeth permitted herself a somewhat grim smile.

"I told Lofty John a few plain truths—he'll not go telling children they're poisoned again in a hurry. I left him fairly dancing with rage."

Worn out, Emily fell asleep as soon as she was in bed; but an hour later she awakened. Aunt Elizabeth had not yet come to bed so the blind was still up and Emily saw a dear, friendly star winking down at her. Far away the sea moaned alluringly. Oh, it was nice just to be alone and to be alive. Life tasted good to her again—"tasted like more," as Cousin Jimmy said. She could have a chance to write more letter-bills, and poetry—Emily already saw a yard of verses entitled "Thoughts of One Doomed to Sudden Death"—and play with Ilse and Teddy—scour the barns with Saucy Sal, watch Aunt Laura skim cream in the dairy and help cousin Jimmy garden,—read books in Emily's Bower and trot along the To-day Road—but NOT visit Lofty John's workshop. She determined that she would never have anything to do with Lofty John again after his diabolical cruelty. She felt so indignant with him for frightening her—after they had been such good friends, too—that she could not go to sleep until she had composed an account of her death by poison, of Lofty John being tried for her murder and condemned to death, and of his being hanged on a gibbet as lofty as himself, Emily being present at the dreadful scene, in spite of the fact that she was dead by his act. When she had finally cut him down and buried him with obloquy—the tears streaming down her face out of sympathy for Mrs. Lofty John—she forgave him. Very likely he was not dod-gasted after all.

She wrote it all down on a letter-bill in the garret the next day.

CHAPTER XIV
FANCY FED

IN October Cousin Jimmy began to boil the pigs' potatoes—unromantic name for a most romantic occupation—or so it appeared to Emily, whose love of the beautiful and picturesque was satisfied as it had never yet been on those long, cool, starry twilights of the waning year at New Moon.

There was a clump of spruce-trees in a corner of the old orchard, and under them an immense iron pot was hung over a circle of large stones—a pot so big that an ox could have been comfortably stewed in it. Emily thought it must have come down from the days of fairy tales and been some giant's porridge pot; but Cousin Jimmy told her that it was only a hundred years old and old Hugh Murray had had it sent out from England.

"We've used it ever since to boil the potatoes for the New Moon pigs," he said. "Blair Water folks think it old-fashioned; they've all got boiler-houses now, with built-in boilers; but as long as Elizabeth's boss at New Moon we'll use this."

Emily was sure no built-in boiler could have the charm of the big pot. She helped Cousin Jimmy fill it full of potatoes after she came from school; then, when supper was over, Cousin Jimmy lighted the fire under it and puttered about it all the evening. Sometimes he poked the fire—Emily loved that part of the performance—sending glorious streams of rosy sparks upward into the darkness; sometimes he stirred the potatoes with a long pole, looking, with his queer, forked grey beard and belted "jumper," just like some old gnome or troll of northland story mixing the contents of a magical caldron; and sometimes he sat beside Emily on the grey granite boulder near the pot and recited his poetry for her. Emily liked this best of all, for Cousin Jimmy's poetry was surprisingly good—at least in spots—and Cousin Jimmy had "fit audience though few" in this slender little maiden with her pale eager face and rapt eyes.

They were an odd couple and they were perfectly happy together. Blair Water people thought Cousin Jimmy a failure and a mental weakling. But he dwelt in an ideal world of which none of them knew anything. He had recited his poems a hundred times thus, as he boiled the pigs' potatoes; the ghosts of a score of autumns haunted the clump of spruces for him. He was an odd, ridiculous figure enough, bent and wrinkled and unkempt, gesticulating awkwardly as he recited. But it was his hour; he was no longer "simple Jimmy Murray" but a prince in his own realm. For a little while he was strong and young and splendid and beautiful, accredited master of song to a listening, enraptured world. None of his prosperous, sensible Blair Water neighbours ever lived through such an hour. He would not have exchanged places with one of them. Emily, listening to him, felt vaguely that if it had not been for that unlucky push into the New Moon well, this queer little man beside her might have stood in the presence of kings.

But Elizabeth HAD pushed him into the New Moon well and as a consequence he boiled pigs' potatoes and recited to Emily—Emily, who wrote poetry too, and loved these evenings so much that she could not sleep after she went to bed until she had composed a minute description of them. The flash came almost every evening over something or other. The Wind Woman swooped or purred in the tossing boughs above them—Emily had never been so near to seeing her; the sharp air was full of the pleasant tang of the burning spruce cones Cousin Jimmy shovelled under the pot; Emily's furry kitten, Mike II, frisked and scampered about like a small, charming demon of the night; the fire glowed with beautiful redness and allure through the gloom; there were nice whispery sounds everywhere; the "great big dark" lay spread around them full of mysteries that daylight never revealed; and over all a purple sky powdered with stars.

Ilse and Teddy came, too, on some evenings. Emily always knew when Teddy was coming, for when he reached the old orchard he whistled his "call"—the one he used just for her—a funny, dear little call, like three clear bird notes, the first just medium pitch, the second higher, the third dropping away into lowness and sweetness long-drawn-out—like the echoes in the *Bugle Song* that went clearer and further in their dying. That call always had an odd effect on Emily; it seemed to her that it fairly drew the heart out of her body—and she HAD to follow it. She thought Teddy could have whistled her clear across the world with those three magic notes. Whenever she heard it she ran quickly through the orchard and told Teddy whether Cousin Jimmy wanted him or not, because it was only on certain nights that Cousin Jimmy wanted anybody but her. He would never recite his poetry to Ilse or Teddy; but he told them fairy stories, and tales about the old dead-and-gone Murrays in the pond graveyard that were as queer, sometimes, as the fairy stories; and Ilse would recite too, doing better there than she ever did anywhere else; and sometimes Teddy lay sprawled out on the ground beside the big pot and drew pictures by the light of the fire—pictures of Cousin Jimmy stirring the potatoes—pictures of Ilse and Emily dancing hand in hand around it like two small witches, pictures of Mike's cunning, little, whiskered face peering around the old boulder, pictures of weird, vague faces crowding in the darkness outside their enchanted circle. They had very wonderful evenings there, those four children.

"Oh, don't you like the world at night, Ilse?" Emily once said rapturously.

Ilse glanced happily around her—poor little neglected Ilse, who found in Emily's companionship what she had hungered for all her short life and who was, even now, being led by love into something of her rightful heritage.

"Yes," she said. "And I always believe there IS a God when I'm here like this."

Then the potatoes were done—and Cousin Jimmy gave each of them one before he mixed in the bran; they broke them in pieces on plates of birch-bark, sprinkled them with salt which Emily had cached in a small box under the roots of the biggest spruce, and ate them with gusto. No banquet of gods was ever as delicious as those potatoes. Then finally came Aunt Laura's kind, silvery voice calling through the frosty dark; Ilse and Teddy scampered homewards; and Emily captured Mike II and shut him up safely for the night in the New Moon dog-house which had held no dog for years, but was still carefully preserved and whitewashed every spring. Emily's heart would have broken if anything had happened to Mike II.

"Old Kelly," the tin pedlar, had given him to her. Old Kelly had come round through Blair Water every fortnight from May to November for thirty years, perched on the seat of a bright red pedlar's wagon and behind a dusty, ambling, red pony of that peculiar gait and appearance pertaining to the ponies of country pedlars—a certain placid, unhasting leanness as of a nag that has encountered troubles of his own and has lived them down by sheer patience and staying power. From the bright red wagon proceeded a certain metallic rumbling and clinking as it bowled along, and two huge nests of tin pans on its flat, rope-encircled roof flashed back the sunlight so dazzlingly that Old Kelly seemed the beaming sun of a little planetary system all his own. A new broom, sticking up aggressively at each of the four corners gave the wagon a resemblance to a triumphal chariot. Emily hankered secretly for a ride in Old Kelly's wagon. She thought it must be very delightful.

Old Kelly and she were great friends. She liked his red, clean-shaven face under his plug hat, his nice, twinkly, blue eyes, his brush of upstanding, sandy hair, and his comical pursed-up mouth, the shape of which was partly due to nature and partly to much whistling. He always had a little three-cornered paper bag of "lemon drops" for her, or a candy stick of many colours, which he smuggled into her pocket when Aunt Elizabeth wasn't looking. And he never forgot to tell her that he supposed she'd soon be thinking of getting married—for Old Kelly thought that the surest way to please a female creature of any age was to tease her about getting married.

One day, instead of candy, he produced a plump grey kitten from the back drawer of his wagon and told her it was for her. Emily received the gift rapturously, but after Old Kelly had rattled and clattered away Aunt Elizabeth told her they did not want any more cats at New Moon.

"Oh, please let me keep it, Aunt Elizabeth," Emily begged. "It won't be a bit of bother to you. I have had experience in bringing up cats. And I'm so lonesome for a kitten. Saucy Sal is getting so wild running with the barn cats that I can't 'sociate with her like I used to do—and she never was nice to cuddle. PLEASE, Aunt Elizabeth."

Aunt Elizabeth would not and did not please. She was in a very bad humour that day, anyhow,—nobody knew just why. In such a mood she was entirely unreasonable. She would not listen to anybody—Laura and Cousin Jimmy had to hold their tongues, and Cousin Jimmy was bidden to take the grey kitten down to the Blair Water and drown it. Emily burst into tears over this cruel command, and this aggravated Aunt Elizabeth still further. She was so cross that Cousin Jimmy dared not smuggle the kitten up to the barn as he had at first planned to do.

"Take that beast down to the pond and throw it in and come back and tell me you've done it," said Elizabeth angrily. "I mean to be obeyed—New Moon is not going to be made a dumping-ground for Old Jock Kelly's superfluous cats."

Cousin Jimmy did as he was told and Emily would not eat any dinner. After dinner she stole mournfully away through the old orchard down the pasture to the pond. Just why she went she could not have told, but she felt that go she must. When she reached the bank of the little creek where Lofty John's brook ran into Blair Water, she heard piteous shrieks; and there, marooned on a tiny islet of sere marsh grass in the creek, was an unhappy little beast, its soaking fur plastered against its sides, shivering and trembling in the wind of the sharp autumnal day. The old oat-bag in which Cousin Jimmy had imprisoned it was floating out into the pond.

Emily did not stop to think, or look for a board, or count the consequences. She plunged in the creek up to her knees, she waded out to the clump of grass and caught the kitten up. She was so hot with indignation that she did not feel the cold of the water or the chill of the wind as she ran back to New Moon. A suffering or tortured animal always filled her with such a surge of sympathy that it lifted her clean out of herself. She burst into the cook-house where Aunt Elizabeth was frying doughnuts.

"Aunt Elizabeth," she cried, "the kitten wasn't drowned after all— and I AM going to keep it."

"You're not," said Aunt Elizabeth.

Emily looked her aunt in the face. Again she felt that odd sensation that had come when Aunt Elizabeth brought the scissors to cut her hair.

"Aunt Elizabeth, this poor little kitten is cold and starving, and oh, so miserable. It has been suffering for hours. It shall NOT be drowned again."

Archibald Murray's look was on her face and Archibald Murray's tone was in her voice. This happened only when the deeps of her being were stirred by some peculiarly poignant emotion. Just now she was in an agony of pity and anger.

When Elizabeth Murray saw her father looking at her out of Emily's little white face, she surrendered without a struggle, rage at herself as she might afterwards for her weakness. It was her one vulnerable point. The thing might not have been so uncanny if Emily had resembled the Murrays. But to see the Murray look suddenly superimposed like a mask over alien features, was such a shock to her nerves that she could not stand up against it. A ghost from the grave could not have cowed her more speedily.

She turned her back on Emily in silence but Emily knew that she had won her second victory. The grey kitten stayed at New Moon and waxed fat and lovable, and Aunt Elizabeth never took the slightest notice of its existence, save to sweep it out of the house when Emily was not about. But it was weeks before Emily was really forgiven and she felt uncomfortable enough over it. Aunt Elizabeth could be a not ungenerous conqueror but she was very disagreeable in defeat. It was really just as well that Emily could not summon the Murray look at will.

CHAPTER XV
VARIOUS TRAGEDIES

EMILY, obedient to Aunt Elizabeth's command, had eliminated the word "bull" from her vocabulary. But to ignore the existence of bulls was not to do away with them—and specifically with Mr. James Lee's English bull, who inhabited the big windy pasture west of Blair Water and who bore a dreadful reputation. He was certainly an awesome looking creature and Emily sometimes had fearful dreams of being chased by him and being unable to move. And one sharp November day these dreams came true.

There was a certain well at the far end of the pasture concerning which Emily felt a curiosity, because Cousin Jimmy had told her a dreadful tale about it. The well had been dug sixty years ago by two brothers who lived in a little house which was built down near the shore. It was a very deep well, which was considered a curious thing in that low-lying land near pond and sea; the brothers had gone ninety feet before they found a spring. Then the sides of the well had been stoned up—but the work never went further. Thomas and Silas Lee had quarrelled over some trivial difference of opinion as to what kind of a hood should be put over it; and in the heat of his anger Silas had struck Thomas on the head with his hammer and killed him.

The well-house was never built. Silas Lee was sent to prison for manslaughter and died there. The farm passed to another brother— Mr. James Lee's father—who moved the house to the other end of it and planked the well over. Cousin Jimmy added that Tom Lee's ghost was supposed to haunt the scene of his tragic death but he couldn't vouch for that, though he had written a poem on it. A very eerie poem it was, too, and made Emily's blood run cold with a fearful joy when he recited it to her one misty night by the big potato pot. Ever since she had wanted to see the old well.

Her chance came one Saturday when she was prowling alone in the old graveyard. Beyond it lay the Lee pasture and there was apparently not a sign of a bull in or about it. Emily decided to pay a visit to the old well and went skimming down the field against the sweep of the north wind racing across the gulf. The Wind Woman was a giantess that day and a mighty swirl she was stirring up along the shore; but as Emily drew near the big sand-dunes they made a little harbour of calmness around the old well.

Emily coolly lifted up one of the planks, knelt on the others and peered down. Fortunately the planks were strong and comparatively new—otherwise the small maiden of New Moon might have explored the well more thoroughly than she desired to do. As it was, she could see little of it; huge ferns grew thickly out of the crevices among the stones of its sides and reached across it, shutting out the view of its gloomy depths. Rather disappointed, Emily replaced the plank and started homeward. She had not gone ten steps before she stopped. Mr. James Lee's bull was coming straight towards her and was less than twenty yards away.

The shore fence was not far behind Emily, and she might possibly have reached it in time had she run. But she was incapable of running; as she wrote that night in her letter to her father she was "parralised" with terror and could no more move than she could in her dreams of this very occurrence. It is quite conceivable that a dreadful thing might have happened then and there had not a certain boy been sitting on the shore fence. He had been sitting there unnoticed all the time Emily had been peering into the well; now he sprang down.

Emily saw, or sensed, a sturdy body dashing past her. The owner thereof ran to within ten feet of the bull, hurled a stone squarely into the monster's hairy face, then sped off at right angles towards the side fence. The bull, thus insulted, turned with a menacing rumble and lumbered off after this intruder.

"Run now!" screamed the boy over his shoulder to Emily.

Emily did not run. Terrified as she was, there was something in her that would not let her run until she saw whether her gallant rescuer made good his escape. He reached his fence in the nick of time. Then and not till then Emily ran too, and scrambled over the shore fence just as the bull started back across the pasture, evidently determined to catch somebody. Trembling, she made her way through the spiky grass of the sand-hills and met the boy at the corner. They stood and looked at each other for a moment.

The boy was a stranger to Emily. He had a cheery, impudent, clean-cut face, with keen, grey eyes and plenty of tawny curls. He wore as few clothes as decency permitted and had only the pretence of a hat. Emily liked him; there was nothing of Teddy's subtle charm in him but he had a certain forceful attraction of his own and he had just saved her from a terrible death.

"Thank you," said Emily shyly, looking up at him with great grey eyes that looked blue under her long lashes. It was a very effective look which lost nothing of effectiveness from being wholly unconscious. Nobody had as yet told Emily how very winsome that shy, sudden, up-glance of hers was.

"Isn't he a rip-snorter?" said the boy easily. He thrust his hands into his ragged pockets and stared at Emily so fixedly that she dropped her eyes in confusion—thereby doing further damage with those demure lids and silken fringes.

"He's dreadful," she said with a shudder. "And I was so scared."

"Were you now? And me thinking you were full of grit to be standing there like that looking at him cool as a cucumber. What's it like to be afraid?"

"Weren't YOU ever afraid?" asked Emily.

"No—don't know what it's like," said the boy carelessly, and a bit boastfully. "What's your name?"

"Emily Byrd Starr."

"Live round here?"

"I live at New Moon."

"Where Simple Jimmy Murray lives?"

"He ISN'T simple," cried Emily indignantly.

"Oh, all right. I don't know him. But I'm going to. I'm going to hire with him for chore boy for the winter."

"I didn't know," said Emily, surprised. "Are you really?"

"Yep. I didn't know it myself till just this minute. He was asking Aunt Tom about me last week but I didn't mean to hire out then. Now I guess I will. Want to know my name?"

"Of course."

"Perry Miller. I live with my old beast of an Aunt Tom down at Stovepipe Town. Dad was a sea-captain and I uster sail with him when he was alive—sailed everywhere. Go to school?"

"Yes."

"I don't—never did. Aunt Tom lives so far away. Anyhow, I didn't think I'd like it. Guess I'll go now, though."

"Can't you read?" asked Emily wonderingly.

"Yes—some—and figger. Dad learned me some when he was alive. I hain't bothered with it since—I'd ruther be down round the harbour. Great fun there. But if I make up my mind to go to school I'll learn like thunder. I s'pose you're awful clever."

"No—not very. Father said I was a genius, but Aunt Elizabeth says I'm just queer."

"What's a genius?"

- 123 -

"I'm not sure. Sometimes it's a person who writes poetry. I write poetry."

Perry stared at her.

"Golly. I'll write poetry too, then."

"I don't believe YOU could write poetry," said Emily—a little disdainfully, it must be admitted. "Teddy can't—and he's VERY clever."

"Who's Teddy?"

"A friend of mine." There was just a trace of stiffness in Emily's voice.

"Then," said Perry, folding his arms across his breast and scowling, "I'm going to punch this friend of yours' head for him."

"You're not," cried Emily. She was very indignant and quite forgot for the moment that Perry had rescued her from the bull. She tossed her own head and started homeward. Perry turned too.

"May as well go up and see Jimmy Murray about hiring 'fore I go home," he said. "Don't be mad, now. If you don't want anybody's head punched I won't punch it. Only you've gotter like me, too."

"Why, of course I'll like you," said Emily, as if there could be no question about it. She smiled her slow, blossoming smile at Perry and thereby reduced him to hopeless bondage.

Two days later Perry Miller was installed as chore boy at New Moon and in a fortnight's time Emily felt as if he must have been there always.

"Aunt Elizabeth didn't want Cousin Jimmy to hire him," she wrote to her father, "because he was one of the boys who did a dreadful thing one night last fall. They changed all the horses that were tied to the fence one Sunday night when preaching was going on and when folks came out the confushun was awful. Aunt Elizabeth said it wouldn't be safe to have him round the place. But Cousin Jimmy said it was awful hard to get a chore boy and that we ode Perry something for saving my life from the bull. So Aunt Elizabeth gave in and lets him sit at the table with us but he has to stay in the kitchen in the evenings. The rest of us are in the sitting-room, but I am allowed to go out and help Perry with his lessons. He can only have one candle and the light is very dim. It keeps us snuffing it all the time. It is great fun to snuff candles. Perry is head of his class in school already. He is only in the third book all-though he is nearly twelve. Miss Brownell said something sarkastik to him the first day in school and he just threw back his head and laughed loud and long. Miss Brownell gave him a whipping for it but she has never been sarkastik to him again. She does not like to be laughed at I can see. Perry isn't afraid of anything. I thought he might not go to school any more when she whipped him but he says a little thing like that isn't going to keep him from getting an educashun since he has made up his mind to it. He is very determined.

"Aunt Elizabeth is determined too. But she says Perry is stubborn. I am teaching Perry grammar. He says he wants to learn to speak properly. I told him he should not call his Aunt Tom an old beast but he said he had to because she wasn't a young beast. He says the place he lives in is called Stovepipe Town because the houses have no chimneys, only pipes sticking out of the roof, but he would live in a manshun some day. Aunt Elizabeth says I ought not to be so friendly with a hired boy. But he is a nice boy though his manners are crood. Aunt Laura says they are crood. I don't know what it means but I guess it means he always says what he thinks right out and eats beans with his knife. I like Perry but in a different way from Teddy. Isn't it funny, dear Father, how many kinds of ways of liking there are? I don't think Ilse likes him. She makes fun of his ignerance and turns up her nose at him because his close are patched though her own close are queer enough. Teddy doesnt like him much and he drew such a funny picture of Perry hanging by his heels from a gallos. The face looked like Perrys and still it didn't. Cousin Jimmy said it was a carrycachure and laughed at it but I dared not show it to Perry for fear he would punch Teddys head. I showed it to Ilse and she got mad and tore it in two. I cant imagine why.

"Perry says he can recite as well as Ilse and could draw pictures too if he put his mind to it. I can see he doesnt like to think anybody can do anything he cant. But he cant see the wallpaper in the air like I can though he tries until I fear he will strane his eyes. He can make better speeches than any of us. He says he used to mean to be a sailer like his father but now he thinks he will be a lawyer when he grows up and go to parlament. Teddy is going to be an artist if his mother will let him, and Ilse is going to be a concert reciter—there is another name but I don't know how it is spelled—and I am going to be a poetess. I think we are a tallented crowd. Perhaps that is a vane thing to say, dear Father.

"A very terrible thing happened the day before yesterday. On Saturday morning we were at family prayers, all kneeling quite solemn around the kitchen. I just looked at Perry once and he made such a funny face at me that I laughed right out loud before I could help it. (THAT was not the terrible thing.) Aunt Elizabeth was VERY angry. I would not tell that it was Perry made me laugh because I was afraid he might be sent away if I did. So Aunt Elizabeth said I was to be punished and I was not let go to Jennie Strangs party in the afternoon. (It was a dreadful disappointment but IT was not the terrible thing either.) Perry was away with Cousin Jimmy all day and when he came home at night he said to me, very feerce, Who has been making you cry. I said I had been crying—a little but not much—because I was not let go to the party because I had laughed at prayers. And Perry marched right up to Aunt Elizabeth and told her it was all his fault that I laughed. Aunt Elizabeth said I should not have laughed anyhow, but Aunt Laura was GREEVOUSLY upset and said my punishment had been far too severe; and she said that she would let me ware her pearl ring to school Monday to make up for it. I was enraptured for it is a lovely ring and no other girl has one. As soon as roll call was over Monday morning I put up my hand to ask Miss Brownell a question but really to show off my ring. That was wikked pride and I was punished. At recess Cora Lee, one of the big girls in the sixth class came and asked me to let her ware the ring for a while. I didnt want to but she said if I didnt she would get all the girls in my class to send me to coventry (which is a dreadful thing, dear Father, and makes you feel like an outcast). So I let her and she kept it on till the afternoon recess and then she came and told me she had lost it in the brook. (This was the terrible thing). Oh, Father dear, I was nearly wild. I dared not go home and face Aunt Laura. I had promised her I would be so careful of the ring. I thought I might earn money to get her another ring but when I figgered it out on my slate I knew I would have to wash dishes for twenty years to do it. I wepped in my despare. Perry saw me and after school he marched up to Cora Lee and said You fork over that ring or I'll tell Miss Brownell about it. And Cora Lee forked it over, very meek and said I was going to give it to her anyhow. I was just playing a joke and Perry said, Dont you play any more jokes on Emily or I'll joke you. It is very comforting to have such a champeen! I tremble to think what it would have been like if I had had to go home and tell Aunt Laura I had lost her ring. But it was crewel of Cora Lee to tell me she had lost it when she had not and harrow up my mind so. I could not be so crewel to an orfan girl.

"When I got home I looked in the glass to see if my hair had turned white. I am told that sometimes hapens. But it hadnt.

"Perry knows more geograffy than any of us because he has been nearly everywhere in the world with his father. He tells me such fassinating stories after his lessons are done. He talks till the candle is burned to the last inch and then he uses that to go to bed with up the black hole into the kitchen loft because Aunt Elizabeth will not let him have more than one candle a night.

"Ilse and I had a fight yesterday about which we'd rather be Joan of Arc or Frances Willard. We didn't begin it as a fight but just as an argewment but it ended that way. I would rather be Frances Willard because she is alive.

"We had the first snow yesterday. I made a poem on it. This is it.

Along the snow the sunbeams glide
Earth is a peerless, gleaming bride,
Dripping with dimonds, clad in traling white,
No bride was ever half so fair and bright.

"I read it to Perry and he said he could make poetry just as good and he said right off,

Mike has made a long row
Of tracks across the snow.

Now isnt that as good as yours. I didnt think it was because you could say it just as well in prose. But when you talk of peerless gleaming brides in prose it sounds funny. Mike DID make a row of little tracks right across the barn field and they looked so pretty, but not so pretty as the mice tracks in some flour Cousin Jimmy spilled on the granary floor. They are the dearest little things. They LOOK like poetry.

"I am sorry winter has come because Ilse and I cant play in our house in Lofty Johns bush any more till spring or outside at the Tansy Patch. Sometimes we play indoors at the Tansy Patch but Mrs. Kent makes us feel queer. She sits and watches us all the time. So we dont go only when Teddy coaxes very hard. And the pigs have been killed, poor things, so Cousin Jimmy doesnt boil for them any more. But there is one consolashun I do not have to ware a sunbonnet to school now. Aunt Laura made me such a pretty red hood with ribbons on it at which Aunt Elizabeth looked skornfully saying it was extravagant. I like school here better every day but I cant like Miss Brownell. She isnt fair. She told us she would give the one who wrote the best composishun a pink ribbon to wear from Friday night to Monday. I wrote The Brooks Story about the brook in Lofty John's bush—all its advenshures and thoughts—and Miss Brownell said I must have copied it and Rhoda Stuart got the ribbon. Aunt Elizabeth said You waste enough time writing trash I think you might have won that ribbon. She was mortifyed (I think) because I had disgraced New Moon by not getting it but I did not tell her what had happened. Teddy says a GOOD SPORT never whines over losing. I want to be a good sport. Rhoda is so hateful to me now. She says she is surprised that a New Moon girl should have a hired boy for a bow. That is very silly because Perry is not my bow. Perry told her she had more gab than sense. That was not polite but it is true. One day in class Rhoda said the moon was situated east of Canada. Perry laughed right out and Miss Brownell made him stay in at recess but she never said anything to Rhoda for saying such a ridiklus thing. But the meanest thing Rhoda said was that she had forgiven me for the way I had used her. That made my blood boil when I hadnt done anything to be forgiven for. The idea.

"We have begun to eat the big beef ham that hung in the southwest corner of the kitchen.

"The other Wednesday night Perry and I helped Cousin Jimmy pick a road through the turnips in the first cellar. We have to go through it to the second cellar because the outside hatch is banked up now. It was great fun. We had a candle stuck up in a hole in the wall and it made such lovely shadows and we could eat all the apples we wanted from the big barrel in the corner and the spirit moved Cousin Jimmy to recite some of his poetry as he threw the turnips.

"I am reading The Alhambra. It belongs to our book case. Aunt Elizabeth does not like to say it isnt fit for me to read because it was one of her fathers books, but I dont believe she aproves because she knits very furiusly and looks black at me over her glasses. Teddy lent me Hans Andersons stories. I love them—only I always think of a different end for the Ice Maiden and save Rudy.

"They say Mrs. John Killegrew has swallowed her wedding-ring. I wonder what she did that for.

"Cousin Jimmy says there is to be an eklips of the sun in December. I hope it wont interfear with Chrismas.

"My hands are chapped. Aunt Laura rubs mutton tallow on them every night when I go to bed. It is hard to write poetry with chapped hands. I wonder if Mrs. Hemans ever had chapped hands. It does not mention anything like that in her biograffy.

"Jimmy Ball has to be a minister when he grows up. His mother told Aunt Laura that she consekrated him to it in his cradle. I wonder how she did it.

"We have brekfast by candlelight now and I like it.

"Ilse was up here Sunday afternoon and we went up in the garret and talked about God, because that is propper on Sundays. We have to be very careful what we do on Sundays. It is a traddishun of New Moon to keep Sundays very holy. Grandfather Murray was very strikt. Cousin Jimmy told me a story about him. They always cut the wood for Sunday on Saturday night, but one time they forgot and there was no wood on Sunday to cook the dinner, so Grandfather Murray said you must not cut wood on Sundays, boys, but just break a little with the back of the axe. Ilse is very curious about God although she doesnt believe in Him most of the time and doesnt like to talk about Him but still wants to find out about Him. She says she thinks she might like Him if she knew Him. She spells his name with a Capital G now because it is best to be on the safe side. I think God is just like my flash, only IT lasts only a second and He lasts always. We talked so long we got hungry and I went down to the sitting-room cubbord and got two donuts. I forgot Aunt Elizabeth had told me I could not have donuts between meals. It was not stealing it was just forgetting. But Ilse got mad at the last and said I was a she jakobite (whatever that is) and a thief and that no Christian would steal donuts from her poor old aunt. So I went and confessed to Aunt Elizabeth and she said I was not to have a donut at supper. It was hard to see the others eating them. I thought Perry et his very quick but after supper he bekoned me out doors and gave me half his donut which he had kept for me. He had rapped it in his hangkerchief which was not very clean but I et it because I did not want to hurt his feelings.

"Aunt Laura says Ilse has a nice smile. I wonder if I have a nice smile. I looked at the glass in Ilse's room and smiled but it did not seem to me very nice.

"Now the nights have got cold Aunt Elizabeth always puts a gin jar full of hot water in the bed. I like to put my toes against it. That is all we use the gin jar for nowadays. But Grandfather Murray used to keep real gin in it.

"Now that the snow has come Cousin Jimmy cant work in his garden any more and he is very lonesome. I think the garden is just as pretty in winter as in summer. There are such pretty dimples and baby hills where the snow has covered up the flower beds. And in the evenings it is all pink and rosy at sunset and by moonlight it is like dreamland. I like to look out of the sitting-room window at it and watch the rabbits candles floting in the air above it and wonder what all the little roots and seeds are thinking of down under the snow. And it gives me a lovely creepy feeling to look at it through the red glass in the front door.

"There is a beautiful fringe of isikles along the cook-house roof. But there will be much more beautiful things in heaven. I was reading about Anzonetta to-day and it made me feel relijus. Good night, my dearest of fathers.

"EMILY.

"P. S. That doesnt mean that I have any other Father. It is just a way of saying VERY VERY dear.

"E. B. S."

CHAPTER XVI
CHECK FOR MISS BROWNELL

EMILY and Ilse were sitting out on the side bench of Blair Water school writing poetry on their slates—at least, Emily was writing poetry and Ilse was reading it as she wrote and occasionally suggesting a rhyme when Emily was momentarily stuck for one. It may as well be admitted here and now that they had no business whatever to be doing this. They should have been "doing sums," as Miss Brownell supposed they were. But Emily never did sums when she took it into her black head to write poetry, and Ilse hated arithmetic on general principles. Miss Brownell was hearing the geography class at the other side of the room, the pleasant sunshine was showering in over them through the big window, and everything seemed propitious for a flight with the muses. Emily began to write a poem about the view from the school window.

It was quite a long time since she had been allowed to sit out on the side bench. This was a boon reserved for those pupils who had found favour in Miss Brownell's cold eyes—and Emily had never been one of those. But this afternoon Ilse had asked for both herself and Emily, and Miss Brownell had let both go, not being able to think of any valid reason for permitting Ilse and refusing Emily—as she would have liked to do, for she had one of those petty natures which never forget or forgive any offence. Emily, on her first day of school, had, so Miss Brownell believed, been guilty of impertinence and defiance—and successful defiance at that. This rankled in Miss Brownell's mind still and Emily felt its venom in a score of subtle ways. She never received any commendation—she was a target for Miss Brownell's sarcasm continually—and the small favours that other girls received never came her way. So this opportunity to sit on the side bench was a pleasing novelty.

There were points about sitting on the side bench. You could see all over the school without turning your head—and Miss Brownell could not sneak up behind you and look over your shoulder to see what you were up to; but in Emily's eyes the finest thing about it was that you could look right down into the "school bush," and watch the old spruces where the Wind Woman played, the long grey-green trails of moss hanging from the branches, like banners of Elfland, the little red squirrels running along the fence, and the wonderful white aisles of snow where splashes of sunlight fell like pools of golden wine; and there was one little opening in the trees through which you could see right over the Blair Water valley to the sand-hills and the gulf beyond. To-day the sand-hills were softly rounded and gleaming white under the snow, but beyond them the gulf was darkly, deeply blue with dazzling white masses of ice like baby icebergs, floating about in it. Just to look at it thrilled Emily with a delight that was unutterable but which she yet must try to utter. She began her poem. Fractions were utterly forgotten—what had numerators and denominators to do with those curving bosoms of white snow—that heavenly blue—those crossed dark fir tips against the pearly skies—those ethereal woodland aisles of pearl and gold? Emily was lost to her world—so lost that she did not know the geography class had scattered to their respective seats and that Miss Brownell, catching sight of Emily's entranced gaze sky-wards as she searched for a rhyme, was stepping softly towards her. Ilse was drawing a picture on her slate and did not see her or she would have warned Emily. The latter suddenly felt her slate drawn out of her hand and heard Miss Brownell saying:

"I suppose you have finished those sums, Emily?"

Emily had not finished even one sum—she had only covered her slate with verses—verses that Miss Brownell must not see—MUST NOT see! Emily sprang to her feet and clutched wildly after her slate. But Miss Brownell, with a smile of malicious enjoyment on her thin lips, held it beyond her reach.

"What is this? It does not look—exactly—like fractions. 'Lines on the View—v-e-w—from the Window of Blair Water School.' Really, children, we seem to have a budding poet among us."

The words were harmless enough, but—oh, the hateful sneer that ran through the tone—the contempt, the mockery that was in it! It seared Emily's soul like a whiplash. Nothing was more terrible to her than the thought of having her beloved "poems" read by stranger eyes—cold, unsympathetic, derisive, stranger eyes.

"Please—please, Miss Brownell," she stammered miserably, "don't read it—I'll rub it off—I'll do my sums right away. Only please don't read it. It—it isn't anything."

Miss Brownell laughed cruelly.

"You are too modest, Emily. It is a whole slateful of—POETRY—think of that, children—POETRY. We have a pupil in this school who can write—POETRY. And she does not want us to read this—

POETRY. I am afraid Emily is selfish. I am sure we should all enjoy this—POETRY."

Emily cringed every time Miss Brownell said "POETRY," with that jeering emphasis and that hateful pause before it. Many of the children giggled, partly because they enjoyed seeing a "Murray of New Moon" grilled, partly because they realized that Miss Brownell expected them to giggle. Rhoda Stuart giggled louder than any one else; but Jennie Strang, who had tormented Emily on her first day at school, refused to giggle and scowled blackly at Miss Brownell instead.

Miss Brownell held up the slate and read Emily's poem aloud, in a sing-song nasal voice, with absurd intonations and gestures that made it seem a very ridiculous thing. The lines Emily had thought the finest seemed the most ridiculous. The other pupils laughed more than ever and Emily felt that the bitterness of the moment could never go out of her heart. The little fancies that had been so beautiful when they came to her as she wrote were shattered and bruised now, like torn and mangled butterflies—"vistas in some fairy dream," chanted Miss Brownell, shutting her eyes and wagging her head from side to side. The giggles became shouts of laughter.

"Oh," thought Emily, clenching her hands, "I wish—I wish the bears that ate the naughty children in the Bible would come and eat YOU."

There were no nice, retributive bears in the school bush, however, and Miss Brownell read the whole "poem" through. She was enjoying herself hugely. To ridicule a pupil always gave her pleasure and when that pupil was Emily of New Moon, in whose heart and soul she had always sensed something fundamentally different from her own, the pleasure was exquisite.

When she reached the end she handed the slate back to the crimson-cheeked Emily.

"Take your—POETRY, Emily," she said.

Emily snatched the slate. No slate "rag" was handy but Emily gave the palm of her hand a fierce lick and one side of the slate was wiped off. Another lick—and the rest of the poem went. It had been disgraced—degraded—it must be blotted out of existence. To the end of her life Emily never forgot the pain and humiliation of that experience.

Miss Brownell laughed again.

"What a pity to obliterate such—POETRY, Emily," she said. "Suppose you do those sums now. They are not—POETRY, but I am in this school to teach arithmetic and I am not here to teach the art of writing—POETRY. Go to your own seat. Yes, Rhoda?"

For Rhoda Stuart was holding up her hand and snapping her fingers.

"Please, Miss Brownell," she said, with distinct triumph in her tones, "Emily Starr has a whole bunch of poetry in her desk. She was reading it to Ilse Burnley this morning while you thought they were learning history."

Perry Miller turned around and a delightful missile, compounded of chewed paper and known as a "spit pill," flew across the room and struck Rhoda squarely in the face. But Miss Brownell was already at Emily's desk, having reached it one jump before Emily herself.

"Don't touch them—you have no RIGHT!" gasped Emily frantically.

But Miss Brownell had the "bunch of poetry" in her hands. She turned and walked up to the platform. Emily followed. Those poems were very dear to her. She had composed them during the various stormy recesses when it had been impossible to play out of doors and written them down on disreputable scraps of paper borrowed from her mates. She had meant to take them home that very evening and copy them on letter-bills. And now this horrible woman was going to read them to the whole jeering, giggling school.

But Miss Brownell realized that the time was too short for that. She had to content herself with reading over the titles, with some appropriate comments.

Meanwhile Perry Miller was relieving his feelings by bombarding Rhoda Stuart with spit pills, so craftily timed that Rhoda had no idea from what quarter of the room they were coming and so could not "tell" on any one. They greatly interfered with her enjoyment of Emily's scrape, however. As for Teddy Kent, who did not wage war with spit pills but preferred subtler methods of revenge, he was busy drawing something on a sheet of paper. Rhoda found the sheet on her desk the next morning; on it was depicted a small, scrawny monkey, hanging by its tail from a branch; and the face of the monkey was as the face of Rhoda Stuart. Whereat Rhoda Stuart waxed wroth, but for the sake of her own vanity tore the sketch to tatters and kept silence regarding it. She did not know that Teddy had made a similar sketch, with Miss Brownell figuring as a vampirish-looking bat, and thrust it into Emily's hand as they left school.

"'The Lost Dimond—a Romantic Tale,'" read Miss Brownell. "'Lines on a Birch Tree'—looks to me more like lines on a very dirty piece of paper, Emily—'Lines Written on a Sundial in our Garden'—ditto—'Lines to my Favourite Cat'—another romantic TAIL, I presume—'Ode to Ilse'—'Thy neck is of a wondrous pearly sheen'—hardly that, I should say. Ilse's neck is very sunburned—'A Deskripshun of Our Parlour,' 'The Violets Spell'—I hope the violet SPELLS better than you do, Emily—'The Disappointed House'—

> "'Lilies lifted up white cups
> For the bees to DR—R—I—I—NK.'"

"I didn't write it that way!" cried tortured Emily.

"'Lines to a Piece of Brokade in Aunt Laura's Burow Drawer,' 'Farewell on Leaving Home,' 'Lines to a Spruce Tree'—'It keeps off heat and sun and glare, Tis a goodly tree I ween'—are you quite sure that you know what 'ween' means, Emily?—'Poem on Mr. Tom Bennet's Field'—'Poem on the Vew from Aunt Elizabeth's Window'—you are strong on 'v-e-w-s,' Emily—'Epitaff on a Drowned Kitten,' 'Meditashuns at the tomb of my great great grandmother'—poor lady—'To my Northern Birds'—'Lines composed on the bank of Blair Water gazing at the stars'—h'm—h'm—

> "'Crusted with uncounted gems,
> Those stars so distant, cold and true,'

Don't try to pass those lines off as your own, Emily. You couldn't have written them."

"I did—I did!" Emily was white with sense of outrage. "And I've written lots far better."

Miss Brownell suddenly crumpled the ragged little papers up in her hand.

"We have wasted enough time over this trash," she said. "Go to your seat, Emily."

She moved towards the stove. For a moment Emily did not realize her purpose. Then, as Miss Brownell opened the stove door, Emily understood and bounded forward. She caught at the papers and tore them from Miss Brownell's hand before the latter could tighten her grasp.

"You SHALL NOT burn them—you shall not have them," gasped Emily. She crammed the poems into the pocket of her "baby apron" and faced Miss Brownell in a kind of calm rage. The Murray look was on her face—and although Miss Brownell was not so violently affected by it as Aunt Elizabeth had been, it nevertheless gave her an unpleasant sensation, as of having roused forces with which she dared not tamper further. This tormented child looked quite capable of flying at her, tooth and claw.

"Give me those papers, Emily,"—but she said it rather uncertainly.

"I will not," said Emily stormily. "They are mine. You have no right to them. I wrote them at recesses—I didn't break any rules. You"—Emily looked defiantly into Miss Brownell's cold eyes—"You are an unjust, tyrannical PERSON."

Miss Brownell turned to her desk.

"I am coming up to New Moon to-night to tell your Aunt Elizabeth of this," she said.

Emily was at first too much excited over saving her precious poetry to pay much heed to this threat. But as her excitement ebbed cold dread flowed in. She knew she had an unpleasant time ahead of her. But at all events they should not get her poems—not one of them, no matter what they did to HER. As soon as she got home from school she flew to the garret and secreted them on the shelf of the old sofa.

She wanted terribly to cry but she would not. Miss Brownell was coming and Miss Brownell should NOT see her with red eyes. But her heart burned within her. Some sacred temple of her being had been desecrated and shamed. And more was yet to come, she felt wretchedly sure. Aunt Elizabeth was certain to side with Miss Brownell. Emily shrank from the impending ordeal with all the dread of a sensitive, fine strung nature facing humiliation. She would not have been afraid of justice; but she knew at the bar of Aunt Elizabeth and Miss Brownell she would not have justice.

"And I can't write Father about it," she thought, her little breast heaving. The shame of it all was too deep and intimate to be written out, and so she could find no relief for her pain.

They did not have supper at New Moon in winter time until Cousin Jimmy had finished his chores and was ready to stay in for the night. So Emily was left undisturbed in the garret.

From the dormer window she looked down on a dreamland scene that would ordinarily have delighted her. There was a red sunset behind the white, distant hills, shining through the dark trees like a great fire; there was a delicate blue tracery of bare branch shadows all over the crusted garden; there was a pale, ethereal alpenglow all over the southeastern sky; and presently there was a little, lovely new moon in the silvery arch over Lofty John's bush. But Emily found no pleasure in any of them.

Presently she saw Miss Brownell coming up the lane, under the white arms of the birches, with her mannish stride.

"If my father was alive," said Emily, looking down at her, "you would go away from this place with a flea in your ear."

The minutes passed, each seeming very long to Emily. At last Aunt Laura came up.

"Your Aunt Elizabeth wants you to come down to the kitchen, Emily."

Aunt Laura's voice was kind and sad. Emily fought down a sob. She hated to have Aunt Laura think she had been naughty, but she could not trust herself to explain. Aunt Laura would sympathize and sympathy would break her down. She went silently down the two long flights of stairs before Aunt Laura and out to the kitchen.

The supper table was set and the candles were lighted. The big black-raftered kitchen looked spookish and weird, as it always did by candlelight. Aunt Elizabeth sat rigidly by the table and her face was very hard. Miss Brownell sat in the rocking-chair, her pale eyes glittering with triumphant malice. There seemed something baleful and poisonous in her very glance. Also, her nose was very red—which did not add to her charm.

Cousin Jimmy, in his grey jumper, was perched on the edge of the wood-box, whistling at the ceiling, and looking more gnome-like than ever. Perry was nowhere to be seen. Emily was sorry for this. The presence of Perry, who was on her side, would have been a great moral support.

"I am sorry to say, Emily, that I have been hearing some very bad things about your behaviour in school to-day," said Aunt Elizabeth.

"No, I don't think you are sorry," said Emily, gravely.

Now that the crisis had come she found herself able to confront it coolly—nay, more, to take a curious interest in it under all her secret fear and shame, as if some part of her had detached itself from the rest and was interestedly absorbing impressions and analyzing motives and describing settings. She felt that when she wrote about this scene later on she must not forget to describe the odd shadows the candle under Aunt Elizabeth's nose cast upward on her face, producing a rather skeletonic effect. As for Miss Brownell, could SHE ever have been a baby—a dimpled, fat, laughing baby? The thing was unbelievable.

"Don't speak impertinently to ME," said Aunt Elizabeth.

"You see," said Miss Brownell, significantly.

"I don't mean to be impertinent, but you are NOT sorry," persisted Emily. "You are angry because you think I have disgraced New Moon, but you are a little glad that you have got some one to agree with you that I'm bad."

"What a GRATEFUL child," said Miss Brownell—flashing her eyes up at the ceiling—where they encountered a surprising sight. Perry Miller's head—and no more of him—was stuck down out of the "black hole" and on Perry Miller's upside-down face was a most disrespectful and impish grimace. Face and head disappeared in a flash, leaving Miss Brownell staring foolishly at the ceiling.

"You have been behaving disgracefully in school," said Aunt Elizabeth, who had not seen this by-play. "I am ashamed of you."

"It was not as bad as that, Aunt Elizabeth," said Emily steadily. "You see it was this way—"

"I don't want to hear anything more about it," said Aunt Elizabeth.

"But you must," cried Emily. "It isn't fair to listen only to HER side. I was a little bad—but not so bad as she says—"

"Not another word! I have heard the whole story," said Aunt Elizabeth grimly.

"You heard a pack of lies," said Perry, suddenly sticking his head down through the black hole again.

Everybody jumped—even Aunt Elizabeth, who at once became angrier than ever because she HAD jumped.

"Perry Miller, come down out of that loft instantly!" she commanded.

"Can't," said Perry laconically.

"At once, I say!"

"Can't," repeated Perry, winking audaciously at Miss Brownell.

"Perry Miller, come down! I WILL be obeyed. I am mistress here YET."

"Oh, all right," said Perry cheerfully. "If I must."

He swung himself down until his toes touched the ladder. Aunt Laura gave a little shriek. Everybody else seemed to be stricken dumb.

"I've just got my wet duds off," Perry was saying cheerfully, waving his legs about to get a foothold on the ladder while he hung to the sides of the black hole with his elbows. "Fell into the brook when I was watering the cows. Was going to put on dry ones—but just as you say—"

"Jimmy," implored poor Elizabeth Murray, surrendering at discretion. SHE could not cope with the situation.

"Perry, get back into that loft and get your clothes on this minute!" ordered Cousin Jimmy.

The bare legs shot up and disappeared. There was a chuckle as mirthful and malicious as an owl's beyond the black hole. Aunt Elizabeth gave a convulsive gasp of relief and turned to Emily. She was determined to regain ascendancy and Emily must be thoroughly humbled.

"Emily, kneel down here before Miss Brownell and ask her pardon for your conduct to-day," she said.

Into Emily's pale cheek came a scarlet protest. She could not do this—she would ask pardon of Miss Brownell but not on her knees. To kneel to this cruel woman who had hurt her so—she could not—would not do it. Her whole nature rose up in protest against such a humiliation.

"Kneel down," repeated Aunt Elizabeth.

Miss Brownell looked pleased and expectant. It would be very satisfying to see this child who had defied her kneeling before her as a penitent. Never again, Miss Brownell felt, would Emily be able to look levelly at her with those dauntless eyes that bespoke a soul untamable and free, no matter what punishment might be inflicted upon body or mind. The memory of this moment would always be with Emily—she could never forget that she had knelt in abasement. Emily felt this as clearly as Miss Brownell did and remained stubbornly on her feet.

"Aunt Elizabeth, PLEASE let me tell my side of the story," she pleaded.

"I have heard all I wish to hear of the matter. You will do as I say, Emily, or you will be outcast in this house until you do. No one will talk to you—play with you—eat with you—have anything to do with you until you have obeyed me."

Emily shuddered. THAT was a punishment she could not face. To be cut off from her world—she knew it would bring her to terms before long. She might as well yield at once—but, oh, the bitterness, the shame of it!

"A human being should not kneel to any one but God," said Cousin Jimmy, unexpectedly, still staring at the ceiling.

A sudden strange change came over Elizabeth Murray's proud, angry face. She stood very still, looking at Cousin Jimmy—stood so long that Miss Brownell made a motion of petulant impatience.

"Emily," said Aunt Elizabeth in a different tone, "I was wrong—I shall not ask you to kneel. But you must apologize to your teacher—and I shall punish you later on."

Emily put her hands behind her and looked straight into Miss Brownell's eyes again.

"I am sorry for anything I did to-day that was wrong," she said, "and I ask your pardon for it."

Miss Brownell got on her feet. She felt herself cheated of a legitimate triumph. Whatever Emily's punishment would be she would not have the satisfaction of seeing it. She could have shaken "simple Jimmy Murray" with a right good will. But it would hardly do to show all she felt. Elizabeth Murray was not a trustee but she was the heaviest ratepayer in New Moon and had great influence with the School Board.

"I shall excuse your conduct if you behave yourself in future, Emily," she said coldly. "I feel that I have only done my duty in putting the matter before your aunt. No, thank you, Miss Murray, I cannot stay to supper—I want to get home before it is too dark."

"God speed all travellers," said Perry cheerfully, climbing down his ladder—this time with his clothes on.

Aunt Elizabeth ignored him—she was not going to have a scene with a hired boy before Miss Brownell. The latter switched herself out and Aunt Elizabeth looked at Emily.

"You will eat your supper alone to-night, Emily, in the pantry—you will have bread and milk only. And you will not speak one word to anyone until to-morrow morning."

"But you won't forbid me to think?" said Emily anxiously.

Aunt Elizabeth made no reply but sat haughtily down at the supper table. Emily went into the pantry and ate her bread and milk, with the odour of the delicious sausages the others were eating for savour. Emily liked sausages, and New Moon sausages were the last word in sausages. Elizabeth Burnley had brought the recipe out from the Old Country and its secret was carefully guarded. And Emily was hungry. But she had escaped the unbearable, and things might be worse. It suddenly occurred to her that she would write an epic poem in imitation of *The Lay Of The Last Minstrel*. Cousin Jimmy had read *The Lay* to her last Saturday. She would begin the first canto right off. When Laura Murray came into the pantry, Emily, her bread and milk only half eaten, was leaning her elbows on the dresser, gazing into space, with faintly moving lips and the light that never was on land or sea in her young eyes. Even the aroma of sausages was forgotten—was she not drinking from a fount of Castaly?

"Emily," said Aunt Laura, shutting the door, and looking very lovingly upon Emily out of her kind blue eyes, "you can talk to ME all you want to. I don't like Miss Brownell and I don't think you were altogether in the wrong—although of course you shouldn't be writing poetry when you have sums to do. And there are some ginger cookies in that box."

"I don't want to talk to any one, dear Aunt Laura—I'm too happy," said Emily dreamily. "I'm composing an epic—it is to be called *The White Lady*, and I've got twenty lines of it made already—and two of them are thrilling. The heroine wants to go into a convent and her father warns her that if she does she will never be able to

Come back to the life you gave
With all its pleasures to the grave.

Oh, Aunt Laura, when I composed those lines the flash came to me. And ginger cookies are nothing to me any more."

Aunt Laura smiled again.

"Not just now perhaps, dear. But when the moment of inspiration has passed it will do no harm to remember that the cookies in the box have not been counted and that they are as much mine as Elizabeth's."

CHAPTER XVII
LIVING EPISTLES

"DEAR FATHER: "O, I have such an exiting thing to tell you. I have been the heroin of an adventure. One day last week Ilse asked me if I would go and stay all night with her because her father was away and wouldn't be home till very late and Ilse said she wasn't fritened but very lonesome. So I asked Aunt Elizabeth if I could. I hardly dared hope, dear Father, that she would let me, for she doesn't aprove of little girls being away from home at night but to my surprise she said I could go very kindly. And then I heard her say in the pantry to Aunt Laura It is a shame the way the doctor leaves that poor child so much alone at nights. It is WIKKED of him. And Aunt Laura said The poor man is warped. You know he was not a bit like that before his wife—and then just as it was getting intresting Aunt Elizabeth gave Aunt Laura a nudge and said s-s-s-h, little pitchers have big ears. I knew she meant me though my ears are not big, only pointed. I do wish I could find out what Ilse's mother did. It worrys me after I go to bed. I lie awake for ever so long thinking about it. Ilse has no idea. Once she asked her father and he told her (in a VOICE OF THUNDER) never to mention THAT WOMAN to him again. And there is something else that worrys me too. I keep thinking of Silas Lee who killed his brother at the old well. How dreadful the poor man must have felt. And what is it to be warped.

"I went over to Ilses and we played in the garret. I like playing there because we dont have to be careful and tidy like we do in our garret. Ilses garret is very untidy and cant have been dusted for years. The rag room is worse than the rest. It is boarded off at one end of the garret and it is full of old close and bags of rags and broken furniture. I dont like the smell of it. The kitchen chimney goes up through it and things hang round it (or did). For all this is in the past now, dear Father.

"When we got tired playing we sat down on an old chest and talked. This is splendid in daytime I said but it must be awful queer at night. Mice, said Ilse,—and spiders and gosts. I dont believe in gosts I said skornfully. There isnt any such thing. (But maybe there is for all that, dear Father.) I believe this garret is hawnted, said Ilse. They say garrets always are. Nonsense I said. You know dear Father it would not do for a New Moon person to believe in gosts. But I felt very queer. Its easy to talk said Ilse beginning to be mad (though I wasnt trying to run down her garret) but you wouldnt stay here alone at night. I wouldnt mind it a bit I said. Then I dare you to do it said Ilse. I dare you to come up here at bedtime and sleep here all night. Then I saw I was in an awful skrape Father dear. It is a foolish thing to bost. I knew not what to do. It was dreadful to think of sleeping alone in that garret but if I didnt Ilse would always cast it up to me whenever we fought and worse than that she would tell Teddy and he would think me a coward. So I said proudly Ill do it Ilse Burnley and Im not afraid to either. (But oh I was—inside.) The mice will run over you said Ilse. O I wouldnt be you for the world. It was mean of Ilse to make things worse than they were. But I could feel she admired me too and that helped me a great deal. We dragged an old feather bed out of the rag room and Ilse gave me a pillow and half her close. It was dark by this time and Ilse wouldnt go up into the garret again. So I said my prayers very carefully and then I took a lamp and started up. I am so used to candles now that the lamp made me nervus. Ilse said I looked scared to death. My knees shook dear Father but for the honnor of the Starrs (and the Murrays too) I went on. I had undressed in Ilses room, so I got right into bed and blew out the lamp. But I couldnt go to sleep for a long time. The moonlight made the garret look weerd. I dont know exactly what weerd means but I feel the garret was it. The bags and old close hanging from the beams looked like creatures. I thought I need not be fritened. The angels are here. But then I felt as if I would be as much fritened of angels as of anything else. And I could hear rats and mice scrambling over things. I thought What if a rat was to run over me, and then I thought that next day I would write out a descripshon of the garret by moonlight and my feelings. At last I heard the doctor driving in and then I heard him knocking round in the kitchen and I felt better and before very long I went to sleep and I dreamed a dreadful dream. I dreamed the door of the rag room opened and a big newspaper came out and chased me all around the garret. And then it went on fire and I could smell the smoke plain as plain and it was just on me when I skreamed and woke up. I was sitting right up in bed and the newspaper was gone but I could smell smoke still. I looked at the rag room door and smoke was coming out under it and I saw firelight through the cracks of the boards. I just yelled at the top of my voice and tore down to Ilses room and she rushed across the hall and woke her father. He said dam but he got right up and then all three of us kept running up and down the garret stairs with pails of water and we made an awful mess but we got the fire out. It was just the bags of wool that had been hanging close to the chimney that had caught fire. When all was over the doctor wiped the persperation from his manly brow and said That was a close call. A few minutes later would have been too late. I put on a fire when I came in to make a cup of tea and I suppose those bags must have caught fire from a spark. I see theres a hole here where the plaster has tumbled out. I must have this whole place cleaned out. How in the world did you come to diskover the fire, Emily. I was sleeping in the garret I said. Sleeping in the garret said the doctor, what in—what the—WHAT were you doing there. Ilse dared me I said. She said Id be too scared to stay there and I said I wouldnt. I fell asleep and woke up and smelled smoke. You little devil, said the doctor. I suppose it was a dreadful thing to be called a devil but the doctor looked at me so admiringly that I felt as if he was paying me a compelment. He has queer ways of talking. Ilse says the only time he ever said a kind thing to her was once when she had a sore throat he called her "a poor little animal" and looked as if he was sorry for her. I feel sure Ilse feels dreadfully bad because her father doesnt like her though she pretends she does not care. But oh dear Father there is more to tell. Yesterday the Shrewsbury *Weekly Times* came and in the Blair Notes it told all about the fire at the doctors and said it had been fortunately diskovered in time by Miss Emily Starr. I cant tell you what I felt like when I saw my name in the paper. I felt FAMUS. And I never was called Miss in ernest before.

"Last Saturday Aunt Elizabeth and Aunt Laura went to Shrewsbury for the day and left Cousin Jimmy and me to keep house. We had such fun and Cousin Jimmy let me skim all the milk pans. But after dinner unexpekted company came and there was no cake in the house. That was a dreadful thing. It never happened before in the annels of New Moon. Aunt Elizabeth had toothache all day yesterday and Aunt Laura was away at Priest Pond visiting Great Aunt Nancy, so no cake was made. I prayed about it and then I went to work and made a cake by Aunt Laura's receet and it turned out all right. Cousin Jimmy helped me set the table and get supper, and I poured the tea and never slopped any over in the saucers. You would have been proud of me Father. Mrs. Lewis took a second piece of cake and said I would know Elizabeth Murrays cake if I found it in central Africa. I said not a word for the honnor of the family. But I felt very proud. I had saved the Murrays from disgrace. When Aunt Elizabeth came home and heard the tale she looked grim and tasted a piece that was left and then she said Well, you have got SOME Murray in you anyway. That is the first time Aunt Elizabeth has ever praised me. She had three teeth out so they will not ache any more. I am glad for her sake. Before I went to bed I got the cook book and picked out all the things Id like to make. Queen Pudding, Sea-foam Sauce, Blackeyed Susans, Pigs In Blankets. They sound just lovely.

"I can see such beautiful fluffy white clouds over Lofty Johns bush. I wish I could sore up and drop right into them. I cant believe they would be wet and messy like Teddy says. Teddy cut my initials and his together on the Monark of The Forest but somebody has cut them out. I don't know whether it was Perry or Ilse.

"Miss Brownell hardly ever gives me good deportment marks now and Aunt Elizabeth is much displeased on Friday nights but Aunt Laura understands. I wrote an account of the afternoon when Miss Brownell made fun of my poems and put it in an old envelope and wrote Aunt Elizabeths name on it and put it among my papers. If I die of consumption Aunt Elizabeth will find it and know the rites of it and mourn that she was so unjust to me. But I don't think I will die because Im getting much fatter and Ilse told me she heard her father tell Aunt Laura I would be handsome if I had more color. Is it wrong to want to be handsome, dearest Father. Aunt Elizabeth says it is and when I said to her Wouldn't YOU like to be handsome, Aunt Elizabeth, she seemed anoyed about something.

"Miss Brownell has had a spite at Perry ever since that evening and treats him very mean but he is meek and says he wont kick up any fuss in school because he wants to learn and get ahead. He keeps saying his rymes are as good as mine and I know they are not and it exassperates me. If I do not pay attention all the time in school Miss Brownell says I suppose you are composing—poetry Emily and then everybody laughs. No not everybody. I must not exagerate. Teddy and Perry and Ilse and Jennie never laugh. It is funny that I like Jennie so well now and I hated her so that first day in school. Her eyes are not piggy after all. They are small but they are jolly and twinkly. She is quite poplar in school. I do hate Frank Barker. He took my new reader and wrote in a big sprawly way all over the front page

Steal not this book for fear of shame
For on it is the owners name
And when you die the Lord will say
Where is that book you stole away
And when you say you do not know
The Lord will say go down below.

"That is not a refined poem and besides it is not the rite way to speak about God. I tore out the leaf and burned it and Aunt Elizabeth was angry and even when I explained why her rath was not apeased. Ilse says she is going to call God Alla after this. I think it is a nicer name myself. It is so soft and doesn't sound so stern. But I fear its not relijus enough.

"MAY 20.

"Yesterday was my birthday dear Father. It will soon be a year since I came to New Moon. I feel as if I had always lived here. I have grown two inches. Cousin Jimmy measured me by a mark on the dairy door. My birthday was very nice. Aunt Laura made a lovely cake and gave me a beautiful new white pettycoat with an embroidered flounce. She had run a blue ribbon through it but Aunt Elizabeth made her pull it out. And Aunt Laura also gave me that piece of pink satin brokade in her burow drawer. I have longed for it ever since I saw it but never hoped to possess it. Ilse asked me what I meant to do with it but I dont mean to do anything with it. Only keep it up here in the garret with my treasures and look at it, because it is beautiful. Aunt Elizabeth gave me a dixonary. That was a useful present. I feel I ought to like it. You will soon notice an improovement in my spelling, I hope. The only trouble is when I am writing something interesting I gct so cxitcd it is just awful to have to stop and hunt up a word to see how it is spelled. I looked up ween in it and Miss Brownell was right. I did not know what it really meant. It rymed so well with sheen and I thought it meant to behold or see but it means to think. Cousin Jimmy gave me a big thick blank book. I am so proud of it. It will be so nice to write pieces in. But I will still use the letter-bills to write to you, dear Father, because I can fold each one up by itself and adress it like a real letter. Teddy gave me a picture of myself. He painted it in water colors and called it The Smiling Girl. I look as if I was listening to something that made me very happy. Ilse says it flatters me. It does make me better looking than I am but not any better looking than I would be if I could have a bang. Teddy says he is going to paint a real big picture of me when he grows up. Perry walked all the way to Shrewsbury to get me a necklace of pearl beads and lost it. He had no more money so he went home to Stovepipe Town and got a young hen from his Aunt Tom and gave me that. He is a very persistent boy. I am to have all the eggs the hen lays to sell the pedler for myself. Ilse gave me a box of candy. I am only going to eat one piece a day to make it last a long time. I wanted Ilse to eat some but she said she wouldnt because it would be mean to help eat a present you had given and I insisted and then we fought over it and Ilse said I was a caterwawling quadruped (which was ridiklus) and didn't know enough to come in when it rained. And I said I knew enough to have some manners at least. Ilse got so mad she went home but she cooled off soon and came back for supper.

"It is raining tonight and it sounds like fairies feet dancing over the garret roof. If it had not rained Teddy was going to come down and help me look for the Lost Dimond. Wouldnt it be splendid if we could find it.

"Cousin Jimmy is fixing up the garden. He lets me help him and I have a little flower bed of my own. I always run out first thing every morning to see how much the things have grown since yesterday. Spring is such a happyfying time isnt it, Father. The little Blue People are all out round the summer house. That is what Cousin Jimmy calls the violets and I think it is lovely. He has names like that for all the flowers. The roses are the Queens and the June lilies are the Snow Ladies and the tulips are the Gay Folk and the daffodils are the Golden Ones and the China Asters are My Pink Friends.

"Mike II is here with me, sitting on the window-sill. Mike is a smee cat. Smee is not in the dictionary. It is a word I invented myself. I could not think of any English word which just describes Mike II so I made this up. It means sleek and glossy and soft and fluffy all in one and something else besides that I cant express.

"Aunt Laura is teaching me to sew. She says I must learn to make a hem on muslin that can't be seen (tradishun). I hope she will teach me how to make point lace some day. All the Murrays of New Moon have been noted for making point lace (I mean all the women Murrays). None of the girls in school can make point lace. Aunt Laura says she will make me a point lace hangkerchief when I get married. All the New Moon brides had point lace hangkerchiefs except my mother who ran away. But you didnt mind her not having one did you Father. Aunt Laura talks a good bit about my mother to me but not when Aunt Elizabeth is around. Aunt Elizabeth never mentions her name. Aunt Laura wants to show me Mothers room but she has never been able to find the key yet because Aunt Elizabeth keeps it hid. Aunt Laura says Aunt Elizabeth loved my mother very much. You would think she would love her daughter some wouldnt you. But she doesnt. She is just bringing me up as a duty.

"JUNE 1.
"DEAR FATHER:

"This has been a very important day. I wrote my first letter, I mean the first letter that was really to go in the mail. It was to Great-Aunt Nancy who lives at Priest Pond and is very old. She wrote Aunt Elizabeth and said I might write now and then to a poor old woman. My heart was touched and I wanted to. Aunt Elizabeth said We might as well let her. And she said to me You must be careful to write a nice letter and I will read it over when it is written. If you make a good impression on Aunt Nancy she may do something for you. I wrote the letter very carefully but it didn't sound a bit like me when it was finished. I couldn't write a good letter when I knew Aunt Elizabeth was going to read it. I felt paralized.

"JUNE 7.

"Dear Father, my letter did not make a good impression on Great-Aunt Nancy. She did not answer it but she wrote Aunt Elizabeth that I must be a very stupid child to write such a stupid letter. I feel insulted because I am not stupid. Perry says he feels like going to Priest Pond and knocking the daylights out of Great-Aunt Nancy. I told him he must not talk like that about my family, and anyhow I dont see how knocking the daylights out of Great-Aunt Nancy would make her change her opinion about me being stupid. (I wonder what daylights are and how you knock them out of people.)

"I have three cantos of *The White Lady* finished. I have the heroin imured in a convent and I dont know how to get her out because I am not a Catholic. I suppose it would have been better if I had a Protestant heroin but there were no Protestants in the days of shivalry. I might have asked Lofty John last year but this year I cant because Ive never spoken to him since he played that horrid joke on me about the apple. When I meet him on the road I look straight ahead just as lofty as he does. I have called my pig after him to get square. Cousin Jimmy has given me a little pig for my own. When it is sold I am to have the money. I mean to give some for missionaries and put the rest in the bank to go to my educashun. And I thought if I ever had a pig I would call it Uncle Wallace. But now it does not seem to me propper to call pigs after your uncles even if you dont like them.

"Teddy and Perry and Ilse and I play we are living in the days of shivalry and Ilse and I are distressed damsels reskued by galant knites. Teddy made a splendid suit of armor out of old barrel staves and then Perry made a better one out of old tin boilers hammered flat with a broken saucepan for a helmit. Sometimes we play at the Tansy Patch. I have a queer feeling that Teddys mother hates me this summer. Last summer she just didnt like me. Smoke and Buttercup are not there now. They disappeared misteriously in the winter. Teddy says he feels sure his mother poisoned them because she thought he was getting too fond of them. Teddy is teaching me to whistle but Aunt Laura says it is unladylike. So many jolly things seem to be unladylike. Sometimes I almost wish my aunts were infidels like Dr. Burnly. HE never bothers whether Ilse is unladylike or not. But no, it would not be good manners to be an infidel. It would not be a New Moon tradishun.

"Today I taught Perry that he must not eat with his knife. He wants to learn all the RULES OF ETIKET. And I am helping him learn a recitation for school examination day. I wanted Ilse to do it but she was mad because he asked me first and she wouldnt. But she should because she is a far better reciter than I am. I am too nervus.

"JUNE 14.

"Dear Father, we have composition in school now and I learned today that you put in things like this " " when you write anything anybody has said. I didnt know that before. I must go over all my letters to you and put them in. And after a question you must put a mark like this ? and when a letter is left out a postroffe which is a comma up in the air. Miss Brownell is sarkastic but she DOES teach you things. I am putting that down because I want to be fair even if I do hate her. And she is interesting although she is not nice. I have written a descripshun of her on a letter-bill. I like writing about people I don't like better than about those I do like. Aunt Laura is nicer to live with than Aunt Elizabeth, but Aunt Elizabeth is nicer to write about. I can deskribe HER fawlts but I feel wikked and ungrateful if I say anything that is not complementary about dear Aunt Laura. Aunt Elizabeth has locked your books away and says I'm not to have them till I'm grown up. Just as if I wouldn't be careful of them, dear Father. She says I wouldn't because she found that when I was reading one of them I put a tiny pencil dot under every beautiful word. It didn't hurt the book a bit, dear Father. Some of the words were dingles, pearled, musk, dappled, intervales, glen, bosky, piping, shimmer, crisp, beechen, ivory. I think those are all lovely words, Father.

"Aunt Laura lets me read her copy of A Pilgrims Progress on Sundays. I call the big hill in the road to White Cross the Delectable Mountain because it is such a beautiful one.

"Teddy lent me 3 books of poetry. One of them was Tennyson and I have learned The Bugle Song off by heart so I will always have it. One was Mrs. Browning. She is lovely. I would like to meet her. I suppose

I will when I die but that may be a long time away. The other was just one poem called Sohrab and Rustum. After I went to bed I cried over it. Aunt Elizabeth said "what are you sniffling about?" I wasn't sniffling—I was weeping sore. She made me tell her and then she said "You must be crazy." But I couldn't go to sleep until I had thought out a different end for it—a happy one.

"JUNE 25.

"DEAR FATHER:

"There has been a dark shadow over this day. I dropped my cent in church. It made a dreadful noise. I felt as if everybody looked at me. Aunt Elizabeth was much annoyed. Perry dropped his too soon after. He told me after church he did it on purpose because he thought it would make me feel better but it didn't because I was afraid the people would think it was me dropping mine again. Boys do such queer things. I hope the minister did not hear because I am beginning to like him. I never liked him much before last Tuesday. His family are all boys and I suppose he doesn't understand little girls very well. Then he called at New Moon. Aunt Laura and Aunt Elizabeth were both away and I was in the kitchen alone. Mr. Dare came in and sat down on Saucy Sal who was asleep in the rocking-chair. He was comfortable but Saucy Sal wasn't. He didn't sit on her stomach. If he had I suppose he would have killed her. He just sat on her legs and tail. Sal yowled but Mr. Dare is a little deaf and didn't hear her and I was too shy to tell him. But Cousin Jimmy came in just as he was asking me if I knew my catechism and said "Catechism, is it? Lawful heart, man, listen to that poor dum beast. Get up if you're a Christian." So Mr. Dare got up and said, "Dear me, this is very remarkable. I thought I felt something moving."

"I thought I would write this to you, dear Father, because it struck me as humerus.

"When Mr. Dare finished asking me questions I thought it was my turn and I would ask him some about some things I've wanted to know for years. I asked him if he thought God was very perticular about every little thing I did and if he thought my cats would go to heaven. He said he hoped I never did wrong things and that animals had no souls. And I asked him why we shouldn't put new wine in old bottles. Aunt Elizabeth does with her dandelion wine and the old bottles do just as well as new ones. He explained quite kindly that the Bible bottles were made of skins and got rotten when they were old. It made it quite clear to me. Then I told him I was worried because I knew I ought to love God better than anything but there were things I loved better than

God. He said "What things?" and I said flowers and stars and the Wind Woman and the Three Princesses and things like that. And he smiled and said "But they are just a part of God, Emily—every beautiful thing is." And all at once I liked him ever so much and didn't feel shy with him any more. He preeched a sermon on heaven last Sunday. It seemed like a dull place. I think it must be more exiting than that. I wonder what I will do when I go to heaven since I cant sing. I wonder if they will let me write poetry. But I think church is interesting. Aunt Elizabeth and Aunt Laura always read their Bibles before the servis begins but I like to stare around and see everybody and wonder what they are thinking of. It's so nice to hear the silk dresses swishing up the isles. Bustles are very fashunable now but Aunt Elizabeth will not wear them. I think Aunt Elizabeth WOULD look funny with a bustle. Aunt Laura wears a very little one.

"Your lovingest daughter,

"EMILY B. STARR.

"P. S. Dear Father, it is lovely to write to you. But O, I never get an answer back.

"E. B. S."

CHAPTER XVIII
FATHER CASSIDY

CONSTERNATION reigned at New Moon. Everybody was desperately unhappy. Aunt Laura cried. Aunt Elizabeth was so cantankerous that there was no living with her. Cousin Jimmy went about as one distracted and Emily gave up worrying about Ilse's mother and Silas Lee's remorseful ghost after she went to bed, and worried over this new trouble. For it had all originated in her disregard of New Moon tradition in making calls on Lofty John, and Aunt Elizabeth did not mince matters in telling her so. If she, Emily Byrd Starr, had never gone to Lofty John's she would never have eaten the Big Sweet apple, and if she had never eaten the Big Sweet apple Lofty John would not have played a joke on her and if he had not played a joke on her Aunt Elizabeth would never have gone and said bitter, Murray-like things to him; and if Aunt Elizabeth had never said bitter Murray-like things to him Lofty John would not have become offended and revengeful; and if Lofty John had not become offended and revengeful he would never have taken it into his lofty head to cut down the beautiful grove to the north of New Moon.

For this was exactly where this house-that-Jack-built progression had landed them all. Lofty John had announced publicly in the Blair Water blacksmith shop that he was going to cut down the bush as soon as harvest was over—every last tree and sapling was to be laid low. The news was promptly carried to New Moon and upset the inhabitants thereof as they had not been upset for years. In their eyes it was nothing short of a catastrophe.

Elizabeth and Laura could hardly bring themselves to believe it. The thing was incredible. That big, thick, protecting bush of spruce and hardwood had ALWAYS been there; it belonged to New Moon MORALLY; even Lofty John Sullivan would not DARE to cut it down. But Lofty John had an uncomfortable reputation for doing what he said he would do; that was a part of his loftiness; and if he did—if he did—

"New Moon will be ruined," wailed poor Aunt Laura. "It will look DREADFUL—ALL its beauty will go—and we will be left open to the north wind and the sea storms—we have always been so warm and sheltered here. And Jimmy's garden will be ruined too."

"This is what comes of bringing Emily here," said Aunt Elizabeth.

It was a cruel thing to say, even when all allowances were made,—cruel and unjust, since her own sharp tongue and Murray sarcasm had had quite as much to do with it as Emily. But she said it and it pierced Emily to the heart with a pang that left a scar for years. Poor Emily did not feel as if she needed any additional anguish. She was already feeling so wretched that she could not eat or sleep. Elizabeth Murray, angry and unhappy as she was, slept soundly at nights; but beside her in the darkness, afraid to move or turn, lay a slender little creature whose tears, stealing silently down her cheeks, could not ease her breaking heart. For Emily thought her heart WAS breaking; she couldn't go on living and suffering like this. Nobody could.

Emily had lived long enough at New Moon for it to get pretty thoroughly into her blood. Perhaps it had even been born there. At any rate, when she came to it she fitted into its atmosphere as a hand into a glove. She loved it as well as if she had lived there all her short life—loved every stick and stone and tree and blade of grass about it—every nail in the old kitchen floor, every cushion of green moss on the dairy roof, every pink and white columbine that grew in the old orchard, every "tradition" of its history. To think of its beauty being in a large measure reft from it was agony to her. And to think of Cousin Jimmy's garden being ruined! Emily loved that garden almost as much as he did; why, it was the pride of Cousin Jimmy's life that he could grow there plants and shrubs that would winter nowhere else in P. E. Island; if the northern shelter were removed they would die. And to think of that beautiful bush itself being cut down—the Today Road and the Yesterday Road and the Tomorrow Road being swept out of existence—the stately Monarch of the Forest discrowned—the little playhouse where she and Ilse had such glorious hours destroyed—the whole lovely, ferny, intimate place torn out of her life at one fell swoop.

Oh, Lofty John had chosen and timed his vengeance well!

When would the blow fall? Every morning Emily listened miserably as she stood on the sandstone doorstep of the kitchen, for the sound of axe blows on the clear September air. Every evening when she returned from school she dreaded to see that the work of destruction had begun. She pined and fretted. There were times when it seemed to her she couldn't bear her life any longer. Every day Aunt Elizabeth said something imputing the whole blame to her and the child grew morbidly sensitive about it. Almost she wished Lofty John would begin and be done with it. If Emily had ever heard the classic story of Damocles she would have heartily sympathized with him. If she had

had any hope that it would do any good she would have swallowed Murray pride and Starr pride and every other kind of pride and gone on her knees to Lofty John to entreat him to hold his revengeful hand. But she believed it would not. Lofty John had left no doubt in anybody's mind as to his bitter determination in the matter. There was much talk about it in Blair Water and some were very well pleased at this blow to New Moon pride and prestige, and some held that it was low and unclean behaviour on Lofty John's part, and all agreed that this was what they had prophesied all along as bound to happen some day when the old Murray-Sullivan feud of three generations should have come to its inevitable head. The only surprising thing was that Lofty John hadn't done it long ago. He had always hated Elizabeth Murray since their schooldays, when her tongue had not spared him.

One day by the banks of Blair Water Emily sat down and wept. She had been sent to trim the dead blossoms off the rosebushes on Grandmother Murray's grave; having finished her task she had not the heart to go back to the house where Aunt Elizabeth was making everybody miserable because she was herself so unhappy. Perry had reported that Lofty John had stated the day before at the blacksmith's that he was going to begin cutting down the big bush on Monday morning.

"I CAN'T bear it," sobbed Emily to the rosebushes.

A few late roses nodded at her; the Wind Woman combed and waved and stirred the long green grasses on the graves where proud Murrays, men and women, slept calmly, unstirred by old feuds and passions; the September sunlight shone beyond on old harvest fields mellowly bright and serene, and very softly against its green, shrub-hung bank, purred and lapped the blue Blair Water.

"I don't see why God doesn't STOP Lofty John," said Emily passionately. Surely the New Moon Murrays had a right to expect that much from Providence.

Teddy came whistling down the pasture, the notes of his tune blowing across the Blair Water like elfin drops of sound, vaulted the graveyard fence and perched his lean, graceful body irreverently on the "Here I stay" of Great-Grandmother Murray's flat tombstone.

"What's the matter?" he said.

"Everything's the matter," said Emily, a little crossly. Teddy had no business to be looking so cheerful. She was used to more sympathy from Teddy and it aggravated her not to find it. "Don't you know Lofty John is going to begin cutting down the bush Monday?"

Teddy nodded.

"Yep. Ilse told me. But look here, Emily, I've thought of something. Lofty John wouldn't dare cut down that bush if the priest told him not to, would he?"

"Why?"

"Because the Catholics have to do just what their priests tell them to, haven't they?"

"I don't know—I don't know anything about them. WE are Presbyterians."

Emily gave her head a little toss. Mrs. Kent was known to be an "English Church" woman and though Teddy went to the Presbyterian Sunday School, that fact gave him scanty standing among bred-in-the-bone Presbyterian circles.

"If your Aunt Elizabeth went to Father Cassidy at White Cross and asked him to stop Lofty John, maybe he'd do it," persisted Teddy.

"Aunt Elizabeth would never do that," said Emily positively. "I'm sure of it. She's too proud."

"Not even to save the bush?"

"Not even for that."

"Then I guess nothing can be done," said Teddy rather crest-fallen. "Look here—see what I've made. This is a picture of Lofty John in purgatory, with three little devils sticking red-hot pitch forks into him. I copied some of it out of one of mother's books—Dante's Infernal, I think it was—but I put Lofty John in place of the man in the book. You can have it."

"I don't want it." Emily uncoiled her legs and got up. She was past the stage when inflicting imaginary torments on Lofty John could comfort her. She had already slain him in several agonizing ways during her night vigils. But an idea had come to her—a daring, breathless idea. "I must go home now, Teddy—it's supper time."

Teddy pocketed his despised sketch—which was really a wonderful bit of work if either of them had had the sense to know it; the expression of anguish in Lofty John's face as a merry little devil touched him up with a pitchfork would have been the despair of many a trained artist. He went home wishing he could help Emily; it was all wrong that a creature like Emily—with soft purple-gray eyes and a smile that made you think of all sorts of wonderful things you couldn't put into words—should be unhappy. Teddy felt so worried about it that he added a few more devils to his sketch of Lofty John in purgatory and lengthened the prongs of their pitchforks quite considerably.

Emily went home with a determined twist to her mouth. She ate as much supper as she could—which wasn't much, for Aunt Elizabeth's face would have destroyed her appetite if she had had any—and then sneaked out of the house by the front door. Cousin Jimmy was working in his garden but he did not call her. Cousin Jimmy was always very sorrowful now. Emily stood a moment on the Grecian porch and looked at Lofty John's bush—green-bosomed, waving, all lovely. Would it be a desecrated waste of stumps by Monday night? Goaded by the thought Emily cast fear and hesitation to the winds and started briskly off down the lane. When she reached the gate she turned to the left on the long red road of mystery that ran up the Delectable Mountain. She had never been on that road before; it ran straight to White Cross; Emily was going to the parish house there to interview Father Cassidy. It was two miles to White Cross and Emily walked it all too soon—not because it was a beautiful road of wind and wild fern, haunted by little rabbits—but because she dreaded what awaited her at the end. She had been trying to think what she should say—how she should say it; but her invention failed her. She had no acquaintance with Catholic priests, and couldn't imagine how you should talk to them at all. They were even more mysterious and unknowable than ministers. Suppose Father Cassidy should be dreadfully angry at her daring to come there and ask a favour. Perhaps it WAS a dreadful thing to do from every point of view. And very likely it would do no good. Very likely Father Cassidy would refuse to interfere with Lofty John, who was a good Catholic, while she was, in his opinion, a heretic. But for any chance, even the faintest, of averting the calamity impending over New Moon, Emily would have faced the entire Sacred College. Horribly frightened, miserably nervous as she was, the idea of turning back never occurred to her. She was only sorry that she hadn't put on her Venetian beads. They might have impressed Father Cassidy.

Although Emily had never been to White Cross she knew the parish house when she saw it—a fine, tree-embowered residence near the big white chapel with the flashing gilt cross on its spire and the four gilt angels, one on each of the little spires at the corners. Emily thought them very beautiful as they gleamed in the light of the lowering sun, and wished they could have some on the plain white church at Blair Water. She couldn't understand why Catholics should have all the angels. But there was not time to puzzle over this, for the door was opening and the trim little maid was looking a question.

"Is—Father Cassidy—at—home?" asked Emily, rather jerkily.

"Yes."

"Can—I—see—him?"

"Come in," said the little maid. Evidently there was no difficulty about seeing Father Cassidy—no mysterious ceremonies such as Emily had half expected, even if she were allowed to see him at all. She was shown into a book-lined room and left there, while the maid went to call Father Cassidy, who, she said, was working in the garden. THAT sounded quite natural and encouraging. If Father Cassidy worked in a garden, he could not be so very terrible.

Emily looked about her curiously. She was in a very pretty room—with cosy chairs, and pictures and flowers. Nothing alarming or uncanny about it—except a huge black cat who was sitting on the top of one of the bookcases. It was really an enormous creature. Emily adored cats and had always felt at home with any of them. But she had never seen such a cat as this. What with its size and its insolent, gold-hued eyes, set like living jewels in its black velvet face, it did not seem to belong to the same species as nice, cuddly, respectable kittens at all. Mr. Dare would never have had such a beast about his manse. All Emily's dread of Father Cassidy returned.

And then in came Father Cassidy, with the friendliest smile in the world. Emily took him in with her level glance as was her habit—or gift—and never again in the world was she the least bit afraid of Father Cassidy. He was big and broad-shouldered, with brown eyes and brown hair; and his very face was so deeply tanned from his inveterate habit of going about bareheaded in merciless sunshine, that it was brown, too. Emily thought he looked just like a big nut—a big, brown, wholesome nut.

Father Cassidy looked at her as he shook hands; Emily had one of her visitations of beauty just then. Excitement had brought a wildrose hue to her face, the sunlight brought out the watered-silk gloss of her black hair; her eyes were softly dark and limpid; but it was at her ears Father Cassidy suddenly bent to look. Emily had a moment of agonized wonder if they were clean.

"She's got pointed ears," said Father Cassidy, in a thrilling whisper. "Pointed ears! I KNEW she came straight from fairyland the minute I saw her. Sit down, Elf—if elves do sit—sit down and give me the latest news av Titania's court."

Emily's foot was now on her native heath. Father Cassidy talked her language, and he talked it in such a mellow, throaty voice, slurring his "ofs" ever so softly as became a proper Irishman. But she shook her head a little sadly. With the burden of her errand on her soul she could not play the part of ambassadress from Elfland.

"I'm only Emily Starr of New Moon," she said; and then gasped hurriedly, because there must be no deception—no sailing under false colours, "and I'm a Protestant."

"And a very nice little Protestant you are," said Father Cassidy. "But for sure I'm a bit disappointed. I'm used to Protestants—the woods hereabouts being full av them—but it's a hundred years since the last elf called on me."

Emily stared. Surely Father Cassidy wasn't a hundred years old. He didn't look more than fifty. Perhaps, though, Catholic priests did live longer than other people. She didn't know exactly what to say so she said, a bit lamely,

"I see you have a cat."

"Wrong." Father Cassidy shook his head and groaned dismally. "A cat has me."

Emily gave up trying to understand Father Cassidy. He was nice but ununderstandable. She let it go at that. And she must get on with her errand.

"You are a kind of minister, aren't you?" she asked timidly. She didn't know whether Father Cassidy would like being called a minister.

"Kind av," he agreed amiably. "And you see ministers and priests can't do their own swearing. They have to keep cats to do it for them. I never knew any cat that could sware as genteelly and effectively as the B'y."

"Is that what you call him?" asked Emily, looking at the black cat in some awe. It seemed hardly safe to discuss him right before his face.

"That's what he calls himself. My mother doesn't like him because he steals the cream. Now, I don't mind his doing that; no, it's his way av licking his jaws after it that I can't stand. Oh, B'y, we've a fairy calling on us. Be excited for once, I implore you—there's a duck av a cat."

The B'y refused to be excited. He winked an insolent eye at Emily.

"Have you any idea what goes on in the head av a cat, elf?"

What queer questions Father Cassidy asked. Yet Emily thought she would like his questions if she were not so worried. Suddenly Father Cassidy leaned across the table and said,

"Now, just what's bothering you?"

"I'm so unhappy," said Emily piteously.

"So are lots av other people. Everybody is unhappy by spells. But creatures who have pointed ears shouldn't be unhappy. It's only mortals who should be that."

"Oh, please—please—" Emily wondered what she should call him. Would it offend him if a Protestant called him "Father"? But she had to risk it—"please, Father Cassidy, I'm in such trouble and I've come to ask a GREAT FAVOUR of you."

Emily told him the whole tale from beginning to end—the old Murray-Sullivan feud, her erstwhile friendship with Lofty John, the Big Sweet apple, the unhappy consequence, and Lofty John's threatened revenge. The B'y and Father Cassidy listened with equal gravity until she had finished. Then the B'y winked at her, but Father Cassidy put his long brown fingers together.

"Humph," he said.

("That's the first time," reflected Emily, "that I've ever heard anyone outside of a book say 'Humph.'")

"Humph," said Father Cassidy again. "And you want me to put a stop to this nefarious deed?"

"If you can," said Emily. "Oh, it would be so splendid if you could. Will you—will you?"

Father Cassidy fitted his fingers still more carefully together.

"I'm afraid I can hardly invoke the power av the keys to prevent Lofty John from disposing as he wishes av his own lawful property, you know, elf."

Emily didn't understand the allusion to the keys but she did understand that Father Cassidy was declining to bring the lever of the Church to bear on Lofty John. There was no hope, then. She could not keep the tears of disappointment out of her eyes.

"Oh, come now, darling, don't cry," implored Father Cassidy. "Elves never cry—they can't. It would break my heart to discover you weren't av the Green Folk. You may call yourself av New Moon and av any religion you like, but the fact remains that you belong to the Golden Age and the old gods. That's why I must save your precious bit av greenwood for you."

Emily stared.

"I think it can be done," Father Cassidy went on. "I think if I go to Lofty John and have a heart-to-heart talk with him I can make him see reason. Lofty John and I are very good friends. He's a reasonable creature, if you know how to take him—which means to flatter his vanity judiciously. I'll put it to him, not as priest to parishoner, but as

- 159 -

man to man, that no decent Irishman carries on a feud with women and that no sensible person is going to destroy for nothing but a grudge those fine old trees that have taken half a century to grow and can never be replaced. Why, the man who cuts down such a tree except when it is really necessary should be hanged as high as Haman on a gallows made from the wood av it."

(Emily thought she would write that last sentence of Father Cassidy's down in Cousin Jimmy's blank book when she got home.)

"But I won't say THAT to Lofty John," concluded Father Cassidy. "Yes, Emily av New Moon, I think we can consider it a settled thing that your bush will not be cut down."

Suddenly Emily felt very happy. Somehow she had entire confidence in Father Cassidy. She was sure he would twist Lofty John around his little finger.

"Oh, I can never thank you enough!" she said earnestly.

"That's true, so don't waste breath trying. And now tell me things. Are there any more av you? And how long have you been yourself?"

"I'm twelve years old—I haven't any brothers or sisters. And I THINK I'd better be going home."

"Not till you've had a bite av lunch."

"Oh, thank you, I've had my supper."

"Two hours ago and a two-mile walk since. Don't tell me. I'm sorry I haven't any nectar and ambrosia on hand—such food as elves eat—and not even a saucer av moonshine—but my mother makes the best plum cake av any woman in P. E. Island. And we keep a cream cow. Wait here a bit. Don't be afraid av the B'y. He eats tender little Protestants sometimes, but he never meddles with leprechauns."

When Father Cassidy came back his mother came with him, carrying a tray. Emily had expected to see her big and brown too, but she was the tiniest woman imaginable, with snow-white, silky hair, mild blue eyes, and pink cheeks.

"Isn't she the sweetest thing in the way av mothers?" asked Father Cassidy. "I keep her to look at. Av course—" Father Cassidy dropped his voice to a pig's whisper—"there's something odd about her. I've known that woman to stop right in the middle av housecleaning, and go off and spend an afternoon in the woods. Like yourself, I'm thinking she has some truck with fairies."

Mrs. Cassidy smiled, kissed Emily, said she must go out and finish her preserving, and trotted off.

"Now you sit right down here, Elf, and be human for ten minutes and we'll have a friendly snack."

Emily WAS hungry—a nice comfortable feeling she hadn't experienced for a fortnight. Mrs. Cassidy's plum cake was all her reverend son claimed, and the cream cow seemed to be no myth.

"What do you think av me now?" asked Father Cassidy suddenly, finding Emily's eyes fixed on him speculatively.

Emily blushed. She had been wondering if she dared ask another favour of Father Cassidy.

"I think you are awfully good," she said.

"I AM awfully good," agreed Father Cassidy. "I'm so good that I'll do what you want me to do—for I feel there's something else you want me to do."

"I'm in a scrape and I've been in it all summer. You see"—Emily was very sober—"I am a poetess."

"Holy Mike! That IS serious. I don't know if I can do much for you. How long have you been that way?"

"Are you making fun of me?" asked Emily gravely.

Father Cassidy swallowed something besides plum cake.

"The saints forbid! It's only that I'm rather overcome. To be after entertaining a lady av New Moon—and an elf—and a poetess all in one is a bit too much for a humble praste like meself. Have another slice av cake and tell me all about it."

"It's like this—I'm writing an epic."

Father Cassidy suddenly leaned over and gave Emily's wrist a little pinch.

"I just wanted to see if you were real," he explained. "Yes—yes, you're writing an epic—go on. I think I've got my second wind now."

"I began it last spring. I called it *The White Lady* first but now I've changed it to *The Child of the Sea*. Don't you think that's a better title?"

"Much better."

"I've got three cantos done, and I can't get any further because there's something I don't know and can't find out. I've been so worried about it."

"What is it?"

"My epic," said Emily, diligently devouring plum cake, "is about a very beautiful high-born girl who was stolen away from her real parents when she was a baby and brought up in a woodcutter's hut."

"One av of the seven original plots in the world," murmured Father Cassidy.

"What?"

"Nothing. Just a bad habit av thinking aloud. Go on."

"She had a lover of high degree but his family did not want him to marry her because she was only a woodcutter's daughter—"

"Another of the seven plots—excuse me."

"—so they sent him away to the Holy land on a crusade and word came back that he was killed and then Editha—her name was Editha—went into a convent—"

Emily paused for a bite of plum cake and Father Cassidy took up the strain.

"And now her lover comes back very much alive, though covered with Paynim scars, and the secret av her birth is discovered through the dying confession av the old nurse and the birthmark on her arm."

"How did you know?" gasped Emily in amazement.

"Oh, I guessed it—I'm a good guesser. But where's your bother in all this?"

"I don't know how to get her out of the convent," confessed Emily. "I thought perhaps you would know how it could be done."

Again Father Cassidy fitted his fingers.

"Let us see, now. It's no light matter you've undertaken, young lady. How stands the case? EDITHA has taken the veil, not because she has a religious vocation but because she imagines her heart is broken. The Catholic Church does not release its nuns from their vows because they happen to think they've made a little mistake av that sort. No, no,—we must have a better reason. Is this Editha the sole child av her real parents?"

"Yes."

"Oh, then the way is clear. If she had had any brothers or sisters you would have had to kill them off, which is a messy thing to do. Well, then, she is the sole daughter and heiress av a noble family who have for years been at deadly feud with another noble family—the family av the lover. Do you know what a feud is?"

"Of course," said Emily disdainfully. "And I've got all that in the poem already."

"So much the better. This feud has rent the kingdom in twain and can only be healed by an alliance between Capulet and Montague."

"Those aren't their names."

"No matter. This, then, is a national affair, with far-reaching issues, therefore an appeal to the Supreme Pontiff is quite in order. What you want," Father Cassidy nodded solemnly, "is a dispensation from Rome."

"Dispensation is a hard word to work into a poem," said Emily.

"Undoubtedly. But young ladies who WILL write epic poems and who WILL lay the scenes thereof amid times and manners av hundreds av years ago, and WILL choose heroines av a religion quite unknown to them, MUST expect to run up against a few snags."

"Oh, I think I'll be able to work it in," said Emily cheerfully. "And I'm so much obliged to you. You don't know what a relief it is to my mind. I'll finish the poem right up now in a few weeks. I haven't done a thing at it all summer. But then of course I've been busy. Ilse Burnley and I have been making a new language."

"Making a—new—excuse me. DID you say LANGUAGE?"

"Yes."

"What's the matter with English? Isn't it good enough for you, you incomprehensible little being?"

"Oh, yes. THAT isn't why we're making a new one. You see in the spring, Cousin Jimmy got a lot of French boys to help plant the potatoes. I had to help too, and Ilse came to keep me company. And it was so annoying to hear those boys talking French when we couldn't understand a word of it. They did it just to make us mad. Such jabbering! So Ilse and I just made up our minds we'd invent a new language that THEY couldn't understand. We're getting on fine and when the potato picking time comes we'll be able to talk to each other and those boys won't be able to understand a word we're saying. Oh, it will be great fun!"

"I haven't a doubt. But two girls who will go to all the trouble av inventing a new language just to get square with some poor little French boys—you're beyond me," said Father Cassidy, helplessly. "Goodness knows what you'll be doing when you grow up. You'll be Red Revolutionists. I tremble for Canada."

"Oh, it isn't a trouble—it's fun. And all the girls in school are just wild because they hear us talking in it and can't make it out. We can talk secrets right before them."

"Human nature being what it is, I can see where the fun comes in all right. Let's hear a sample av your language."

"Nat millan O ste dolman bote ta Shrewsbury fernas ta poo litanos," said Emily glibly. "That means, 'Next summer I am going to Shrewsbury woods to pick strawberries.' I yelled that across the playground to Ilse the other day at recess and oh, how everybody stared."

"Staring, is it? I should say so. My own poor old eyes are all but dropping out av me head. Let's hear a bit more av it."

"Mo tral li dead seb ad li mo trene. Mo bertral seb mo bertrene das sten dead e ting setra. THAT means 'My father is dead and so is my mother. My grandfather and grandmother have been dead a long time.' We haven't invented a word for 'dead' yet. I think I will soon be able to write my poems in our language and then Aunt Elizabeth will not be able to read them if she finds them."

"Have you written any other poetry besides your epic?"

"Oh, yes—but just short pieces—dozens of them."

"H'm. Would you be so kind as to let me hear one av them?"

Emily was greatly flattered. And she did not mind letting Father Cassidy hear her precious stuff.

"I'll recite my last poem," she said, clearing her throat importantly. "It's called *Evening Dreams*."

Father Cassidy listened attentively. After the first verse a change came over his big brown face, and he began patting his fingertips together. When Emily finished she hung down her lashes and waited tremblingly. What if Father Cassidy said it was no good? No, he wouldn't be so impolite—but if he bantered her as he had done about her epic—she would know what THAT meant.

Father Cassidy did not speak all at once. The prolonged suspense was terrible to Emily. She was afraid he could not praise and did not want to hurt her feelings by dispraise. All at once her "Evening Dreams" seemed trash and she wondered how she could ever have been silly enough to repeat it to Father Cassidy.

Of course, it WAS trash. Father Cassidy knew that well enough. All the same, for a child like this—and rhyme and rhythm were flawless—and there was one line—just one line—"the light of faintly golden stars"—for the sake of that line Father Cassidy suddenly said,

"Keep on,—keep on writing poetry."

"You mean?"—Emily was breathless.

"I mean you'll be able to do something by and by. Something—I don't know how much—but keep on—keep on."

Emily was so happy she wanted to cry. It was the first word of commendation she had ever received except from her father—and a father might have too high an opinion of one. THIS was different. To the end of her struggle for recognition Emily never forgot Father Cassidy's "Keep on" and the tone in which he said it.

"Aunt Elizabeth scolds me for writing poetry," she said wistfully. "She says people will think I'm as simple as Cousin Jimmy."

"The path of genius never did run smooth. But have another piece av cake—do, just to show there's something human about you."

"Ve, merry ti. O del re dolman cosey aman ri sen ritter. THAT means, 'No, thank you. I must be going home before it gets dark.'"

"I'll drive you home."

"Oh, no, no. It's very kind of you"—the English language was quite good enough for Emily now. "But I'd rather WALK. It's—it's—such good exercise."

"Meaning," said Father Cassidy with a twinkle in his eye, "that we must keep it from the old lady. Good-bye, and may you always see a happy face in your looking-glass!"

Emily was too happy to be tired on the way home. There seemed to be a bubble of joy in her heart—a shimmering, prismatic bubble. When she came to the top of the big hill and looked across to New Moon, her eyes were satisfied and loving. How beautiful it was, lying embowered in the twilight of the old trees; the tips of the loftiest spruces came out in purple silhouette against the northwestern sky of rose and amber; down behind it the Blair Water dreamed in silver; the Wind Woman had folded her misty bat-wings in a valley of sunset and stillness lay over the world like a blessing. Emily felt sure everything would be all right. Father Cassidy would manage it in some way.

And he had told her to "keep on."

CHAPTER XIX
FRIENDS AGAIN

EMILY listened very anxiously on Monday morning, but "no sound of axe, no ponderous hammer rang" in Lofty John's bush. That evening on her way home from school, Lofty John himself overtook her in his buggy and for the first time since the night of the apple stopped and accosted her.

"Will ye take a lift, Miss Emily av New Moon?" he said affably.

Emily climbed in, feeling a little bit foolish. But Lofty John looked quite friendly as he clucked to his horse.

"So you've clean wiled the heart out av Father Cassidy's body," he said. "'The sweetest scrap av a girl I've iver seen,' says he to me. Sure an' ye might lave the poor prastes alone."

Emily looked at Lofty John out of the corner of her eye. He did not seem angry.

"Ye've put ME in a nice tight fix av it," he went on. "I'm as proud as any New Moon Murray av ye all and your Aunt Elizabeth said a number av things that got under my skin. I've many an old score to settle with her. So I thought I'd get square by cutting av the bush down. And you had to go and quare me wid me praste bekase av it and now I make no doubt I'll not be after daring to cut a stick av kindling to warm me shivering carcase without asking lave av the Pope."

"Oh, Mr. Sullivan, are you going to leave the bush alone?" said Emily breathlessly.

"It all rests with yourself, Miss Emily av New Moon. Ye can't be after expecting a Lofty John to be too humble. I didn't come by the name bekase av me makeness."

"What do you want me to do?"

"First, then, I'm wanting you to let bygones be bygones in that matter av the apple. And be token av the same come over and talk to me now and then as ye did last summer. Sure now, and I've missed ye—ye and that spit-fire av an Ilse who's never come aither bekase she thinks I mistrated you."

"I'll come of course," said Emily doubtfully, "if only Aunt Elizabeth will let me."

"Tell her if she don't the bush'll be cut down—ivery last stick av it. That'll fetch her. And there's wan more thing. Ye must ask me rale make and polite to do ye the favour av not cutting down the bush. If ye do it pretty enough sure niver a tree will I touch. But if ye don't down they go, praste or no praste," concluded Lofty John.

Emily summoned all her wiles to her aid. She clasped her hands, she looked up through her lashes at Lofty John, she smiled as slowly and seductively as she knew how—and Emily had considerable native knowledge of that sort. "Please, Mr. Lofty John," she coaxed, "won't you leave me the dear bush I love?"

Lofty John swept off his crumpled old felt hat. "To be sure an' I will. A proper Irishman always does what a lady asks him. Sure an' it's been the ruin av us. We're at the mercy av the petticoats. If ye'd come and said that to me afore ye'd have had no need av your walk to White Cross. But mind ye keep the rest av the bargin. The reds are ripe and the scabs soon will be—and all the rats have gone to glory."

Emily flew into the New Moon kitchen like a slim whirlwind.

"Aunt Elizabeth, Lofty John isn't going to cut down the bush—he told me he wouldn't—but I have to go and see him sometimes—if you don't object."

"I suppose it wouldn't make much difference to you if I did," said Aunt Elizabeth. But her voice was not so sharp as usual. She would not confess how much Emily's announcement relieved her; but it mellowed her attitude considerably. "There's a letter here for you. I want to know what it means."

Emily took the letter. It was the first time she had ever received a real letter through the mail and she tingled with the delight of it. It was addressed in a heavy black hand to "Miss Emily Starr, New Moon, Blair Water." But—

"You opened it!" she cried indignantly.

"Of course I did. You are not going to receive letters I am not to see, Miss. What I want to know is—how comes Father Cassidy to be writing to you—and writing such nonsense?"

"I went to see him Saturday," confessed Emily, realizing that the cat was out of the bag. "And I asked him if he couldn't prevent Lofty John from cutting down the bush."

"Emily—Byrd—Starr!"

"I TOLD him I was a Protestant," cried Emily. "He understands all about it. And he was just like anybody else. I like him BETTER than Mr. Dare."

Aunt Elizabeth did not say much more. There did not seem to be much she COULD say. Besides the bush wasn't going to be cut down. The bringer of good news is forgiven much. She contented herself with glaring at Emily—who was too happy and excited to mind glares. She carried her letter off to the garret dormer and gloated over the stamp and the superscription a bit before she took out the enclosure.

"Dear Pearl of Emilys," wrote Father Cassidy. "I've seen our lofty friend and I feel sure your green outpost of fairyland will be saved for your moonlit revels. I know you DO dance there by light o' moon when mortals are snoring. I think you'll have to go through the form of asking Mr. Sullivan to spare those trees, but you'll find him quite reasonable. It's all in the knowing how and the time of the moon. How goes the epic and the language? I hope you'll have no trouble in freeing the *Child of The Sea* from her vows. Continue to be the friend of all good elves, and of

"Your admiring friend,

"JAMES CASSIDY.

"P. S. The B'y sends respects. What word have you for 'cat' in your language? Sure and you can't get anything cattier than 'cat' can you, now?"

Lofty John spread the story of Emily's appeal to Father Cassidy far and wide, enjoying it as a good joke on himself. Rhoda Stuart said she always knew Emily Starr was a bold thing and Miss Brownell said she would be surprised at NOTHING Emily Starr would do, and Dr. Burnley called her a Little Devil more admiringly than ever, and Perry said she had pluck and Teddy took credit for suggesting it, and Aunt Elizabeth endured, and Aunt Laura thought it might have been worse. But Cousin Jimmy made Emily feel very happy.

"It would have spoiled the garden and broken my heart, Emily," he told her. "You're a little darling girl to have prevented it."

One day a month later, when Aunt Elizabeth had taken Emily to Shrewsbury to fit her out with a winter coat, they met Father Cassidy in a store. Aunt Elizabeth bowed with great stateliness, but Emily put out a slender paw.

"What about the dispensation from Rome?" whispered Father Cassidy.

One Emily was quite horrified lest Aunt Elizabeth should overhear and think she was having sly dealings with the Pope, such as no good Presbyterian half-Murray of New Moon should have. The other Emily thrilled to her toes with the dramatic delight of a secret understanding of mystery and intrigue. She nodded gravely, her eyes eloquent with satisfaction.

"I got it without any trouble," she whispered back.

"Fine," said Father Cassidy. "I wish you good luck, and I wish it hard. Good-bye."

"Farewell," said Emily, thinking it a word more in keeping with dark secrets than good-bye. She tasted the flavour of that half-stolen interview all the way home, and felt quite as if she were living in an epic herself. She did not see Father Cassidy again for years—he was soon afterwards removed to another parish; but she always thought of him as a very agreeable and understanding person.

CHAPTER XX
BY AERIAL POST

"DEAREST FATHER: "My heart is very sore to night. Mike died this morning. Cousin Jimmy says he must have been poisoned. Oh, Father dear, I felt so bad. He was such a lovely cat. I cried and cried and cried. Aunt Elizabeth was disgusted. She said, "You did not make half so much fuss when your father died." What a crewel speech. Aunt Laura was nicer but when she said, "Don't cry dear. I will get you another kitten," I saw she didn't understand either. I don't want another kitten. If I had MILLIONS of kittens they wouldn't make up for Mike.

"Ilse and I buried him in Lofty John's bush. I am so thankful the ground wasn't frozen yet. Aunt Laura gave me a shoe box for a coffin, and some pink tissue paper to wrap his poor little body in. And we put a stone over the grave and I said "Blessed are the dead who die in the Lord." When I told Aunt Laura about it she was horrified and said, "Oh, Emily, that was a dreadful thing. You should not have said that over a cat." And Cousin Jimmy said, "Don't you think, Laura, that an innocent little dum creature has a share in God? Emily loved him and all love is part of God." And Aunt Laura said, "Maybe you are right, Jimmy. But I am thankful Elizabeth did not hear her."

"Cousin Jimmy may not be all there, but what is there is very nice.

"But oh, Father, I am so lonesome for Mike tonight. Last night he was here playing with me, so cunning and pretty and SMEE, and now he is cold and dead in Lofty John's bush.

"DECEMBER 18.

"DEAR FATHER:

"I am here in the garret. The Wind Woman is very sorry about something tonight. She is sying so sadly around the window. And yet the first time I heard her tonight the flash came—I felt as if I had just seen something that happened long, long ago—something so lovely that it hurt me.

"Cousin Jimmy says there will be a snow storm tonight. I am glad. I like to hear a storm at night. It's so cozy to snuggle down among the blankets and feel it can't get at you. Only when I snuggle Aunt Elizabeth says I skwirm. The idea of any one not knowing the difference between snuggling and skwirming.

"I am glad we will have snow for Christmas. The Murray dinner is to be at New Moon this year. It is our turn. Last year it was at Uncle Oliver's but Cousin Jimmy had grippe and couldn't go so I stayed home with him. I will be right in the thick of it this year and it exites me. I will write you all about it after it is over, dearest.

"I want to tell you something, Father. I am ashamed of it, but I think I'll feel better if I tell you all about it. Last Saturday Ella Lee had a birthday party and I was invited. Aunt Elizabeth let me put on my new blue cashmere dress. It is a very pretty dress. Aunt Elizabeth wanted to get a dark brown but Aunt Laura insisted on blue. I looked at myself in my glass and I remembered that Ilse had told me her father told her I would be handsome if I had more colour. So I pinched my cheeks to make them red. I looked ever so much nicer but it didn't last. Then I took an old red velvet flower that had once been in Aunt Laura's bonnet and wet it and then rubbed the red on my cheeks. I went to the party and the girls all LOOKED at me but nobody said anything, only Rhoda Stuart giggled and giggled. I meant to come home and wash the red off before Aunt Elizabeth saw me. But she took a notion to call for me on her way home from the store. She did not say anything there but when we got home she said, "What have you been doing to your face, Emily?" I told her and I expected an awful scolding, but all she said was, "Don't you know that you have made yourself CHEAP?" I did know it, too. I had felt that all along although I couldn't think of the right word for it before. "I will never do such a thing again, Aunt Elizabeth," I said. "You'd better not," she said. "Go and wash your face this instant." I did and I was not half so pretty but I felt ever so much better. Strange to relate, dear Father, I heard Aunt Elizabeth laughing about it in the pantry to Aunt Laura afterwards. You never can tell what will make Aunt Elizabeth laugh. I am sure it was ever so much funnier when Saucy Sal followed me to prayer meeting last Wednesday night, but Aunt Elizabeth never laughed a bit then. I don't often go to prayer meeting but Aunt Laura couldn't go that night so Aunt Elizabeth took me because she doesn't like to go alone. I didn't know Sal was following us till just as we got to the church I saw her. I shooed her away but after we went in I suppose Sal sneaked in when someone opened the door and got upstairs into the galery. And just as soon as Mr. Dare began to pray Sal began to yowl. It sounded awful up in that big empty galery. I felt so gilty and miserable. I did not need to paint my face. It was just burning red and Aunt Elizabeth's eyes glittered feendishly. Mr. Dare prayed a long time. He is deaf, so he did not hear Sal any more than when he sat on her. But everyone else did and the boys giggled. After the prayer Mr. Morris went up to the galery and chased Sal out. We could hear her skrambling over the seats and

Mr. Morris after her. I was wild for fear he'd hurt her. I ment to spank her myself with a shingle next day but I did not want her to be kicked. After a long time he got her out of the galery and she tore down the stairs and into the church, up one isle and down the other two or three times as fast as she could go and Mr. Morris after her with a broom. It is awfully funny to think of it now but I did not think it so funny at the time I was so ashamed and so afraid Sal would be hurt.

"Mr. Morris chased her out at last. When he sat down I made a face at him behind my hymn book. Coming home Aunt Elizabeth said, "I hope you have disgraced us enough tonight, Emily Starr. I shall never take you to prayer meeting again." I am sorry I disgraced the Murrays but I don't see how I was to blame and anyway I don't like prayer meeting because it is dull.

"But it wasn't dull that night, dear Father.

"Do you notice how my spelling is improved? I have thought of such a good plan. I write my letter first and then I look up all the words I'm not sure of and correct them. Sometimes though I think a word is all right when it isn't.

"Ilse and I have given up our language. We fought over the verbs. Ilse didn't want to have any tenses for the verbs. She just wanted to have a different word altogether for every tense. I said if I was going to make a language it was going to be a proper one and Ilse got mad and said she had enough bother with grammer in English and I could go and make my old language by myself. But that is no fun so I let it go too. I was sorry because it was very interesting and it was such fun to puzzle the other girls in school. We weren't able to get square with the French boys after all for Ilse had sore throat all through potato picking time and couldn't come over. It seems to me that life is full of disappointments.

"We had examinations in school this week. I did pretty well in all except arithmetic. Miss Brownell explained something about the questions but I was busy composing a story in my mind and did not hear her so I got poor marks. The story is called *Madge MacPherson's Secret*. I am going to buy four sheets of foolscap with my egg money and sew them into a book and write the story in it. I can do what I like with my egg money. I think maybe I'll write novels when I grow up as well as poetry. But Aunt Elizabeth won't let me read any novels so how can I find out how to write them? Another thing that worries me, if I do grow up and write a wonderful poem, perhaps people won't see how wonderful it is.

"Cousin Jimmy says that a man in Priest Pond says the end of the world is coming soon. I hope it won't come till I've seen everything in it.

"Poor Elder MacKay has the mumps.

"I was over sleeping with Ilse the other night because her father was away. Ilse says her prayers now and she said she'd bet me anything she could pray longer than me. I said she couldn't and I prayed ever so long about everything I could think of and when I couldn't think of anything more I thought at first I'd begin over again. Then I thought, "No, that would not be honerable. A Starr must be honerable." So I got up and said "You win" and Ilse never answered. I went around the bed and there she was asleep on her knees. When I woke her up she said we'd have to call the bet off because she could have gone on praying for ever so long if she hadn't fell asleep.

"After we got into bed I told her a lot of things I wished afterwards I hadn't. Secrets.

"The other day in history class Miss Brownell read that Sir Walter Raleigh had to lie in the Tower for fourteen years. Perry said "Wouldn't they let him get up sometimes?" Then Miss Brownell punished him for impertinence, but Perry was in earnest. Ilse was mad at Miss Brownell for whipping Perry and mad at Perry for asking such a fool question as if he didn't know anything. But Perry says he is going to write a history book some day that won't have such puzzling things in it.

"I am finishing the Disappointed House in my mind. I'm furnishing the rooms like flowers. I'll have a rose room all pink and a lily room all white and silver and a pansy room, blue and gold. I wish the Disappointed House could have a Christmas. It never has any Christmasses.

"Oh, Father, I've just thought of something nice. When I grow up and write a great novel and make lots of money, I will buy the Disappointed House and finish it. Then it won't be Disappointed any more.

"Ilse's Sunday School teacher, Miss Willeson, gave her a Bible for learning 200 verses. But when she took it home her father laid it on the floor and kicked it out in the yard. Mrs. Simms says a judgment will come on him but nothing has happened yet. The poor man is warped. That is why he did such a wicked thing.

"Aunt Laura took me to old Mrs. Mason's funeral last Wednesday. I like funerals. They are so dramatic.

"My pig died last week. It was a GREAT FINANSHUL LOSS to me. Aunt Elizabeth says Cousin Jimmy fed it too well. I suppose I should not have called it after Lofty John.

"We have maps to draw in school now. Rhoda Stuart always gets the most marks. Miss Brownell doesn't know that Rhoda just puts the map up against a window pane and the paper over it and copies it off. I like drawing maps. Norway and Sweden look like a tiger with mountains for stripes and Ireland looks like a little dog with its back turned on England, and its paws held up against its breast, and Africa looks like a big pork ham. Australia is a lovely map to draw.

"Ilse is getting on real well in school now. She says she isn't going to have me beating her. She can learn like the dickins, as Perry says, when she tries, and she has won the silver metal for Queen's County. The W.C.T.U. in Charlottetown gave it for the best reciter. They had the contest in Shrewsbury and Aunt Laura took Ilse because Dr. Burnley wouldn't and Ilse won it. Aunt Laura told Dr. Burnley when he was here one day that he ought to give Ilse a good education. He said "I'm not going to waste money educating any she-thing." And he looked black as a thunder cloud. Oh, I wish Dr. Burnley would love Ilse. I'm so glad YOU loved ME, Father.

"DEC. 22.

"Dear Father: We had our school examination today. It was a great occasion. Almost everybody was there except Dr. Burnley and Aunt Elizabeth. All the girls wore their best dresses but me. I knew Ilse had nothing to wear but her shabby old last winter's plaid that is too short for her, so to keep her from feeling bad, I put on my old brown dress, too. Aunt Elizabeth did not want to let me do it at first because New Moon Murrays should be well dressed but when I explained about Ilse she looked at Aunt Laura and then said I might.

"Rhoda Stuart made fun of Ilse and me but I heaped coals of fire on her head. (That is what is called a figure of speech.) She got stuck in her recitation. She had left the book home and nobody else knew the piece but me. At first I looked at her triumphantly. But then a queer feeling came into me and I thought "What would I feel like if I was stuck before a big crowd of people like this? And besides the honour of the school is at stake," so I whispered it to her because I was quite close. She got through the rest all right. The strange thing is, dear Father, that now I don't feel any more as if I hated her. I feel quite kindly to her and it is much nicer. It is uncomfortable to hate people.

"DEC. 28.

"DEAR FATHER:

"Christmas is over. It was pretty nice. I never saw so many good things cooked all at once. Uncle Wallace and Aunt Eva and Uncle Oliver and Aunt Addie and Aunt Ruth were here. Uncle Oliver didn't bring any of his children and I was much disappointed. We had Dr. Burnley and Ilse too. Everyone was dressed up. Aunt Elizabeth wore her black satin dress with a pointed lace collar and cap. She looked quite handsome and I was proud of her. You like your relations to look well even if you don't like THEM. Aunt Laura wore her brown silk and Aunt Ruth had on a grey dress. Aunt Eva was VERY elegant. Her dress had a train. But it smelled of moth balls.

"I had on my blue cashmere and wore my hair tied with blue ribbons, and Aunt Laura let me wear mother's blue silk sash with the pink daisies on it that she had when she was a little girl at New Moon. Aunt Ruth sniffed when she saw me. She said, "You have grown a good deal, Em'ly. I hope you are a better girl."

"But she DIDN'T hope it (really). I saw that quite plain. Then she told me my bootlace was untyed.

"She looks better," said Uncle Oliver. "I wouldn't wonder if she grew up into a strong, healthy girl after all."

"Aunt Eva sighed and shook her head. Uncle Wallace didn't say anything but shook hands with me. His hand was as cold as a fish. When we went out to the sitting room for dinner I stepped on Aunt Eva's train and I could hear some stitches rip somewhere. Aunt Eva pushed me away and Aunt Ruth said, "What a very awkward child you are, Emily." I stepped behind Aunt Ruth and stuck out my tongue at her. Uncle Oliver makes a noise eating his soup. We had all the good silver spoons out. Cousin Jimmy carved the turkeys and he gave me two slices of the breast because he knows I like the white meat best. Aunt Ruth said "When I was a little girl the wing was good enough for me," and Cousin Jimmy put ANOTHER white slice on my plate. Aunt Ruth didn't say anything more then till the carving was done, and then she said, "I saw your school teacher in Shrewsbury last Saturday, Em'ly, and she did not give me a very good account of you. If you were MY daughter I would expect a different report."

"I am very glad I am not your daughter," I said in my mind. I didn't say it out loud of course but Aunt Ruth said, "Please do not look so sulky when I speak to you, Em'ly." And Uncle Wallace said, "It is a pity she has such an unattractive expression."

"YOU are conceited and domineering and stingy," I said, still in my mind. "I heard Dr. Burnley say you were."

"I see there is an ink-stain on her finger," said Aunt Ruth. (I had been writing a poem before dinner.)

"And then a most surprising thing happened. Relations are always surprising you. Aunt Elizabeth spoke up and said, "I DO WISH, RUTH, THAT YOU AND WALLACE WOULD LEAVE THAT CHILD ALONE." I could hardly believe my ears. Aunt Ruth looked annoyed but she DID leave me alone after that and only sniffed when Cousin Jimmy slipped a bit more white meat on my plate.

"After that the dinner was nice. And when they got as far as the pudding they all began to talk and it was splendid to listen to. They told stories and jokes about the Murrays. Even Uncle Wallace laughed and Aunt Ruth told some things about Great-Aunt Nancy. They were sarcastic but they were interesting. Aunt Elizabeth opened Grandfather Murray's desk and took out an old poem that had been written to Aunt Nancy BY A LOVER when she was young and Uncle Oliver read it. Great-Aunt Nancy must have been very beautiful. I wonder if anyone will ever write a poem to me. If I could have a bang somebody might. I said, "Was Great Aunt Nancy really as pretty as that?" and Uncle Oliver said, "They say she was 70 years ago" and Uncle Wallace said, "She hangs on well—she'll see the century mark yet," and Uncle Oliver said, "Oh, she's got so in the habit of living she'll never die."

"Dr. Burnley told a story I didn't understand. Uncle Wallace hawhawed right out and Uncle Oliver put his napkin up to his face. Aunt Addie and Aunt Eva looked at each other sidewise and then at their plates and smiled a little bit. Aunt Ruth seemed offended and Aunt Elizabeth looked COLDLY at Dr. Burnley and said, "I think you forget that there are children present." Dr. Burnley said, "I beg your pardon, Elizabeth," VERY politely. He can speak with a GRAND AIR when he likes. He is very handsome when he is dressed up and shaved. Ilse says she is proud of him even if he hates her.

"After dinner was over the presents were given. That is a Murray tradishun. We never have stockings or trees but a big bran pie is passed all around with the presents buried in it and ribbons hanging out with names on them. It was fun. My relations all gave me useful presents except Aunt Laura. She gave me a bottle of perfume. I love it. I love nice smells. Aunt Elizabeth does not approve of perfumes. She gave me a new apron but I am thankful to say not a baby one. Aunt Ruth gave me a New Testament and said "Em'ly, I hope you will read a portion of that every day until you have read it through," and I said, "Why, Aunt Ruth, I've read the whole New Testament a dozen times (and so I have) I LOVE Revelations." (And I DO. When I read the verse "and the twelve gates were twelve pearls" I just SAW them and the flash came.) "The Bible is not to be read as a story book," Aunt Ruth said coldly. Uncle Wallace and Aunt Eva gave me a pair of black mits and Uncle Oliver and Aunt Addie gave me a whole dollar in nice new silver dimes and Cousin Jimmy gave me a hair ribbon. Perry had left a silk bookmark for me. He had to go home to spend Christmas day with his Aunt Tom at Stovepipe Town but I saved a lot of nuts and raisins for him. I gave him and Teddy handkerchiefs (Teddy's was a LITTLE the nicest) and I gave Ilse a hair ribbon. I bought them myself out of my egg money. (I will not have any more egg money for a long time because my hen has stopped laying.) Everybody was happy and once Uncle Wallace smiled right at me. I did not think him so ugly when he smiled.

"After dinner Ilse and I played games in the kitchen and Cousin Jimmy helped us make taffy. We had a big supper but nobody could eat much because they had had such a dinner. Aunt Eva's head ached and Aunt Ruth said she didn't see why Elizabeth made the sausages so rich. But the rest were good humored and Aunt Laura kept things pleasant. She is good at making things pleasant. And after it was all over Uncle Wallace said (this is another Murray tradishun) "Let us think for a few moments of those who have gone before." I liked the way he said it—very solemnly and kind. It was one of the times when I am glad the blood of the Murrays flows in my vains. And I thought of YOU, darling Father, and Mother and poor little Mike and Great-great-Grandmother Murray, and of my old account book that Aunt Elizabeth burned, because it seemed just like a person to me. And then we all joined hands and sung "For Auld Lang Syne" before they went home. I didn't feel like a stranger among the Murrays any more. Aunt Laura and I stood out on the porch to watch them go. Aunt Laura put her arm around me and said, "Your mother and I used to stand like this long ago, Emily, to watch the Christmas guests go away." The snow creaked and the bells rang back through the trees and the frost on the pighouse roof sparkled in the moonlight. And it was all so lovely (the bells and the frost and the big shining white night) that THE FLASH came and that was best of all."

CHAPTER XXI
"ROMANTIC BUT NOT COMFORTABLE"

A CERTAIN thing happened at New Moon because Teddy Kent paid Ilse Burnley a compliment one day and Emily Starr didn't altogether like it. Empires have been overturned for the same reason.

Teddy was skating on Blair Water and taking Ilse and Emily out in turns for "slides." Neither Ilse nor Emily had skates. Nobody was sufficiently interested in Ilse to buy skates for her, and as for Emily, Aunt Elizabeth did not approve of girls skating. New Moon girls had never skated. Aunt Laura had a revolutionary idea that skating would be good exercise for Emily and would, moreover, prevent her from wearing out the soles of her boots sliding. But neither of these arguments was sufficient to convince Aunt Elizabeth, in spite of the thrifty streak that came to her from the Burnleys. The latter, however, caused her to issue an edict that Emily was not to "slide." Emily took this very hardly. She moped about in a woe-begone fashion and she wrote to her father, "I HATE Aunt Elizabeth. She is so unjust. She never plays fair." But one day Dr. Burnley stuck his head in at the door of the New Moon kitchen and said gruffly, "What's this I hear about you not letting Emily slide, Elizabeth?"

"She wears out the soles of her boots," said Elizabeth.

"Boots be—" the doctor remembered that ladies were present just in time. "Let the creature slide all she wants to. She ought to be in the open air all the time. She ought"—the doctor stared at Elizabeth ferociously—"she ought to sleep out of doors."

Elizabeth trembled lest the doctor should go on to insist on this unheard-of proceeding. She knew he had absurd ideas about the proper treatment of consumptives and those who might become such. She was glad to appease him by letting Emily stay out-of-doors in daytime and do what seemed good to her, if only he would say no more about staying out all night too.

"He is much more concerned about Emily than he is about his own child," she said bitterly to Laura.

"Ilse is too healthy," said Aunt Laura with a smile. "If she were a delicate child Allan might forgive her for—for being her mother's daughter."

"S—s—h," said Aunt Elizabeth. But she "s—s—s—h'd" too late. Emily, coming into the kitchen, had heard Aunt Laura and puzzled over what she had said all day in school. Why had Ilse to be forgiven for being her mother's daughter? Everybody was her mother's daughter, wasn't she? Wherein did the crime consist? Emily worried over it so much that she was inattentive to her lessons and Miss Brownell raked her fore and aft with sarcasm.

It is time we got back to Blair Water where Teddy was just bringing Emily in from a glorious spin clear round the great circle of ice. Ilse was waiting for her turn, on the bank. Her golden cloud of hair aureoled her face and fell in a shimmering wave over her forehead under the faded, little red tam she wore. Ilse's clothes were always faded. The stinging kiss of the wind had crimsoned her cheeks and her eyes were glowing like amber pools with fire in their hearts. Teddy's artistic perception saw her beauty and rejoiced in it.

"Isn't Ilse handsome?" he said.

Emily was not jealous. It never hurt her to hear Ilse praised. But somehow she did not like this. Teddy was looking at Ilse altogether TOO admiringly. It was all, Emily believed, due to that shimmering fringe on Ilse's white brows.

"If I had a bang Teddy might think me handsome too," she thought resentfully. "Of course, black hair isn't as pretty as gold. But my forehead is too high—everybody says so. And I DID look nice in Teddy's picture because he drew some curls over it."

The matter rankled. Emily thought of it as she went home over the sheen of the crusted snow-field slanting to the light of the winter sunset, and she could not eat her supper because she did not have a bang. All her long hidden yearning for a bang seemed to come to a head at once. She knew there was no use in coaxing Aunt Elizabeth for one. But when she was getting ready for bed that night she stood on a chair so that she could see little Emily-in-the-glass, then lifted the curling ends of her long braid and laid them over her forehead. The effect, in Emily's eyes at least, was very alluring. She suddenly thought—what if she cut a bang herself? It would take only a minute. And once done what could Aunt Elizabeth do? She would be very angry and doubtless inflict some kind of punishment. But the bang would be there—at least until it grew out long.

Emily, her lips set, went for the scissors. She unbraided her hair and parted the front tresses. Snip—snip—went the scissors. Glistening locks fell at her feet. In a minute Emily had her long-desired bang. Straight across her brows fell the lustrous, softly curving fringe. It changed the whole character of her face. It made it arch, provocative, elusive. For one brief moment Emily gazed at her reflection in triumph.

And then—sheer terror seized her. Oh, what had she done? How angry Aunt Elizabeth would be! Conscience suddenly awoke and added its pang also. She had been wicked. It was wicked to cut a bang when Aunt Elizabeth had forbidden it. Aunt Elizabeth had given her a home at New Moon—hadn't Rhoda Stuart that very day in school twitted her again with "living on charity"? And she was repaying her by disobedience and ingratitude. A Starr should not have done that. In a panic of fear and remorse Emily snatched the scissors and cut the bang off—cut it close against the hair line. Worse and worse! Emily beheld the result in dismay. Any one could see that a bang HAD been cut, so Aunt Elizabeth's anger was still to face. And she had made a terrible fright of herself. Emily burst into tears, snatched up the fallen locks and crammed them into the waste-basket, blew out her candle and sprang into bed, just as Aunt Elizabeth came in.

Emily burrowed face downward in the pillows, and pretended to be asleep. She was afraid Aunt Elizabeth would ask her some question and insist on her looking up while she answered it. That was a Murray tradition—you looked people in the face when you spoke to them. But Aunt Elizabeth undressed in silence and came to bed. The room was in darkness—thick darkness. Emily sighed and turned over. There was a hot gin-jar in the bed, she knew, and her feet were cold. But she did not think she ought to have the privilege of the gin-jar. She was too wicked—too ungrateful.

"DO stop squirming," said Aunt Elizabeth.

Emily squirmed no more—physically at least. Mentally she continued to squirm. She could not sleep. Her feet or her conscience— or both—kept her awake. And fear, also. She dreaded the morning. Aunt Elizabeth would see then what had happened. If it were only over—if the revelation were only over. Emily forgot and squirmed.

"What makes you so restless tonight?" demanded Aunt Elizabeth, in high displeasure. "Are you taking a cold?"

"No, ma'am."

"Then go to sleep. I can't bear such wriggling. One might as well have an eel in bed—O—W!"

Aunt Elizabeth, in squirming a bit herself, had put her own foot against Emily's icy ones.

"Goodness, child, your feet are like snow. Here, put them on the gin-jar."

Aunt Elizabeth pushed the gin-jar over against Emily's feet. How lovely and warm and comforting it was!

Emily worked her toes against it like a cat. But she suddenly knew she could not wait for morning.

"Aunt Elizabeth, I've got something to confess."

Aunt Elizabeth was tired and sleepy and did not want confessions just then. In no very gracious tone she said,

"What have you been doing?"

"I—I cut a bang, Aunt Elizabeth."

"A bang?"

Aunt Elizabeth sat up in bed.

"But I cut it off again," cried Emily hurriedly. "Right off—close to my head."

Aunt Elizabeth got out of bed, lit a candle, and looked Emily over.

"Well you HAVE made a sight of yourself," she said grimly. "I never saw any one as ugly as you are this minute. And you have behaved in a most underhanded fashion."

This was one of the times Emily felt compelled to agree with Aunt Elizabeth.

"I'm sorry," she said, lifting pleading eyes.

"You will eat your supper in the pantry for a week," said Aunt Elizabeth. "And you will not go to Uncle Oliver's next week when I go. I had promised to take you. But I shall take no one who looks as you do anywhere with me."

This was hard. Emily had looked forward to that visit to Uncle Oliver's. But on the whole she was relieved. The worst was over and her feet were getting warm. But there was one thing yet. She might as well unburden her heart completely while she was at it.

"There's another thing I feel I ought to tell you."

Aunt Elizabeth got into bed again with a grunt. Emily took it for permission.

"Aunt Elizabeth, you remember that book I found in Dr. Burnley's bookcase and brought home and asked you if I could read it? It was called 'The History of Henry Esmond.' You looked at it and said you had no objections to my reading history. So I read it. But, Aunt Elizabeth, it wasn't history—it was a novel. And I KNEW IT WHEN I BROUGHT IT HOME."

"You know that I have forbidden you to read novels, Emily Starr. They are wicked books and have ruined many souls."

"It was very dull," pleaded Emily, as if dullness and wickedness were quite incompatible. "And it made me feel unhappy. Everybody seemed to be in love with the wrong person. I have made up my mind, Aunt Elizabeth, that I will never fall in love. It makes too much trouble."

"Don't talk of things you can't understand, and that are not fit for children to think about. This is the result of reading novels. I shall tell Dr. Burnley to lock his bookcase up."

"Oh, don't do that, Aunt Elizabeth," exclaimed Emily. "There are no more novels in it. But I'm reading such an interesting book over there. It tells about everything that's inside of you. I've got as far along as the liver and its diseases. The pictures are so interesting. Please let me finish it."

This was worse than novels. Aunt Elizabeth was truly horrified. Things that were inside of you were not to be read about.

"Have you no shame, Emily Starr? If you have not I am ashamed for you. Little girls do not read books like that."

"But, Aunt Elizabeth, why not? I HAVE a liver, haven't I—and heart and lungs—and stomach—and—"

"That will do, Emily. Not another word."

Emily went to sleep unhappily. She wished she had never said a word about 'Esmond.' And she knew she would never have a chance to finish that other fascinating book. Nor had she. Dr. Burnley's bookcase was locked thereafter and the doctor gruffly ordered her and Ilse to keep out of his office. He was in a very bad humour about it for he had words with Elizabeth Murray over the matter.

Emily was not allowed to forget her bang. She was twitted and teased in school about it and Aunt Elizabeth looked at it whenever she looked at Emily and the contempt in her eyes burned Emily like a flame. Nevertheless, as the mistreated hair grew out and began to curl in soft little ringlets, Emily found consolation. The bang was tacitly permitted, and she felt that her looks were greatly improved thereby. Of course, as soon as it grew long enough she knew Aunt Elizabeth would make her brush it back. But for the time being she took comfort in her added beauty.

The bang was just about at its best when the letter came from Great-Aunt Nancy.

It was written to Aunt Laura—Great-Aunt Nancy and Aunt Elizabeth were not over-fond of each other—and in it Great-Aunt Nancy said, "If you have a photograph of that child Emily send it along. I don't want to see HER; she's stupid—I know she's stupid. But I want to see what Juliet's child looks like. Also the child of that fascinating young man, Douglas Starr. He WAS fascinating. What fools you all were to make such a fuss about Juliet running away with him. If you and Elizabeth had BOTH run away with somebody in your running days it would have been better for you."

This letter was not shown to Emily. Aunt Elizabeth and Aunt Laura had a long secret consultation and then Emily was told that she was to be taken to Shrewsbury to have her picture taken for Aunt Nancy. Emily was much excited over this. She was dressed in her blue cashmere and Aunt Laura put a point lace collar on it and hung her Venetian beads over it. And new buttoned boots were got for the occasion.

"I'm so glad this has happened while I still have my bang," thought Emily happily.

But in the photographer's dressing-room, Aunt Elizabeth grimly proceeded to brush back her bang and pin it with hairpins.

"Oh, please, Aunt Elizabeth, let me have it down," Emily begged. "Just for the picture. After this I'll brush it back."

Aunt Elizabeth was inexorable. The bang was brushed back and the photograph taken. When Aunt Elizabeth saw the finished result she was satisfied.

"She looks sulky; but she is neat; and there is a resemblance to the Murrays I never noticed before," she told Aunt Laura. "That will please Aunt Nancy. She is very clannish under all her oddness."

Emily would have liked to throw every one of the photographs in the fire. She hated them. They made her look hideous. Her face seemed to be ALL forehead. If they sent Aunt Nancy that Aunt Nancy would think her stupider than ever. When Aunt Elizabeth did the photograph up in cardboard and told Emily to take it to the office Emily already knew what she meant to do. She went straight to the garret and took out of her box the water-colour Teddy had made of her. It was just the same size as the photograph. Emily removed the latter from its wrappings, spurning it aside with her foot.

"That isn't ME," she said. "I looked sulky because I felt sulky about the bang. But I hardly ever look sulky, so it isn't fair."

She wrapped Teddy's sketch up in the cardboard and then sat down and wrote a letter.

"DEAR GREAT-AUNT NANCY:

"Aunt Elizabeth had my picture taken to send you but I don't like it because it makes me look too ugly and I am putting another picture in instead. An ARTIST FRIEND made it for me. It is just like me when I'm smiling and have a bang. I am only LENDING it to you, not GIVING it, because I valew it very highly.

"Your obedient grand niece,
  "EMILY BYRD STARR.
"P. S. I am not so stupid as you think.
"E. B. S.
"P. S. No. 2. I am not stupid AT ALL."

Emily put her letter in with the picture—thereby unconsciously cheating the post-office—and slipped out of the house to mail it. Once it was safely in the post-office she drew a breath of relief. She found the walk home very enjoyable. It was a bland day in early April and spring was looking at you round the corners. The Wind Woman was laughing and whistling over the wet sweet fields; freebooting crows held conferences in the tree tops; little pools of sunshine lay in the mossy hollows; the sea was a blaze of sapphire beyond the golden dunes; the maples in Lofty John's bush were talking about red buds. Everything Emily had ever read of dream and myth and legend seemed a part of the charm of that bush. She was filled to her finger-tips with a rapture of living.

"Oh, I smell spring!" she cried as she danced along the brook path.

Then she began to compose a poem on it. Everybody who has ever lived in the world and could string two rhymes together has written a poem on spring. It is the most be-rhymed subject in the world—and always will be, because it is poetry incarnate itself. You can never be a real poet if you haven't made at least one poem about spring.

Emily was wondering whether she would have elves dancing on the brookside by moonlight, or pixies sleeping in a bed of ferns in her poem, when something confronted her at a bend in the path which was neither elf nor pixy, but seemed odd and weird enough to belong to some of the tribes of Little People. Was it a witch? Or an elderly fay of evil intentions—the bad fairy of all christening tales?

"I'm the b'y's Aunt Tom," said the appearance, seeing that Emily was too amazed to do anything but stand and stare.

"Oh!" Emily gasped in relief. She was no longer frightened. But what a VERY peculiar looking lady Perry's Aunt Tom was. Old—so old that it seemed quite impossible that she could ever have been young; a bright red hood over crone-like, fluttering grey locks; a little face seamed by a thousand fine, criss-cross wrinkles; a long nose with a knob on the end of it; little twinkling, eager, grey eyes under bristly brows; a ragged man's coat covering her from neck to feet; a basket in one hand and a black knobby stick in the other.

"Staring wasn't thought good breeding in my time," said Aunt Tom.

"Oh!" said Emily again. "Excuse me— How do you do!" she added, with a vague grasp after her manners.

"Polite—and not too proud," said Aunt Tom, peering curiously at her. "I've been up to the big house with a pair of socks for the b'y but 'twas yourself I wanted to see."

"Me?" said Emily blankly.

"Yis. The b'y has been talking a bit of you and a plan kem into my head. Thinks I to myself it's no bad notion. But I'll make sure before I waste my bit o' money. Emily Byrd Starr is your name and Murray is your nature. If I give the b'y an eddication will ye marry him when ye grow up?"

"Me!" said Emily again. It seemed to be all she could say. Was she dreaming? She MUST be.

"Yis—you. You're half Murray and it'll be a great step up f'r the b'y. He's smart and he'll be a rich man some day and boss the country. But divil a cent will I spend on him unless you promise."

"Aunt Elizabeth wouldn't let me," cried Emily, too frightened of this odd old body to refuse on her own account.

"If you've got any Murray in you you'll do your own choosing," said Aunt Tom, thrusting her face so close to Emily's that her bushy eyebrows tickled Emily's nose. "Say you'll marry the b'y and to college he goes."

Emily seemed to be rendered speechless. She could think of nothing to say—oh, if she could ONLY wake up! She could not even run.

"Say it!" insisted Aunt Tom, thumping her stick sharply on a stone in the path.

Emily was so horrified that she might have said something— anything—to escape. But at this moment Perry bounded out of the spruce copse, his face white with rage, and seized his Aunt Tom most disrespectfully by the shoulder.

"You go home!" he said furiously.

"Now, b'y dear," quavered Aunt Tom deprecatingly. "I was only trying to do you a good turn. I was asking her to marry ye after a bit an—"

"I'll do my own asking!" Perry was angrier than ever. "You've likely spoiled everything. Go home—go home, I say!"

Aunt Tom hobbled off muttering, "Then I'll know better than to waste me bit o' money. No Murray, no money, me b'y."

When she had disappeared down the brook path Perry turned to Emily. From white he had gone very red.

"Don't mind her—she's cracked," he said. "Of course, when I grow up I mean to ask you to marry me but—"

"I couldn't—Aunt Elizabeth—"

"Oh, she will then. I'm going to be premier of Canada some day."

"But I wouldn't want—I'm sure I wouldn't—"

"You will when you grow up. Ilse is better looking of course, and I don't know why I like you best but I do."

"Don't you ever talk to me like this again!" commanded Emily, beginning to recover her dignity.

"Oh, I won't—not till we grow up. I'm as ashamed of it as you are," said Perry with a sheepish grin. "Only I had to say something after Aunt Tom butted in like that. I ain't to blame for it so don't you hold it against me. But just you remember that I'm going to ask you some day. And I believe Teddy Kent is too."

Emily was walking haughtily away but she turned at this to say coolly over her shoulder,

"If he does I'll marry him."

"If you do I'll knock his head off," shouted Perry in a prompt rage.

But Emily walked steadily on home and went to the garret to think things over.

"It has been romantic but not comfortable," was her conclusion. And that particular poem on spring was never finished.

CHAPTER XXII
WYTHER GRANGE

NO reply or acknowledgement came from Great-Aunt Nancy Priest regarding Emily's picture. Aunt Elizabeth and Aunt Laura, knowing Great-Aunt Nancy's ways tolerably well, were not surprised at this, but Emily felt rather worried over it. Perhaps Great-Aunt Nancy did not approve of what she had done; or perhaps she still thought her too stupid to bother with.

Emily did not like to lie under the imputation of stupidity. She wrote a scathing epistle to Great-Aunt Nancy on a letter-bill in which she did not mince her opinions as to that ancient lady's knowledge of the rules of epistolary etiquette; the letter was folded up and stowed away on the little shelf under the sofa but it served its purpose in blowing off steam and Emily had ceased to think about the matter when a letter came from Great-Aunt Nancy in July.

Elizabeth and Laura talked the matter over in the cook-house, forgetful or ignorant of the fact that Emily was sitting on the kitchen doorstep just outside. Emily was imagining herself attending a drawing-room of Queen Victoria. Robed in white, with ostrich plumes, veil, and court train, she had just bent to kiss the Queen's hand when Aunt Elizabeth's voice shattered her dream as a pebble thrown into a pool scatters the fairy reflection.

"What is your opinion, Laura," Aunt Elizabeth was saying, "of letting Emily visit Aunt Nancy?"

Emily pricked up her ears. What was in the wind now?

"From her letter she seems very anxious to have the child," said Laura.

Elizabeth sniffed.

"A whim—a whim. You know what her whims are. Likely by the time Emily got there she'd be quite over it and have no use for her."

"Yes, but on the other hand if we don't let her go she will be dreadfully offended and never forgive us—or Emily. Emily should have her chance."

"I don't know that her chance is worth much. If Aunt Nancy really has any money beyond her annuity—and that's what neither you nor I nor any living soul knows, unless it's Caroline—she'll likely leave it all to some of the Priests—Leslie Priest's a favourite of hers, I understand. Aunt Nancy always liked her husband's family better than her own, even though she's always slurring at them. Still—she MIGHT take a fancy to Emily—they're both so odd they might suit each other—but you know the way she talks—she and that abominable old Caroline."

"Emily is too young to understand," said Aunt Laura.

"I understand more than you think," cried Emily indignantly.

Aunt Elizabeth jerked open the cook-house door.

"Emily Starr, haven't you learned by this time not to listen?"

"I wasn't listening. I thought you knew I was sitting here—I can't help my ears HEARING. Why didn't you WHISPER? When you whisper I know you're talking secrets and I don't try to hear them. Am I going to Great-Aunt Nancy's for a visit?"

"We haven't decided," said Aunt Elizabeth coldly, and that was all the satisfaction Emily got for a week. She hardly knew herself whether she wanted to go or not. Aunt Elizabeth had begun making cheese— New Moon was noted for its cheeses—and Emily found the whole process absorbing, from the time the rennet was put in the warm new milk till the white curds were packed away in the hoop and put under the press in the old orchard, with the big, round, grey "cheese" stone to weight it down as it had weighed down New Moon cheeses for a hundred years. And then she and Ilse and Teddy and Perry were absorbed heart and soul in "playing out" the "Midsummer Night's Dream" in Lofty John's bush and it was very fascinating. When they entered Lofty John's bush they went out of the realm of daylight and things known into the realm of twilight and mystery and enchantment. Teddy had painted wonderful scenery on old boards and pieces of sails, which Perry had got at the Harbor. Ilse had fashioned delightful fairy wings from tissue paper and tinsel, and Perry had made an ass's head for BOTTOM out of an old calf-skin that was very realistic. Emily had toiled happily for many weeks copying out the different parts and adapting them to circumstances. She had "cut" the play after a fashion that would have harrowed Shakespeare's soul but after all the result was quite pretty and coherent. It did not worry them that four small actors had to take six times as many parts. Emily was TITANIA and HERMIA and a job lot of fairies besides, Ilse was HIPPOLYTA and HELENA, plus some more fairies, and the boys were anything that the dialogue required. Aunt Elizabeth knew nothing of it all; she would promptly have put a stop to the whole thing, for she thought play-acting exceedingly wicked; but Aunt Laura was privy to the plot, and Cousin Jimmy and Lofty John had already attended a moonlight rehearsal.

To go away and leave all this, even for a time, would be a hard wrench, but on the other hand Emily had a burning curiosity to see Great-Aunt Nancy and Wyther Grange, her quaint, old house at Priest Pond with the famous stone dogs on the gateposts. On the whole, she thought she would like to go; and when she saw Aunt Laura doing up her starched white petticoats and Aunt Elizabeth grimly dusting off a small, black, nail-studded trunk in the garret she knew, before she was told, that the visit to Priest Pond was going to come off; so she took out the letter she had written to Aunt Nancy and added an apologetic postscript.

Ilse chose to be disgruntled because Emily was going for a visit. In reality Ilse felt appalled at the lonely prospect of a month or more without her inseparable chum. No more jolly evenings of play-acting in Lofty John's bush, no more pungent quarrels. Besides, Ilse herself had never been anywhere for a visit in her whole life and she felt sore over this fact.

"I wouldn't go to Wyther Grange for anything," said Ilse. "It's haunted."

"'Tisn't."

"Yes! It's haunted by a ghost you can FEEL and HEAR but never SEE. Oh, I wouldn't be YOU for the world! Your Great-Aunt Nancy is an AWFUL CRANK and the old woman who lives with her is a WITCH. She'll put a spell on you. You'll pine away and die."

"I won't—she isn't!"

"IS! Why, she makes the stone dogs on the gateposts howl every night if any one comes near the place. They go, 'WO-OR-OO-OO.'"

Ilse was not a born elocutionist for nothing. Her "wo-or-oo-oo" was extremely gruesome. But it was daylight, and Emily was as brave as a lion in daylight.

"You're jealous," she said, and walked off.

"I'm not, you blithering centipede," Ilse yelled after her. "Putting on airs because your aunt has stone dogs on her gateposts! Why, I know a woman in Shrewsbury who has dogs on her posts that are ten times stonier than your aunt's!"

But next morning Ilse was over to bid Emily good-bye and entreat her to write every week. Emily was going to drive to Priest Pond with Old Kelly. Aunt Elizabeth was to have driven her but Aunt Elizabeth was not feeling well that day and Aunt Laura could not leave her. Cousin Jimmy had to work at the hay. It looked as if she could not go, and this was rather serious, for Aunt Nancy had been told to expect her that day and Aunt Nancy did not like to be disappointed. If Emily did not turn up at Priest Pond on the day set Great-Aunt Nancy was quite capable of shutting the door in her face when she did appear and telling her to go back home. Nothing less than this conviction would have induced Aunt Elizabeth to fall in with Old Kelly's suggestion that Emily should ride to Priest Pond with him. His home was on the other side of it and he was going straight there.

Emily was quite delighted. She liked Old Kelly and thought that a drive on his fine red wagon would be quite an adventure. Her little black box was hoisted to the roof and tied there and they went clinking and glittering down the New Moon lane in fine style. The tins in the bowels of the wagon behind them rumbled like a young earthquake.

"Get up, my nag, get up," said Old Kelly. "Sure, an' I always like to drive the pretty gurrls. An' when is the wedding to be?"

"Whose wedding?"

"The slyness av her! Your own, av coorse."

"I have no intention of being married—immediately," said Emily, in a very good imitation of Aunt Elizabeth's tone and manner.

"Sure, and ye're a chip av the ould block. Miss Elizabeth herself couldn't have said it better. Get up, my nag, get up."

"I only meant," said Emily, fearing that she had insulted Old Kelly, "that I am too young to be married."

"The younger the better—the less mischief ye'll be after working with them come-hither eyes. Get up, my nag, get up. The baste is tired. So we'll let him go at his own swate will. Here's a bag av swaties for ye. Ould Kelley always trates the ladies. Come now, tell me all about him."

"About who?"—but Emily knew quite well.

"Your beau, av coorse."

"I haven't ANY beau. Mr. Kelly, I wish you wouldn't talk to me about such things."

"Sure, and I won't if 'tis a sore subject. Don't ye be minding if ye haven't got one—there'll be scads av them after a while. And if the right one doesn't know what's good for him, just ye come to Ould Kelly and get some toad ointment."

Toad ointment! It sounded horrible. Emily shivered. But she would rather talk about toad ointment than beaux.

"What is that for?"

"It's a love charm," said Old Kelly mysteriously. "Put a li'l smooch on his eyelids and he's yourn for life with never a squint at any other gurrl."

"It doesn't SOUND very nice," said Emily. "How do you make it?"

"You bile four toads alive till they're good and soft and then mash—"

"Oh, stop, stop!" implored Emily, putting her hands to her ears. "I don't want to hear any more—you couldn't be so cruel!"

"Cruel is it? You were after eating lobsters this day that were biled alive—"

"I don't believe it. I don't. If it's true I'll never, never eat one again. Oh, Mr. Kelly, I thought you were a nice kind man—but those poor toads!"

"Gurrl dear, it was only me joke. An' you won't be nading toad ointment to win your lad's love. Wait you now—I've something in the till behind me for a prisent for you."

Old Kelly fished out a box which he put into Emily's lap. She found a dainty little hairbrush in it.

"Look at the back av it," said Old Kelly. "You'll see something handsome—all the love charm ye'll ever nade."

Emily turned it over. Her own face looked back at her from a little inset mirror surrounded by a scroll of painted roses.

"Oh, Mr. Kelly—how pretty—I mean the roses and the glass," she cried. "Is it really for me? Oh, thank you, thank you! Now, I can have Emily-in-the-glass whenever I want her. Why, I can carry her round with me. And you were really only in fun about the toads!"

"Av coorse. Get up, my nag, get up. An' so ye're going to visit the ould lady over at Praste Pond? Ever been there?"

"No."

"It's full of Prastes. Ye can't throw a stone but ye hit one. And hit one—hit all. They're as proud and lofty as the Murrays themselves. The only wan I know is Adam Praste—the others hold too high. He's the black shape and quite sociable. But if ye want to see how the world looked on the morning after the flood go into his barnyard on a rainy day. Look a-here, gurrl dear"—Old Kelly lowered his voice mysteriously—"don't ye ever marry a Praste."

"Why not?" asked Emily, who had never thought of marrying a Priest but was immediately curious as to why she shouldn't.

"They're ill to marry—ill to live with. The wives die young. The ould lady of the Grange fought her man out and buried him but she had the Murray luck. I wouldn't trust it too far. The only dacent Praste among them is the wan they call Jarback Praste and he's too ould for you."

"Why do they call him Jarback?"

"Wan av his shoulders is a l'il bit higher than the other. He's got a bit of money and doesn't be after having to work. A book worrum, I'm belaving. Have ye got a bit av cold iron about you?"

"No; why?"

"Ye should have. Old Caroline Praste at the Grange is a witch if ever there was one."

"Why, that's what Ilse said. But there are no such thing as witches really, Mr. Kelly."

"Maybe that's thrue but it's better to be on the safe side. Here, put this horseshoe-nail in your pocket and don't cross her if ye can help it. Ye don't mind if I have a bit av a smoke, do ye?"

Emily did not mind at all. It left her free to follow her own thoughts, which were more agreeable than Old Kelly's talk of toads and witches. The road from Blair Water to Priest Pond was a very lovely one, winding along the gulf shore, crossing fir fringed rivers and inlets, and coming ever and anon on one of the ponds for which that part of the north shore was noted—Blair Water, Derry Pond, Long Pond, Three Ponds where three blue lakelets were strung together like three great sapphires held by a silver thread; and then Priest Pond, the largest of all, almost as round as Blair Water. As they drove down towards it Emily drank the scene in with avid eyes—as soon as possible she must write a description of it; she had packed the Jimmy blank book in her box for just such purposes.

The air seemed to be filled with opal dust over the great pond and the bowery summer homesteads around it. A western sky of smoky red was arched over the big Malvern Bay beyond. Little grey sails were drifting along by the fir-fringed shores. A sequestered side road, fringed thickly with young maples and birches, led down to Wyther Grange. How damp and cool the air was in the hollows! And how the ferns did smell! Emily was sorry when they reached Wyther Grange and climbed in between the gateposts whereon the big stone dogs sat very stonily, looking grim enough in the twilight.

The wide hall door was open and a flood of light streamed out over the lawn. A little old woman was standing in it. Old Kelly seemed suddenly in something of a hurry. He swung Emily and her box to the ground, shook hands hastily and whispered, "Don't lose that bit av a nail. Good-bye. I wish ye a cool head and a warm heart," and was off before the little old woman could reach them.

"So this is Emily of New Moon!" Emily heard a rather shrill, cracked voice saying. She felt a thin, claw-like hand grasp hers and draw her towards the door. There were no witches, Emily knew,—but she thrust her hand into her pocket and touched the horseshoe-nail.

CHAPTER XXIII
DEALS WITH GHOSTS

"YOUR aunt is in the back parlor," said Caroline Priest. "Come this way. Are you tired?"

"No," said Emily, following Caroline and taking her in thoroughly. If Caroline were a witch she was a very small one. She was really no taller than Emily herself. She wore a black silk dress and a little string cap of black net edged with black ruching on her yellowish white hair. Her face was more wrinkled than Emily had ever supposed a face could be and she had the peculiar grey-green eyes which, as Emily afterwards discovered, "ran" in the Priest clan.

"You may be a witch," thought Emily, "but I think I can manage YOU."

They went through the spacious hall, catching glimpses on either side of large, dim, splendid rooms, then through the kitchen end out of it into an odd little back hall. It was long and narrow and dark. On one side was a row of four, square, small-paned windows, on the other were cupboards, reaching from floor to ceiling, with doors of black shining wood. Emily felt like one of the heroines in Gothic romance, wandering at midnight through a subterranean dungeon, with some unholy guide. She had read "The Mysteries of Udolpho" and "The Romance of the Forest" before the taboo had fallen on Dr. Burnley's bookcase. She shivered. It was awful but interesting.

At the end of the hall a flight of four steps led up to a door. Beside the steps was an immense black grandfather's clock reaching almost to the ceiling.

"We shut little girls up in that when they're bad," whispered Caroline, nodding at Emily, as she opened the door that led into the back parlour.

"I'll take good care you won't shut ME up in it," thought Emily.

The back parlour was a pretty, quaint old room where a table was laid for supper. Caroline led Emily through it and knocked at another door, using a quaint old brass knocker that was fashioned like a chessy-cat, with such an irresistible grin that you wanted to grin, too, when you saw it. Somebody said, "Come in," and they went down another four steps—was there ever such a funny house?—into a bedroom. And here at last was Great-Aunt Nancy Priest, sitting in her arm-chair, with her black stick leaning against her knee, and tiny white hands, still pretty, and sparkling with fine rings, lying on her purple silk apron.

Emily felt a distinct shock of disappointment. After hearing that poem in which Nancy Murray's beauty of nut-brown hair and starry brown eyes and cheek of satin rose had been be-rhymed she had somehow expected Great-Aunt Nancy, in spite of her ninety years, to be beautiful still. But Aunt Nancy was white-haired and yellow-skinned and wrinkled and shrunken, though her brown eyes were still bright and shrewd. Somehow, she looked like an old fairy—an impish, tolerant old fairy, who might turn suddenly malevolent if you rubbed her the wrong way—only fairies never wore long, gold-tasselled earrings that almost touched their shoulders, or white lace caps with purple pansies in them.

"So this is Juliet's girl!" she said, giving Emily one of her sparkling hands. "Don't look so startled, child. I'm not going to kiss you. I never held with inflicting kisses on defenseless creatures simply because they were so unlucky as to be my relatives. Now, who does she look like, Caroline?"

Emily made a mental grimace. Now for another ordeal of comparisons, wherein dead-and-gone noses and eyes and foreheads would be dragged out and fitted on her. She was thoroughly tired of having her looks talked over in every gathering of the clans.

"Not much like the Murrays," said Caroline, peering so closely into her face that Emily involuntarily drew back. "Not so handsome as the Murrays."

"Nor the Starrs either. Her father was a handsome man—so handsome that I'd have run away with him myself if I'd been fifty years younger. There's nothing of Juliet in her that I can see. Juliet was pretty. You are not as good-looking as that picture made you out but I didn't expect you would be. Pictures and epitaphs are never to be trusted. Where's your bang gone, Emily?"

"Aunt Elizabeth combed it back."

"Well, you comb it down again while you're in my house. There's something of your Grandfather Murray about your eye-brows. Your grandfather was a handsome man—and a darned bad-tempered one— almost as bad-tempered as the Priests,—hey, Caroline?"

"If you please, Great-Aunt Nancy," said Emily deliberately, "I don't like to be told I look like other people. I look just like myself."

Aunt Nancy chuckled.

"Spunk, I see. Good. I never cared for meek youngsters. So you're not stupid, eh?"

"No, I'm not."

Great-Aunt Nancy grinned this time. Her false teeth looked uncannily white and young in her old, brown face.

"Good. If you've brains it's better than beauty—brains last, beauty doesn't. Me, for example. Caroline here, now, never had either brains nor beauty, had you, Caroline? Come, let's go to supper. Thank goodness, my stomach has stood by me if my good looks haven't."

Great-Aunt Nancy hobbled, by the aid of her stick, up the steps and over to the table. She sat at one end, Caroline at the other, Emily between, feeling rather uncomfortable. But the ruling passion was still strong in her and she was already composing a description of them for the blank book.

"I wonder if anybody will be sorry when you die," she thought, looking intently at Caroline's wizened old face.

"Come now, tell me," said Aunt Nancy. "If you're not stupid, why did you write me such a stupid letter that first time. Lord, but it was stupid! I read it over to Caroline to punish her whenever she is naughty."

"I couldn't write any other kind of a letter because Aunt Elizabeth said she was going to read it."

"Trust Elizabeth for that. Well, you can write what you like here—and say what you like—and do what you like. Nobody will interfere with you or try to bring you up. I asked you for a visit, not for discipline. Thought likely you'd have enough of that at New Moon. You can have the run of the house and pick a beau to your liking from the Priest boys—not that the young fry are what they were in my time."

"I don't want a beau," retorted Emily. She felt rather disgusted. Old Kelly had ranted about beaux half the way over and here was Aunt Nancy beginning on the same unnecessary subject.

"Don't you tell me," said Aunt Nancy, laughing till her gold tassels shook. "There never was a Murray of New Moon that didn't like a beau. When I was your age I had half a dozen. All the little boys in Blair Water were fighting about me. Caroline here now never had a beau in her life, had you, Caroline?"

"Never wanted one," snapped Caroline.

"Eighty and twelve say the same thing and both lie," said Aunt Nancy. "What's the use of being hypocrites among ourselves? I don't say it isn't well enough when men are about. Caroline, do you notice what a pretty hand Emily has? As pretty as mine when I was young. And an elbow like a cat's. Cousin Susan Murray had an elbow like that. It's odd—she has more Murray points than Starr points and yet she looks like the Starrs and not like the Murrays. What odd sums in addition we all are—the answer is never what you'd expect. Caroline, what a pity Jarback isn't home. He'd like Emily—I have a feeling he'd like Emily. Jarback's the only Priest that'll ever go to heaven, Emily. Let's have a look at your ankles, puss."

Emily rather unwillingly put out her foot. Aunt Nancy nodded her satisfaction.

"Mary Shipley's ankle. Only one in a generation has it. I had it. The Murray ankles are thick. Even your mother's ankles were thick. Look at that instep, Caroline. Emily, you're not a beauty but if you learn to use your eyes and hands and feet properly you'll pass for one. The men are easily fooled and if the women say you're not 'twill be held for jealousy."

Emily decided that this was a good opportunity to find out something that had puzzled her.

"Old Mr. Kelly said I had come-hither eyes, Aunt Nancy. Have I? And WHAT are come-hither eyes?"

"Jock Kelly's an old ass. You haven't come-hither eyes—it wouldn't be a Murray tradish." Aunt Nancy laughed. "The Murrays have keep-your-distance eyes—and so have you—though your lashes contradict them a bit. But sometimes eyes like that—combined with certain other points—are quite as effective as come-hither eyes. Men go by contraries oftener than not—if you tell them to keep off they'll come on. My own Nathaniel now—the only way to get him to do anything was to coax him to do the opposite. Remember, Caroline? Have another cooky, Emily?"

"I haven't had one yet," said Emily, rather resentfully.

Those cookies looked very tempting and she had been wishing they might be passed. She didn't know why Aunt Nancy and Caroline both laughed. Caroline's laugh was unpleasant—a dry, rusty sort of laugh—"no juice in it," Emily decided. She thought she would write in her description that Caroline had a "thin, rattling laugh."

"What do you think of us?" demanded Aunt Nancy. "Come now, what DO you think of us?"

Emily was dreadfully embarrassed. She had just been thinking of writing that Aunt Nancy looked "withered and shrivelled;" but one couldn't say that—one COULDN'T.

"Tell the truth and shame the devil," said Aunt Nancy.

"That isn't a fair question," cried Emily.

"You think," said Aunt Nancy, grinning, "that I'm a hideous old hag and that Caroline isn't quite human. She isn't. She never was—but you should have seen ME seventy years ago. I was handsomest of all the handsome Murrays. The men were mad about me. When I married Nat Priest his three brothers could have cut his throat. One cut his own. Oh, I played havoc in my time. All I regret is I can't live it over. 'Twas a grand life while it lasted. I queened it over them. The women hated me, of course—all but Caroline here. You worshipped me, didn't you, Caroline? And you worship me yet, don't you, Caroline? Caroline, I WISH you didn't have a wart on your nose."

"I wish you had one on your tongue," said Caroline waspishly.

Emily was beginning to feel tired and bewildered. It was interesting—and Aunt Nancy was kind enough in her queer way; but at home Ilse and Perry and Teddy would be foregathering in Lofty John's bush for their evening revel, and Saucy Sal would be sitting on the dairy steps, waiting for Cousin Jimmy to give her the froth. Emily suddenly realized that she was as homesick for New Moon as she had been for Maywood her first night at New Moon.

"The child's tired," said Aunt Nancy. "Take her to bed, Caroline. Put her in the Pink Room."

Emily followed Caroline through the back hall, through the kitchen, through the front hall, up the stairs, down a long hall, through a long side hall. Where on earth was she being taken? Finally they reached a large room. Caroline set down the lamp, and asked Emily if she had a nightgown.

"Of course I have. Do you suppose Aunt Elizabeth would have let me come without one?"

Emily was quite indignant.

"Nancy says you can sleep as long as you like in the morning," said Caroline. "Good-night. Nancy and I sleep in the old wing, of course, and the rest of us sleep well in our graves."

With this cryptic remark Caroline trotted out and shut the door.

Emily sat down on an embroidered ottoman and looked about her. The window curtains were of faded pink brocade and the walls were hung with pink paper decorated with diamonds of rose chains. It made a very pretty fairy paper, as Emily found by cocking her eyes at it. There was a green carpet on the floor, so lavishly splashed with big pink roses that Emily was almost afraid to walk on it. She decided that the room was a very splendid one.

"But I have to sleep here alone, so I must say my prayers very carefully," she reflected.

She undressed rather hastily, blew out the light and got into bed. She covered herself up to her chin and lay there, staring at the high, white ceiling. She had grown so used to Aunt Elizabeth's curtained bed that she felt curiously unsheltered in this low, modern one. But at least the window was wide open—evidently Aunt Nancy did not share Aunt Elizabeth's horror of night air. Through it Emily could see summer fields lying in the magic of a rising yellow moon. But the room was big and ghostly. She felt horribly far away from everybody. She was lonesome—homesick. She thought of Old Kelly and his toad ointment. Perhaps he DID boil the toads alive after all. This hideous thought tormented her. It was AWFUL to think of toads—or anything—being boiled alive. She had never slept alone before. Suddenly she was frightened. How the window rattled. It sounded terribly as if somebody—or SOMETHING—were trying to get in. She thought of Ilse's ghost—a ghost you couldn't SEE but could HEAR and FEEL was something especially spooky in the way of ghosts—she thought of the stone dogs that went "Wo—or—oo—oo" at midnight. A dog DID begin to howl somewhere. Emily felt a cold perspiration on her brow. WHAT had Caroline meant about the rest of them sleeping well in their graves? The floor creaked. Wasn't there somebody—or SOMETHING—tiptoeing round outside the door? Didn't something move in the corner? There were mysterious sounds in the long hall.

"I WON'T be scared," said Emily. "I WON'T think of those things, and tomorrow I'll write down all about how I feel now."

And then—she DID hear something—right behind the wall at the head of her bed. There was no mistake about it. It was not imagination. She heard distinctly strange uncanny rustles—as if stiff silk dresses were rubbing against each other—as if fluttering wings fanned the air—and there were soft, low, muffled sounds like tiny children's cries or moans. They lasted—they kept on. Now and then they would die away—then start up again.

Emily cowered under the bedclothes, cold with real terror. Before, her fright had been only on the surface—she had KNOWN there was nothing to fear, even while she feared. Something in her braced her to endure. But THIS was no mistake—no imagination. The rustles and flutterings and cries and moans were all too real. Wyther Grange suddenly became a dreadful, uncanny place. Ilse was right—

it WAS haunted. And she was all alone here, with miles of rooms and halls between her and any human being. It was cruel of Aunt Nancy to put her in a haunted room. Aunt Nancy must have known it was haunted—cruel old Aunt Nancy with her ghoulish pride in men who had killed themselves for her. Oh, if she were back in dear New Moon, with Aunt Elizabeth beside her. Aunt Elizabeth was not an ideal bedfellow but she was flesh-and-blood. And if the windows were hermetically sealed they kept out spooks as well as night air.

"Perhaps it won't be so bad if I say my prayers over again," thought Emily.

But even this didn't help much.

To the end of her life Emily never forgot that first horrible night at Wyther Grange. She was so tired that sometimes she dozed fitfully off only to be awakened in a few minutes in panic horror, by the rustling and muffled moans behind her bed. Every ghost and groan, every tortured spirit and bleeding nun of the books she had read came into her mind.

"Aunt Elizabeth was right—novels aren't fit to read," she thought. "Oh, I will die here—of fright—I know I will. I know I'm a coward—I can't be brave."

When morning came the room was bright with sunshine and free from mysterious sounds. Emily got up, dressed and found her way to the old wing. She was pale, with black-ringed eyes, but resolute.

"Well, and how did you sleep?" asked Aunt Nancy graciously.

Emily ignored the question.

"I want to go home today," she said.

Aunt Nancy stared.

"Home? Nonsense! Are you such a homesick baby as that?"

"I'm not homesick—not VERY—but I must go home."

"You can't—there's no one here to take you. You don't expect Caroline can drive you to Blair Water, do you?"

"Then I will walk."

Aunt Nancy thumped her stick angrily on the floor.

"You will stay right here until I'm ready for you to go, Miss Puss. I never tolerate any whims but my own. Caroline knows that, don't you, Caroline? Sit down to your breakfast—and eat—EAT."

Aunt Nancy glared at Emily.

"I won't stay here," said Emily. "I won't stay another night in that horrible haunted room. It was cruel of you to put me there. If—" Emily gave Aunt Nancy glare for glare—"if I was Salome I'd ask for YOUR head on a charger."

"Hoity-toity! What nonsense is this about a haunted room? We've no ghosts at Wyther Grange. Have we, Caroline? We don't consider them hygienic."

"You have something DREADFUL in that room—it rustled and moaned and cried all night long right in the wall behind my bed. I won't stay—I won't—."

Emily's tears came in spite of her efforts to repress them. She was so unstrung nervously that she couldn't help crying. It lacked but little of hysterics with her already.

Aunt Nancy looked at Caroline and Caroline looked back at Aunt Nancy.

"We should have told her, Caroline. It's all our fault. I clean forgot—it's so long since any one slept in the Pink Room. No wonder she was frightened. Emily, you poor child, it was a shame. It would serve me right to have my head on a charger, you vindictive scrap. We should have told you."

"Told me—what?"

"About the swallows in the chimney. That was what you heard. The big central chimney goes right up through the walls behind your bed. It is never used now since the fireplaces were built in. The swallows nest there—hundreds of them. They do make an uncanny noise—fluttering and quarrelling as they do."

Emily felt foolish and ashamed—much more ashamed than she needed to feel, for her experience had really been a very trying one, and older folks than she had been woefully frightened o' nights in the Pink Room at Wyther Grange. Nancy Priest HAD put people into that room sometimes expressly to scare them. But to do her justice she really had forgotten in Emily's case and was sorry.

Emily said no more about going home; Caroline and Aunt Nancy were both very kind to her that day; she had a good nap in the afternoon; and when the second night came she went straight to the Pink Room and slept soundly the night through. The rustles and cries were as distinct as ever but swallows and spectres were two entirely different things.

"After all, I think I'll like Wyther Grange," said Emily.

CHAPTER XXIV
A DIFFERENT KIND OF HAPPINESS

"JULY 20th.

"DEAR FATHER:

"I have been a fortnight at Wyther Grange and I have not written to you once. But I thought of you every day. I had to write to Aunt Laura and Ilse and Teddy and Cousin Jimmy and Perry and between times I am having such fun. The first night I was here I did not think I was going to be happy. But I am—only it's a different kind from New Moon happiness.

"Aunt Nancy and Caroline are very good to me and let me do exactly as I like. This is very agreeable. They are very sarcastic to each other. But I think they are a good bit like Ilse and me—they fight quite frequently but love each other very hard between times. I am sure Caroline isn't a witch but I would like to know what she thinks of when she is all alone by herself. Aunt Nancy is not pretty any longer but she is very ARISTOCRATIC LOOKING. She doesn't walk much because of her roomatism, so she sits mostly in her back parlor and reads and knits lace or plays cards with Caroline. I talk to her a great deal because she says it amuses her and I have told her a great many things but I have never told her that I write poetry. If I did I know she would make me recite it to her and I feel she is not the right person to recite your poetry to. And I do not talk about you or Mother to her, though she tries to make me. I told her all about Lofty John and his bush and going to Father Cassidy. She chuckled over that and said she always liked to talk to the Catholic Priests because they were the only men in the world a woman could talk to for more than ten minutes without other women saying she was throwing herself at their heads.

"Aunt Nancy says a great many things like that. She and Caroline talk a great deal to each other about things that happened in the Priest and Murray families. I like to sit and listen. They don't stop just as things are getting interesting the way Aunt Elizabeth and Aunt Laura do. A good many things I don't understand but I will remember them and will find out about them sometime. I have written descriptions of Aunt Nancy and Caroline in my Jimmy-book. I keep the book hid behind the wardrobe in my room because I found Caroline rummidging in my trunk one day. I must not call Aunt Nancy Great-Aunt. She says it makes her feel like Methoosaleh. She tells me all about the men who were in love with her. It seems to me they all behaved pretty much the same. I don't think that was exciting but she says it was. She tells me about all the parties and dances they used to have here long ago. Wyther Grange is bigger than New Moon and the furniture is much handsomer but it is harder to feel acquainted with it.

"There are many interesting things in this house. I love to look at them. There is a Jakobite glass on a stand in the parlor. It was a glass AN OLD ANSESTER of the Priests had long ago in Scotland and it has a thistle and a rose on it and they used it to drink Prince Charlie's health with and for NO OTHER PURPOSE. It is a very VALEWABLE AIRLOOM and Aunt Nancy prizes it highly. And she has a pickled snake in a big glass jar in the china cabinet. It is hideous but fascinating. I shiver when I see it but yet I go to look at it every day. Something seems to drag me to it. Aunt Nancy has a bureau in her room with GLASS KNOBS and a vase shaped like a green fish sitting up on end and a Chinese draggon with a curly tail, and a case of sweet little stuffed humming birds and a sand-glass for boiling eggs by and a framed wreath made out of the hair of all the dead Priests and lots of old dagerrotipes. But the thing I like the best of all is a great silvery shining ball hanging from the lamp in the parlour. It reflects everything like a little fairy world. Aunt Nancy calls it a gazing-ball, and says that when she is dead I am to have it. I wish she hadn't said that because I want the ball so much that I can't help wondering when she will die and that makes me feel wicked. I am to have the chessy-cat door knocker and her gold earrings, too. These are Murray airlooms. Aunt Nancy says the Priest airlooms must go to the Priests. I will like the chessy-cat but I don't want the earrings. I'd rather not have people notice my ears.

"I have to sleep alone. I feel frightened but I think if I could get over being frightened I'd like it. I don't mind the swallows now. It's just being alone so far away from any one. But it is lovely to be able to stretch out your legs just as you like and not have anybody scold you for skwirming. And when I wake up in the night and think of a splendid line of poetry (because the things that you think of like that always seem the best) I can get right out of bed and write it right down in my Jimmy-book. I couldn't do that at home and then by morning I'd likely forget it. I thought of such a nice line last night. "Lilies lifted pearly chaluses (a chalus is a kind of cup only more poetical) where bees were drowned in sweetness" and I felt happy because I was sure they were two better lines than any I had composed yet.

"I am allowed to go into the kitchen and help Caroline cook. Caroline is a good cook but sometimes she makes a mistake and this vexes Aunt Nancy because she likes nice things to eat. The other day Caroline made the barley soup far too thick and when Aunt Nancy looked at her plate she said "Lord, is this a dinner or a poltis?" Caroline said "It is good enough for a Priest and what is good enough for a Priest is good enough for a Murray," and Aunt Nancy said "Woman, the Priests eat of the crumbs that fall from the Murrays' tables," and Caroline was so mad she cried. And Aunt Nancy said to me "Emily, never marry a Priest"—just like Old Kelly, when I have no notion of marrying one of them. I don't like any of them I've seen very much but they seem to me a good deal like other people. Jim is the best of them but impident.

"I like the Wyther Grange breakfasts better than the New Moon breakfasts. We have toast and bacon and marmalade—nicer than porridge.

"Sunday is more amusing here than at New Moon but not so holy. Nice for a change. Aunt Nancy can't go to church or knit lace so she and Caroline play cards all day but she says I must never do it—that she is just a bad example. I love to look at Aunt Nancy's big parlor Bible because there are so many interesting things in it—pieces of dresses and hair and poetry and old tintipes and accounts of deaths and weddings. I found a piece about my own birth and it gave me a queer feeling.

"In the afternoon some of the Priests come to see Aunt Nancy and stay to supper. Leslie Priest always comes. He is Aunt Nancy's faverite neffew, so Jim says. I think that is because he pays her compliments. But I saw him wink at Isaac Priest once when he paid her one. I don't like him. He treats me as if I was a meer child. Aunt Nancy says terrible things to them all but they just laugh. When they go away Aunt Nancy makes fun of them to Caroline. Caroline doesn't like it, because she is a Priest and so she and Aunt Nancy always quarrel Sunday evening and don't speak again till Monday morning.

"I can read all the books in Aunt Nancy's bookcase except the row on the top shelf. I wonder why I can't read them. Aunt Nancy said they were French novels but I just peeped into one and it was English. I wonder if Aunt Nancy tells lies.

"The place I love best is down at bay shore. Some parts of the shore are very steep and there are such nice, woodsy, UNEXPECTED places all along it. I wander there and compose poetry. I miss Ilse and Teddy and Perry and Saucy Sal a great deal. I had a letter from Ilse today. She wrote me that they couldn't do anything more about the Midsummer Night's Dream till I got back. It is nice to feel so necessary.

"Aunt Nancy doesn't like Aunt Elizabeth. She called her a "tyrant" one day and then she said "Jimmy Murray was a very clever boy. Elizabeth Murray killed his intellect in her temper—and nothing was done to her. If she had killed his body she would have been a murderess. The other was worse, if you ask me." I do not like Aunt Elizabeth at times myself but I felt, dear Father, that I must stand up for MY FAMILY and I said "I do not want to hear such things said of my Aunt Elizabeth."

"And I just gave Aunt Nancy a LOOK. She said "Well, Saucebox, my brother Archibald will never be dead as long as you're alive. If you don't want to hear things don't hang around when Caroline and I are talking. I notice there are plenty of things you like to hear."

"This was sarcasm, dear Father, but still I feel Aunt Nancy likes me but perhaps she will not like me very long. Jim Priest says she is fikkle and never liked anyone, even her husband, very long. But after she has been sarcastic to me she always tells Caroline to give me a piece of pie so I don't mind the sarcasm. She lets me have real tea, too. I like it. At New Moon Aunt Elizabeth won't give me anything but cambric tea because it is best for my health. Aunt Nancy says the way to be healthy is to eat just what you want and never think about your stomach. But then she was never threttened with consumption. She says I needn't be a bit frightened of dying of consumption because I have too much ginger in me. That is a comforting thought. The only time I don't like Aunt Nancy is when she begins talking about the different parts of me and the effect they will have on the men. It makes me feel so silly.

"I will write you oftener after this, dear Father. I feel I have been neglecting you.

"P. S. I am afraid there are some mistakes in spelling in this letter. I forgot to bring my dictionary with me.

"JULY 22.

"Oh, dear Father, I am in a dreadful scrape. I don't know what I am to do. Oh, Father, I have broken Aunt Nancy's Jakobite glass. It seems to me like a dreadful dream.

"I went into the parlor today to look at the pickled snake and just as I was turning away my sleeve caught the Jakobite glass and over it went on the harth and SHIVERED INTO FRAGMENTS. At first I rushed out and left them there but afterwards I went back and carefully gathered them up and hid them in a box behind the sofa. Aunt Nancy never goes into the parlor now and Caroline not very often and perhaps they may not miss the glass until I go home. But it HAUNTS me. I keep thinking of it all the time and I cannot enjoy anything. I know Aunt Nancy will be furious and never forgive me if she finds out. I could not sleep all night for worrying about it. Jim Priest came down to play with me today but he said there was no fun in me and went home. The Priests mostly say what they think. Of course there was no fun in me. How could there be? I wonder if it would do any good to pray about it. I don't feel as if it would be right to pray because I am deceiving Aunt Nancy.

"JULY 24.

"Dear Father, this is a very strange world. Nothing ever turns out just like what you expect. Last night I couldn't sleep again. I was so worried. I thought I was a coward, and doing an underhanded thing and not living up to my tradishuns. At last it got so bad I couldn't stand it. I can bear it when other people have a bad opinion of me but it hurts too much when I have a bad opinion of myself. So I got out of bed and went right back through all those halls to the back parlor. Aunt Nancy was still there all alone playing Solitare. She said what on earth was I out of bed for at such an hour. I just said, short and quick to get the worst over, "I broke your Jakobite glass yesterday and hid the pieces behind the sofa." Then I waited for the STORM TO BURST. Aunt Nancy said "What a blessing. I've often wanted to smash it but never had the courage. All the Priest clan are waiting for me to die to get that glass and quarrel over it and I'm tickled to think none of them can have it now and yet can't pick a fuss with me over smashing it. Get off to bed and get your beauty sleep." I said "And aren't you mad at all, Aunt Nancy?" "If it had been a Murray airloom I'd have torn up the turf" Aunt Nancy said. "But I don't care a hoot about the Priest things."

"So I went back to bed, dear Father, and felt very releeved, but not so heroyik.

"I had a letter from Ilse today. She says Saucy Sal has had kittens at last. I feel that I ought to be home to see about them. Likely Aunt Elizabeth will have them all drowned before I get back. I had a letter from Teddy too, not much of a letter but all filled with dear little pictures of Ilse and Perry and the Tansy Patch and Lofty John's bush. They made me feel homesick.

"JULY 28.

"Oh, Father dear, I have found out all about the mistery of Ilse's mother. It is so terrible I can't write it down even to you. I cannot believe it but Aunt Nancy says it is true. I did not think there could be such terrible things in the world. No, I can't believe it and I won't believe it no matter who says it is true. I KNOW Ilse's mother COULDN'T have done anything like that. There must have been a fearful mistake somewhere. I am so unhappy and feel as if I could never be happy any more. Last night I wept on my pillow, like the heroins in Aunt Nancy's books do."

CHAPTER XXV
"SHE COULDN'T HAVE DONE IT"

GREAT-AUNT NANCY and Caroline Priest were wont to colour their grey days with the remembered crimsons of old, long-past delights and merry-makings, but they went further than this and talked over any number of old family histories before Emily with a total disregard of her youth. Loves, births, deaths, scandals, tragedies—anything that came into their old heads. Nor did they spare details. Aunt Nancy revelled in details. She forgot nothing, and sins and weaknesses that death had covered and time shown mercy to were ruthlessly dragged out and dissected by this ghoulish old lady.

Emily was not quite certain whether she really liked it or not. It WAS fascinating—it fed some dramatic hunger in her—but it made her feel unhappy somehow, as if something very ugly were concealed in the darkness of the pit they opened before her innocent eyes. As Aunt Laura had said, her youth protected her to some extent, but it could not save her from a dreadful understanding of the pitiful story of Ilse's mother on the afternoon when it seemed good to Aunt Nancy to resurrect that tale of anguish and shame.

Emily was curled up on the sofa in the back parlour, reading *The Scottish Chiefs* because it was a breathlessly hot July afternoon—too hot to haunt the bay shore. Emily was feeling very happy. The Wind Woman was ruffling over the big maple grove behind the Grange, turning the leaves until every tree seemed to be covered with strange, pale, silvery blossoms; fragrances drifted in from the garden; the world was lovely; she had had a letter from Aunt Laura saying that one of Saucy Sal's kittens had been saved for her. Emily had felt when Mike II died that she would never want another cat. But now she found she did. Everything suited her very well; she was so happy that she should have sacrificed her dearest possession to the jealous gods if she had known anything about the old pagan belief.

Aunt Nancy was tired of playing solitaire. She pushed the cards away and took up her knitting.

"Emily," she said, "has your Aunt Laura any notion of marrying Dr. Burnley?"

Emily, recalled thus abruptly from the field of Bannockburn, looked bored. Blair Water gossip had often asked or hinted this question; and now it met her in Priest Pond.

"No, I'm sure she hasn't," she said. "Why, Aunt Nancy, Dr. Burnley HATES women."

Aunt Nancy chuckled.

"Thought perhaps he'd got over that. It's eleven years now since his wife ran away. Few men hold to one idea for anything like eleven years. But Allan Burnley always was stubborn in anything—love or hate. He still loves his wife—and that is why he hates her memory and all other women."

"I never heard the rights of that story," said Caroline. "Who was his wife?"

"Beatrice Mitchell—one of the Shrewsbury Mitchells. She was only eighteen when Allan married her. He was thirty-five. Emily, never you be fool enough to marry a man much older than yourself."

Emily said nothing. *The Scottish Chiefs* was forgotten. Her finger-tips were growing cold as they always did in excitement, her eyes turning black. She felt that she was on the verge of solving the mystery that had so long worried and puzzled her. She was desperately afraid that Aunt Nancy would branch off to something else.

"I've heard she was a great beauty," said Caroline.

Aunt Nancy sniffed.

"Depends on your taste in style. Oh, she was pretty—one of your golden-haired dolls. She had a little birthmark over her left eyebrow—just like a tiny red heart—I never could see anything but that mark when I looked at her. But her flatterers told her it was a beauty spot—'the Ace of Hearts' they called her. Allan was mad about her. She had been a flirt before her marriage. But I WILL say—for justice among women is a rare thing, Caroline—YOU, for instance, are an unjust old hag—that she didn't flirt after marrying—openly, at least. She was a sly puss—always laughing and singing and dancing—no wife for Allan Burnley if you ask me. And he could have had Laura Murray. But between a fool and a sensible woman did a man ever hesitate? The fool wins every time, Caroline. That's why YOU never got a husband. You were too sensible. I got mine by pretending to be a fool. Emily, you remember that. You have brains—hide them. Your ankles will do more for you than your brains ever will."

"Never mind Emily's ankles," said Caroline, keen on a scandal hunt. "Go on about the Burnleys."

"Well, there was a cousin of hers—Leo Mitchell from Shrewsbury. You remember the Mitchells, don't you, Caroline? This Leo was a handsome fellow—a sea-captain. He had been in love with Beatrice, so gossip ran. Some said Beatrice wanted him but that her people made her marry Allan Burnley because he was the better match. Who knows? Gossip lies nine times and tells a half truth the tenth. She pretended to be in love with Allan anyhow, and he believed it. When Leo came home from a voyage and found Beatrice married he took it coolly enough. But he was always over at Blair Water. Beatrice had plenty of excuses. Leo was her cousin—they had been brought up together—they were like brother and sister—she was so lonesome in Blair Water after living in a town—he had no home except with a brother. Allan took it all down—he was so infatuated with her she could have made him believe anything. She and Leo were always together there when Allan was away seeing his patients. Then came the night Leo's vessel—*The Lady of Winds*—was to sail from Blair Harbour for South America. He went— and my lady Beatrice went with him."

A queer little strangled sound came from Emily's corner. If Aunt Nancy or Caroline had looked at her they would have seen that the child was white as the dead, with wide, horror-filled eyes. But they did not look. They knitted and gossiped on, enjoying themselves hugely.

"How did the doctor take it?" asked Caroline.

"Take it—take it—nobody knows. Everybody knows what kind of a man he's been ever since, though. He came home that night at dusk. The baby was asleep in its crib and the servant girl was watching it. She told Allan that Mrs. Burnley had gone to the harbour with her cousin for a good-bye walk and would be back at ten. Allan waited for her easily enough—he never doubted her—but she didn't come back. She had never intended to come back. In the morning *The Lady of Winds* was gone—had sailed out of the harbour at dark the night before. Beatrice had gone on board with him—that was all anybody knew. Allan Burnley SAID nothing, beyond forbidding her name ever to be mentioned in his hearing again. But *The Lady of Winds* was lost with all on board off Hatteras and that was the end of that elopement, and the end of Beatrice with her beauty and her laughter and her Ace of Hearts."

"But not the end of the shame and wretchedness she brought to her home," said Caroline shrewishly. "I'd tar and feather such a woman."

"Nonsense—if a man can't look after his wife—if he blinds his own eyes— Mercy on us, child, what is the matter?"

For Emily was standing up, holding out her hands as if pushing some loathly thing from her.

"I don't believe it," she cried, in a high, unnatural voice. "I don't believe Ilse's mother did THAT. She didn't—she couldn't have—not Ilse's MOTHER."

"Catch her, Caroline!" cried Aunt Nancy.

But Emily, though the back parlour had whirled about her for a second, had recovered herself.

"Don't touch me!" she cried passionately. "Don't touch me! You—you—you LIKED hearing that story!"

She rushed out of the room. Aunt Nancy looked ashamed for a moment. For the first time it occurred to her that her scandal-loving old tongue had done a black thing. Then she shrugged her shoulders.

"She can't go through life in cotton wool. Might as well learn spades are spades now as ever. I would have thought she'd have heard it all long ago if Blair Water gossip is what it used to be. If she goes home and tells this I'll have the indignant virgins of New Moon coming down on me in holy horror as a corrupter of youth. Caroline, don't you ask me to tell you any more family horrors before my niece, you scandalous old woman. At your age! I'm surprised at you!"

Aunt Nancy and Caroline returned to their knitting and their spicy reminiscences, and upstairs in the Pink Room Emily lay face downwards on her bed and cried for hours. It was so horrible—Ilse's mother had run away and left her little baby. To Emily that was the awful thing—the strange, cruel, heartless thing that Ilse's mother had done. She could not bring herself to believe it—there was some mistake somewhere—there WAS.

"Perhaps she was kidnapped," said Emily, trying desperately to explain it. "She just went on board to look around—and he weighed anchor and carried her off. She COULDN'T have gone away of her own accord and left her dear little baby."

The story haunted Emily in good earnest. She could think of nothing else for days. It took possession of her and worried and gnawed at her with an almost physical pain. She dreaded going back to New Moon and meeting Ilse with this consciousness of a dark secret which she must hide from her. Ilse knew nothing. She had asked Ilse once where her mother was buried and Ilse had said, "Oh, I don't know. At Shrewsbury, I guess—that's where all the Mitchells are buried."

Emily wrung her slim hands together. She was as sensitive to ugliness and pain as she was to beauty and pleasure, and this thing was both hideous and agonizing. Yet she could not keep from thinking about it, day and night. Life at Wyther Grange suddenly went stale.

Aunt Nancy and Caroline all at once gave up talking family history, even harmless history, before her. And as it was painful repression for them, they did not encourage her hanging round. Emily began to feel that they were glad when she was out of hearing, so she kept away and spent most of her days wandering on the bay shore. She could not compose any poetry—she could not write in her Jimmy-book—she could not even write to her father. Something seemed to hang between her and her old delights. There was a drop of poison in every cup. Even the filmy shadows on the great bay, the charm of its fir-hung cliffs and its little purple islets that looked like outposts of fairyland, could not bring to her the old "fine, careless rapture." She was afraid she could never be happy again—so intense had been her reaction to her first revelation of the world's sin and sorrow. And under it all, persisted the same incredulity—Ilse's mother COULDN'T have done it—and the same helpless longing to prove she couldn't have done it. But how could it be proved? It couldn't. She had solved one "mystery" but she had stumbled into a darker one—the reason why Beatrice Burnley had never come back on that summer twilight of long ago. For, all the evidence of facts to the contrary notwithstanding, Emily persisted in her secret belief that whatever the reason WAS, it was NOT that she had gone away in *The Lady of Winds* when that doomed ship sailed out into the starlit wonder of the gulf beyond Blair Harbour.

CHAPTER XXVI
ON THE BAY SHORE

"IWONDER," thought Emily, "how much longer I have to live."

She had prowled that evening further down the bay shore than she had ever gone before. It was a warm, windy evening; the air was resinous and sweet; the bay a misty turquoise. That part of the shore whereon she found herself seemed as lonely and virgin as if no human foot had ever trodden it, save for a tiny, tricksy path, slender as red thread and bordered by great, green, velvety sheets of moss, that wound in and out of the big firs and scrub spruces. The banks grew steeper and rockier as she went on and finally the little path vanished altogether in a plot of bracken. Emily was just turning to go back when she caught sight of a magnificent spray of farewell summer, growing far out on the edge of the bank. She must get it—she had never seen farewell-summers of so dark and rich a purple. She stepped out to reach them—the treacherous mossy soil gave way under her feet and slid down the steep slope. Emily made a frantic attempt to scramble back but the harder she tried, the faster went the landslide, carrying her with it. In a moment it would pass the slope and go over the brink of the rocks, straight to the boulder-strewn shore thirty feet below. Emily had one dreadful moment of terror and despair; and then she found that the clump of mossy earth which had broken away had held on a narrow ledge of rock, half hanging over it; and she was lying on the clump. It seemed to her that the slightest movement on her part would send it over, straight to the cruel boulders underneath.

She lay very still, trying to think—trying not to be afraid. She was far, far away from any house—nobody could hear her if she screamed. And she did not even dare to scream lest the motion of her body dislodge the fragment on which she lay. How long could she lie there motionless? Night was coming on. Aunt Nancy would grow anxious when the dark fell and would send Caroline to look for her. But Caroline would never find her here. Nobody would ever think of looking here for her, so far away from the Grange, in the spruce barrens of the Lower Bay. To lie there alone all night—to fancy the earth was slipping over—waiting for help that would never come—Emily could hardly restrain a shudder that might have been ruinous.

She had faced death once before, or thought she had, on the night when Lofty John had told her she had eaten a poisoned apple—but this was even harder. To die here, all alone, far away from home! They might never know what had become of her—never find her. The crows or the gulls would pick her eyes out. She dramatized the thing so vividly that she almost screamed with the horror of it. She would just disappear from the world as Ilse's mother had disappeared.

WHAT HAD BECOME OF ILSE'S MOTHER? Even in her own desperate plight Emily asked herself that question. And she would never see dear New Moon again and Teddy and the dairy and the Tansy Patch and Lofty John's bush and the mossy old sundial and her precious little heap of manuscripts on the sofa shelf in the garret.

"I must be very brave and patient," she thought. "My only chance is to lie still. And I can pray in my mind—I'm sure God can hear thoughts as well as words. It is nice to think He can hear me if nobody else can. O God—Father's God—please work a miracle and save my life, because I don't think I'm fit to die yet. Excuse my not being on my knees—You can see I can't move. And if I die please don't let Aunt Elizabeth find my letter-bills ever. Please let Aunt Laura find them. And please don't let Caroline move out the wardrobe when she house-cleans because then she would find my Jimmy-book and read what I wrote about her. Please forgive all my sins, especially not being grateful enough and cutting a bang, and please don't let Father be very far away. Amen."

Then, characteristically she thought of a postscript. "And oh, PLEASE let somebody find out that Ilse's mother didn't do THAT."

She lay very still. The light on the water began to turn warm gold and rose. A great pine on a bluff in front of her overflowed in a crest of dark boughs against the amber splendour behind it—a part of the beauty of the beautiful world that was slipping away from her. The chill of the evening gulf breeze began to creep over her. Once a bit of earth broke off at her side and went down—Emily heard the thud of the little pebbles in it on the boulders below. The portion upon which one of her legs lay was quite loose and pendent also. She knew it might break off, too, at any moment. It would be very dreadful to be there when it got dark. She could see the big spray of farewell-summer that had lured her to her doom, waving unplucked above her, wonderfully purple and lovely.

Then, beside it, she saw a man's face looking down at her!

She heard him say, "My God!" softly to himself. She saw that he was slight and that one shoulder was a trifle higher than the other. This must be Dean Priest—Jarback Priest. Emily dared not call to him. She lay still and her great, grey-purple eyes said, "Save me."

"How can I help you?" said Dean Priest hoarsely, as if to himself. "I cannot reach you—and it looks as if the slightest touch or jar would send that broken earth over the brink. I must go for a rope—and to leave you here alone—like this. Can you wait, child?"

"Yes," breathed Emily. She smiled at him to encourage him—the little soft smile that began at the corners of her mouth and spread over her face. Dean Priest never forgot that smile—and the steadfast child-eyes looking out through it from the little face that seemed so perilously near the brink.

"I'll be as quick as I can," he said. "I can't go very fast—I'm a bit lame, you see. But don't be frightened—I'll save you. I'll leave my dog to keep you company. Here, Tweed."

He whistled—a great, tawny-gold dog came in sight.

"Sit right there, Tweed, till I come back. Don't stir a paw—don't wag a tail—talk to her only with your eyes."

Tweed sat down obediently and Dean Priest disappeared.

Emily lay there and dramatized the whole incident for her Jimmy-book. She was a little frightened still, but not too frightened to see herself writing it all out the next day. It would be quite a thrilling bit.

She liked to know the big dog was there. She was not so learned in lore of dogs as in lore of cats. But he looked very human and trusty watching her with great kindly eyes. A grey kitten was an adorable thing—but a grey kitten would not have sat there and encouraged her. "I believe," thought Emily, "that a dog is better than a cat when you're in trouble."

It was half an hour before Dean Priest returned.

"Thank God you haven't gone over," he muttered. "I hadn't to go as far as I feared—I found a rope in an empty boat up-shore and took it. And now—if I drop the rope down to you, are you strong enough to hold it while the earth goes and then hang on while I pull you up?"

"I'll try," said Emily.

Dean Priest knotted a loop at the end and slid it down to her. Then he wound the rope around the trunk of a heavy fir.

"Now," he said.

Emily said inwardly, "Dear God, PLEASE—" and caught the swaying loop. The next moment the full weight of her body swung from it, for at her first movement the broken soil beneath her slipped down—slipped over. Dean Priest sickened and shivered. Could she cling to the rope while he drew her up?

Then he saw she had got a little knee-hold on the narrow shelf. Carefully he drew on the rope. Emily, full of pluck, helped him by digging her toes into the crumbling bank. In a moment she was within his reach. He grasped her arms and pulled her up beside him into safety. As he lifted her past the farewell-summer Emily reached out her hand and broke off the spray.

"I've got it, anyhow," she said jubilantly. Then she remembered her manners. "I'm much obliged to you. You saved my life. And—and—I think I'll sit down a moment. My legs feel funny and trembly."

Emily sat down, all at once more shaky than she had been through all the danger. Dean Priest leaned against the gnarled old fir. He seemed "trembly" too. He wiped his forehead with his handkerchief. Emily looked curiously at him. She had learned a good deal about him from Aunt Nancy's casual remarks—not always good-natured remarks, for Aunt Nancy did not wholly like him, it seemed. She always called him "Jarback" rather contemptuously, while Caroline scrupulously called him Dean. Emily knew he had been to college, that he was thirty-six years old—which to Emily seemed a venerable age—and well-off; that he had a malformed shoulder and limped slightly; that he cared for nothing save books nor ever had; that he lived with an older brother and travelled a great deal; and that the whole Priest clan stood somewhat in awe of his ironic tongue. Aunt Nancy had called him a "cynic." Emily did not know what a cynic was but it sounded interesting. She looked him over carefully and saw that he had delicate, pale features and tawny-brown hair. His lips were thin and sensitive, with a whimsical curve. She liked his mouth. Had she been older she would have known why—because it connoted strength and tenderness and humour.

In spite of his twisted shoulder there was about him a certain aloof dignity of presence which was characteristic of many of the Priests and which was often mistaken for pride. The green Priest eyes, that were peering and uncanny in Caroline's face and impudent in Jim Priest's, were remarkably dreamy and attractive in his.

"Well, do you think me handsome?" he said, sitting down on another stone and smiling at her. His voice was beautiful—musical and caressing.

Emily blushed. She knew staring was not etiquette, and she did not think him at all handsome, so she was very thankful that he did not press his question, but asked another.

"Do you know who your knightly rescuer is?"

"I think you must be Jar—Mr. Dean Priest." Emily flushed again with vexation. She had come so near to making another terrible hole in her manners.

"Yes, Jarback Priest. You needn't mind the nickname. I've heard it often enough. It's a Priest idea of humour." He laughed rather unpleasantly. "The reason for it is obvious enough, isn't it? I never got anything else at school. How came you to slide over that cliff?"

"I wanted this," said Emily, waving her farewell-summer.

"And you have it! Do you always get what you go after, even with death slipping a thin wedge between? I think you're born lucky. I see the signs. If that big aster lured you into danger it saved you as well, for it was through stepping over to investigate it that I saw you. Its size and colour caught my eye. Otherwise I should have gone on and you—what would have become of you? Whom do you belong to that you are let risk your life on these dangerous banks? What is your name—if you have a name! I begin to doubt you—I see you have pointed ears. Have I been tricked into meddling with fairies, and will I discover presently that twenty years have passed and that I am an old man long since lost to the living world with nothing but the skeleton of my dog for company?"

"I am Emily Byrd Starr of New Moon," said Emily, rather coldly. She was beginning to be sensitive about her ears. Father Cassidy had remarked on them—and now Jarback Priest. Was there really something uncanny about them?

And yet there was a flavour about the said Jarback that she liked—liked decidedly. Emily never was long in doubt about any one she met. In a few minutes she always knew whether she liked, disliked, or was indifferent to them. She had a queer feeling that she had known Jarback Priest for years—perhaps because it had seemed so long when she was lying on that crumbling earth waiting for him to return. He was not handsome but she liked that lean, clever face of his with its magnetic green eyes.

"So you're the young lady visitor at the Grange!" said Dean Priest, in some astonishment. "Then my dear Aunt Nancy should look after you better—my VERY dear Aunt Nancy."

"You don't like Aunt Nancy, I see," said Emily coolly.

"What is the use of liking a lady who won't like me? You have probably discovered by this time that my Lady Aunt detests me."

"Oh, I don't think it's as bad as that," said Emily. "She must have some good opinions about you—she says you're the only Priest who will ever go to heaven."

"She doesn't mean that as a compliment, whatever you in your innocence believe it to be. And you are Douglas Starr's daughter? I knew your father. We were boys together at Queen's Academy—we drifted apart after we left it—he went into journalism, I to McGill. But he was the only friend I had at school—the only boy who would bother himself about Jarback Priest, who was lame and hunchbacked and couldn't play football or hockey. Emily Byrd Starr—Starr should be your first name. You look like a star—you have a radiant sort of personality shining through you—your proper habitat should be the evening sky just after sunset—or the morning sky just before sunrise. Yes. You'd be more at home in the morning sky. I think I shall call you Star."

"Do you mean that you think me pretty?" asked Emily directly.

"Why, it hadn't occurred to me to wonder whether you were pretty or not. Do you think a star should be pretty?"

Emily reflected.

"No," she said finally, "the word doesn't suit a star."

"I perceive you are an artist in words. Of course it doesn't. Stars are prismatic—palpitating—elusive. It is not often we find one made flesh and blood. I think I'll wait for you."

"Oh, I'm ready to go now," said Emily, standing up.

"H'm. That wasn't what I meant. Never mind. Come along, Star— if you don't mind walking a bit slowly. I'll take you back from the wilderness at least—I don't know that I'll venture to Wyther Grange to-night. I don't want Aunt Nancy to take the edge off YOU. And so you don't think me handsome?"

"I didn't say so," cried Emily.

"Not in words. But I can read your thoughts, Star—it won't ever do to think anything you don't want me to know. The gods gave me that gift—when they kept back everything else I wanted. You don't think me handsome but you think me nice. Do you think you are pretty yourself?"

"A little—since Aunt Nancy lets me wear my bang," said Emily frankly.

Jarback Priest made a grimace.

"Don't call it by such a name. It's a worse name even than bustle. Bangs and bustles—they hurt me. I like that black wave breaking on your white brows—but don't call it a bang—ever again."

"It IS a very ugly word. I never use it in my poetry, of course."

Whereby Dean Priest discovered that Emily wrote poetry. He also discovered pretty nearly everything else about her in that charming walk back to Priest Pond in the fir-scented dusk, with Tweed walking between them, his nose touching his master's hand softly every now and then, while the robins in the trees above them whistled blithely in the afterlight.

With nine out of ten people Emily was secretive and reserved, but Dean Priest was sealed of her tribe and she divined it instantly. He had a right to the inner sanctuary and she yielded it unquestioningly. She talked to him freely.

Besides, she felt ALIVE again—she felt the wonderful thrill of living again, after that dreadful space when she had seemed to hang between life and death. She felt, as she wrote to her father afterwards, "as if a little bird was singing in my heart." And oh, how good the green sod felt under her feet!

She told him all about herself and her doings and beings. Only one thing she did not tell him—her worry over Ilse's mother. THAT she could not speak of to any one. Aunt Nancy need not have been frightened that she would carry tales to New Moon.

"I wrote a whole poem yesterday when it rained and I couldn't get out," she said. "It began,

> I sit by the western window
> That looks on Malvern Bay—"

"Am I not to hear the whole of it?" asked Dean, who knew perfectly well that Emily was hoping that he would ask it.

Emily delightedly repeated the whole poem. When she came to the two lines she liked best in it,

> Perhaps in those wooded islands
> That gem the proud bay's breast—

she looked up sidewise at him to see if he admired them. But he was walking with eyes cast down and an absent expression on his face. She felt a little disappointed.

"H'm," he said when she had finished. "You're twelve, didn't you say? When you're ten years older I shouldn't wonder—but let's not think of it."

"Father Cassidy told me to keep on," cried Emily.

"There was no need of it. You WOULD keep on anyhow—you have the itch for writing born in you. It's quite incurable. What are you going to do with it?"

"I think I shall be either a great poetess or a distinguished novelist," said Emily reflectively.

"Having only to choose," remarked Dean dryly. "Better be a novelist—I hear it pays better."

"What worries me about writing novels," confided Emily, "is the love talk in them. I'm sure I'll never be able to write it. I've tried," she concluded candidly, "and I can't think of ANYTHING to say."

"Don't worry about that. I'LL teach you some day," said Dean.

"Will you—will you really?" Emily was very eager. "I'll be so obliged if you will. I THINK I could manage EVERYTHING else very nicely."

"It's a bargain then—don't forget it. And don't go looking for another teacher, mind. What do you find to do at the Grange besides writing poetry? Are you never lonesome with only those two old survivals?"

"No. I enjoy my own company," said Emily gravely.

"You would. Stars are said to dwell apart, anyhow, sufficient unto themselves—ensphered in their own light. Do you really like Aunt Nancy?"

"Yes, indeed. She is very kind to me. She doesn't make me wear sunbonnets and she lets me go barefooted in the forenoons. But I have to wear my buttoned boots in the afternoons, and I hate buttoned boots."

"Naturally. You should be shod with sandals of moonshine and wear a scarf of sea-mist with a few fireflies caught in it over your hair. Star, you don't look like your father, but you suggest him in several ways. Do you look like your mother? I never saw her."

All at once Emily smiled demurely. A real sense of humour was born in her at that moment. Never again was she to feel quite so unmixedly tragic over anything.

"No," she said, "it's only my eyelashes and smile that are like Mother's. But I've got Father's forehead, and Grandma Starr's hair and eyes, and Great-Uncle George's nose, and Aunt Nancy's hands, and Cousin Susan's elbows, and Great-great-Grandmother Murray's ankles, and Grandfather Murray's eyebrows."

Dean Priest laughed.

"A rag-bag—as we all are," he said. "But your soul is your own, and fire-new, I'll swear to that."

"Oh, I'm so glad I like you," said Emily impulsively. "It would be HATEFUL to think any one I didn't like had saved my life. I don't mind YOUR saving it a bit."

"That's good. Because you see your life belongs to me henceforth. Since I saved it it's mine. Never forget that."

Emily felt an odd sensation of rebellion. She didn't fancy the idea of her life belonging to anybody but herself—not even to anybody she liked as much as she liked Dean Priest. Dean, watching her, saw it and smiled his whimsical smile that always seemed to have so much more in it than mere smiling.

"That doesn't quite suit you? Ah, you see one pays a penalty when one reaches out for something beyond the ordinary. One pays for it in bondage of some kind or other. Take your wonderful aster home and keep it as long as you can. It has cost you your freedom."

He was laughing—he was only joking, of course—yet Emily felt as if a cobweb fetter had been flung round her. Yielding to a sudden impulse she flung the big aster on the ground and set her foot on it.

Dean Priest looked on amusedly. His strange eyes were very kindly as he met hers.

"You rare thing—you vivid thing—you starry thing! We are going to be good friends—we ARE good friends. I'm coming up to Wyther Grange to-morrow to see those descriptions you've written of Caroline and my venerable Aunt in your Jimmy-book. I feel sure they're delicious. Here's your path—don't go roaming again so far from civilization. Good-night, my Star of the Morning."

He stood at the crossroad and watched her out of sight.

"What a child!" he muttered. "I'll never forget her eyes as she lay there on the edge of death—the dauntless little soul—and I've never seen a creature who seemed so full of sheer joy in existence. She is Douglas Starr's child—HE never called me Jarback."

He stooped and picked up the broken aster. Emily's heel had met it squarely and it was badly crushed. But he put it away that night between the leaves of an old volume of *Jane Eyre*, where he had marked a verse—

All glorious rose upon my sight
That child of shower and gleam.

CHAPTER XXVII
THE VOW OF EMILY

IN Dean Priest Emily found, for the first time since her father had died, a companion who could fully sympathize. She was always at her best with him, with a delightful feeling of being understood. To love is easy and therefore common—but to UNDERSTAND—how rare it is! They roamed wonderlands of fancy together in the magic August days that followed upon Emily's adventure on the bay shore, talked together of exquisite, immortal things, and were at home with "nature's old felicities" of which Wordsworth so happily speaks.

Emily showed him all the poetry and "descriptions" in her "Jimmy-book" and he read them gravely, and, exactly as Father had done, made little criticisms that did not hurt her because she knew they were just. As for Dean Priest, a certain secret well-spring of fancy that had long seemed dry bubbled up in him sparklingly again.

"You make me believe in fairies, whether I will or no," he told her, "and that means youth. As long as you believe in fairies you can't grow old."

"But I can't believe in fairies myself," protested Emily sorrowfully. "I wish I could."

"But YOU are a fairy yourself—or you wouldn't be able to find fairyland. You can't buy a ticket there, you know. Either the fairies themselves give you your passport at your christening—or they don't. That is all there is to it."

"Isn't 'Fairyland' the LOVELIEST word?" said Emily dreamily.

"Because it means everything the human heart desires," said Dean.

When he talked to her Emily felt as if she were looking into some enchanted mirror where her own dreams and secret hopes were reflected back to her with added charm. If Dean Priest were a cynic he showed no cynicism to Emily. But in her company he was not a cynic; he had shed his years and became a boy again with a boy's untainted visions. She loved him for the world he opened to her view.

There was such fun in him, too,—such sly, surprising fun. He told her jokes—he made her laugh. He told her strange old tales of forgotten gods who were very beautiful—of court festivals and the bridals of kings. He seemed to have the history of the whole world at his fingers' ends. He described things to her in unforgettable phrases as they walked by the bay shore or sat in the overgrown, shadowy old garden of Wyther Grange. When he spoke of Athens as "the City of the Violet Crown" Emily realized afresh what magic is made when the right words are wedded; and she loved to think of Rome as "the City of the Seven Hills." Dean had been in Rome and Athens—and almost everywhere else.

"I didn't know any one ever talked as you do except in books," she told him.

Dean laughed—with a little note of bitterness that was so often present in his laughter—though less often with Emily than with other people. It was really his laughter that had won Dean his reputation for cynicism. People so often felt that he was laughing AT them instead of WITH them.

"I've had only books for companions most of my life," he said. "Is it any wonder I talk like them?"

"I'm sure I'll like studying history after this," said Emily; "except Canadian History. I'll never like IT—it's so dull. Not just at the first, when we belonged to France and there was plenty of fighting, but after that it's nothing but politics."

"The happiest countries, like the happiest women, have no history," said Dean.

"I hope I'LL have a history," cried Emily. "I want a THRILLING career."

"We all do, foolish one. Do you know what makes history? Pain— and shame—and rebellion—and bloodshed and heartache. Star, ask yourself how many hearts ached—and broke—to make those crimson and purple pages in history that you find so enthralling. I told you the story of Leonidas and his Spartans the other day. They had mothers, sisters and sweethearts. If they could have fought a bloodless battle at the polls wouldn't it have been better—if not so dramatic."

"I—can't—FEEL—that way," said Emily confusedly. She was not old enough to think or say, as she would say ten years later, "The heroes of Thermopylæ have been an inspiration to humanity for centuries. What squabble around a ballot-box will ever be that?"

"And, like all female creatures, you form your opinions by your feelings. Well, hope for your thrilling career—but remember that if there is to be drama in your life SOMEBODY must pay the piper in the coin of suffering. If not you—then some one else."

"Oh, no, I wouldn't like THAT."

"Then be content with fewer thrills. What about your tumble over the bank down there? That came near being a tragedy. What if I hadn't found you?"

"But you DID find me," cried Emily. "I like near escapes—after they're over," she added. "If everybody had always been happy there'd be nothing to read about."

Tweed made a third in their rambles and Emily grew very fond of him, without losing any of her loyalty to the pussy folk.

"I like cats with one part of my mind and dogs with another part," she said.

"I like cats but I never keep one," Dean said. "They're too exacting—they ask too much. Dogs want only love but cats demand worship. They have never got over the Bubastis habit of godship."

Emily understood this—he had told her all about old Egypt and the goddess Pasht—but she did not quite agree with him.

"Kittens don't want to be worshipped," she said. "They just want to be cuddled."

"By their priestesses—yes. If you had been born on the banks of the Nile five thousand years ago, Emily, you would have been a priestess of Pasht—an adorable, slim, brown creature with a fillet of gold around your black hair and bands of silver on those ankles Aunt Nancy admires, with dozens of sacred little godlings frisking around you under the palms of the temple courts."

"Oh," gasped Emily rapturously, "that gave me THE FLASH. And," she added wonderingly, "just for a moment it made me HOMESICK, too. Why?"

"Why? Because I haven't a doubt you WERE just such a priestess in a former incarnation and my words reminded your soul of it. Do you believe in the doctrine of the transmigration of souls, Star? But of course not—brought up by the true-blue Calvinists of New Moon."

"What does it mean?" asked Emily, and when Dean explained it to her she thought it a very delightful belief but was quite sure Aunt Elizabeth would not approve of it.

"So I won't believe it—yet," she said gravely.

Then it all came to an end quite suddenly. It had been taken for granted by all concerned that Emily was to stay at Wyther Grange until the end of August. But in mid-August Aunt Nancy said suddenly to her one day,

"Go home, Emily. I'm tired of you. I like you very well—you're not stupid and you're passably pretty and you've behaved exceedingly well—tell Elizabeth you do the Murrays credit—but I'm tired of you. Go home."

Emily's feelings were mixed. It hurt her to be told Aunt Nancy was tired of her—it would hurt any one. It rankled in her for several days until she thought of a sharp answer she might have made Aunt Nancy and wrote it down in her Jimmy-book. She felt quite as relieved then as if she had really said it.

And she was sorry to leave Wyther Grange; she had grown to love the old beautiful house, with its flavour of hidden secrets—a flavour that was wholly a trick of its architecture, for there had never been anything in it but the simple tale of births and deaths and marriages and everyday living that most houses have. She was sorry to leave the bay shore and the quaint garden and the gazing-ball and the chessy-cat and the Pink Room bed of freedom; and most of all she was sorry to leave Dean Priest. But on the other hand it was delightful to think of going back to New Moon and all the loved ones there—Teddy and his dear whistle, Ilse and her stimulating comradeship, Perry with his determined reaching up for higher things, Saucy Sal and the new kitten that must be needing proper training now, and the fairy world of the *Midsummer Night's Dream*. Cousin Jimmy's garden would be in its prime of splendour, the August apples would be ripe. Suddenly, Emily was very ready to go. She packed her little black box jubilantly and found it an excellent chance to work in neatly a certain line from a poem Dean had recently read to her which had captured her fancy.

"'Good-bye, proud world, I'm going home,'" she declaimed feelingly, standing at the top of the long, dark, shining staircase and apostrophizing the row of grim Priest photographs hanging on the wall.

But she was much annoyed over one thing. Aunt Nancy would not give her back the picture Teddy had painted.

"I'm going to keep it," Aunt Nancy said, grinning and shaking her gold tassels. "Some day that picture will be worth something as the early effort of a famous artist."

"I only lent it to you—I told you I only lent it to you," said Emily indignantly.

"I'm an unscrupulous old demon," said Aunt Nancy coolly. "That is what the Priests all call me behind my back. Don't they, Caroline? May as well have the game as the name. I happen to have a fancy for that picture, that's all. I'm going to frame it and hang it here in my parlour. But I'll leave it to you in my will—that and the chessy-cat and the gazing-ball and my gold earrings. Nothing else—I'm not going to leave you a cent of my money—never count on that."

"I don't want it," said Emily loftily. "I'm going to earn heaps of money for myself. But it isn't fair of you to keep my picture. It was given to me."

"I never was fair," said Aunt Nancy. "Was I, Caroline?"

"No," said Caroline shrewishly.

"You see. Now don't make a fuss, Emily. You've been a very good child but I feel that I've done my duty by you for this year. Go back to New Moon and when Elizabeth won't let you do things tell her I always let you. I don't know if it will do any good but try it. Elizabeth, like every one else related to me, is always wondering what I'm going to do with my money."

Cousin Jimmy came over for Emily. How glad she was to see his kind face with its gentle, elfish eyes and forked beard again! But she felt very badly when she turned to Dean.

"If you like I'll kiss you good-bye," she said chokily.

Emily did not like kissing people. She did not really want to kiss Dean but she liked him so much she thought she ought to extend all the courtesies to him.

Dean looked down smiling into her face, so young, so pure, so softly curved.

"No, I don't want you to kiss me—yet. And our first kiss mustn't have the flavour of good-bye. It would be a bad omen. Star O' Morning, I'm sorry you're going. But I'll see you again before long. My oldest sister lives in Blair Water, you know, and I feel a sudden access of brotherly affection towards her. I seem to see myself visiting her very often henceforth. In the meantime remember you have promised to write me every week. And I'll write you."

"Nice fat letters," coaxed Emily. "I love fat letters."

"Fat! They'll be positively corpulent, Star. Now, I'm not even going to SAY good-bye. Let's make a pact, Star. We'll never SAY good-bye to each other. We'll just smile and go."

Emily made a gallant effort—smiled—and went. Aunt Nancy and Caroline returned to the back parlour and their cribbage. Dean Priest whistled for Tweed and went to the bay shore. He was so lonely that he laughed at himself.

Emily and Cousin Jimmy had so much to talk of that the drive home seemed very short.

New Moon was white in the evening sunshine which also lay with exceeding mellowness on the grey old barns. The Three Princesses, shooting up against the silvery sky, were as remote and princessly as ever. The old gulf was singing away down over the fields.

Aunt Laura came running out to meet them, her lovely blue eyes shining with pleasure. Aunt Elizabeth was in the cook-house preparing supper and only shook hands with Emily, but looked a trifle less grim and stately than usual, and she had made Emily's favourite cream-puffs for supper. Perry was hanging about, barefooted and sunburned, to tell her all the gossip of kittens and calves and little pigs and the new foal. Ilse came swooping over, and Emily discovered she had forgotten how vivid Ilse was—how brilliant her amber eyes, how golden her mane of spun-silk hair, looking more golden than ever under the bright blue silk tam Mrs. Simms had bought her in Shrewsbury. As an article of dress, that loud tam made Laura Murray's eyes and sensibilities ache, but its colour certainly did set off Ilse's wonderful hair. She engulfed Emily in a rapturous embrace and quarrelled bitterly with her ten minutes later over the fact that Emily refused to give her Saucy Sal's sole surviving kitten.

"I ought to have it, you doddering hyena," stormed Ilse. "It's as much mine as yours, pig! Our old barn cat is its father."

"Such talk is not decent," said Aunt Elizabeth, pale with horror. "And if you two children are going to quarrel over that kitten I'll have it drowned—remember that."

Ilse was finally appeased by Emily's offering to let her name the kitten and have a half interest in it. Ilse named it Daffodil. Emily did not think this suitable, since, from the fact of Cousin Jimmy referring to it as Little Tommy, she suspected it was of the sterner sex. But rather than again provoke Aunt Elizabeth's wrath by discussing tabooed subjects, she agreed.

"I can call it Daff," she thought. "That sounds more MASCULINE."

The kitten was a delicate bit of striped greyness that reminded Emily of her dear lost Mikes. And it smelled so nice—of warmth and clean furriness, with whiffs of the clover hay where Saucy Sal had made her mother-nest.

After supper she heard Teddy's whistle in the old orchard—the same enchanting call. Emily flew out to greet him—after all, there was nobody just like Teddy in the world. They had an ecstatic scamper up to the Tansy Patch to see a new puppy that Dr. Burnley had given Teddy. Mrs. Kent did not seem very glad to see Emily—she was colder and more remote than ever, and she sat and watched the two children playing with the chubby little pup with a smouldering fire in her dark eyes that made Emily vaguely uncomfortable whenever she happened to glance up and encounter it. Never before had she sensed Mrs. Kent's dislike for her so keenly as that night.

"Why doesn't your mother like me?" she asked Teddy bluntly, when they carried little Leo to the barn for the night.

"Because I do," said Teddy briefly. "She doesn't like ANYTHING I like. I'm afraid she'll poison Leo very soon. I—I wish she wasn't so fond of me," he burst out, in the beginning of a revolt against this abnormal jealousy of love, which he felt rather than understood to be a fetter that was becoming galling. "She says she won't let me take up Latin and Algebra this year—you know Miss Brownell said I might—because I'm not to go to college. She says she can't bear to part from me—ever. I don't care about the Latin and stuff—but I want to learn to be an artist—I want to go away some day to the schools where they teach that. She won't let me—she hates my pictures now because she thinks I like them better than her. I DON'T—I love Mother—she's awful sweet and good to me every other way. But she thinks I do—and she's burned some of them. I know she has. They're missing from the barn wall and I can't find them anywhere. If she does anything to Leo—I'll—I'll HATE her."

"Tell her that," said Emily coolly, with some of the Murray shrewdness coming uppermost in her. "She doesn't know that YOU know she poisoned Smoke and Buttercup. Tell her you do know it and that if she does anything to Leo you won't love her any more. She'll be so frightened of your NOT loving her that she won't meddle with Leo—I KNOW. Tell her gently—don't hurt her feelings—but TELL her. It will," concluded Emily, with a killing imitation of Aunt Elizabeth delivering an ultimatum, "be better for all concerned."

"I believe I will," said Teddy, much impressed. "I CAN'T have Leo disappear like my cats did—he's the only dog I've ever had and I've always wanted a dog. Oh, Emily, I'm glad you're back!"

It was very nice to be told this—especially by Teddy. Emily went home to New Moon happily. In the old kitchen the candles were lighted and their flames were dancing in the winds of the August night blowing through door and window.

"I suppose you'll not like candles very well, Emily, after being used to lamps at Wyther Grange," said Aunt Laura with a little sigh. It was one of the bitter, small things in Laura Murray's life that Elizabeth's tyranny extended to candles.

Emily looked around her thoughtfully. One candle sputtered and bobbed at her as if greeting her. One, with a long wick, glowed and smouldered like a sulky little demon. One had a tiny flame—a sly, meditative candle. One swayed with a queer fiery grace in the draught from the door. One burned with a steady upright flame like a faithful soul.

"I—don't know—Aunt Laura," she answered slowly. "You can be—friends—with candles. I believe I like the candles best after all."

Aunt Elizabeth, coming in from the cook-house, heard her. Something like pleasure gleamed in her gulf-blue eyes.

"You have some sense in you," she said.

"That's the second compliment she has paid me," thought Emily.

"I think Emily has grown taller since she went to Wyther Grange," Aunt Laura said, looking at her rather wistfully.

Aunt Elizabeth, snuffing the candles, glanced sharply over her glasses.

"I can't see it," she said. "Her dress is just the same length on her."

"I'm sure she has," persisted Laura.

Cousin Jimmy, to settle the dispute, measured Emily by the sitting-room door. She just touched the former mark.

"You see," said Aunt Elizabeth triumphantly, liking to be right even in this small matter.

"She looks—different," said Laura with a sigh.

Laura, after all, was right. Emily HAD grown, taller and older, in soul, if not in body. It was this change which Laura felt, as close and tender affection swiftly feels. The Emily who returned from Wyther Grange was not the Emily who had gone there. She was no longer wholly the child. Aunt Nancy's family histories over which she had pondered, her enduring anguish over the story of Ilse's mother, that terrible hour when she had lain cheek by jowl with death on the cliffs of the bay shore, her association with Dean Priest, all had combined to mature her intelligence and her emotions. When she went to the garret next morning and pulled out her precious little bundle of manuscripts to read them lovingly over she was amazed and rather grieved to find that they were not half so good as she had believed they were. Some of them were positively silly, she thought; she was ashamed of them—so ashamed that she smuggled them down to the cook-house stove and burned them, much to Aunt Elizabeth's annoyance when she came to prepare dinner and found the fire-box all choked up with charred paper.

Emily no longer wondered that Miss Brownell had made fun of them—though this did not mellow her bitterness of remembrance in regard to that lady in any degree. The rest she put back on the sofa shelf, including "The Child of the Sea," which still impressed her as fairly good, though not just the wonderful composition she had once deemed it. She felt that many passages could be re-written to their advantage. Then she immediately began writing a new poem, "On Returning Home After Weeks' Absence." As everything and everybody connected with New Moon had to be mentioned in this poem it promised to be quite long and to furnish agreeable occupation for spare minutes in many weeks to come. It was very good to be home again.

"There is no place just like dear New Moon," thought Emily.

One thing that marked her return—one of those little household "epochs" that make a keener impression on the memory and imagination than perhaps their real importance warrants—was the fact that she was given a room of her own. Aunt Elizabeth had found her unshared slumber too sweet a thing to be again surrendered. She decided that she could not put up any longer with a squirming bedfellow who asked unearthly questions at any hour of the night she took it into her head to do so.

So, after a long conference with Laura, it was settled that Emily was to have her mother's room—the "lookout" as it was called, though it was not really a lookout. But it occupied the place in New Moon, looking over the front door to the garden, that the real lookouts did in other Blair Water houses, so it went by that name. It had been prepared for Emily's occupancy in her absence and when bedtime came on the first evening of her return Aunt Elizabeth curtly told her that henceforth she was to have her mother's room.

"All to myself?" exclaimed Emily.

"Yes. We will expect you to take care of it yourself and keep it very tidy."

"It has never been slept in since the night before your mother—went away," said Aunt Laura, with a queer sound in her voice—a sound of which Aunt Elizabeth disapproved.

"Your mother," she said, looking coldly at Emily over the flame of the candle—an attitude that gave a rather gruesome effect to her acquiline features—"RAN away—flouted her family and broke her father's heart. She was a silly, ungrateful, disobedient girl. I hope YOU will never disgrace your family by such conduct."

"Oh, Aunt Elizabeth," said Emily breathlessly, "when you hold the candle down like that it makes your face look just like a corpse! Oh, it's so interesting."

Aunt Elizabeth turned and led the way upstairs in grim silence. There was no use in wasting perfectly good admonitions on a child like this.

Left alone in her lookout, lighted dimly by the one small candle, Emily gazed about her with keen and thrilling interest. She could not get into bed until she had explored every bit of it. The room was very old-fashioned, like all the New Moon rooms. The walls were papered with a design of slender gilt diamonds enclosing golden stars and hung with worked woollen mottoes and pictures that had been "supplements" in the girlhood of her aunts. One of them, hanging over the head of the bed, represented two guardian angels. In its day this had been much admired but Emily looked at it with distaste.

"I don't like feather wings on angels," she said decidedly. "Angels should have rainbowy wings."

On the floor was a pretty homespun carpet and round braided rugs. There was a high black bedstead with carved posts, a fat feather-bed, and an Irish chain quilt, but, as Emily was glad to see, no curtains. A little table, with funny claw-feet and brass-knobbed drawers, stood by the window, which was curtained with muslin frills; one of the window-panes contorted the landscape funnily, making a hill where no hill was. Emily liked this—she couldn't have told why, but it was really because it gave the pane an individuality of its own. An oval mirror in a tarnished gilt frame hung above the table; Emily was delighted to find she could see herself in it—"all but my boots"—without craning or tipping it. "And it doesn't twist my face or turn my complexion green," she thought happily. Two high-backed, black chairs with horsehair seats, a little washstand with a blue basin and pitcher, and a faded ottoman with woollen roses cross-stitched on it, completed the furnishing. On the little mantel were vases full of dried and coloured grasses and a fascinating pot-bellied bottle filled with West Indian shells. On either side were lovable little cupboards with leaded-glass doors like those in the sitting-room. Underneath was a small fireplace.

"I wonder if Aunt Elizabeth will ever let me have a little fire here," thought Emily.

The room was full of that indefinable charm found in all rooms where the pieces of furniture, whether old or new, are well acquainted with each other and the walls and floors are on good terms. Emily felt it all over her as she flitted about examining everything. This was her room—she loved it already—she felt perfectly at home.

"I belong here," she breathed happily.

She felt deliciously NEAR to her mother—as if Juliet Starr had suddenly become real to her. It thrilled her to think that her mother had probably crocheted the lace cover on the round pincushion on the table. And that fat, black jar of pot-pourri on the mantel—her mother must have compounded it. When Emily lifted the lid a faint spicy odour floated out. The souls of all the roses that had bloomed through many olden summers at New Moon seemed to be prisoned there in a sort of flower purgatory. Something in the haunting, mystical, elusive odour gave Emily THE FLASH—and her room had received its consecration.

There was a picture of her mother hanging over the mantel—a large daguerreotype taken when she was a little girl. Emily looked at it lovingly. She had the picture of her mother which her father had left, taken after their marriage. But when Aunt Elizabeth had brought that from Maywood to New Moon she had hung it in the parlour where Emily seldom saw it. This picture, in her bedroom, of the golden-haired, rose-cheeked girl, was all her own. She could look at it—talk to it at will.

"Oh, Mother," she said, "what did you think of when you were a little girl here like me? I wish I could have known you THEN. And to think nobody has ever slept here since that last night you did before you ran away with Father. Aunt Elizabeth says you were wicked to do it but I don't think you were. It wasn't as if you were running away with a STRANGER. Anyway, I'm glad you DID, because if you hadn't there wouldn't have been any ME."

Emily, very glad that there was an Emily, opened her lookout window as high as it would go, got into bed and drifted off to sleep, feeling a happiness that was so deep as to be almost pain as she listened to the sonorous sweep of the night wind among the great trees in Lofty John's bush. When she wrote to her father a few days later she began the letter "Dear Father and Mother."

"And I'll always write the letter to YOU as well as Father after this, Mother. I'm sorry I left you out so long. But you didn't seem REAL till that night I came home. I made the bed beautifully next morning—

Aunt Elizabeth didn't find a bit of fault with it—and I dusted EVERYTHING—and when I went out I knelt down and kissed the doorstep. I didn't think Aunt Elizabeth saw me but she did and said had I gone crazy. Why does Aunt Elizabeth think any one is crazy who does something she never does? I said 'No, it's only because I love my room so much' and she sniffed and said 'You'd better love your God.' But so I do, dear Father—and Mother—and I love Him better than ever since I have my dear room. I can see all over the garden from it and into Lofty John's bush and one little bit of the Blair Water through the gap in the trees where the Yesterday Road runs. I like to go to bed early now. I love to lie all alone in my own room and make poetry and think out descriptions of things while I look through the open window at the stars and the nice, big, kind, quiet trees in Lofty John's bush.

"Oh, Father dear and Mother, we are going to have a new teacher. Miss Brownell is not coming back. She is going to be married and Ilse says that when her father heard it he said 'God help the man.' And the new teacher is a Mr. Carpenter. Ilse saw him when he came to see her father about the school—because Dr. Burnley is a trustee this year—and she says he has bushy grey hair and whiskers. He is married, too, and is going to live in that little old house down in the hollow below the school. It seems so funny to think of a teacher having a wife and whiskers.

"I am glad to be home. But I miss Dean and the gazing-ball. Aunt Elizabeth looked very cross when she saw my bang but didn't say anything. Aunt Laura says just to keep quiet and go on wearing it. But I don't feel comfortable going against Aunt Elizabeth so I have combed it all back except a LITTLE fringe. I don't feel QUITE comfortable about it even yet, but I have to put up with being a little uncomfortable for the sake of my looks. Aunt Laura says bustles are going out of style so I'll never be able to have one but I don't care because I think they're ugly. Rhoda Stuart will be cross because she was just longing to be old enough to wear a bustle. I hope I'll be able to have a gin-jar all to myself when the weather gets cold. There is a row of gin-jars on the high shelf in the cook-house.

"Teddy and I had the nicest ADVENTURE yesterday evening. We are going to keep it a secret from everybody—partly because it was so nice, and partly because we think we'd get a fearful scolding for one thing we did.

"We went up to the Disappointed House, and we found one of the boards on the windows loose. So we pried it off and crawled in and went all over the house. It is lathed but not plastered, and the shavings are lying all over the floors just as the carpenters left them years ago. It seemed more disappointed than ever. I just felt like crying. There was a dear little fireplace in one room so we went to work and kindled a fire in it with shavings and pieces of boards (this is the thing we would be scolded for, likely) and then sat before it on an old carpenter's bench and talked. We decided that when we grew up we would buy the Disappointed House and live here together. Teddy said he supposed we'd have to get married, but I thought maybe we could find a way to manage without going to all that bother. Teddy will paint pictures and I will write poetry and we will have toast and bacon and marmalade EVERY MORNING for breakfast—just like Wyther Grange—but NEVER porridge. And we'll always have lots of nice things to eat in the pantry and I'll make lots of jam and Teddy is always going to help me wash the dishes and we'll hang the gazing-ball from the middle of the ceiling in the fireplace room—because likely Aunt Nancy will be dead by then.

"When the fire burned out we jammed the board into place in the window and came away. Every now and then to-day Teddy would say to me "Toast and bacon and marmalade" in the MOST MYSTERIOUS tones and Ilse and Perry are wild because they can't find out what he means.

"Cousin Jimmy has got Jimmy Joe Belle to help with the harvest. Jimmy Joe Belle comes from over Derry Pond way. There are a great many French there and when a French girl marries they call her mostly by her husband's first name instead of Mrs. like the English do. If a girl named Mary marries a man named Leon she will always be called Mary Leon after that. But in Jimmy Joe Belle's case, it is the other way and he is called by his wife's name. I asked Cousin Jimmy why, and he said it was because Jimmy Joe was a poor stick of a creature and Belle wore the britches. But still I don't understand. Jimmy Joe wears britches himself—that means trousers—and why should he be called Jimmy Joe Belle instead of her being called Belle Jimmy Joe just because she wears them too! I won't rest till I find out.

"Cousin Jimmy's garden is splendid now. The tiger lilies are out. I am trying to love them because nobody seems to like them at all but deep down in my heart I know I love the late roses best. You just can't help loving the roses best.

"Ilse and I hunted all over the old orchard to-day for a four-leaved clover and couldn't find one. Then I found one in a clump of clover by the dairy steps to-night when I was straining the milk and never thinking of clovers. Cousin Jimmy says that is the way luck always comes, and it is no use to look for it.

"It is lovely to be with Ilse again. We have only fought twice since I came home. I am going to try not to fight with Ilse any more because I don't think it is dignified, although quite interesting. But it is hard not to because even when I keep quiet and don't say a word Ilse thinks that's a way of fighting and gets madder and says worse things than ever. Aunt Elizabeth says it always takes two to make a quarrel but she doesn't know Ilse as I do. Ilse called me a sneaking albatross to-day. I wonder how many animals are left to call me. She never repeats the same one twice. I wish she wouldn't clapper-claw Perry so much. (Clapper-claw is a word I learned from Aunt Nancy. Very striking, I think.) It seems as if she couldn't bear him. He dared Teddy to jump from the henhouse roof across to the pighouse roof. Teddy wouldn't. He said he would try it if it had to be done or would do anybody any good but he wasn't going to do it just to show off. Perry did it and landed safe. If he hadn't he might have broken his neck. Then he bragged about it and said Teddy was afraid and Ilse turned red as a beet and told him to shut up or she would bite his snout off. She can't bear to have anything said against Teddy, but I guess he can take care of himself.

"Ilse can't study for the Entrance either. Her father won't let her. But she says she doesn't care. She says she's going to run away when she gets a little older and study for the stage. That sounds wicked, but interesting.

"I felt very queer and guilty when I saw Ilse first, because I knew about her mother. I don't know why I felt guilty because I had nothing to do with it. The feeling is wearing away a little now but I am so unhappy by spells over it. I wish I could either forget it altogether or find out the rights of it. Because I am sure nobody knows them.

"I had a letter from Dean to-day. He writes lovely letters—just as if I was grown up. He sent me a little poem he had cut out of a paper called *The Fringed Gentian*. He said it made him think of me. It is all lovely but I like the last verse best of all. This is it:

> Then whisper, blossom, in thy sleep
> How I may upward climb
> The Alpine Path, so hard, so steep,

That leads to heights sublime.
How I may reach that far-off goal
Of true and honored fame
And write upon its shining scroll
A woman's humble name.

"When I read that THE FLASH came, and I took a sheet of paper—I forgot to tell you Cousin Jimmy gave me a little box of paper and envelopes—ON THE SLY—and I wrote on it:

I, Emily Byrd Starr, do solemnly vow this day that I will climb the Alpine Path and write my name on the scroll of fame.

"Then I put it in the envelope and sealed it up and wrote on it THE VOW OF EMILY BYRD STARR, AGED 12 YEARS AND 3 MONTHS, and put it away on the sofa shelf in the garret.

"I am writing a murder story now and I am trying to feel how a man would feel who was a murderer. It is creepy, but thrilling. I almost feel as if I HAD murdered somebody.

"Good night, dear Father and Mother.

"Your lovingest daughter,

"EMILY.

"P. S. I have been wondering how I'll sign my name when I grow up and print my pieces. I don't know which would be best—Emily Byrd Starr in full or Emily B. Starr, or E. B. Starr, or E. Byrd Starr. Sometimes I think I'll have a *nom-de-plume*—that is, another name you pick for yourself. It's in my dictionary among the "French phrases" at the back. If I did that then I could hear people talking of my pieces right before me, never suspecting, and say just what they really thought of them. That would be interesting but perhaps not always comfortable. I think I'll be,

"E. BYRD STARR."

CHAPTER XXVIII
A WEAVER OF DREAMS

IT took Emily several weeks to make up her mind whether she liked Mr. Carpenter or not. She knew she did not DISlike him, not even though his first greeting, shot at her on the opening day of school in a gruff voice, accompanied by a startling lift of his spiky grey brows was, "So you're the girl that writes poetry, eh? Better stick to your needle and duster. Too many fools in the world trying to write poetry and failing. I tried it myself once. Got better sense now."

"You don't keep your nails clean," thought Emily.

But he upset every kind of school tradition so speedily and thoroughly that Ilse, who gloried in upsetting things and hated routine, was the only scholar that liked him from the start. Some never liked him—the Rhoda Stuart type for example—but most of them came to it after they got used to never being used to anything. And Emily finally decided that she liked him tremendously.

Mr. Carpenter was somewhere between forty and fifty—a tall man, with an upstanding shock of bushy grey hair, bristling grey moustache and eyebrows, a truculent beard, bright blue eyes out of which all his wild life had not yet burned the fire, and a long, lean, greyish face, deeply lined. He lived in a little two-roomed house below the school with a shy mouse of a wife. He never talked of his past or offered any explanation of the fact that at his age he had no better profession than teaching a district school for a pittance of salary, but the truth leaked out after a while; for Prince Edward Island is a small province and everybody in it knows something about everybody else. So eventually Blair Water people, and even the school children, understood that Mr. Carpenter had been a brilliant student in his youth and had had his eye on the ministry. But at college he had got in with a "fast set"—Blair Water people nodded heads slowly and whispered the dreadful phrase portentously—and the fast set had ruined him. He "took to drink" and went to the dogs generally. And the upshot of it all was that Francis Carpenter, who had led his class in his first and second years at McGill, and for whom his teachers had predicted a great career, was a country school-teacher at forty-five with no prospect of ever being anything else. Perhaps he was resigned to it—perhaps not. Nobody ever knew, not even the brown mouse of a wife. Nobody in Blair Water cared—he was a good teacher, and that was all that mattered. Even if he did go on occasional "sprees" he always took Saturday for them and was sober enough by Monday. Sober, and especially dignified, wearing a rusty black frock coat which he never put on any other day of the week. He did not invite pity and he did not pose as a tragedy. But sometimes, when Emily looked at his face, bent over the arithmetic problems of Blair Water School, she felt horribly sorry for him without in the least understanding why.

He had an explosive temper which generally burst into flame at least once a day, and then he would storm about wildly for a few minutes, tugging at his beard, imploring heaven to grant him patience, abusing everybody in general and the luckless object of his wrath in particular. But these tempers never lasted long. In a few minutes Mr. Carpenter would be smiling as graciously as a sun bursting through a storm-cloud on the very pupil he had been rating. Nobody seemed to cherish any grudge because of his scoldings. He never said any of the biting things Miss Brownell was wont to say, which rankled and festered for weeks; his hail of words fell alike on just and unjust and rolled off harmlessly.

He could take a joke on himself in perfect good nature. "Do you hear me? Do you hear me, sirrah?" he bellowed to Perry Miller one day. "Of course I hear you," retorted Perry coolly, "they could hear you in Charlottetown." Mr. Carpenter stared for a moment, then broke into a great, jolly laugh.

His methods of teaching were so different from Miss Brownell's that the Blair Water pupils at first felt as if he had stood them on their heads. Miss Brownell had been a martinet for order. Mr. Carpenter never tried to keep order apparently. But somehow he kept the children so busy that they had no time to do mischief. He taught history tempestuously for a month, making his pupils play the different characters and enact the incidents. He never bothered any one to learn dates—but the dates stuck in the memory just the same. If, as Mary Queen of Scots, you were beheaded by the school axe, kneeling blindfolded at the doorstep, with Perry Miller, wearing a mask made out of a piece of Aunt Laura's old black silk, for executioner, wondering what would happen if he brought the axe down TOO hard, you did not forget the year it happened; and if you fought the battle of Waterloo all over the school playground, and heard Teddy Kent shouting, "Up, Guards and at 'em!" as he led the last furious charge you remembered 1815 without half trying to.

Next month history would be thrust aside altogether and geography would take its place, when school and playground were mapped out into countries and you dressed up as the animals inhabiting them or traded in various commodities over their rivers and cities. When Rhoda Stuart had cheated you in a bargain in hides, you remembered that she had bought the cargo from the Argentine Republic, and when Perry Miller would not drink any water for a whole hot summer day because he was crossing the Arabian Desert with a caravan of camels and could not find an oasis, and then drank so much that he took terrible cramps and Aunt Laura had to be up all night with him—you did not forget where the said desert was. The trustees were quite scandalized over some of the goings on and felt sure that the children were having too good a time to be really learning anything.

If you wanted to learn Latin and French you had to do it by talking your exercises, not writing them, and on Friday afternoons all lessons were put aside and Mr. Carpenter made the children recite poems, make speeches and declaim passages from Shakespeare and the Bible. This was the day Ilse loved. Mr. Carpenter pounced on her gift like a starving dog on a bone and drilled her without mercy. They had endless fights and Ilse stamped her foot and called him names while the other pupils wondered why she was not punished for it but at last had to give in and do as he willed. Ilse went to school regularly—something she had never done before. Mr. Carpenter had told her that if she were absent for a day without good excuse she could take no part in the Friday "exercises" and this would have killed her.

One day Mr. Carpenter had picked up Teddy's slate and found a sketch of himself on it, in one of his favourite if not exactly beautiful attitudes. Teddy had labelled it "The Black Death"—half of the pupils of the school having died that day of the Great Plague, and having been carried out on stretchers to the Potter's Field by the terrified survivors.

Teddy expected a roar of denunciation, for the day before Garrett Marshall had been ground into figurative pulp on being discovered with the picture of a harmless cow on his slate—at least, Garrett said he meant it for a cow. But now this amazing Mr. Carpenter only drew his beetling brows together, looked earnestly at Teddy's slate, put it down on the desk, looked at Teddy, and said,

"I don't know anything about drawing—I can't help you, but, by gad, I think hereafter you'd better give up those extra arithmetic problems in the afternoon and draw pictures."

Whereupon Garrett Marshall went home and told his father that "old Carpenter" wasn't fair and "made favourites" over Teddy Kent.

Mr. Carpenter went up to the Tansy Patch that evening and saw the sketches in Teddy's old barn-loft studio. Then he went into the house and talked to Mrs. Kent. What he said and what she said nobody ever knew. But Mr. Carpenter went away looking grim, as if he had met an unexpected match. He took great pains with Teddy's general school work after that and procured from somewhere certain elementary text books on drawing which he gave him, telling him not to take them home—a caution Teddy did not require. He knew quite well that if he did they would disappear as mysteriously as his cats had done. He had taken Emily's advice and told his mother he would not love HER if anything happened to Leo, and Leo flourished and waxed fat and doggy. But Teddy was too gentle at heart and too fond of his mother to make such a threat more than once. He knew she had cried all that night after Mr. Carpenter had been there, and prayed on her knees in her little bedroom most of the next day, and looked at him with bitter, haunting eyes for a week. He wished she were more like other fellows' mothers but they loved each other very much and had dear hours together in the little grey house on the tansy hill. It was only when other people were about that Mrs. Kent was queer and jealous.

"She's always lovely when we're alone," Teddy had told Emily.

As for the other boys, Perry Miller was the only one Mr. Carpenter bothered much with in the way of speeches—and he was as merciless with him as with Ilse. Perry worked hard to please him and practiced his speeches in barn and field—and even by nights in the kitchen loft—until Aunt Elizabeth put a stop to THAT. Emily could not understand why Mr. Carpenter would smile amiably and say, "Very good" when Neddy Gray rattled off a speech glibly, without any expression whatever, and then rage at Perry and denounce him as a dunce and a nincompoop, by gad, because he had failed to give just the proper emphasis on a certain word, or had timed his gesture a fraction of a second too soon.

Neither could she understand why he made red pencil corrections all over her compositions and rated her for split infinitives and too lavish adjectives and strode up and down the aisle and hurled objurgations at her because she didn't know "a good place to stop when she saw it, by gad," and then told Rhoda Stuart and Nan Lee that their compositions were very pretty and gave them back without so much as a mark on them. Yet, in spite of it all, she liked him more and more as time went on and autumn passed and winter came with its beautiful bare-limbed trees, and soft pearl-grey skies that were slashed with rifts of gold in the afternoons, and cleared to a jewelled pageantry of stars over the wide white hills and valleys around New Moon.

Emily shot up so that winter that Aunt Laura had to let down the tucks in her dresses. Aunt Ruth, who had come for a week's visit, said she was outgrowing her strength—consumptive children always did.

"I am NOT consumptive," Emily said. "The Starrs are tall," she added, with a touch of subtle malice hardly to be looked for in near-thirteen.

Aunt Ruth, who was sensitive in regard to her dumpiness, sniffed.

"It would be well if THAT were the only thing in which you resemble them," she said. "How are you getting on in school?"

"Very well. I am the smartest scholar in my class," answered Emily composedly.

"You conceited child!" said Aunt Ruth.

"I'm NOT conceited." Emily looked scornful indignation. "Mr. Carpenter said it and HE doesn't flatter. Besides, I can't help seeing it myself."

"Well, it is to be hoped you have some brains, because you haven't much in the way of looks," said Aunt Ruth. "You've no complexion to speak of—and that inky hair around your white face is startling. I see you're going to be a plain girl."

"You wouldn't say that to a grown-up person's face," said Emily with a deliberate gravity which always exasperated Aunt Ruth because she could not understand it in a child. "I don't think it would hurt you to be as polite to me as you are to other people."

"I'm telling you your faults so you may correct them," said Aunt Ruth frigidly.

"It ISN'T my fault that my face is pale and my hair black," protested Emily. "I can't correct that."

"If you were a different girl," said Aunt Ruth, "I would—"

"But I don't WANT to be a different girl," said Emily decidedly. She had no intention of lowering the Starr flag to Aunt Ruth. "I wouldn't want to be anybody but myself even if I am plain. Besides," she added impressively as she turned to go out of the room, "though I may not be very good-looking now, when I go to heaven I believe I'll be very beautiful."

"Some people think Emily quite pretty," said Aunt Laura, but she did not say it until Emily was out of hearing. She was Murray enough for that.

"I don't know where they see it," said Aunt Ruth. "She's vain and pert and says things to be thought smart. You heard her just now. But the thing I dislike most in her is that she is un-childlike—and deep as the sea. Yes, she is, Laura—deep as the sea. You'll find it out to your cost one day if you disregard my warning. She's capable of anything. Sly is no word for it. You and Elizabeth don't keep a tight enough rein over her."

"I've done my best," said Elizabeth stiffly. She herself did think she had been much too lenient with Emily—Laura and Jimmy were two to one—but it nettled her to have Ruth say so.

Uncle Wallace also had an attack of worrying over Emily that winter.

He looked at her one day when he was at New Moon and remarked that she was getting to be a big girl.

"How old are you, Emily?" He asked her that every time he came to New Moon.

"Thirteen in May."

"H'm. What are you going to do with her, Elizabeth?"

"I don't know what you mean," said Aunt Elizabeth coldly—or as coldly as is possible to speak when one is pouring melted tallow into candle-moulds.

"Why, she'll soon be grown up. She can't expect you to provide for her indefinitely"—

"I don't," Emily whispered resentfully under her breath.

"—and it's time we decided what is best to be done for her."

"The Murray women have never had to work out for a living," said Aunt Elizabeth, as if that disposed of the matter.

"Emily is only half Murray," said Wallace. "Besides, times are changing. You and Laura will not live forever, Elizabeth, and when you are gone New Moon goes to Oliver's Andrew. In my opinion Emily should be fitted to support herself if necessary."

Emily did not like Uncle Wallace but she was very grateful to him at that moment. Whatever his motives were he was proposing the very thing she secretly yearned for.

"I would suggest," said Uncle Wallace, "that she be sent to Queen's Academy to get a teacher's license. Teaching is a genteel, lady-like occupation. I will do my share in providing for the expense of it."

A blind person might have seen that Uncle Wallace thought this very splendid of himself.

"If you do," thought Emily, "I'll pay every cent back to you as soon as I'm able to earn it."

But Aunt Elizabeth was adamant.

"I do not believe in girls going out into the world," she said. "I don't mean Emily to go to Queen's. I told Mr. Carpenter so when he came to see me about her taking up the Entrance work. He was very rude—school-teachers knew their place better in my father's time. But I made him understand, I think. I'm rather surprised at YOU, Wallace. You did not send your own daughter out to work."

"MY daughter had parents to provide for her," retorted Uncle Wallace pompously. "Emily is an orphan. I imagined from what I had heard about her that she would prefer earning her own living to living on charity."

"So I would," cried out Emily. "So I would, Uncle Wallace. Oh, Aunt Elizabeth, please let me study for the Entrance. Please! I'll pay you back every cent you spend on it—I will indeed. I pledge you my word of honour."

"It does not happen to be a question of money," said Aunt Elizabeth in her stateliest manner. "I undertook to provide for you, Emily, and I will do it. When you are older I may send you to the High School in Shrewbury for a couple of years. I am not decrying education. But you are not going to be a slave to the public—no Murray girl ever was THAT."

Emily realising the uselessness of pleading, went out in the same bitter disappointment she had felt after Mr. Carpenter's visit. Then Aunt Elizabeth looked at Wallace.

"Have you forgotten what came of sending Juliet to Queen's?" she asked significantly.

If Emily was not allowed to take up the Entrance classes, Perry had no one to say him nay and he went at them with the same dogged determination he showed in all other matters. Perry's status at New Moon had changed subtly and steadily. Aunt Elizabeth had ceased to refer scornfully to him as "a hired boy." Even she recognised that though he was still indubitably a hired boy he was not going to remain one, and she no longer objected to Laura's patching up his ragged bits of clothing, or to Emily's helping him with his lessons in the kitchen after supper, nor did she growl when Cousin Jimmy began to pay him a certain small wage—though older boys than Perry were still glad to put in the winter months choring for board and lodging in some comfortable home. If a future premier was in the making at New Moon Aunt Elizabeth wanted to have some small share in the making. It was credible and commendable that a boy should have ambitions. A girl was an entirely different matter. A girl's place was at home.

Emily helped Perry work out algebra problems and heard his lessons in French and Latin. She picked up more thus than Aunt Elizabeth would have approved and more still when the Entrance pupils talked those languages in school. It was quite an easy matter for a girl who had once upon a time invented a language of her own. When George Bates, by way of showing off, asked her one day in French—HIS French, of which Mr. Carpenter had once said doubtfully that perhaps God might understand it—"Have you the ink of my grandmother and the shoebrush of my cousin and the umbrella of my aunt's husband in your desk?" Emily retorted quite as glibly and QUITE as Frenchily, "No, but I have the pen of your father and the cheese of the innkeeper and the towel of your uncle's maidservant in my basket."

To console herself for her disappointment in regard to the Entrance class Emily wrote more poetry than ever. It was especially delightful to write poetry on a winter evening when the storm winds howled without and heaped the garden and orchard with big ghostly drifts, starred over with rabbits' candles. She also wrote several stories—desperate love affairs wherein she struggled heroically against the difficulties of affectionate dialogue; tales of bandits and pirates—Emily liked these because there was no necessity for bandits and pirates to converse lovingly; tragedies of earls and countesses whose conversation she dearly loved to pepper with scraps of French; and a dozen other subjects she didn't know anything about. She also meditated beginning a novel but decided it would be too hard to get enough paper for it. The letter-bills were all done now and the Jimmy-books were not big enough, though a new one always appeared mysteriously in her school basket when the old one was almost full. Cousin Jimmy seemed to have an uncanny prescience of the proper time—that was part of his Jimmyness.

Then one night, as she lay in her lookout bed and watched a full moon gleaming lustrously from a cloudless sky across the valley, she had a sudden dazzling idea.

She would send her latest poem to the Charlottetown *Enterprise*.

The *Enterprise* had a Poet's Corner where "original" verses were frequently printed. Privately Emily thought her own were quite as good—as probably they were, for most of the *Enterprise* "poems" were sad trash.

Emily was so excited over the idea that she could not sleep for the greater part of the night—and didn't want to. It was glorious to lie there, thrilling in the darkness, and picture the whole thing out. She saw her verses in print signed E. Byrd Starr—she saw Aunt Laura's eyes shining with pride—she saw Mr. Carpenter pointing them out to strangers—"the work of a pupil of mine, by gad"—she saw all her schoolmates envying her or admiring, according to type—she saw herself with one foot at least firmly planted on the ladder of fame—one hill at least of the Alpine Path crested, with a new and glorious prospect opening therefrom.

Morning came. Emily went to school, so absent-minded because of her secret that she did badly in everything and was raged at by Mr. Carpenter. But it all slipped off her like the proverbial water off a duck's back. Her body was in Blair Water school but her spirit was in kingdoms empyreal.

As soon as school was out she betook herself to the garret with half a sheet of blue-lined notepaper. Very painstakingly she copied down the poem, being especially careful to dot every I and cross every T. She wrote it on both sides of the paper, being in blissful ignorance of any taboo thereon. Then she read it aloud delightedly, not omitting the title *Evening Dreams*. There was one line in it she tasted two or three times:

The haunting elfin music of the air.

"I think that line is VERY good," said Emily. "I wonder now how I happened to think of it."

She mailed her poem the next day and lived in a delicious mystic rapture until the following Saturday. When the *Enterprise* came she opened it with tremulous eagerness and ice-cold fingers, and turned to the Poet's Corner. Now for her great moment!

There was not a sign of an Evening Dream about it!

Emily threw down the *Enterprise* and fled to the garret dormer where, face downward on the old haircloth sofa, she wept out her bitterness of disappointment. She drained the draught of failure to the very dregs. It was horribly real and tragic to her. She felt exactly as if she had been slapped in the face. She was crushed in the very dust of humiliation and was sure she could never rise again.

How thankful she was that she hadn't told Teddy anything about it—she had been so strongly tempted to, and only refrained because she didn't want to spoil the dramatic surprise of the moment when she would show him the verses with her name signed to them.

She HAD told Perry, and Perry was furious when he saw her tear-stained face later on in the dairy, as they strained the milk together. Ordinarily Emily loved this, but to-night the savour had gone out of the world. Even the milky splendour of the still, mild winter evening and the purple bloom over the hillside woods that presaged a thaw could not give her the accustomed soul-thrill.

"I'm going to Charlottetown if I have to walk and I'll bust that *Enterprise* editor's head," said Perry, with the expression which, thirty years later, warned the members of his party to scatter for cover.

"That wouldn't be any use," said Emily drearily. "He didn't think it good enough to print—that is what hurts me so, Perry—he didn't think it any good. Busting his head wouldn't change THAT."

It took her a week to recover from the blow. Then she wrote a story in which the editor of the *Enterprise* played the part of a dark and desperate villain who found lodging eventually behind prison bars. This got the venom out of her system and she forgot all about him in the delight of writing a poem addressed to "Sweet Lady April." But I question if she ever really forgave him—even when she discovered eventually that you must NOT write on both sides of the paper—even when she read over *Evening Dreams* a year later and wondered how she could ever have thought it any good.

This sort of thing was happening frequently now. Every time she read her little hoard of manuscripts over she found some of which the fairy gold had unaccountably turned to withered leaves, fit only for the burning. Emily burned them,—but it hurt her a little. Outgrowing things we love is never a pleasant process.

CHAPTER XXIX
SACRILEGE

THERE had been several clashes between Aunt Elizabeth and Emily that winter and spring. Generally Aunt Elizabeth came out victorious; there was that in her that would not be denied the satisfaction of having her own way even in trifling matters. But once in a while she came up against that curious streak of granite in Emily's composition which was unyielding and unbendable and unbreakable. Mary Murray, of a hundred years agone, had been, so family chronicle ran, a gentle and submissive creature generally; but she had that same streak in her, as her "Here I Stay" abundantly testified. When Aunt Elizabeth tried conclusions with that element in Emily she always got the worst of it. Yet she did not learn wisdom therefrom but pursued her policy of repression all the more rigorously; for it occasionally came home to her, as Laura let down tucks, that Emily was on the verge of beginning to grow up and that various breakers and reefs loomed ahead, ominously magnified in the mist of unseen years. Emily must not be allowed to get out of hand now, lest later on she make shipwreck as her mother had done—or as Elizabeth Murray firmly believed she had done. There were, in short, to be no more elopements from New Moon.

One of the things they fell out about was the fact that Emily, as Aunt Elizabeth discovered one day, was in the habit of using more of her egg money to buy paper than Aunt Elizabeth approved of. What did Emily do with so much paper? They had a fuss over this and eventually Aunt Elizabeth discovered that Emily was writing stories. Emily had been writing stories all winter under Aunt Elizabeth's very nose and Aunt Elizabeth had never suspected it. She had fondly supposed that Emily was writing school compositions. Aunt Elizabeth knew in a vague way that Emily wrote silly rhymes which she called "poetry" but this did not worry her especially. Jimmy made up a lot of similar trash. It was foolish but harmless and Emily would doubtless outgrow it. Jimmy had not outgrown it, to be sure, but then his accident— Elizabeth always went a little sick in soul when she remembered it— had made him more or less a child for life.

But writing stories was a very different thing and Aunt Elizabeth was horrified. Fiction of any kind was an abominable thing. Elizabeth Murray had been trained up in this belief in her youth and in her age she had not departed from it. She honestly thought that it was a wicked and sinful thing in anyone to play cards, dance, or go to the theatre, read or write novels, and in Emily's case there was a worse feature—it was the Starr coming out in her—Douglas Starr especially. No Murray of New Moon had ever been guilty of writing "stories" or of ever wanting to write them. It was an alien growth that must be pruned off ruthlessly. Aunt Elizabeth applied the pruning shears; and found no pliant, snippable root but that same underlying streak of granite. Emily was respectful and reasonable and above-board; she bought no more paper with egg money; but she told Aunt Elizabeth that she could not give up writing stories and she went right on writing them, on pieces of brown wrapping paper and the blank backs of circulars which agricultural machinery firms sent Cousin Jimmy.

"Don't you know that it is wicked to write novels?" demanded Aunt Elizabeth.

"Oh, I'm not writing novels—yet," said Emily. "I can't get enough paper. These are just short stories. And it isn't wicked—Father liked novels."

"Your father—" began Aunt Elizabeth, and stopped. She remembered that Emily had "acted up" before now when anything derogatory was said of her father. But the very fact that she felt mysteriously compelled to stop annoyed Elizabeth, who had said what seemed good to her all her life at New Moon without much regard for other people's feelings.

"You will not write any more of THIS STUFF," Aunt Elizabeth contemptuously flourished "The Secret of the Castle" under Emily's nose. "I forbid you—remember, I forbid you."

"Oh, I must write, Aunt Elizabeth," said Emily gravely, folding her slender, beautiful hands on the table and looking straight into Aunt Elizabeth's angry face with the steady, unblinking gaze which Aunt Ruth called unchildlike. "You see, it's this way. It is IN me. I can't help it. And Father said I was ALWAYS to keep on writing. He said I would be famous some day. Wouldn't you like to have a famous niece, Aunt Elizabeth?"

"I am not going to argue the matter," said Aunt Elizabeth.

"I'm not arguing—only explaining." Emily was exasperatingly respectful. "I just want you to understand how it is that I HAVE to go on writing stories, even though I am so very sorry you don't approve."

"If you don't give up this—this worse than nonsense, Emily, I'll—I'll—"

Aunt Elizabeth stopped, not knowing what to say she would do. Emily was too big now to be slapped or shut up; and it was no use to say, as she was tempted to, "I'll send you away from New Moon," because Elizabeth Murray knew perfectly well she would not send Emily away from New Moon—COULD not send her away, indeed, though this knowledge was as yet only in her feelings and had not been translated into her intellect. She only felt that she was helpless and it angered her; but Emily was mistress of the situation and calmly went on writing stories. If Aunt Elizabeth had asked her to give up crocheting lace or making molasses taffy, or eating Aunt Laura's delicious drop cookies, Emily would have done so wholly and cheerfully, though she loved these things. But to give up writing stories—why, Aunt Elizabeth might as well have asked her to give up breathing. WHY couldn't she understand? It seemed so simple and indisputable to Emily.

"Teddy can't help making pictures and Ilse can't help reciting and I can't help writing. DON'T you see, Aunt Elizabeth?"

"I see that you are an ungrateful and disobedient child," said Aunt Elizabeth.

This hurt Emily horribly, but she could not give in; and there continued to be a sense of soreness and disapproval between her and Aunt Elizabeth in all the little details of daily life that poisoned existence more or less for the child, who was so keenly sensitive to her environment and to the feelings with which her kindred regarded her. Emily felt it all the time—except when she was writing her stories. THEN she forgot everything, roaming in some enchanted country between the sun and moon, where she saw wonderful beings whom she tried to describe and wonderful deeds which she tried to record, coming back to the candle-lit kitchen with a somewhat dazed sense of having been years in No-Man's Land.

She did not even have Aunt Laura to back her up in the matter. Aunt Laura thought Emily ought to yield in such an unimportant matter and please Aunt Elizabeth.

"But it's not unimportant," said Emily despairingly. "It's the most important thing in the world to me, Aunt Laura. Oh, I thought YOU would understand."

"I understand that you like to do it, dear, and I think it's a harmless enough amusement. But it seems to annoy Elizabeth some way and I do think you might give it up on that account. It is not as if it was anything that mattered much—it IS really a waste of time."

"No—no," said distressed Emily. "Why, some day, Aunt Laura, I'll write real books—and make lots of money," she added, sensing that the businesslike Murrays measured the nature of most things on a cash basis.

Aunt Laura smiled indulgently.

"I'm afraid you'll never grow rich that way, dear. It would be wiser to employ your time preparing yourself for some useful work."

It was maddening to be condescended to like this—maddening that nobody could see that she HAD to write—maddening to have Aunt Laura so sweet and loving and stupid about it.

"Oh," thought Emily bitterly, "if that hateful *Enterprise* editor had printed my piece they'd have believed THEN."

"At any rate," advised Aunt Laura, "don't let Elizabeth SEE you writing them."

But somehow Emily could not take this prudent advice. There HAD been occasions when she had connived with Aunt Laura to hoodwink Aunt Elizabeth on some little matter, but she found she could not do it in this. THIS had to be open and above-board. She MUST write stories—and Aunt Elizabeth MUST know it—that was the way it had to be. She could not be false to herself in this—she could not PRETEND to be false.

She wrote her father all about it—poured out her bitterness and perplexity to him in what, though she did not suspect it at the time, was the last letter she was to write him. There was a large bundle of letters by now on the old sofa shelf in the garret—for Emily had written many letters to her father besides those which have been chronicled in this history. There were a great many paragraphs about Aunt Elizabeth in them, most of them very uncomplimentary and some of them, as Emily herself would have owned when her first bitterness was past, overdrawn and exaggerated. They had been written in moments when her hurt and angry soul demanded some outlet for its emotion and barbed her pen with venom. Emily was mistress of a subtly malicious style when she chose to be. After she had written them the hurt had ceased and she thought no more about them. But they remained.

And one spring day, Aunt Elizabeth, housecleaning in the garret while Emily played happily with Teddy at the Tansy Patch, found the bundle of letters on the sofa shelf, sat down, and read them all.

Elizabeth Murray would never have read any writing belonging to a grown person. But it never occurred to her that there was anything dishonourable in reading the letters wherein Emily, lonely and—sometimes—misunderstood, had poured out her heart to the father she had loved and been loved by, so passionately and understandingly. Aunt Elizabeth thought she had a right to know everything that this pensioner on her bounty did, said, or thought. She read the letters and she found out what Emily thought of her—of her, Elizabeth Murray, autocrat unchallenged, to whom no one had ever dared to say anything uncomplimentary. Such an experience is no pleasanter at sixty than at sixteen. As Elizabeth Murray folded up the last letter her hands trembled—with anger, and something underneath it that was not anger.

"Emily, your Aunt Elizabeth wants to see you in the parlour," said Aunt Laura, when Emily returned from the Tansy Patch, driven home by the thin grey rain that had begun to drift over the greening fields. Her tone—her sorrowful look—warned Emily that mischief was in the wind. Emily had no idea what mischief—she could not recall anything she had done recently that should bring her up before the tribunal Aunt Elizabeth occasionally held in the parlour. It must be serious when it was in the parlour. For reasons best known to herself Aunt Elizabeth held super-serious interviews like this in the parlour. Possibly it was because she felt obscurely that the photographs of the Murrays on the walls gave her a backing she needed when dealing with this hop-out-of-kin; for the same reason Emily detested a trial in the parlour. She always felt on such occasions like a very small mouse surrounded by a circle of grim cats.

Emily skipped across the big hall, pausing, in spite of her alarm, to glance at the charming red world through the crimson glass; then pushed open the parlour door. The room was dim, for only one of the slat blinds was partially raised. Aunt Elizabeth was sitting bolt upright in Grandfather Murray's black horsehair-chair. Emily looked at her stern, angry face first—and then at her lap.

Emily understood.

The first thing she did was to retrieve her precious letters. With the quickness of light she sprang to Aunt Elizabeth, snatched up the bundle and retreated to the door; there she faced Aunt Elizabeth, her face blazing with indignation and outrage. Sacrilege had been committed—the most sacred shrine of her soul had been profaned.

"How dare you?" she said. "How dare you touch MY PRIVATE PAPERS, Aunt Elizabeth?"

Aunt Elizabeth had not expected THIS. She had looked for confusion—dismay—shame—fear—for anything but this righteous indignation, as if SHE, forsooth, were the guilty one. She rose.

"Give me those letters, Emily."

"No, I will not," said Emily, white with anger, as she clasped her hands around the bundle. "They are mine and Father's—not yours. You had no right to touch them. I will NEVER forgive you!"

This was turning the tables with a vengeance. Aunt Elizabeth was so dumfounded that she hardly knew what to say or do. Worst of all, a most unpleasant doubt of her own conduct suddenly assailed her—driven home perhaps by the intensity and earnestness of Emily's accusation. For the first time in her life it occurred to Elizabeth Murray to wonder if she had done rightly. For the first time in her life she felt ashamed; and the shame made her furious. It was intolerable that SHE should be made to feel ashamed.

For the moment they faced each other, not as aunt and niece, not as child and adult, but as two human beings each with hatred for the other in her heart—Elizabeth Murray, tall and austere and thin-lipped; Emily Starr, white of face, her eyes pools of black flame, her trembling arms hugging her letters.

"So THIS is your gratitude," said Aunt Elizabeth. "You were a penniless orphan—I took you to my home—I have given you shelter and food and education and kindness—and THIS is my thanks."

As yet Emily's tempest of anger and resentment prevented her from feeling the sting of this.

"You did not WANT to take me," she said. "You made me draw lots and you took me because the lot fell to you. You knew some of you had to take me because you were the proud Murrays and couldn't let a relation go to an orphan asylum. Aunt Laura loves me now but you don't. So why should I love you?"

"Ungrateful, thankless child!"

"I'm NOT thankless. I've tried to be good—I've tried to obey you and please you—I do all the chores I can to help pay for my keep. And you had NO BUSINESS to read my letters to Father."

"They are disgraceful letters—and must be destroyed," said Aunt Elizabeth.

"No," Emily clasped them tighter. "I'd sooner burn myself. You shall not have them, Aunt Elizabeth."

She felt her brows drawing together—she felt the Murray look on her face—she knew she was conquering.

Elizabeth Murray turned paler, if that were possible. There were times when she could give the Murray look herself; it was not that which dismayed her—it was the uncanny something which seemed to peer out behind the Murray look that always broke her will. She trembled—faltered—yielded.

"Keep your letters," she said bitterly, "and scorn the old woman who opened her home to you."

She went out of the parlour. Emily was left mistress of the field. And all at once her victory turned to dust and ashes in her mouth.

She went up to her own room, hid her letters in the cupboard over the mantel, and then crept up on her bed, huddling down in a little heap with her face buried in her pillow. She was still sore with a sense of outrage—but underneath another pain was beginning to ache terribly.

Something in her was hurt because she had hurt Aunt Elizabeth— for she felt that Aunt Elizabeth, under all her anger, was HURT. This surprised Emily. She would have expected Aunt Elizabeth to be angry, of course, but she would never have supposed it would affect her in any other way. Yet she had seen something in Aunt Elizabeth's eyes when she had flung that last stinging sentence at her—something that spoke of bitter hurt.

"Oh! Oh!" gasped Emily. She began to cry chokingly into her pillow. She was so wretched that she could not get out of herself and watch her own suffering with a sort of enjoyment in its drama—set her mind to analyse her feelings—and when Emily was as wretched as that she was very wretched indeed and wholly comfortless. Aunt Elizabeth would not keep her at New Moon after a poisonous quarrel like this. She would send her away, of course. Emily believed this. Nothing was too horrible to believe just then. How could she live away from dear New Moon?

"And I may have to live eighty years," Emily moaned.

But worse even than this was the remembrance of that look in Aunt Elizabeth's eyes.

Her own sense of outrage and sacrilege ebbed away under the remembrance. She thought of all the things she had written her father about Aunt Elizabeth—sharp, bitter things, some of them just, some of them unjust. She began to feel that she should not have written them. It was true enough that Aunt Elizabeth had not loved her—had not wanted to take her to New Moon. But she HAD taken her and though it had been done in duty, not in love, the fact remained. It was no use for her to tell herself that it wasn't as if the letters were written to any one living, to be seen and read by others. While she was under Aunt Elizabeth's roof—while she owed the food she ate and the clothes she wore to Aunt Elizabeth—she should not say, even to her father, harsh things of her. A Starr should not have done it.

"I must go and ask Aunt Elizabeth to forgive me," thought Emily at last, all the passion gone out of her and only regret and repentance left. "I suppose she never will—she'll hate me always now. But I must go."

She turned herself about—and then the door opened and Aunt Elizabeth entered. She came across the room and stood at the side of the bed, looking down at the grieved little face on the pillow—a face that in the dim, rainy twilight, with its tear-stains and black shadowed eyes, looked strangely mature and chiseled.

Elizabeth Murray was still austere and cold. Her voice sounded stern; but she said an amazing thing.

"Emily, I had no right to read your letters. I admit I was wrong. Will you forgive me?"

"Oh!" The word was almost a cry. Aunt Elizabeth had at last discerned the way to conquer Emily. The latter lifted herself up, flung her arms about Aunt Elizabeth, and said chokingly,

"Oh—Aunt Elizabeth—I'm sorry—I'm sorry—I shouldn't have written those things—but I wrote them when I was vexed—and I didn't mean them ALL—truly, I didn't mean the worst of them. Oh, you'll believe THAT, won't you, Aunt Elizabeth?"

"I'd like to believe it, Emily." An odd quiver passed through the tall, rigid form. "I—don't like to think you—HATE me—my sister's child—little Juliet's child."

"I don't—oh, I don't," sobbed Emily. "And I'll LOVE you, Aunt Elizabeth, if you'll let me—if you WANT me to. I didn't think you cared. DEAR Aunt Elizabeth."

Emily gave Aunt Elizabeth a fierce hug and a passionate kiss on the white, fine-wrinkled cheek. Aunt Elizabeth kissed her gravely on the brow in return and then said, as if closing the door on the whole incident,

"You'd better wash your face and come down to supper."

But there was yet something to be cleared up.

"Aunt Elizabeth," whispered Emily. "I CAN'T burn those letters, you know—they belong to Father. But I'll tell you what I will do. I'll go over them all and put a star by anything I said about you and then I'll add an explanatory footnote saying that I was mistaken."

Emily spent her spare time for several days putting in her "explanatory footnotes," and then her conscience had rest. But when she again tried to write a letter to her father she found that it no longer meant anything to her. The sense of reality—nearness—of close communion had gone. Perhaps she had been outgrowing it gradually, as childhood began to merge into girlhood—perhaps the bitter scene with Aunt Elizabeth had only shaken into dust something out of which the spirit had already departed. But, whatever the explanation, it was not possible to write such letters any more. She missed them terribly but she could not go back to them. A certain door of life was shut behind her and could not be re-opened.

CHAPTER XXX
WHEN THE CURTAIN LIFTED

IT would be pleasant to be able to record that after the reconciliation in the lookout Emily and Aunt Elizabeth lived in entire amity and harmony. But the truth was that things went on pretty much the same as before. Emily went softly, and tried to mingle serpent's wisdom and dove's harmlessness in practical proportions, but their points of view were so different that there were bound to be clashes; they did not speak the same language, so there was bound to be misunderstanding.

And yet there was a difference—a very vital difference. Elizabeth Murray had learned an important lesson—that there was not one law of fairness for children and another for grown-ups. She continued to be as autocratic as ever—but she did not do or say to Emily anything she would not have done or said to Laura had occasion called for it.

Emily, on her side, had discovered the fact that, under all her surface coldness and sternness, Aunt Elizabeth really had an affection for her; and it was wonderful what a difference this made. It took the sting out of Aunt Elizabeth's "ways" and words and healed entirely a certain little half-conscious sore spot that had been in Emily's heart ever since the incident of the drawn slips at Maywood.

"I don't believe I'm a duty to Aunt Elizabeth any more," she thought exultantly.

Emily grew rapidly that summer in body, mind and soul. Life was delightful, growing richer every hour, like an unfolding rose. Forms of beauty filled her imagination and were transferred as best she could to paper, though they were never so lovely there, and Emily had the heartbreaking moments of the true artist who discovers that

> "Never on painter's canvas lives
> The charm of his fancy's dream."

Much of her "old stuff" she burned; even the *Child of the Sea* was reduced to ashes. But the little pile of manuscripts in the mantel cupboard of the lookout was growing steadily larger. Emily kept her scribblings there now; the sofa shelf in the garret was desecrated; and, besides, she felt somehow that Aunt Elizabeth would never meddle with her "private papers" again, no matter where they were kept. She did not go now to the garret to read or write or dream; her own dear lookout was the best place for that. She loved that quaint, little old room intensely; it was almost like a living thing to her—a sharer in gladness—a comforter in sorrow.

Ilse was growing, too, blossoming out into strange beauty and brilliance, knowing no law but her own pleasure, recognizing no authority but her own whim. Aunt Laura worried over her.

"She will be a woman so soon—and WHO will look after her? Allan won't."

"I've no patience with Allan," said Aunt Elizabeth grimly. "He is always ready to hector and advise other people. He'd better look at home. He'll come over here and order me to do this or that, or NOT to do it, for Emily; but if I say one word to him about Ilse he blows the roof off. The idea of a man turning against his daughter and neglecting her as he has neglected Ilse simply because her mother wasn't all she ought to be—as if the poor child was to blame for THAT."

"S—s—sh," said Aunt Laura, as Emily crossed the sitting-room on her way upstairs.

Emily smiled sadly to herself. Aunt Laura needn't be "s-s-sh'ing." There was nothing left for her to find out about Ilse's mother—nothing, except the most important thing of all, which neither she nor anybody else living knew. For Emily had never surrendered her conviction that the whole truth about Beatrice Burnley was not known. She often worried about it when she lay curled up in her black walnut bed o'nights, listening to the moan of the gulf and the Wind Woman singing in the trees, and drifted into sleep wishing intensely that she could solve the dark old mystery and dissolve its legend of shame and bitterness.

Emily went rather languidly upstairs to the lookout. She meant to write some more of her story, *The Ghost of the Well*, wherein she was weaving the old legend of the well in the Lee field; but somehow interest was lacking; she put the manuscript back into the mantel cupboard; she read over a letter from Dean Priest which had come that day, one of his fat, jolly, whimsical, delightful letters wherein he had told her that he was coming to stay a month with his sister at Blair Water. She wondered why this announcement did not excite her more. She was tired—her head was aching. Emily couldn't remember ever having had a headache before. Since she could not write she decided to lie down and be LADY TREVANION for awhile. Emily was LADY TREVANION very often that summer, in one of the dream lives she had begun to build up for herself. LADY TREVANION was the wife of an English earl and, besides being a famous novelist, was a member of the British House of Commons—where she always appeared in black velvet with a stately coronet of pearls on her dark hair. She was the only woman in the House and, as this was before the days of the suffragettes, she had to endure many sneers and innuendoes and insults from the ungallant males around her. Emily's favourite dream scene was where she rose to make her first speech—a wonderfully thrilling event. As Emily found it difficult to do justice to the scene in any ideas of her own, she always fell back on "Pitt's reply to Walpole," which she had found in her *Royal Reader*, and declaimed it, with suitable variations. The insolent speaker who had provoked LADY TREVANION into speech had sneered at her as a WOMAN, and LADY TREVANION, a magnificent creature in her velvet and pearls, rose to her feet, amid hushed and dramatic silence, and said,

"The atrocious crime of being a WOMAN which the honourable member has, with such spirit and decency, charged upon me, I shall attempt neither to palliate nor deny, but shall content myself with wishing that I may be one of those whose follies cease with their SEX and NOT one of that number who are ignorant in spite of MANHOOD and experience."

(Here she was always interrupted by thunders of applause.)

But the savour was entirely lacking in this scene today and by the time Emily had reached the line, "But WOMANHOOD, Sir, is not my only crime"—she gave up in disgust and fell to worrying over Ilse's mother again, mixed up with some uneasy speculations regarding the climax of her story about the ghost of the well, mingled with her unpleasant physical sensations.

Her eyes hurt her when she moved them. She was chilly, although the July day was hot. She was still lying there when Aunt Elizabeth came up to ask why she hadn't gone to bring the cows home from the pasture.

"I—I didn't know it was so late," said Emily confusedly. "I—my head aches, Aunt Elizabeth."

Aunt Elizabeth rolled up the white cotton blind and looked at Emily. She noted her flushed face—she felt her pulse. Then she bade her shortly to stay where she was, went down, and sent Perry for Dr. Burnley.

"Probably she's got the measles," said the doctor as gruffly as usual. Emily was not yet sick enough to be gentle over. "There's an outbreak of them at Derry Pond. Has she had any chance to catch them?"

"Jimmy Joe Belle's two children were here one afternoon about ten days ago. She played with them—she's always playing round with people she's no business to associate with. I haven't heard that they were or have been sick though."

Jimmy Joe Belle, when asked plainly, confessed that his "young ones" had come out with measles the very day after they had been at New Moon. There was therefore not much doubt as to Emily's malady.

"It's a bad kind of measles apparently," the doctor said. "Quite a number of the Derry Pond children have died of it. Mostly French though—the kids would be out of bed when they had no business to be and caught cold. I don't think you need worry about Emily. She might as well have measles and be done with it. Keep her warm and keep the room dark. I'll run over in the morning."

For three or four days nobody was much alarmed. Measles was a disease everybody had to have. Aunt Elizabeth looked after Emily well and slept on a sofa which had been moved into the lookout. She even left the window open at night. In spite of this—perhaps Aunt Elizabeth thought because of it—Emily grew steadily sicker, and on the fifth day a sharp change for the worse took place. Her fever went up rapidly, delirium set in; Dr. Burnley came, looked anxious, scowled, changed the medicine.

"I'm sent for to a bad case of pneumonia at White Cross," he said, "and I have to go to Charlottetown in the morning to be present at Mrs. Jackwell's operation. I promised her I would go. I'll be back in the evening. Emily is very restless—that high-strung system of hers is evidently very sensitive to fever. What's that nonsense she's talking about the Wind Woman?"

"Oh, I don't know," said Aunt Elizabeth worriedly. "She's always talking nonsense like that, even when she's well. Allan, tell me plainly—is there any danger?"

"There's always danger in this type of measles. I don't like these symptoms—the eruption should be out by now and there's no sign of it. Her fever is very high—but I don't think we need be alarmed yet. If I thought otherwise I wouldn't go to town. Keep her as quiet as possible—humour her whims if you can—I don't like that mental disturbance. She looks terribly distressed—seems to be worrying over something. Has she had anything on her mind of late?"

"Not that I know of," said Aunt Elizabeth. She had a sudden bitter realisation that she really did not know much about the child's mind. Emily would never have come to her with any of her little troubles and worries.

"Emily, what is bothering you?" asked Dr. Burnley softly—very softly. He took the hot, tossing, little hand gently, oh, so gently, in his big one.

Emily looked up with wild, fever-bright eyes.

"She couldn't have done it—she COULDN'T have done it."

"Of course she couldn't," said the doctor cheerily. "Don't worry—she didn't do it."

His eyes telegraphed, "What does she mean?" to Elizabeth, but Elizabeth shook her head.

"Who are you talking about—dear?" she asked Emily. It was the first time she had called Emily "dear."

But Emily was off on another tack. The well in Mr. Lee's field was open, she declared. Someone would be sure to fall into it. Why didn't Mr. Lee shut it up? Dr. Burnley left Aunt Elizabeth trying to reassure Emily on that point and hurried away to White Cross.

At the door he nearly fell over Perry who was curled up on the sandstone slab, hugging his sunburned legs desperately. "How is Emily?" he demanded, grasping the skirt of the doctor's coat.

"Don't bother me—I'm in a hurry," growled the doctor.

"You tell me how Emily is or I'll hang on to your coat till the seams go," said Perry stubbornly. "I can't get one word of sense out of them old maids. YOU tell me."

"She's a sick child but I'm not seriously alarmed about her yet." The doctor gave his coat another tug—but Perry held on for a last word.

"You've GOT to cure her," he said. "If anything happens to Emily I'll drown myself in the pond—mind that."

He let go so suddenly that Dr. Burnley nearly went headlong on the ground. Then Perry curled up on the doorstep again. He watched there until Laura and Cousin Jimmy had gone to bed and then he sneaked through the house and sat on the stairs, where he could hear any sound in Emily's room. He sat there all night, with his fists clenched, as if keeping guard against an unseen foe.

Elizabeth Murray watched by Emily until two o'clock, and then Laura took her place.

"She has raved a great deal," said Aunt Elizabeth. "I wish I knew what is worrying her—there IS something, I feel sure. It isn't all mere delirium. She keeps repeating 'She couldn't have done it' in such imploring tones. I wonder oh, Laura, you remember the time I read her letters? Do you think she means me?"

Laura shook her head. She had never seen Elizabeth so moved.

"If the child—doesn't get—better—" said Aunt Elizabeth. She said no more but went quickly out of the room.

Laura sat down by the bed. She was pale and drawn with her own worry and fatigue—for she had not been able to sleep. She loved Emily as her own child and the awful dread that had possessed her heart would not lift for an instant. She sat there and prayed mutely. Emily fell into a troubled slumber which lasted until the grey dawn crept into the lookout. Then she opened her eyes and looked at Aunt Laura— looked through her—looked beyond her.

"I see her coming over the fields," she said in a high, clear voice. "She is coming so gladly—she is singing—she is thinking of her baby— oh, keep her back—keep her back—she doesn't see the well—it's so dark she doesn't see it—oh, she's gone into it—she's gone into it!"

Emily's voice rose in a piercing shriek which penetrated to Aunt Elizabeth's room and brought her flying across the hall in her flannel nightgown.

"What is wrong, Laura?" she gasped.

Laura was trying to soothe Emily, who was struggling to sit up in bed. Her cheeks were crimson and her eyes had still the same far, wild look.

"Emily—Emily, darling, you've just had a bad dream. The old Lee well isn't open—nobody has fallen into it."

"Yes, somebody has," said Emily shrilly. "SHE has—I saw her—I saw her—with the ace of hearts on her forehead. Do you think I don't know her?"

She fell back on her pillow, moaned, and tossed the hands which Laura Murray had loosened in her surprise.

The two ladies of New Moon looked at each other across her bed in dismay—and something like terror.

"Who did you see, Emily?" asked Aunt Elizabeth.

"Ilse's mother—of course. I always knew she didn't do that dreadful thing. She fell into the old well—she's there now—go—go and get her out, Aunt Laura. PLEASE."

"Yes—yes, of course we'll get her out, darling," said Aunt Laura, soothingly.

Emily sat up in bed and looked at Aunt Laura again. This time she did not look through her—she looked into her. Laura Murray felt that those burning eyes read her soul.

"You are lying to me," cried Emily. "You don't mean to try to get her out. You are only saying it to put me off. Aunt Elizabeth," she suddenly turned and caught Aunt Elizabeth's hand, "you'll do it for me, won't you? You'll go and get her out of the old well, won't you?"

Elizabeth remembered that Dr. Burnley had said that Emily's whims must be humoured. She was terrified by the child's condition.

"Yes, I'll get her out if she is in there," she said. Emily released her hand and sank down. The wild glare left her eyes. A great sudden calm fell over her anguished little face.

"I know YOU'LL keep your word," she said. "You are very hard—but YOU never lie, Aunt Elizabeth."

Elizabeth Murray went back to her own room and dressed herself with her shaking fingers. A little later, when Emily had fallen into a quiet sleep, Laura went down stairs and heard Elizabeth giving Cousin Jimmy some orders in the kitchen.

"Elizabeth, you don't really mean to have that old well searched?"

"I do," said Elizabeth resolutely. "I know it's nonsense as well as you do. But I had to promise it to quiet her down—and I'll keep my promise. You heard what she said—she believed I wouldn't lie to her. Nor will I. Jimmy, you will go over to James Lee's after breakfast and ask him to come here."

"How has she heard the story?" said Laura.

"I don't know—oh, some one has told her, of course—perhaps that old demon of a Nancy Priest. It doesn't matter who. She HAS heard it and the thing is to keep her quiet. It isn't so much of a job to put ladders in the well and get some one to go down it. The thing that matters is the absurdity of it."

"We'll be laughed at for a pair of fools," protested Laura, whose share of Murray pride was in hot revolt. "And besides, it will open up all the old scandal again."

"No matter. I'll keep my word to the child," said Elizabeth stubbornly.

Allan Burnley came to New Moon at sunset, on his way home from town. He was tired, for he had been going night and day for over a week; he was more worried than he had admitted over Emily; he looked old and rather desolate as he stepped into the New Moon kitchen.

Only Cousin Jimmy was there. Cousin Jimmy did not seem to have much to do, although it was a good hay-day and Jimmy Joe Belle and Perry were hauling in the great fragrant, sun-dried loads. He sat by the western window with a strange expression on his face.

"Hello, Jimmy, where are the girls? And how is Emily?"

"Emily is better," said Cousin Jimmy. "The rash is out and her fever has gone down. I think she's asleep."

"Good. We couldn't afford to lose that little girl, could we, Jimmy?"

"No," said Jimmy. But he did not seem to want to talk about it. "Laura and Elizabeth are in the sitting-room. They want to see you." He paused a minute and then added in an eerie way, "There is nothing hidden that shall not be revealed."

It occurred to Allan Burnley that Jimmy was acting mysteriously. And if Laura and Elizabeth wanted to see him why didn't they come out? It wasn't like them to stand on ceremony in this fashion. He pushed open the sitting-room door impatiently.

Laura Murray was sitting on the sofa, leaning her head on its arm. He could not see her face but he felt that she was crying. Elizabeth was sitting bolt upright on a chair. She wore her second-best black silk and her second-best lace cap. And she, too, had been crying. Dr. Burnley never attached much importance to Laura's tears, easy as those of most women, but that Elizabeth Murray should cry—had he ever seen her cry before?

The thought of Ilse flashed into his mind—his little neglected daughter. Had anything happened to Ilse?

In one dreadful moment Allan Burnley paid the price of his treatment of his child.

"What is wrong?" he exclaimed in his gruffest manner.

"Oh, Allan," said Elizabeth Murray. "God forgive us—God forgive us all!"

"It—is—Ilse," said Dr. Burnley, dully.

"No—no—not Ilse."

Then she told him—she told him what had been found at the bottom of the old Lee well—she told him what had been the real fate of the lovely, laughing young wife whose name for twelve bitter years had never crossed his lips.

It was not until the next evening that Emily saw the doctor. She was lying in bed, weak and limp, red as a beet with the measles rash, but quite herself again. Allan Burnley stood by the bed and looked down at her.

"Emily—dear little child—do you know what you have done for me? God knows how you did it."

"I thought you didn't believe in God," said Emily, wonderingly.

"You have given me back my faith in Him, Emily."

"Why, what have I done?"

Dr. Burnley saw that she had no remembrance of her delirium. Laura had told him that she had slept long and soundly after Elizabeth's promise and had awakened with fever gone and the eruption fast coming out. She had asked nothing and they had said nothing.

"When you are better we will tell you all," he said, smiling down at her. There was something very sorrowful in the smile—and yet something very sweet.

"He is smiling with his eyes as well as his mouth now," thought Emily.

"How—how did she know?" whispered Laura Murray to him when he went down. "I—can't understand it, Allan."

"Nor I. These things are beyond us, Laura," he answered gravely. "I only know this child has given Beatrice back to me, stainless and beloved. It can be explained rationally enough perhaps. Emily has evidently been told about Beatrice and worried over it—her repeated 'she couldn't have done it' shows that. And the tales of the old Lee well naturally made a deep impression on the mind of a sensitive child keenly alive to dramatic values. In her delirium she mixed this all up with the well-known fact of Jimmy's tumble into the New Moon well— and the rest was coincidence. I would have explained it all so myself once—but now—now, Laura, I only say humbly, 'A little child shall lead them.'"

"Our stepmother's mother was a Highland Scotchwoman. They said she had the second sight," said Elizabeth. "I never believed in it— before."

The excitement of Blair Water had died away before Emily was deemed strong enough to hear the story. That which had been found in the old Lee well had been buried in the Mitchell plot at Shrewsbury and a white marble shaft, "Sacred to the memory of Beatrice Burnley, beloved wife of Allan Burnley," had been erected. The sensation caused by Dr. Burnley's presence every Sunday in the old Burnley pew had died away. On the first evening that Emily was allowed to sit up Aunt Laura told her the whole story. Her manner of telling stripped it forever of the taint and innuendo left by Aunt Nancy.

"I KNEW Ilse's mother couldn't have done it," said Emily triumphantly.

"We blame ourselves now for our lack of faith," said Aunt Laura. "We should have known too—but it DID seem black against her at the time, Emily. She was a bright, beautiful, merry creature—we thought her close friendship with her cousin natural and harmless. We know now it was so—but all these years since her disappearance we have believed differently. Mr. James Lee remembers clearly that the well was open the night of Beatrice's disappearance. His hired man had taken the old rotten planks off it that evening, intending to put the new ones on at once. Then Robert Greerson's house caught fire and he ran with everybody else to help save it. By the time it was out it was too dark to finish with the well, and the man said nothing about it until the morning. Mr. Lee was angry with him—he said it was a scandalous thing to leave a well uncovered like that. He went right down and put the new planks in place himself. He did not look down in the well— had he looked he could have seen nothing, for the ferns growing out from the sides screened the depths. It was just after harvest. No one was in the field again before the next spring. He never connected Beatrice's disappearance with the open well—he wonders now that he didn't. But you see—dear—there had been much malicious gossip— and Beatrice was KNOWN to have gone on board *The Lady of Winds*. It was taken for granted she never came off again. But she did—and went to her death in the old Lee field. It was a dreadful ending to her bright young life—but not so dreadful, after all, as what we believed. For twelve years we have wronged the dead. But—Emily—how could you KNOW?"

"I—don't—know. When the doctor came in that day I couldn't remember anything—but now it seems to me that I remember something—just as if I'd dreamed it—of SEEING Ilse's mother coming over the fields, singing. It was dark—and yet I could see the ace of hearts—oh, Aunty, I don't know—I don't like to think of it, some way."

"We won't talk of it again," said Aunt Laura gently. "It is one of the things best not talked of—one of God's secrets."

"And Ilse—does her father love her now?" asked Emily eagerly.

"Love her! He can't love her enough. It seems as if he were pouring out on her at once all the shut-up love of those twelve years."

"He'll likely spoil her now as much with indulgence as he did before with neglect," said Elizabeth, coming in with Emily's supper in time to hear Laura's reply.

"It will take a lot of love to spoil Ilse," laughed Laura. "She's drinking it up like a thirsty sponge. And she loves him wildly in return. There isn't a trace of grudge in her over his long neglect."

"All the same," said Elizabeth grimly, tucking pillows behind Emily's back with a very gentle hand, oddly in contrast with her severe expression, "he won't get off so easily. Ilse has run wild for twelve years. He won't find it so easy to make her behave properly now—if he ever does."

"Love will do wonders," said Aunt Laura softly. "Of course, Ilse is dying to come and see you, Emily. But she must wait until there is no danger of infection. I told her she might write—but when she found I would have to read it because of your eyes she said she'd wait till you could read it yourself. Evidently"—Laura laughed again—"evidently Ilse has much of importance to tell you."

"I didn't know anybody could be as happy as I am now," said Emily. "And oh, Aunt Elizabeth, it is SO nice to feel hungry again and to have something to CHEW."

CHAPTER XXXI
EMILY'S GREAT MOMENT

EMILY'S convalescence was rather slow. Physically she recovered with normal celerity but a certain spiritual and emotional languor persisted for a time. One cannot go down to the depths of hidden things and escape the penalty. Aunt Elizabeth said she "moped." But Emily was too happy and contented to mope. It was just that life seemed to have lost its savour for a time, as if some spring of vital energy had been drained out of it and refilled slowly.

She had, just then, no one to play with. Perry, Ilse and Teddy had all come down with measles the same day. Mrs. Kent at first declared bitterly that Teddy had caught them at New Moon, but all three had contracted them at a Sunday School picnic where Derry Pond children had been. That picnic infected all Blair Water. There was a perfect orgy of measles. Teddy and Ilse were only moderately ill, but Perry, who had insisted on going home to Aunt Tom at the first symptoms, nearly died. Emily was not allowed to know his danger until it had passed, lest it worry her too much. Even Aunt Elizabeth worried over it. She was surprised to discover how much they missed Perry round the place.

It was fortunate for Emily that Dean Priest was in Blair Water during this forlorn time. His companionship was just what she needed and helped her wonderfully on the road to complete recovery. They went for long walks together all over Blair Water, with Tweed woofing around them, and explored places and roads Emily had never seen before. They watched a young moon grow old, night by night; they talked in dim scented chambers of twilight over long red roads of mystery; they followed the lure of hill winds; they saw the stars rise and Dean told her all about them—the great constellations of the old myths. It was a wonderful month; but on the first day of Teddy's convalescence Emily was off to the Tansy Patch for the afternoon and Jarback Priest walked—if he walked at all—alone.

Aunt Elizabeth was extremely polite to him, though she did not like the Priests of Priest Pond overmuch, and never felt quite comfortable under the mocking gleam of "Jarback's" green eyes and the faint derision of his smile, which seemed to make Murray pride and Murray traditions seem much less important than they really were.

"He has the Priest flavour," she told Laura, "though it isn't as strong in him as in most of them. And he's certainly helping Emily—she has begun to spunk up since he came."

Emily continued to "spunk up" and by September, when the measles epidemic was spent and Dean Priest had gone on one of his sudden swoops over to Europe for the autumn, she was ready for school again—a little taller, a little thinner, a little less childlike, with great grey shadowy eyes that had looked into death and read the riddle of a buried thing, and henceforth would hold in them some haunting, elusive remembrance of that world behind the veil. Dean Priest had seen it—Mr. Carpenter saw it when she smiled at him across her desk at school.

"She's left the childhood of her soul behind, though she is still a child in body," he muttered.

One afternoon amid the golden days and hazes of October he asked her gruffly to let him see some of her verses.

"I never meant to encourage you in it," he said. "I don't mean it now. Probably you can't write a line of real poetry and never will. But let me see your stuff. If it's hopelessly bad I'll tell you so. I won't have you wasting years striving for the unattainable—at least I won't have it on my conscience if you do. If there's any promise in it, I'll tell you so just as honestly. And bring some of your stories, too—THEY'RE trash yet, that's certain, but I'll see if they show just and sufficient cause for going on."

Emily spent a very solemn hour that evening, weighing, choosing, rejecting. To the little bundle of verse she added one of her Jimmy-books which contained, as she thought, her best stories. She went to school next day, so secret and mysterious that Ilse took offense, started in to call her names—and then stopped. Ilse had promised her father that she would try to break herself of the habit of calling names. She was making fairly good headway and her conversation, if less vivid, was beginning to approximate to New Moon standards.

Emily made a sad mess of her lessons that day. She was nervous and frightened. She had a tremendous respect for Mr. Carpenter's opinion. Father Cassidy had told her to keep on—Dean Priest had told her that some day she might really write—but perhaps they were only trying to be encouraging because they liked her and didn't want to hurt her feelings. Emily knew Mr. Carpenter would not do this. No matter if he did like her he would nip her aspirations mercilessly if he thought the root of the matter was not in her. If, on the contrary, he bade her Godspeed, she would rest content with that against the world and never lose heart in the face of any future criticism. No wonder the day seemed fraught with tremendous issues to Emily.

When school was out Mr. Carpenter asked her to remain. She was so white and tense that the other pupils thought she must have been found out by Mr. Carpenter in some especially dreadful behaviour and knew she was going to "catch it." Rhoda Stuart flung her a significantly malicious smile from the porch—which Emily never even saw. She was, indeed, at a momentous bar, with Mr. Carpenter as supreme judge, and her whole future career—so she believed—hanging on his verdict.

The pupils disappeared and a mellow sunshiny stillness settled over the old schoolroom. Mr. Carpenter took the little packet she had given him in the morning out of his desk, came down the aisle and sat in the seat before her, facing her. Very deliberately he settled his glasses astride his hooked nose, took out her manuscripts and began to read—or rather to glance over them, flinging scraps of comments, mingled with grunts, sniffs and hoots, at her as he glanced. Emily folded her cold hands on her desk and braced her feet against the legs of it to keep her knees from trembling. This was a very terrible experience. She wished she had never given her verses to Mr. Carpenter. They were no good—of course they were no good. Remember the editor of the *Enterprise*.

"Humph!" said Mr. Carpenter. "SUNSET—Lord, how many poems have been written on 'Sunset'—

>   'The clouds are massed in splendid state
>   At heaven's unbarred western gate
>   Where troops of star-eyed spirits wait'—

By gad, what does that mean?"

"I—I—don't know," faltered startled Emily, whose wits had been scattered by the sudden swoop of his spiked glance.

Mr. Carpenter snorted.

"For heaven's sake, girl, don't write what you can't understand yourself. And this—TO LIFE—'Life, as thy gift I ask no rainbow joy'—is that sincere? Is it, girl. Stop and think. DO you ask 'no rainbow joy' of life?"

He transfixed her with another glare. But Emily was beginning to pick herself up a bit. Nevertheless, she suddenly felt oddly ashamed of the very elevated and unselfish desires expressed in that sonnet.

"No—o," she answered reluctantly. "I DO want rainbow joy—lots of it."

"Of course you do. We all do. We don't get it—you won't get it—but don't be hypocrite enough to pretend you don't want it, even in a sonnet. *Lines to a Mountain Cascade*— 'On its dark rocks like the whiteness of a veil around a bride'—Where did you see a mountain cascade in Prince Edward Island?"

"Nowhere—there's a picture of one in Dr. Burnley's library."

"A WOOD STREAM—

> 'The threading sunbeams quiver,
> The bending bushes shiver,
> O'er the little shadowy river'—

There's only one more rhyme that occurs to me and that's 'liver.' Why did you leave it out?"

Emily writhed.

"WIND SONG—

> 'I have shaken the dew in the meadows
> From the clover's creamy gown'—

Pretty, but weak. JUNE—June, for heaven's sake, girl, don't write poetry on June. It's the sickliest subject in the world. It's been written to death."

"No, June is immortal," cried Emily suddenly, a mutinous sparkle replacing the strained look in her eyes. She was not going to let Mr. Carpenter have it all his own way.

But Mr. Carpenter had tossed JUNE aside without reading a line of it.

"'I weary of the hungry world'—what do you know of the hungry world?—you in your New Moon seclusion of old trees and old maids—but it IS hungry. ODE TO WINTER—the seasons are a sort of disease all young poets must have, it seems—ha! 'Spring will not forget'—THAT'S a good line—the only good line in it. H'm'm—WANDERINGS—

> 'I've learned the secret of the rune
> That the somber pines on the hillside croon'—

Have you—HAVE you learned that secret?"

"I think I've always known it," said Emily dreamily. That flash of unimaginable sweetness that sometimes surprised her had just come and gone.

"AIM AND ENDEAVOUR—too didactic—too didactic. You've no right to try to teach until you're old—and then you won't want to—

'Her face was like a star all pale and fair'—
Were you looking in the glass when you composed that line?"

"No—" indignantly.

"'When the morning light is shaken like a banner on the hill'—a good line—a good line—

'Oh, on such a golden morning
To be living is delight'—

Too much like a faint echo of Wordsworth. THE SEA IN SEPTEMBER—'blue and austerely bright'—'austerely bright'—child, how can you marry the right adjectives like that? MORNING—'all the secret fears that haunt the night'—what do YOU know of the fears that haunt the night?"

"I know something," said Emily decidedly, remembering her first night at Wyther Grange.

"TO A DEAD DAY—

'With the chilly calm on her brow
That only the dead may wear'—

Have you ever SEEN the chilly calm on the brow of the dead, Emily?"

"Yes," said Emily softly, recalling that grey dawn in the old house in the hollow.

"I thought so—otherwise you couldn't have written THAT—and even as it is—how old are you, jade?"

"Thirteen, last May."

"Humph! LINES TO MRS. GEORGE IRVING'S INFANT SON—you should study the art of titles, Emily—there's a fashion in them as in everything else. Your titles are as out of date as the candles of New Moon—

'Soundly he sleeps with his red lips pressed
Like a beautiful blossom close to her breast'—

The rest isn't worth reading. SEPTEMBER—is there a month you've missed?—'Windy meadows harvest-deep'—good line. BLAIR WATER BY MOONLIGHT—gossamer, Emily, nothing but gossamer. THE GARDEN OF NEW MOON—

'Beguiling laughter and old song
Of merry maids and men'—

Good line—I suppose New Moon IS full of ghosts. 'Death's fell minion well fulfilled its part'—that might have passed in Addison's day but not now—not now, Emily—

'Your azure dimples are the graves
Where million buried sunbeams play'—

Atrocious, girl—atrocious. Graves aren't playgrounds. How much would YOU play if you were buried?"

Emily writhed and blushed again. WHY couldn't she have seen that herself? ANY goose could have seen it.

"'Sail onward, ships—white wings, sail on,
Till past the horizon's purple bar
You drift from sight.—In flush of dawn
Sail on, and 'neath the evening star'—

Trash—trash—and yet there's a picture in it—

'Lap softly, purple waves. I dream,
And dreams are sweet—I'll wake no more'—

Ah, but you'll have to wake if you want to accomplish anything. Girl, you've used PURPLE twice in the same poem.

'Buttercups in a golden frenzy'—

'a golden frenzy'—girl, I SEE the wind shaking the buttercups.

'From the purple gates of the west I come'—

You're too fond of purple, Emily."

"It's such a lovely word," said Emily.

"'Dreams that seem too bright to die'—

SEEM but never ARE, Emily—

'The luring voice of the echo, fame'—

So you've heard it, too? It IS a lure and for most of us only an echo. And that's the last of the lot."

Mr. Carpenter swept the little sheets aside, folded his arms on the desk, and looked over his glasses at Emily.

Emily looked back at him mutely, nervelessly. All the life seemed to have been drained out of her body and concentrated in her eyes.

"Ten good lines out of four hundred, Emily—comparatively good, that is—and all the rest balderdash—balderdash, Emily."

"I—suppose so," said Emily faintly.

Her eyes brimmed with tears—her lips quivered. She could not help it. Pride was hopelessly submerged in the bitterness of her disappointment. She felt exactly like a candle that somebody had blown out.

"What are you crying for?" demanded Mr. Carpenter.

Emily blinked away the tears and tried to laugh.

"I—I'm sorry—you think it's no good—" she said.

Mr. Carpenter gave the desk a mighty thump.

"No good! Didn't I tell you there were ten good lines? Jade, for ten righteous men Sodom had been spared."

"Do you mean—that—after all—" The candle was being relighted again.

"Of course, I mean. If at thirteen you can write ten good lines, at twenty you'll write ten times ten—if the gods are kind. Stop messing over months, though—and don't imagine you're a genius either, if you HAVE written   ten   decent   lines.   I   think there's SOMETHING trying to speak through you—but you'll have to make yourself a fit instrument for it. You've got to work hard and sacrifice—by gad, girl, you've chosen a jealous goddess. And she never lets her votaries go—not even when she shuts her ears forever to their plea. What have you there?"

Emily, her heart thrilling, handed him her Jimmy-book. She was so happy that it shone through her whole being with a positive radiance. She saw her future, wonderful, brilliant—oh, her goddess would listen to HER—"Emily B. Starr, the distinguished poet"—"E. Byrd Starr, the rising young novelist"—

She was recalled from her enchanting reverie by a chuckle from Mr. Carpenter. Emily wondered a little uneasily what he was laughing at. She didn't think there was anything funny in THAT book. It contained only three or four of her latest stories—THE BUTTERFLY QUEEN, a little fairy tale; THE DISAPPOINTED HOUSE, wherein she had woven a pretty dream of hopes come true after long years; THE SECRET OF THE GLEN, which, in spite of its title, was a fanciful little dialogue between the Spirit of the Snow, the Spirit of the Grey Rain, the Spirit of Mist, and the Spirit of Moonshine.

"So you think I am not beautiful when I say my prayers?" said Mr. Carpenter.

Emily gasped—realized what had happened—made a frantic grab at her Jimmy-book—missed it. Mr. Carpenter held it up beyond her reach and mocked at her.

She had given him the wrong Jimmy-book! And this one, oh, horrors, what was in it? Or rather, what wasn't in it? Sketches of everyone in Blair Water—and a full—a very full—description of Mr. Carpenter himself. Intent on describing him exactly, she had been as mercilessly lucid as she always was, especially in regard to the odd faces he made on mornings when he opened the school day with a prayer. Thanks   to   her   dramatic   knack   of   word   painting,   Mr. Carpenter LIVED in that sketch. Emily did not know it, but HE did— he saw himself as in a glass and the artistry of it pleased him so that he cared for nothing else. Besides, she had drawn his good points quite as clearly as his bad ones. And there were some sentences in it—"He looks as if he knew a great deal that can never be any use to him"—"I think he wears the black coat Mondays because it makes him feel that he hasn't been drunk at all." Who or what had taught the little jade these things? Oh, her goddess would not pass Emily by!

"I'm—sorry," said Emily, crimson with shame all over her dainty paleness.

"Why, I wouldn't have missed this for all the poetry you've written or ever will write! By gad, it's literature—LITERATURE—and you're only thirteen. But you don't know what's ahead of you—the stony hills—the steep ascents—the buffets—the discouragements. Stay in the valley if you're wise. Emily, WHY do you want to write? Give me your reason."

"I want to be famous and rich," said Emily coolly.

"Everybody does. Is that all?"

"No. I just LOVE to write."

"A better reason—but not enough—not enough. Tell me this—if you knew you would be poor as a church mouse all your life—if you knew you'd never have a line published—would you still go on writing—WOULD you?"

"Of course I would," said Emily disdainfully. "Why, I HAVE to write—I can't help it by times—I've just GOT to."

"Oh—then I'd waste my breath giving advice at all. If it's IN you to climb you must—there are those who MUST lift their eyes to the hills—they can't breathe properly in the valleys. God help them if there's some weakness in them that prevents their climbing. You don't understand a word I'm saying—yet. But go on—climb! There, take your book and go home. Thirty years from now I will have a claim to distinction in the fact that Emily Byrd Starr was once a pupil of mine. Go—go—before I remember what a disrespectful baggage you are to write such stuff about me and be properly enraged."

Emily went, still a bit scared but oddly exultant behind her fright. She was so happy that her happiness seemed to irradiate the world with its own splendour. All the sweet sounds of nature around her seemed like the broken words of her own delight. Mr. Carpenter watched her out of sight from the old worn threshold.

"Wind—and flame—and sea!" he muttered. "Nature is always taking us by surprise. This child has—what I have never had and would have made any sacrifice to have. But 'the gods don't allow us to be in their debt'—she will pay for it—she will pay."

At sunset Emily sat in the lookout room. It was flooded with soft splendour. Outside, in sky and trees, were delicate tintings and aerial sounds. Down in the garden Daffy was chasing dead leaves along the red walks. The sight of his sleek, striped sides, the grace of his movements, gave her pleasure—as did the beautiful, even, glossy furrows of the ploughed fields beyond the lane, and the first faint white star in the crystal-green sky.

The wind of the autumn night was blowing trumpets of fairyland on the hills; and over in Lofty John's bush was laughter—like the laughter of fauns. Ilse and Perry and Teddy were waiting there for her—they had made a tryst for a twilight romp. She would go to them— presently—not yet. She was so full of rapture that she must write it out before she went back from her world of dreams to the world of reality. Once she would have poured it into a letter to her father. She could no longer do that. But on the table before her lay a brand-new Jimmy-book. She pulled it towards her, took up her pen, and on its first virgin page she wrote.

New Moon,

Blair Water,

P. E. Island.

October 8th.

I am going to write a diary, that it may be published when I die.

THE END

DETAILED HISTORICAL CONTEXT

Emily of New Moon

During the period this book was originally written, the world was a very different place. The events of the time produced an impact on the authorship, style and content of this work. In order for you the reader to better appreciate and connect with this book, it is therefore important to have some context on world events during this timeframe. To this end, we have included a detailed events calendar for the *20th* century for your reference.

Please give consideration in particular to the era around *1923*, the year in which this work was first published.

Disclaimer: Some scenes throughout history may not be suitable for children, for example, in relation to war or violence. Please use your own discretion before reading this section to your child or allowing your child to read it.

The nineteenth century was a fascinating and crucial formative period in Western literature since it served as the primary context for the future evolution and emergence of modern literary traditions and styles as we know them. Additional study, for example, demonstrates that the Romantic, Symbolist, and Realist movements, as well as numerous social and economic situations that dominated the twentieth century, had their origins and ancestors in the nineteenth century.

Movements and Literature

Romanticism: The nineteenth century brought a fresh method in the form of Romanticism, with a contrastive emphasis on sensation and the irrational. Whereas the 18th century was seen to be the age of intelligence, logic, and the mind. Romanticism, which arose from the late-nineteenth-century German Sturm und Drang ("Stress and Storm") movement and whose renowned members included Goethe and Friedrich Schiller, was distinguished by a stress on the individual, the subjective, the mystical, the emotional, and inner life. It had an enormous influence on literature, art, music, and even architecture.

Rousseau: With his focus on the individual and the value of inspiration, 18th-century Swiss philosopher Jean-Jacques Rousseau influenced the Preromantic and Romantic movements, as well as the Age of Enlightenment and some parts of the French Revolution.

Early Romantic poets: The late 18th and early 19th century Romantic English poets William Wordsworth and Samuel Taylor Coleridge, who published their Lyrical Ballads collection of poetry in 1798, are regarded the forerunners of this style. The Romantic poetry movement was popular and flourished throughout Europe and beyond, as seen by the works of Pushkin in Russia, Ugo Foscolo and Giacomo Leopardi in Italy, José de Espronceda in Spain, and Giacomo Leopardi.

American Romanticism: The historical adventure novels of James Fenimore Cooper, Edgar Allan Poe's supernatural and mystical works, Walt Whitman's poetry, and Emerson and Henry David Thoreau's Transcendentalist scriptures are just a few instances of the Romantic movement's effect and growth in America.

Second Generation Romantic poets: The Romantics turned to people's emotions, which were anchored in and exemplified by interaction with nature and the primordial self, rather than intellectual examination, to uncover the "truth" of things. The works of second-generation Romantic poets John Keats, Lord Byron, and Percy Bysshe Shelley are good illustrations of these points of view.

Post Romanticism – Parnassianism: The works of French poets Théophile Gautier and Charles Baudelaire are examples of Parnassianism, which may be seen of as an extension of early Romantic perspectives with its emphasis on aesthetics and the concept of art for the sake of art. Schopenhauer's philosophical concepts had an influence as well. Devotees aimed to treat their exotic and old topics of attraction in a more controlled, formal manner, moving from the excess emotion and sentimentality of the Romantic movement.

Impressionism and Symbolism: Claude Monet and other Paris-based painters helped to establish impressionism, which initially appeared in painting and subsequently in music in France near the end of the nineteenth century. Impressionism was a painting technique that sought to depict the visual world as precisely as possible by utilizing the fluctuating properties of light and color as seen via human perception and experience.

Symbolism may be defined as a shift away from naturalism and realism and toward a harsher, more realistic depiction of the world, with an emphasis on the ordinary rather than the spectacular. Symbolist poets, such as Gustave Kahn and Ezra Pound, employed a lighter, freer verse form and used imagery to "evoke" rather than portray or describe.

The Gothic Novel: This was a popular subgenre of European Romantic fiction that began in the late 18th century with novels like Horace Walpole's Castle of Otranto (1765) and Ann Radcliffe's Mysteries of Udolpho. The term "gothic" refers to Gothic architecture, which commonly served as the backdrop and setting for early works in this genre. It set itself distinct from previous supernatural or ghost stories by focusing on the characters' present-day lives being plagued by their pasts. Famous and beloved 19th-century gothic novels include Frankenstein by Mark Shelley, Bride of Lammermoor by Walter Scott, The Devil's Elixirs by E.T.A. Hoffmann, Wuthering Heights by Emily Bronte, The Strange Case of Dr. Jekyll and Mr. Hyde by Robert Louis Stevenson, and Dracula by Bram Stoker. Other well-known Victorian books, such as Charles Dickens' Bleak House and Great Expectations, exhibit the influence of the gothic genre.

Popular Philosophy

German Idealism: This school of thought included Johann Gottlieb Fichte, who developed Kantian metaphysics and argued for a self that is a "self-producing and changing process," Georg Wilhelm Friedrich Hegel, whose writings emphasized the significance of the historical thinking process in which the spirit conceives of itself, and Arthur Schopenhauer, who, in contrast to Hegel, argued for a return to Kantian transcendentalism.

Marxism: Karl Marx and Friedrich Engels created and expanded a school of thought. Their Communist Manifesto (1848), which asserted that capitalism will inevitably self-destruct and be replaced by socialism and finally communism, laid the groundwork for the modern communist movement.

Positivism: August Comte's empiricist philosophical theory argued that genuine knowledge can be seen to be true by definition or positive—that is, an a posteriori fact determined by using reason and logic, from sensory experience, as opposed to instinct or theology.

Social Darwinism: Natural selection and survival of the fittest principles, such as those developed and detailed in Charles Darwin's On the Origin of Species, were attempted to be applied to social Darwinism views. Francis Galton was among those who claimed that mental qualities, like physical ability, were inherited and that over-breeding by "less fit" members of society should be discouraged. Herbert Spencer, whose book The Social creature (1860) sees society as a living creature that evolves and develops in the same way, as well as Francis Spencer, were both supporters.

Social, Economic, and Political Impacts

The Industrial Revolution: The Industrial Revolution, which occurred between the late 18th century and the years 1820–1840, was a period of great social, political, and economic upheaval and change that involved the difficult transition from largely manual production methods to mechanical manufacturing methods, particularly in the fields of textiles, steam power, iron making, and the invention of machine tools. Agriculture had previously formed the cornerstone of the European economy, and it was also a time when fundamental political, scientific, and religious ideals were dismantled.

As a result of this mechanisation, a considerable number of people were transported from rural villages to metropolitan regions, resulting in a major rise in population and the establishment of new, bigger cities. The advancement of new technology resulted in the establishment of factories, a dehumanizing and horrifying manner of labor, particularly child labor, and a capitalist way of life. Because cities were unable to handle the rapidly rising population, there were overcrowded slums and terribly deplorable living conditions, as described in publications such as Friedrich Engels' The Condition of the Working Class in England, published in 1844.

Elizabeth Barrett Browning's The Cry of the Children, Thomas Hardy's Tess of the D'Urbervilles, and works by author and philosopher Thomas Carlyle warned of the threat to society posed by these inhumane conditions and the profit-focused, materialistic ideals of what Carlyle referred to as the "mechanical age".

Science and influential Non-Fiction works: Throughout the nineteenth century, Victorians' ambition to comprehend and categorize the natural world played an important part in the development of scientific theory and understanding. Charles Darwin's works, such as the well-known On the Origin of Species (1859), would have a dramatic and far-reaching impact due to their innovative theory of evolution, which contradicted many of the time's established assumptions and religious beliefs.

The French Revolution: A History, published in 1837, and On Heroes, Hero-Worship, and the Heroic in History, published in 1841, are two additional important non-fiction works from the time that influenced political thinking in the mid-nineteenth century.

Key Historical Events

The Acts of Union and Treaty of Amiens: Following the French Revolution and the Irish Rebellion in the late 18th century, which ushered in times of unpredictability and instability, the Acts of Union were approved in 1800, uniting Britain and Ireland to form the United Kingdom.

The Treaty of Amiens ended the Second Coalition French Revolutionary War, as well as the issues between France and the United Kingdom. However, the effect was very ephemeral, as the Napoleonic Wars began in just three years.

US expansion: With their freshly obtained independence, the United States decided to double their size and expand their rule over the Mississippi River by acquiring the Louisiana Purchase in 1803. Native Americans inhabit a sizable chunk of the territory, which purchased from the French First Republic for $15 million.

Napoleonic Wars: In 1805, Napoleon destroyed the Russian and

Austrian armies, but his plans to invade England were thwarted when Admiral Nelson soundly defeated the French and Spanish armies at the Battle of Trafalgar, solidifying the nation's dominion over the oceans.

The French army sustained significant losses during the invasion of Russia—up to 380,000 troops died—and Napoleon's prior reputation as an unstoppable leader was destroyed. As a result of his defeat in the War of the Sixth Coalition in 1814, the French monarch abdicated and was banished to Elba.

British and Russian empire expansion: Following France's defeat, the British and Russian empires came to prominence as the world's two greatest powers, with Russia expanding its sphere of influence to include Central Asia and the Caucasus and Britain expanding its foreign holdings to include Canada, Australia, South Africa, and Africa. The British East India Company was defunct as a result of the Indian Rebellion of 1857, a broad revolt against its rule. Later, direct governance by the British Crown and the establishment of the British Raj were established.

Opium wars: By the middle of the nineteenth century, China had major opium problems due to the opening of commerce with the West and the illicit traffic in the drug organized by British businesspeople eager to make money at the trade ports. On the basis of free trade principles, Britain fought the emperor's attempt to ban its sale, resulting in the First Opium War and the Treaty of Nanking in 1842, which allowed the drug trade to continue and resulted in the British assuming control of Hong Kong.

The Taiping Rebellion of 1856 provided a violent background for the second Opium War, in which the French and British allied. The 1860 Peking Convention, which legalized the opium trade and compelled the transfer of further regions, led to the fall of the Qing empire in the early nineteenth century.

The 1848 Revolutions: The 1848 Revolutions, also known as the Springtime of the Nations, were a series of political upheavals that occurred practically simultaneously throughout Europe and the rest of the world in 1848. The primary goal of these uprisings was to depose past monarchical power and create free nation governments.

In order to build a liberal government and break free from Austrian authority, nationalists in Italy launched revolutions in Sicily and the Italian peninsula republics. The February Revolution in France took place in Paris following the crackdown on the campagne des banquets, a violent insurrection against the monarchy that resulted in the overthrow of King Louis Philippe. Other countries that had revolutions against the Habsburg Monarchy were Germany, Denmark, Hungary, Galicia, Sweden, and Switzerland.

Abolitionism and the end of slavery: The Atlantic slave trade was prohibited in the United States in 1808, and the Slavery Abolition Act of 1833 prohibited slavery across the British Empire. The nineteenth century saw the triumph of Abolitionism. Abolitionism remained in the United States until the Civil War ended in 1865, leading to the Thirteenth Amendment to the Constitution, which effectively abolished slavery there.

Women's Suffrage movement: The demand for universal women's suffrage became stronger and louder in the 1840s, with the Seneca Falls Convention in the United States and the National Women's Rights Convention in 1850. Margaret Fuller's seminal American feminist work Woman in the Nineteenth Century was published in 1839, while Sarah Grimké's The Equality of the Sexes on the Condition of Women was published in 1845.

Following the failure of suffragists to get the right to vote in the early 1870s, a protracted and relentless effort was launched in each state in favor of a constitutional amendment on women's rights and suffrage. Wyoming was the first state to provide women the right to vote in 1869. Emmeline Pankhurst joined and helped lead the UK suffragette movement in 1880.

This concludes the historical context.

Thank you for your interest in our publications. Please don't forget to check out our other books and leave a review if you enjoyed this book.

Made in the USA
Middletown, DE
20 January 2024